SWUNG

Ewan Morrison was an award-winning television director before turning to fiction. His widely acclaimed first collection of short stories, *The Last Book You Read*, was published by Black and White in 2005.

By the same author

The Last Book You Read

EWAN MORRISON

SWUNG

JONATHAN CAPE
LONDON

Published by Jonathan Cape 2007

Copyright © Ewan Morrison 2007

2 4 6 8 10 9 7 5 3 1

Ewan Morrison has asserted his right under the Copyright, Designs
and Patents Act 1988 to be identified as the author of this work

The author is grateful for permission to reprint lines from
Revolutionary Road by Richard Yates (Methuen Publishing Ltd).
Copyright © The Estate of Richard Yates.

First published in Great Britain in 2007 by
Jonathan Cape
Random House, 20 Vauxhall Bridge Road,
London SW1V 2SA

www.randomhouse.co.uk

Addresses for companies within The Random House Group Limited
can be found at:
www.randomhouse.co.uk/offices.htm

The Random House Group Limited Reg. No. 954009

A CIP catalogue record for this book is available from the British Library

ISBN 9780224078764

The Random House Group Limited makes every effort to ensure that the
papers used in its books are made from trees that have been legally sourced
from well-managed and credibly certified forests. Our paper procurement
policy can be found at: www.randomhouse.co.uk/paper.htm

Typeset by Palimpsest Book Production Limited, Grangemouth, Stirlingshire

Printed and bound in Great Britain by
Mackays of Chatham plc, Chatham, Kent

ID # 3561411

SCREENNAME: WONDERLAND

Alice + White Rabbit – Bi-curious couple – seek W/E Kings + Queens to join us 4 adventures in Wonderland – Full swaps, Parties, Orgies, Role playing O and A. Can travel or accom. W/End Glasgow. Week nights only. Age and size not important. No one-offs. Looking to develop long-term friendship w/like-minded people. No Timewasters / Pic collectors. Step through the mirror w/us. Face/ nude pics + phone # guarantee reply.

CONTENTS

'Everything you said was based on this great premise of ours that we were somehow special and superior to the whole thing, and I wanted to say – but we're not! Look at us, we're just like the people you're talking about. We are the people you're talking about.'

Richard Yates
Revolutionary Road

SWUNG

1
WINDOW

She hung her picture on the wall as he uncorked the wine. It was the old one, the painting she'd been dabbling with since he'd met her but never finished, the abstract.

'My dear Alice,' he said in the parody of a posh voice he'd been putting on for the last twenty minutes. 'Truly, it is a work of inspired genius.'

She stifled a laugh. 'Oh, no, no, no,' she said, elongating her vowels in imitation, which sounded hilarious and she knew it, with her remaining trace of a Californian accent. 'What we need here, given the space, if we are to be totally feng shui about it, is something . . .'

'Something radical,' he said, struggling not to laugh. 'Given that we have now moved into our delectable bourgeois heaven.'

'Absolutely. A modernist master. A Picasso perhaps.'

'Ah, but one must always be conscious of the cost.'

'Not at all. Picasso is now available from Homeworld. £22.99.'

'How charmingly philistine.'

Then they were laughing and hugging over the wonderfully awful 80s yuppie breakfast bar that had been there when they moved in. He cleared his throat, theatrically, to let her know that the act must continue. He poured the way-too-expensive wine into the cups in a witty parody of a wine tasting. They'd moved in today and couldn't be bothered unpacking just to look for wine glasses, so they were using a couple of cups the previous owners had left behind in one of the Ikea kitchen units. Hers read 'I am the boss'. His had a picture of a stag on it. He loved that, the way they always busked it. Made do. He filled them up and raised his cup.

'To the West End,' he said. 'To my beautiful baby.'

'I think you'll find that "darling" is the correct terminology.'

'I see, so she prefers to be called darling. Cheers then, darling.'

They fell silent for a second.

'Oh Daddy,' she said. 'But we are happy aren't we?'

'Darling,' he said with a sly nod. The game had to be played out. 'But yet, I fear one cannot be truly happy without . . .'

'What do you need, Daddy?'

'I need a thirty-eight-inch flat-screen digital surround-sound television and 200 channels to go with the wonderful stripped-pine home entertainment unit that I found in the living room.'

She was choking on wine and giggles. 'God yeah, and a . . . what we really need is . . .'

He jumped in. 'The collected works of Jamie Oliver.'

'Yeah, yeah . . . and a Walberg juicer slash food processor, so we can "be smooth with a smoothie."'

The way she put everything in inverted commas. Her hands flying up to the sides of her face, quoting the air. The way her laughter seemed to explode from within her, flying through the quotation marks. So unlike Hannah. And yes it was funny, when he looked around, them sitting there in this big empty flat on their first night. For a second their eyes drifted into the hallway. The pile of crap they had there. Hardly worth paying a mover to shift. What few things they'd separately accumulated over a decade. So sad it was funny. The things left over after his separation. After her ten wasted years. Everything stuffed into the wine boxes he'd picked up in the street. Not real packing crates.

His three boxes of old grunge records for which they didn't have a record player.

The hi-fi which was really just the remnants of three other hi-fis he'd got in second-hand shops and hot-wired together. The two mismatched speakers that weren't quite stereo.

The old orange 70s sofa covered in scratch marks from the last owners' cat, that they'd bought in the Salvation Army, and carried together for a whole mile uphill to her bedsit near the uni, stopping every block to sit on it and laugh, as the students passed by and thought they were crazy. That wouldn't sit right when they got it to hers. That had to be propped up with her books where the castors were missing.

'Oh Daddy,' she said as she reached for his hand across the breakfast bar. 'It's so hard to believe we're really here.'

'Baby,' he said. Their ironic names for each other. Others would think it sick, a separated man with a five-year-old child calling his new girlfriend baby, her calling him Daddy. But still, Daddy for her was more. It was an American expression, came from some Joni Mitchell song or something. 'Oh, you're a mean ole Daddy.' The way she said these things you could analyse forever.

They sat in silence for seconds, smiling at each other, set against the dimensions of the big white kitchen slash dining room. His eyes drifted out through the large bay windows and he sensed her gaze following his. The light was fading and the neighbour's kitchen slash dining room faced theirs. Lights on. They were moving around.

'Doctor I'd say . . .' she said.

He looked out at Mr Neighbour through the big uncurtained windows. About thirty-five, David guessed. Worked-out body. Some old T-shirt with a university logo on it, moving into the kitchen with a box.

'Nah, lawyer,' he said.

'Quite the new man. Cooks. Le Creuset it seems.'

'I've got competition then.'

She entered the frame. His wife slash partner, standing in the window, head obscured. Standing on a chair and starting to take down the curtains. He wasn't sure whether they were moving in or out but there were signs. The curtains from the previous occupants maybe. So moving in, like them, or maybe taking them down to move out. Never had a chance to say hello. A split second and Alice made her assessment.

'Private school. Ex-high-school vamp turned hausfrau.'

'Absolutely. Career?'

'Nurse, private definitely.'

'Naw, doctors and nurses. Too easy.'

'What then?'

Attractive. Yes, she was. Brown slash auburn hair just visible over her shoulder. Long. Looks real, not dyed red like Alice's. Curvaceous, large breasts, yes, but firm. Her old T-shirt too tight but very flattering. Some old rock band thing. She folded the curtains and stood down, oblivious it seemed to being watched. By her movements, even from twenty yards away David surmised that she was not wearing a bra. Look at us, he thought, looking at them.

'OK. Used to work in PR,' she said. 'Something about her hair. He wasn't her first choice but she's what – thirty-six?'

'Thirty-eight, I'd say,' he said, Alice being thirty-five.

'Gave it up to have a baby. Looks like she could be pregnant already.'

'No, she's just big.'

'Stop looking at her tits!'

'I'm not. OK, I am, but so are you.'

Alice leaned forward. Their tongues met. They no longer messed around with the initial stages. No lips. French kissing instead, diving in deep, second after second circling each other, then she pulled away and looked at him in that playful way of hers.

'Really, Daddy!' she said.

'Baby,' he said. 'I mean darling.'

'Hmm,' she said, looking at him, in some mode that might have been breaking with the game. Then flicking it off, that way she did.

'Think I may try out the new jacuzzi.'

'Bath slash jacuzzi unit is, I think you'll find, the correct bourgeois terminology.'

'Would Daddy like to join me in the bath slash jacuzzi unit?'

More laughter as already she was stripping off.

'In the name of decency, darling. What will the neighbours think?'

She pulled her T-shirt over her head and put on some kind of Hollywood 50s starlet kind of voice. Who? Monroe, Marilyn. No, smarter. Hepburn, Audrey.

'Would you be a good little Daddy and make my bed?' She twirled her T-shirt in the air and walked away from him in her bra and jeans. That way she wiggled her tiny ass in that caricature of sexy. Clever the way she made sex into something playful, almost laughable. These devices she'd found to deal with his impotence.

'Don't put bubble bath in,' he shouted after her. 'Not in a bath slash jacuzzi unit.'

Her laughter danced along the corridor as she tippy-toed past the boxes. Like she didn't like to touch the ground. Like she was wearing heels although she never did.

He was left alone. Since he'd first seen it he'd been drawn to this room. It was what made the place different from most West End flats, which were generally square, subdivided into eighteen-by-fifteen boxes, like the one he'd had with Hannah. He must remember to make sure the direct debit was still in place for the child-support payments. He also must remember to try to work out what he was going to call her now – Hannah – the ex – the ex-wife – the former wife.

Yes, even calling it the West End at all was another joke. Sure, that was what the estate agents liked you to think it was so they could squeeze another 10K out of you. But they'd been smarter and got it for fifteen under. It was fringy, borderline and arty. An isolated street of run-down Victorian tenements by the side of the motorway. Spatially eccentric. The long dark corridor, the L-shaped layout, the kitchen at the end. You could sit there and feel you were in a space cut off from the rest of your life. Contemplative. The light flooding in from the big bay windows on two sides. The sound of the motorway. The only unsettling thing about it was, since the whole street was the same, everyone's kitchen slash dining room looked directly into the neighbours'. It was, in fact, almost impossible not to sit there and look at them as you were gazing into space. He poured himself another cup of the £12.99 wine and his eyes drifted out again.

The lawyer slash doctor with his boxes. Yes, Alice was right, so hard to believe they were actually here. It was a joke. But he wasn't laughing. Felt melancholy actually, sitting there alone. The light from the bathroom came on and lit up the outside wall. He craned his neck slightly and glimpsed Alice's silhouette in the bathroom window. Amazing really how she'd stayed with him despite his problem. How, in some way, she even seemed to love him more because of it. Maybe it was the £12.99 wine from the ridiculously exclusive wine shop, or maybe he was getting sentimental.

'Hey,' she shouted through from the bathroom. 'What we really need is a . . .'

He couldn't hear. Jesus this place was big. 'A what?'

'A bidet. A bee-day. You know. Water up your ass.'

He sat there smirking for a second, swilling the wine round his mouth. Yes, it did taste better than the usual cheap Bulgarian Merlot they drank in her bedsit. He couldn't help but look. The next-door window again. She was straightening a picture on the facing wall, just like Alice had done earlier. Nice the way her T-shirt was riding up to show her waist as she went up on her tippy-toes. It was whatsisname. Popper. Hopper. That one of the two strangers, a guy who looked like Bogart and a dame like Monroe, sitting alone, ten feet apart, not talking, in an all-night café. *The Night Watch*, no, fuck, that was Rembrandt. He made a mental note to ask Alice tomorrow. So yeah. She's an ex-artist, he told himself. Went to art school, like Alice did. Had ten bad years, like Alice did. Gave it all up to have kids. So unlike Alice.

So quiet there in the empty room. Nothing but the ticking of the thermostat. He wished he could hear what they were saying next door. She was asking him something. Perhaps, like Alice had done earlier, to see if the picture was hanging right. Getting it ready for the buyers maybe. He was ignoring her. Mr Lawyer slash Doctor. Too concerned with his pots and pans, arranging, re-arranging, packing, unpacking. Look at them. Him in one window, her framed by the other. Like that Hopper on their back wall. So much the caricature couple. So like he'd been with Hannah. To hell with it. Maybe they'd go round, him and Alice, and say hello in the next few days. To be 'neighbourly', of course, but really just to find out if he really was a doctor or a lawyer. No. All the fake smiles and platitudes were too exhausting even to think about and it wasn't worth the bet. The glowing satisfaction slash dissatisfaction of finding out that your cynical one-liners turned out to be right. Always.

He walked down the corridor. Alice had let her jeans stay where they fell. So Alice. It made him laugh that she could be so intellectually rigorous and at the same time so messy in every other aspect of her life. What the hell. He enjoyed cleaning up after her.

He folded her jeans. How small she was. Again her contradictions. That someone so tiny, only five foot and so skinny, could be so intimidating to so many men. Her T-shirt and bra were lying by the bathroom door. The T-shirt read 'HATE YOUR FRIENDS'. Part of her vast slacker collection. She liked to turn people's heads for reasons different than the usual. At least they're not looking at my tits, she said. She had a thing about her tits too. Yes, they were small, but he liked that. Small but incredibly sensitive, so unlike Hannah's. David held Alice's non-frilly sports B-cup to his nose.

And her red hair. That slight annoyance of hers earlier at seeing that the neighbour was real auburn. He couldn't recall if he'd ever told Alice that his ex-wife had long red hair, that when he thought of her now it was the hair, not the face, that remained. Alice's hair was dyed, bright red, cropped short. It had been a surprise when he discovered that she was a natural redhead too. Why spoil your real hair colour? he'd asked. As usual, she explained, it was a critique. A big fat fuck off to your biological inheritance.

But why, he'd asked, not just dye it white or green or
whatever? She'd done all those before, she said. So now
her hair was this caricature of itself. He'd said that the
nuances would be lost on most Scots, was probably some
clever American thing. Yes, he loved that about her too,
that she was a real Californian slacker. That being with
her in some way felt like a holiday, every day. That short
of escaping from Scotland she gave him a sense of not
being trapped. Alice. She even had a problem with her
name. Her mother, a hippie, had named her after the books
by Lewis Carroll. She'd said in passing more than a few
times that she'd wanted to change it. Preferred 'Baby',
because it was corny and kind of sexist. But how could
Alice not be Alice, when there were so many things he
now thought of as Alice-ish, Alice-like, so typically Alice.

The corridor. Her boxes of books. All she seemed to
own. *Das Kapital. The Women's Room. 120 days of Sodom.*
Academic textbooks on art, philosophy, psychology.
R. D. Laing. Foucault. Freud. His angry intellectual
Alice, his Alice.

He stood there in the corridor looking at her silhouette through the frosted glass. Times like this. Her
humming to herself in the bathroom, in that world all
of her own. She always felt she was like a kid, she'd said,
not just a kid, a boy. People's first impressions were the
usual clichés, thought she was a snob. An angry ball-
breaking dyke. But they'd never seen her walking on her
tippy-toes. Never spent the night with her and listened
to her stories. Alice. He could stand there all night just
watching her without her knowing. His bookish boy-girl,
singing, laughing at the jacuzzi bubbles tickling her feet.

He stepped away and headed for their bedroom.
Stopped on the threshold. It was the wrong room. As if
the imprint for every home was burned into his brain,

was the flat he'd lived in with Hannah. The sound of the light switch echoed round the empty walls. The second bedroom, the kids' one. It was going to be Alice's studio. For months he'd been encouraging her to give it a second go with her art. Thomas the Tank Engine wallpaper. Kids' room. They'd had a pregnancy scare after their first year, what, six months ago. His impotence had made her a little lazy with her Pill and her periods were always irregular. That was what got them thinking. Felt time getting on. That and the merger at work. The possibility that she might lose her job. Most women her age would have seen it as a sign. Baby-making time. But they'd read the signs differently. Time to get back to what she'd really always wanted to be. So the artist's studio was what they'd agreed to call it. She was on two weeks' annual leave saved up after two years. They'd timed it perfectly. Invested the money they'd saved. Wisely, promptly. If she lost her job, she would have her art. They wouldn't be like those sad ex-employees who had to become free-lances, kissing any ass they could to get a ten-day contract. She was going to be an artist.

He stepped in. Look at it. How many kids had been in there? There were crayon marks on the wall at knee height. Like his daughter, Amy, two, three years ago. Two kids probably, the norm round here. He and Hannah had planned to have two. The norm. Boy and girl if you were lucky. Kids are a form of consensual slavery, Alice said. Women have them because they can't create anything of value in their own lives. These things Alice said made him feel so much better about so many things. Like why it was he left his wife and child in the first place. The things Alice didn't say. As loud as the things she did. Like their silent agreement that they wouldn't be having kids. Ever.

He looked up at the ceiling. Alice was definitely wrong about the cornicing. Not authentic Victorian at all. B&Q was his guess. Fake Victoriana. He worried for a second that the two weeks Alice had given herself off work wouldn't be enough to make a real start with her art. They'd already wasted one week with the move and she still hadn't started and things had been getting scary at work. He reminded himself that no matter what happened with the merger, he would still have a job. Human Resources were always the last to go. No, their set-up was perfect. He'd do his kiss-ass corporate job and she'd do her radical avant-garde art and it would be more than enough for them both.

He was back in the corridor and Alice was still singing to herself in the bathroom. What the fuck was that? 'Teenage Kicks'. She couldn't sing for shit. But that made it even better.

Standing there, spying almost, made him feel guilty so he went through to the other room. The one they'd picked as their bedroom. It faced the back. From the window he could see their kitchen and the neighbours' and glimpse her studio. Bed. Right. Make the bed. Another one of her little jokes. Make it, but not with sheets. Bloody thing still had to be constructed. Was still in its Habitat box. He started tearing away the cardboard. Forty-five screws, eight bolts, seventeen wooden plugs. Phillips screwdriver. Fuck it. He tore the plastic wrapping off the new, their first, queen-sized mattress. Pushed it against the wall. The bed frame could wait. And the duvet. Another box somewhere. To sleep naked on the mattress. Like squatters in their own bourgeois home, as she told him his bedtime story.

Her stories. Every third night or so. Stories about couples fucking, them watching. As they lay in bed together, jerking off as she spoke. Like that for so many months. Fictions, a fictional sex life, but still holding each other. 'I can't tell you how crazy I am about you,' she'd said. 'Ever.'

As he stood there staring at their new unmade bed, he worried about her stories. Her latest theory was his problem was something to do with his ex-wife. He worried that that might have been the reason she'd insisted on moving to within half a mile of Hannah's home.

He felt awkward being in the bedroom by himself. The overhead light without a shade maybe. The tiny marks on the floor that showed the imprints of the last occupants' bed. The vague memory of his own marital bed. No, it was the bloody heating. It was too hot in there. Alice's place didn't have heating.

Alice was still in the bath, singing some Nirvana song. He went back through to the kitchen slash dining room and tried to locate the thermostat. Opened the wall-fitted cupboards, searched under the sink. We really can't afford to have the heating on full blast all the time like this, he thought. The mortgage is a stretch as it is. Although the merger was nothing to really worry about, and it had been coming for months, and he'd studied comparable histories of local takeovers by multinational conglomerates, he still couldn't help but worry. There had been sixty-five redundancies in the last two weeks. His boss had taken a holiday at exactly the wrong time. There were signs that the thing was more aggressive than predicted. He'd hidden it all from Alice, kept nipping in to work in the last week just to make sure things were OK. But she'd read his mind. Losing his job. She'd said he could always go back to his acting again, but realistically, what kind of work would he get now, aged thirty-seven? Some 'extra' work maybe, more than likely just corporate videos. The same crap he had to show employees in his HR exercises. If he was to be honest he'd have told her that he'd long since given up on the prospect of being an actor. That even if he did lose his job, he'd do any shitty job he could find just to be able to subsidise her and her art. I can't tell you how crazy I am about you, she'd said. Ever. And so he couldn't tell her either. Ever.

He'd walked back through to the kitchen, poured himself the last cupful of Rioja and was watching the neighbours again. She was calling out to him, putting a set of kitchen utensils into a packing box. Somehow he was still busy fussing over his goddamn pans. Yes, their kitchen is better than ours, he thought. Stainless steel splashbacks. Fucking stainless steel splashbacks. Never again.

He walked back past the bathroom, the door was open, she was no longer there so he walked to the bedroom with his cup of wine. The lights were off. He expected to find her under the sheet or in a towel but she was lying on top of the bare mattress, wearing a padded bra, a thong and hold-ups.

'Whaddya think?' she said, grinning. 'Swinging wives?'

A joke but he couldn't laugh. When they'd been packing to move, she'd backed up everything on his hard drive and there had been a virus in his secret swinging folder – pictures of horny housewives and couples. His excuses had been pathetic and she'd laughed in a forgiving way. It was OK, she said. At least he was flawed, wasn't doing the whole clichéd new-man routine. He tried to explain that there was this guy at work who got fired for looking at the site and it was really just this office in-joke, and how really . . . 'It's OK. Kinda cool,' she'd said, joking about how adultery was no big problem and how he hadn't yet reached the end of the two years' mandatory separation period and was still technically married and so she was technically his mistress.

'Come here, Daddy,' she said with that voice that might now have been Mae West. He moved closer but couldn't get the thoughts from his head. That he'd been an adulterer, had already tried, many times, to confess to the minutiae of his infidelities, and now, maybe, she'd taken them on board, made them hers. And then for some reason, on one of their usual weekend strolls three months ago, she'd led him to the West End. Like it was another game. 'Look at those saddo couples hugging each other at the real-estate window,' she'd said. 'C'mon, let's do it, for a laugh.' She'd taken his arm and put on a posh accent. 'Three bedrooms. Original features. Offers over one seven seven. Oh, darling, we simply must have it.'

She gave up her pose and slowly raised herself on the bed. Her hands climbing up his legs. She rubbed her face against his crotch through his jeans. She smiled up at him, with an expression that could only have come from his swinging sites. 'C'mon, let's try it in the kitchen so the neighbours can see.' This idea was haunting him, that this whole move here, it had started as a joke.

'You don't like your horny housewife?'

A whole month it had taken them to make the choice, the move. To get the courage up to invest in something resembling a future. The dozens of houses checked out after work. Walking into people's lives and looking at the dimensions. He had thought she'd come to terms with his impotence, but now it was clear. They were here and she was wearing lingerie.

'Mmmm,' she said, licking her lips in a bored housewife kind of way as she undid his fly. 'Oh, Daddy.'

He backed off. Apologised. 'I'm tired, it's the move,' he said. 'It's just. I dunno – can't we just get all spoony and just . . .'

The wrong thing to say. She'd gone to all this bother, buying these things, dressing up. Her little surprise. She lay back on the bed. Even in the dark he could tell. The effort it must have taken. The sound of her breath as she lay down. Deflated.

'Sorry,' she said.

'No, no, it's just. I'm knackered. And back at work tomorrow and there's a lot going on, I guess I'm a little anxious.'

She silently took off the hold-ups and he took that as his cue to get undressed. She'd never worn them before. He'd hurt her feelings. This special occasion for them both. The fear of it all. How smart of her to pass it off as a joke. A role-play adultery on your first night in the West End. He should have played along. Should have called her darling.

'It was just,' she said. 'I thought. It'd be funny.'

He reached to touch her face. But she moved away and pulled the single sheet over herself. He climbed in beside her.

Put his hand on her thigh as he always did. She fell asleep more quickly than usual. The stress of the move, no doubt. Usually they fell asleep within seconds of each other. His hand cupping her tiny breasts, her hand holding his flaccid dick. But tonight she had rolled away and his fingers fell to the bare mattress.

They lay there, for the first time alone on the same bed. The new bed. The marital cliché. To be alone together. Like with Hannah, like the neighbours, no doubt. Alice was snoring. She always snored after wine. Another one of those things he loved about her. So unlike

Hannah, who slept silently, fucked silently, argued silently. Usually Alice's snoring lulled him to sleep but tonight it was keeping him awake. The room was so dark. The thermostat clicked on again. The radiators started creaking.

There was no way he could sleep. Not now. Not here. He lifted the sheet gently so as not to make a draught. She rolled away, moaning and gripping it round herself. He got to his feet.

He walked naked to the kitchen window and picked up the cup he'd left behind, sipping the last of the Rioja. But then he was conscious of his own reflection in the glass. Thinning on top, bloating at the gut, so nearly forty, naked. The neighbours might see him. She was still there. In the window. Twenty yards away, packing sheets into a box. So they were definitely moving out. He hit the light switch off and moved back. Her husband must have been in the room but out of sight, because she turned and said something to him. She closed the packing box, and left the window frame. David waited. Thirty, forty seconds. He felt stupid standing there naked in the shadows waiting for another glimpse. But then he saw it, her hand, by the edge of the window frame, reaching for the bottle of wine. No she couldn't be pregnant, no self-respecting West End woman would drink while pregnant. She poured some into a tumbler. Her hand, the tumbler, the bottle, then she walked to the centre of the room. The window frame momentarily obscuring her face. Seeing her drink made David want to drink. He reached for his cup again on the edge of the breakfast bar. As his eyes adjusted to the darkness he noticed that the light from her kitchen was reaching into theirs. His cup and his bottle were lit by her light. He lifted them away.

She sat there on her chair by their Habitat table and leaned towards the window looking in his direction. For a second he was scared she'd spotted him. He grabbed a kitchen towel and fastened it round his waist. Look at you, he thought. Whatever your name is. Shona. Charlotte. Hollie. Look at you. You are staring. That expression on your face. Those temples you stroke that are signs of a headache. That face you rest in your hands. The hands that rub your neck, that bring the glass again to your mouth. 'A bird in a gilded cage.' As Alice would have said. You and your husband are drifting apart, like me and Hannah did.

He conducted a little experiment. Her eyes were staring out at him, so he waved. Once, twice. Then ridiculously, again and again. But the look on her face told him that she saw nothing. Her lights were on and his were off. Her window had become a mirror. She was staring at herself. Look at you, looking at yourself. Beautiful woman. He's ignoring you, isn't he? Running back and forward, with his boxes, his toolkit. Every time he passes, you lean over and drink more from your glass. You've reached that stage now, haven't you, when you no longer talk or kiss. Just deal with practical things, make plans, accumulate possessions to fight the dissatisfaction. But now tonight, as you sit there, ready to move out, wine in hand, staring at yourself, you're thinking of leaving him, aren't you, as you run your fingers through your hair.

David ran his fingers through his hair just to see what it felt like. For the first time in months he could feel himself getting hard.

He should go through to Alice now and try to make love to her. Maybe she'd been right, that moving here would be a fresh start for them both. She'd be asleep, but he'd wake her gently. There would be no more need for her bedtime stories. No more masturbating together while she whispered in his ear about secretly watching some couple fucking on a sand dune, or some woman playing with herself in the changing room at Marks & Sparks, no more stories or sorrys. He'd wake her gently and for the first time ever, properly, they would.

He seems to have left the room now, because you look round and refill your glass.

Tomorrow, he told himself, we'll go and visit. Bring over another bottle of this nice Rioja. Sit in your slightly better Habitat kitchen slash dining room and compare stories. You will no doubt talk about how weird it feels to be here, like Hannah once said. So damned claustrophobic. How you like to joke with your hubby about the whole damned thing. It's amazing, you'll say to Alice, how predictable people are round here, how awful it is, even though everyone is so nice, that all the women round here have given up their careers to become mothers, and how you'd never do that yourself but you can understand. How you've been thinking about it, the biological clock and all. Like Hannah once said. But all these damned three-wheel strollers. Makes you realise that time really is running out. And how great it is to find some other people, so close by, who are real people. Pity we're moving away because it would have been so nice to get to know you. And Alice will have a problem with you, because you are too knowing. Pretending to be different from everyone else. Though you're not. Not really, not like us. Like me and Hannah once said.

I watch you lift your wine to your mouth as I lift mine to mine. For a second I taste what you taste, or some brand so similar the differences count for little. Look at you. Sarah, Hollie, Hannah. The hunger with which you lift that glass to your mouth.

*   *   *

They'd done the hilarious housewife-kissing-bread-winning-husband-at-front-door routine and he'd 'wished her luck' and now she was standing there with her third coffee staring at the room.

The problem though was that even with the easel assembled, the four pre-stretched canvases stacked against the wall, the five sketchbooks, hammer, nails, tacks, charcoals, pencils, erasers and the selection of professional-grade Rowney oil paints, the room didn't say 'artist's studio', it said 'Mothercare'. It was, for sure, the ideologically questionable Thomas the Tank Engine wallpaper, the matching Conservative bright blue carpet. The original Victorian fireplace brutally painted by the last occupants to make it match. Blue is for boys.

But don't judge, don't become complacent and smug. All this predictable ugliness is just all the more reason for trying to make something of beauty. So get to it, Alice, stop passing judgement, do something. Stop staring at the goddamn wallpaper. Turn a problem into an opportunity, as David would have said in his piss-take of HR speak.

Her first drawing would be of the room itself. An empty child's bedroom. A damning critique of the middle-class indoctrination of children. But also rather moving. A child's room without a child. She carefully copied a section of wall in light pencil. It took forty-five minutes of concentration, line after line, and she was glad to find that the old skills hadn't totally abandoned her. And as she drew, it came to her that she had never had a child's bedroom when she was growing up. She'd always been on the move with her mother, sleeping on sofas, in caravans, in back rooms and closets, on the camp beds and futons that belonged to her 'uncles'. These men who took her mother in, these men Alice now knew were her mother's lovers. Uncle John, Sam, Joe and Uncle Tom Cobbley and all. Who put up with her mother and her drinking and drugs and fucking for only so long before they threw her out and they were both back on the road again. '79 to '89. Jesus. Hilarious. Maybe all she'd ever wanted was a real bedroom like this. Jesus.

But as the image appeared on the page, it started to freak her out. Thirty-five and two abortions and this image of a child's empty bedroom, yes, it would upset David too, remind him of his ex. And she wasn't sure why the hell she was attempting realism anyway. So she drew a hard dark mark across the drawing and abandoned it.

She set her sketchbook on the easel and the white page stared at her and she laughed at that old artist's cliché – 'The fear of the empty page.' But after twenty minutes of ideas rushing at her she still hadn't made that first mark. Just as she was about to cover the entire surface with random scrawls, her mobile phone rang in the kitchen. David maybe, Pauline probably, yeah, totally, doing her work-buddy routine, wanting to ask her how it was going, gossiping about who'd been fired and yah-de-yah. She did as David suggested, and let it ring.

Magritte. That was the second big idea she had. The empty page on the easel against the kids' wallpaper. A picture in negative. No image, just white, framed by a border of children's wallpaper. Surrealism and Freud. We are empty, everything we will ever try to create is framed by our parents. A little po-mo. An anti-image. White square in the centre. An absence where identity should be. Brilliant in its simplicity.

She started sketching the wallpaper, then fuck it, why the hell not? She got one of the palette knives and dug into Thomas the Tank Engine's grinning face. Bad DIY job, the paper came away almost too easily. She pulled off a section. Then another. Fuck it, the place would be a mess when she got a few canvases on the go anyway. After twenty minutes of tearing off Thomas and glueing him to the edge of the white page, she set the thing on the easel and had a good look.

You had to laugh. She did. Fuck. It was like something the other girls in lifestyle programming would have come up with on a dull day and tried to pass off as a programme idea. 'Don't throw away your old wallpaper – turn it into an interesting collage to contrast and highlight your new decor.' Jesus. So she abandoned it.

Half the day had gone and she should have called it lunch but instead she sat on the floor staring at the two pictures she'd discarded. One, a carefully drawn image destroyed, the other an image with a hole in its centre. Really, it was all she'd ever done, made images then destroyed them. She told herself over and over that it wasn't just her. It was classic 90s art school stuff. Back then, if you were smart, po-mo, you spent weeks drawing something then erased it, you did a wild angry abstract and then painted an incompatibly delicate flower in the middle of it. You took a beautiful photograph and sprayed graffiti over it. You took someone else's work and you signed it. Because. Because Jackson Pollock was now available in five colours of Formica. Because Picasso really was for sale in Homeworld. Because every genre was dead. Because things that were made with love and belief were always going to be betrayed. Because destruction was now the only legitimate creative act. Because . . .

She'd lost it. Fuck it. Reading too much into everything again. C'mon. Give it up. Abort, abort. It was the wallpaper. That was it. Every idea she'd had so far had been to do with the wallpaper. Really. C'mon. It had to come down before she could start.

Thankfully David had had the foresight to buy all the stuff at Homeworld. Wallpaper scrapers, steam stripper. Another forty-five minutes wasted, reading instructions, filling the stripper with water, and then she was there, as the instructions had said, pressing the steamer against the wall. Remove all distractions, the surrealists had said. Pushing the button, as the steam scalded her skin. Keep on. Just to get rid of a square, four by four. So there was nothing distracting in the field of vision. Shit. Pain. Fuck. She pulled her hand away and the wet layers were stripping by themselves, falling off the wall. Four layers, talking to her as she sucked her knuckles. And it was amazing. Beneath Thomas, a layer of bright yellow, the happy yuppie years no doubt, then beneath that striped silver and gold, the 70s. Beneath that, tiny flowers in repeat pattern. The war years. Pretty flowers, tweed skirts and the A-bomb. Beneath that. Hard to believe. The original plaster. Terracotta. Craftsmen painting into wet plaster. 19. What, 18? 1890. Awesome.

So the third idea she had was to take all of the bits of wallpaper she had and turn them into some kind of collage slash painting. What could be a more appropriate form? No need to make a mark of your own. We are all products of our history. Like Marx said. Let the wallpaper speak for itself. One layer of Thomas, one of 80s yuppies, one of 70s glitz, one of wartime flowers, and one of Victorian austerity. What could be a more telling image? Layer under layer. Let the sociologists and art critics work it out. Seriously. Words, phrases. Paper over the cracks, start again, design a life.

But after three hours of wallpaper stripping, and collaging, and making tentative then bold charcoal marks, then erasing them, then collaging on more, she found herself again staring up at the wall she'd torn away at,

then back down at the collages she'd made from the fragments. And she felt giddy. Not with excitement.

Look at it. The wall looked more like an artwork than
her attempts. Laughing again, she abandoned the collage
and set a new sketchbook page on the easel and stared
at the white square. Only this time she wasn't laughing
at the old cliché of the artist staring at the white page
in fear. She was actually. No she wasn't. C'mon Alice.
No you're not. Such a cliché. To be scared of making
art.

*   *   *

Nine ten, and there he was on the desert island again –
the little name he and Alice had for the TV company,
based on one of the HR games he played with the
recently redundant, called 'Survivor'. And it did look a
lot like an island. The old 70s four-floor concrete
monstrosity, surrounded on all sides by motorway, its
dated corporate logo rusting on the wall. Stuck in the
kind of past you only found in Scotland. Scotia TV. The
desert island – because it barely survived as a TV channel
at all. Had very little time left before it was consumed
by the American slash Australian corporation that had
been buying up all the local stations in the UK, hacking
out the dead wood to make the necessary rafts to float
on the new international market.

Nine fifteen. He walked through the corporate-
friendly reception and the new corporate-unfriendly
security guards, flashing his badge. Sam and Willie were
no longer there, joking about the football, letting him in
with a wave of the hand. Instead there were the two new
Schwarzenegger types from the private security firm that
was brought in last week, no doubt to stop disgruntled
former employees firebombing the building. As the

mirrored walls of the elevator reflected his face into solitary infinity and he ascended past the first and second
floors, he tried not to imagine the scenes of despair
unfolding as the remaining staff walked through their
generic hundred-foot open plan offices to their desks and
inboxes to find the redundancy notices he'd mailed last
Friday. Two hundred staff and almost half of them were
gone, going or up for review. The studio directors – gone,
the cameramen, the lighting department, grips, make-up
and wardrobe, all being invited to reapply for their old
jobs with a non-union buyout that made them available
for work 24/7 with a thirty per cent pay cut. That they
hadn't seen this coming was astounding. But then they
didn't sit all day reading corporate reports and laughing
at the world. Didn't know or want to know that the staff
would be reduced to a skeletal structure before being
built up again to about half its size with everyone being
expected to treble their productivity through multitasking. Didn't know that the events on their little island
were a duplicate of what had happened at Canary Wharf,
LTV, YTV and even the BBC.

Floor three. Alice's. Research. On a whim he hit the
button. Just in time. Just a peek to reassure himself that
they had done the right thing making their own raft
before the deluge. Maybe get a bit of gossip from Alice's
friend Pauline to float his boat.

The old cheery ching. The smell of new carpet and
polystyrene packaging. As he stepped out of the elevator
he almost walked into two guys from facilities carrying
a new desk. Yes, things were progressing as predicted.
Just look at it.

The refurbishment had started early last week, and
he'd been checking its progress as Alice took time off.
Nipping into work for the bare minimum hours every

day, reluctantly forcing himself to do the last of the dirty work. Finalising and co-signing the hundred or so severance packages. Alice's name had not been on his list. And he'd calmed himself every day by taking a lunchtime stroll down to her floor to look at the new furnishings.

But best not to tell her the details. He'd told her it was just as she'd predicted.

Now the hundred-foot space had been divided in two. To the left it was the old order. Fluorescent overhead lights, regulation pine-veneered desks, purple hessian-covered partitions which went up to chest height and were used for segregating departments. The old fat oyster-coloured PCs and monitors. The old metal venetian blinds that always seemed jammed halfway. The Facilities guys were heaving the old desks and PCs into a corner as, to the right, in the place where Alice's desk used to be, another bunch of guys were installing funky ultra-thin digital monitors on new semi-circular bright-coloured desks which could no doubt be turned into all kinds of interesting shapes, snakes, figure eights, as you fluidly exchanged ideas with other short-term freelancers in other short-term departments and lounged around on the new multicoloured upmarket Ikea-type sofas. Every image can be taken two ways, Alice said. Most people would be happy to get a new desk and monitor, to have a big fat injection of capital into their underperforming parochial channel, but there was a sinister side to the makeover. Whenever I sniff Ikea, she said, I hear the word 'temp'. She'd made him read this book. Some big sociology text. The future is temporary it said, employment, housing, relationships, marriage. The social plan for society has collapsed. Every man for himself, till you're too old to compete. And it had been the trigger, four months ago when they heard about the merger. Hi, welcome to Tempworld. Freelance contracts reduced from a year to two months – get the new graduates only too keen to work round the clock 'cos they wanna be in TV – get a series or a couple of shows out of them, budgets slashed – use 'em up, burn 'em up, spit 'em out, bring on the new ones, even younger, hungrier, cheaper, even more anti-union, burn 'em up even faster. There was no future in TV. And if you were thirty or so how could you compete? She was right. The plan for life was dead. They'd play the survivor game and find another way to be together without buying into what other people thought of as 'a life'. That was the plan. The irony being that this world of temps meant a more secure future for him in HR. Someone had to deal with the sheer number of freelancers being hired and fired. They'd read the signs right. Knew the smell of Ikea. Thus their deal. She'd make art and he'd subsidise her with his job. A clever inverted caricature of a happy 50s couple. Still, be nice to sneak home one of those funky new sofas.

Elevator. He was glad not to have bumped into Pauline. She would only have disturbed his peace of mind with questions. Floor four. Home. HR, PR and Accounts. Yes, they were the only floor that still had permanent glass-walled partitions. Reading the signs, that counted for a lot. But as he did the old walk to his office, he couldn't help notice that a new office junior was packing the contents of Sally's desk in Accounts. Sally gone. Sally's walls had been solid.

The usual stroll past the water cooler and there was Pauline with her conspiracists. He tried to avoid her but was conscious that she was avoiding him too. None of her usual drag-him-over-get-the-news-update routine. He walked on and Boss John's glass-walled office was empty. Portentous. No, just late maybe.

As he threw his suit jacket over his leather swivel chair
and flicked the nodding head of his Homer Simpson desk
toy he tried not to think about Pauline's silent conspir-
acies and hit 'Start' on his PC. There was nothing in his
in-tray, and as Windows started up and he sipped his
Starbucks, he thought he might just do what he usually
did, which was to have a quick peek at the forbidden site
before starting work.

Two months ago Archie Mackay had been caught by
IT using his work email to post ads on some site called
swinging-paradise.com. Hot'n'Hung. Fifty-two. Looking
for couples and single women for parties, orgies, oral and
anal. Archie had won three BAFTAs for editing social
agenda documentaries, worked for the company for thirty
years, and been union shop steward for ten, but as soon
as his redundancy notice came in he'd lost the plot. Hit
the bottle and the net. IT found it first, the photo he'd
taken on the work webcam, standing naked in his editing
suite with a beer and belly to match. IT passed it to HR
with a memo asking whether this was, as the handbook
said, 'Inappropriate use of Internet access.'

He and Boss John had had to decide whether Archie
was guilty of misconduct, which required disciplinary
action, or gross misconduct which meant instant
dismissal. They'd checked the handbook and the photo.
Although it wasn't easy to make out, and was not particularly impressive, Archie did have an erection. This made
his misconduct gross, apparently.

So Archie had been fired, but as a member of HR,
David was still permitted to visit forbidden sites. So it
had been this running joke with his boss since then. Every
morning, Starbucks in hand, logging on to swinging-
paradise with Archie's password and seeing if the old man
had managed to score. Replies to his ad had been pitiful.

An overeager overweight transvestite from Bearsden
called Wanda; a couple called Pussy-galore – mid thirties, looking for single men and couples. Threesomes,
foursomes, and mutual DIY. DIY. That'd made him
laugh. Think jerking off in Homeworld. He and John
had joked about how it would be so easy to log on as
Archie and send off a few emails. Archie would be on
the dole now, aged fifty-two, and with nothing else left
to live for. A few witty messages might help get him laid.
Call it a gift from HR.

There was a new reply from Pussy-galore. They'd sent
a pic and wanted some in return. It was a ridiculous waste
of time but David checked over his shoulder to see if
anyone was walking by his glass partition before clicking
'Open'.

Freaky. That they would do that. Their new picture.
A wedding photograph, with their faces blanked out with
white squares. These people, Jesus. Be just the thing to
show John when he turned up. If he did. Definitely, he
was late.

Internal mail – a new message. John, surely, an out-
of-office memo with the new list of redundancies. Alice's
name would no doubt be on it, as they had predicted.
Twenty-two-point azure blue bold Helvetica. They'd
paid some designer a couple of grand to choose the font.
Bold was big and friendly and blue was calming but
serious.

> John McDonald has resigned his post as head of Human
> Resources. We wish him luck with his future endeavours.

Fuck. So this was John's 'holiday'. Imagine if people got
married the same way they got hired and fired these days.
We thank you for your commitment to this relationship

and wish you luck with your etc. Yup, Alice was right. We apologise for the temporary break in signal but would like to inform you that the future is temporary.

Ten thirty. He felt like calling Alice, to ask her how her art was coming on. No. He mustn't hassle her. Art needed time, was a life project, maybe the only one left. He'd call her in the lunch break. Back to work. But, shit, why hadn't John told him he'd been fired, and did this mean David was now, by default, the new head of HR?

Eleven, role-playing time, and he was heading towards floor three again. Conference room C. It had the same 70s matching repeat pattern of company logo on the walls and well-worn carpets that all the other conference rooms had. No windows. An overhead projector that hadn't been used in more than a decade. A lingering smell of sweat, feet, and pre-packed sandwiches. The same room, or one comparably anonymous to the one he'd been in for his interview six years ago, when he'd lied about his quali-fications and told himself that it was very much like one of the hundreds of auditions he'd been to as an actor and if you could just tell yourself that you were acting a role, be method and stay in character, the job would be yours. And they'd bought it. His fake CV and his passionate belief in HR. Telling them, the five suits, that Human Resources was basically – well how can I put this – well, like a human drama – very much like being a director on a TV show – and the employees are your actors and the handbook is the script. And, even though he thought he'd overplayed it, he still hadn't let it slip that actually he was kind of excited about working for a TV company, because even though the job was in HR, he was sure that someday someone would notice his talent and he'd walk into the film studio when they were recording the below

average parochial soap opera, and they'd be short of extras
and could he just do a walk-on? And then, over time,
they'd see. And before anyone knew he'd be taking long
lunches and there'd be real speaking parts and then he'd
be where he wanted to be. On TV. He said none of this,
but they gave him the job and after eight years of failure
as an avant-garde fringe actor and six of temping and call
centres, the only role he'd performed consistently was
this one. Al Pacino plays lead as assistant head of HR in
a movie called *Survivor*. Great title. One of those Hollywood numbers where the masses rise up against their
dictatorial leader. Where a solitary Pacino, or maybe De
Niro, screams near the end, 'I am not a resource, goddamn
it, I am a human.'

Opening the door to 3C. There he was again and there
they were. Twitching on their plastic chairs. Six recent
layoffs who'd been invited to reapply for their old jobs,
who now had to go through this humiliating role-playing
exercise and pick four out of eight objects which could
help them survive on a fictional desert island. The person
who could manage the others and delegate would be the
last remaining survivor. Ironic, really, that the last person
would have no one left to manage or delegate to. But
these little contradictions were what made corporate life
such a rich and challenging role.

Shona (Bookings), John (IT), James (Editing), Yvonne
(Research), Wendy and Todd (Sales). That's what the list
in front of him and the name tags they had on told him.

Their faces. People who all knew each other already.
Who'd been there years longer than him and now were
here having to play catch-ball and shout their names.
He wanted to apologise to them all, explain that in the
last few hours he'd been more than a little unnerved by
the fact that his boss had been fired, but if he did the

whole thing would become impossible. The only choice
was to ham it up and at least make it entertaining for
himself and for any of the others who still had a sense
of humour.

'Right,' he said. 'So here's the story.'

The way they looked at him. Like he was a clock.
Counting the minutes. Doing their obligatory sighs to
show their disdain. Understandable, of course, but still.
They all knew that this had to be got through so there
was no point in drawing it out by resisting. They should
have planned ahead for this like he and Alice had. If he
could just get back to his PC and check his email.
Promotion? Demotion?

'OK,' he said, '747. International flight. The food trolleys are just about to start their run when there is a huge
explosion in a baggage compartment in first class.' How
apt.

Todd shook his head. Yes, the irony was not lost on
him either.

'The pilot, due to his history in training as a fighter
pilot in the last Gulf War, managed a water landing. But
as it hit the plane broke in two.' These words were not
on his scripted page but no one was to know. Yvonne,
the large girl from Research wearing Dorothy Perkins,
started biting her rag nails. John, from IT, started picking
some breakfast from the knee and crotch area of his
chinos. Ketchup probably.

'You were all sitting in the last row. Todd, you were
in the toilet, doing whatever. Yvonne, you were an air
hostess, preparing the baked Alaska.'

'How'd they do that?' she asked. 'Is it a microwave?'

'Baked fucking Alaska,' muttered Todd.

Yvonne blushed. 'Well, I don't know,' she said, snapping at him. 'Do you?'

Todd was obviously the self-appointed joker in the pack. He'd score high on individuality but low on team spirit. The two would cancel each other out.

David let the silence stand for a second. Stared back at them. Unable to deal with the pressing question on the heating of foodstuffs, they all turned to face him again.

'OK, so all of you, you six, are the only survivors, and by clinging to the food trolleys and baggage, you somehow manage to float safely, through the night, in the warm tropical waters somewhere near Samoa or possibly Fiji.' Food trolleys and the exact locale of the desert island were not on his list either.

'Tiger sharks,' said John from IT. 'The tropics right? We'd never make it past the tiger sharks. They have these lids man, come over their eyes, like shutters, before they bite.' Everyone looked at him. Todd shot him a glance that said 'Idiot!'

'Good point, John,' said David. 'But thankfully, the tiger sharks are busy and so are the hammerheads,' he paused, regaining composure, 'with the 200 or so dead floating amongst the wreckage.' Everyone seemed either reassured or baffled. OK, perhaps he'd taken it too far.

'So you wake to find yourselves on the scorching sand. Individually you scour the beach looking for food and shelter but the vegetation is sparse and it seems there are few or no animals. Finally you all meet each other, under the searing heat, and there are scenes of despair and hope. Crushing, desperate tears, strangers holding each other.' OK, back to the script. There was no point in spinning this out. He just wanted to get to his PC and check. Would they offer him John's post or bring in a new head? If they did he'd lose his job. A new regime. That was always the way.

'As the waves recede, you discover remnants from the air crash, washed up on the beach.' Eight objects. He read them out from the list. This was the fifty-third time he'd done this now and each time the objects seemed to get more and more Beckettian.

1. A tarpaulin
2. Salt tablets
3. Three bottles of vodka

'Where the fuck did the vodka come from?' laughed Todd. David already had it in his notes that Todd had a disciplinary for drinking at work. He ticked the box that read: Obstructive.

'My apologies, Todd,' David said. Say their first names – the American way. 'It's not three but three hundred, and not just vodka.' The drinks trolley. Mini bottles. 'A hundred and seventy-five Smirnoff. Fifty Whyte & Mackay.' He did the quick mental arithmetic. 'Seventy-five Gordon's gin. No mixers.' It was totally improvised, and credible. The number of drinks involved kept Todd quiet for a moment.

4. Flares (usually David joked about how they weren't the denim variety, but the joke was well worn and this was the wrong audience)
5. Razors
6. A magnifying glass
7. A mirror
8. A mobile phone

The group stared at him – was that all? Todd still seemed to be working out how long the alcohol would last. John went back to picking at his food stains. If he could just

get back to his PC and check the email. There would
be the memo with the list of new redundancies. Alice's
name would be on it. Not his. He'd wait till Friday before
telling her. By then she'd have made an incredible artwork
and would almost be glad to not have to come back to
all of this. Six, seven minutes then he'd make up some
excuse to get out for five and check.

'No way you'd get a signal,' John said. 'Not even with
Virgin.'

'Good point, John, and as you've guessed the purpose
of this exercise is to decide on what objects should be
used or discarded. You have to pick four.' Grateful that
the guy had given him the opportunity to skip three pages
and he could easily paraphrase the rest. 'You have no
food and no fresh water and so you have to choose
between different strategies. Without water, in this heat,
I'd give you three days. If you all take an object each and
do your own thing you'll probably run out of time and
die, so you have to decide which objects and strategies
to prioritise.'

Moving on swiftly. Skip another page. No point in
explaining the purpose of the exercise. The two quiet
ones maybe understood. Names? He'd check again later.
Yes, the silent man with the stay-press Gaps and the army
haircut. Survivalist. Looked like he could eat human flesh.
Start a fire with a piece of broken glass and cook the
others, throw it all back with a cocktail of Gordon's and
Whyte & Mackay.

'So, if you could make your choices and just fill these
in. No need to give reasons.' He handed out the forms.

OK, now was his chance. Ten minutes they'd need. It
wouldn't be seen as sneaking away. Get back to his desk.
The email, the offer of promotion perhaps, the contract
to look over. Hilarious that he now wanted promotion,

in this job that he had hated for so long, but this was
the plan. To do this for Alice. To just get back to the
PC.

'No conferring,' he said as he got to his feet, 'you all
have to do it by yourselves.' As he headed to the door
he noticed that the cannibal from IT had taken his seat
to the corner of the room and was devouring his pen.

Out the door, down the corporate-coloured corridor.
Elevator, corridor, glass partitions, desk. The usual, but
arriving there unusual. No emails. Nothing. Usually he
got one every five minutes. His boss had been fired and
there was nothing. It was a sign, from on high. That was
the way it worked here, everywhere. SILENCE EQUALS
DEATH. If a merger is going through and no one tells
you anything, then you're dead. That was the way. The
water-cooler conspiracists knew before you did, and they
had fallen silent as he'd passed.

As he headed back towards room 3C, he remembered.
Tonight was childminding night. Shit. How had he
forgotten? The move probably. He'd have to call Alice
and tell her, apologise, he'd have to go straight to
Hannah's from work. Damn it, Alice's first day doing her
art and he was dying to get back and see what she'd done.
But then maybe, sitting down to dinner after, chatting
and joking, she'd see it in his face. His new worries about
work. My God, he'd have to put on this act for her all
week.

Reaching for the door handle of conference room 3C
he reminded himself again that he was still a fine actor.
The method. Think method. Objects. A milk bottle, a
T-shirt, a glass. Brando, Dean. Take an object in your
hand, feel it, crush it, caress it. Feel the role through the
object. The method. Running over the first line he would
say to them all, 'So, anyone pick the tarpaulin?' As usual

no one would have, so there would be nothing to catch the rainwater in and they would all die of thirst. He took the handle in his hand, turned it slowly, and when the door opened the face they saw was that of a man with a secure career in Human Resources.

*   *   *

I stepped closer to the door and peered inside, she was on her hands and knees and my boss Tony was pumping away at her. No, too like the one last week. *Steve was my hubby's work chum and I always thought he was a bit of a hunk.* No, hunks intimidated David. *Me and Joe have always been great in bed, but recently.* No, best to start with positive reinforcement.

She was on the net, looking through his porn sites, to find a real life amateur confession. Whenever he came back from babysitting he was always incredibly tense and needed his bedtime story. It wasn't exactly the typical textbook way of dealing with impotence, but they'd never been a typical textbook couple, and straight after that first night together she'd made a point of buying all the textbooks just to make sure. *Coping with Erectile Dysfunction. Love Matters: A Holistic View. ED: Five case studies. Psychopathia Sexualis. Impotence and the New Man.*

> Since the sexual revolution of the 60s, many men still feel enormous pressure to 'perform' sexually.

They'd laughed about that one 'cos she hated the 60s and he was an actor and getting through every day, he said, was a kind of performance. As they read the books together it became increasingly apparent that there was no real cure.

Relaxing together is a must. Enjoy a meal, or visit a
theatre or cinema. Leave each other affectionate notes.
Or enjoy a shared walk in a park or the countryside.
Cook a favourite meal. It can also help to look at photos
of you both throughout your relationship to remind yourselves how far you have come.

For the first few months they were compulsory bedside
reading, and they laughed themselves senseless at how it
all sounded so much like the kind of shit David had to
say on his Human Resources courses.

Think positive. You have not been fired – you've been
freed.

The fact that he could get hard by himself was proof that
it was psychological.

It's important that you avoid using technical terms like
'Impotence' or 'Erectile Dysfunction (ED)'. Try to find
your own intimate words. Suggestions are 'Mr droopy
drawers' or 'Sleepy sausage' or 'Our little problem'.
Try using the word 'We' rather than 'I' or 'You' as this
reassures your partner that you are dealing with the
condition together.

It was only after they'd finished all the books that she
discovered that joking, laughing and cuddling in bed were
quote-unquote *powerful ways of building the intimacy
required to take the first steps*. They'd laughed then about
how you weren't supposed to be laughing at the books
which were supposed to cure you. And then they took it
one step further and started getting off on the case
studies. *Tony is well endowed but can only get hard with oral.*

At about the six-month mark she'd made her first mistake. They'd got drunk and she just wanted to get laid. They'd done the usual. She'd read him a couple of pages from the case studies and they'd both started jerking off together. But then she reached over and touched him and he was hard and he was still hard as she climbed on top and guided him inside. But then.

'Same ole same ole,' he'd said. 'Sorry.' And she'd done all the things the books said she shouldn't. She felt rejected, angry. She said you, she said I, not we.

> Most men experience a period of **psychological impotence** at one time in their lives, either due to stress, substance abuse, medication, fatigue, ill health, depression, relationship issues, or change of partner particularly after a loss. It is important that this is seen as an isolated event. If the male becomes anxious about his 'performance' after the occasional episode, this will lead to **performance anxiety** before the sexual event, which results in the formation of a vicious circle: anxiety – failure – more anxiety – more failure. This is called the **impotence domino effect.**

Every time he tried to enter her it was the same story. So then she had the idea of an altogether different kind of story. At first they lay there and she made them up but, all too soon, she found the limits of her imagination. So she'd secretly started looking at his porno sites and memorising stories so she could recount them to him. There were other nuances too. Stories about 'We', about 'Me' and 'You' – 'You're fucking me so hard', 'Give it to me' – only seemed to increase his anxiety and make it all too clear that they weren't actually fucking each other. So the stories became about watching. And as they

lay together, eyes closed, and she recounted her stories
and he whispered 'Yeah, go on, tell me', it wasn't so difficult for them to imagine that they were really there, in
some car park, some hotel, some changing room in a
chain store, on a beach, at a party, watching another
couple fucking. There was little point in analysing what
it meant, as little as there was in questioning him about
the origin of 'their' problem. It was obviously something
to do with his ex-wife but at the same time was like that
thing with her mother – no point asking an alcoholic
why they drink, better to find strategies for coping. And
it did work. They jerked off together and as she heard
him starting to come she could bring herself quickly to
a climax, and they would hold each other afterwards, to
all the world like a real couple who'd just had sex.

*I couldn't believe it when Sylvia came home and told me
what she'd seen her friend Sharon doing at work today. So
when Sharon and her boyfriend invited us for dinner I knew
I couldn't resist the temptation.* Yup. That one would be
just fine. He'd be back in a few hours. He'd want to see
her art but she'd lead him to the bed, tell him, Shh,
undress him and read him his bedtime story.

*   *   *

'Can I see your new house, Daddy?'

The three little pigs were to blame, their houses of
straw, wood and brick. He was grateful that Amy hadn't
asked why it was he lived in a different house. But still
she was just doing her little trick with him again. Asking
her questions so she could stay up. He'd told her three
times that it was well past sleepy time and he'd already
read her five stories even though Mummy said she should
only have three.

'Yes, you can come to my house sometime soon,' he

said, although he worried that it wasn't time just yet for Amy to know about or meet Alice. Or for Alice to meet Amy.

'Can I play in your garden?'

'Well we don't, I don't, have a garden, really.'

'Mummy says some people don't have houses. That's silly, isn't it, Daddy?'

This last month, every time he'd been childminding it had been the questions. Hundreds of them, pouring from her five-year-old mind: 'Why can't we play in the other park?'; 'Why doesn't Jamie have a daddy?'; 'Why don't men wear skirts?'; 'Why are there so many cars, Daddy?'

In so many ways they were the same angry questions Alice still asked. Why are things the way they are? Chomsky, Foucault. Unlike Alice he found he had few answers.

'Well, darling, things are. Just are. The way they are.'

'Are you the boss, Daddy?'

Having children. The terror of it, when you have to have answers to give but still have so many things unresolved in your own life.

'No, I'm not the boss.'

'Jemma's daddy says he's the boss.'

'Well maybe he is.'

'Is he your boss, Daddy?'

Much as he hated to have to do it, he had to be strict with her. There would be other times for her questions but now it was nine o'clock and forty-five minutes after sleepy time. He tucked her in, held her hand and put on his almost-cross voice, although it was hard not to smile.

'Sleepy time, darling.'

'Can you stay beside me, Daddy?'

Yes, he wanted to, to feel her snuggling against his arm, to hear her breath slowing, her little yawns, to feel her eyelids tickling his arm as they grew heavy and sleep came to her. But then there was the fear. That he'd close his eyes too. That he'd be woken by Hannah's key in the door and would rise to see her staring at him in the doorway. Her ex-husband lying beside her daughter. So he sat on the edge of her bed and stroked her head. 'Nah-night, darling. Sleepy time.'

Moments like this. He had to lift his eyes from her face, to look away, at anything other than her sleepy face. So it was the room. The antique rocking horse. The doll's house from Ikea. The big polar bear he'd got for a pound in a car boot sale, just before he left, which Hannah said took up too much space and wanted him to take with him but which Amy had named Tom-Tom and couldn't be separated from. As if she knew. Look at the space. Amy's bedroom was bigger than the kids' bedroom in the new place. Thankfully, the wallpaper was orange, not pink or blue, although even since his visit last week there had been an increase in pink girly toys. This unspoken ideological battle with Hannah. She'd insisted that he stopped bringing Amy presents on every visit. The implicit criticism being that they could never make up for the damage he'd done. He always made a point of making his toys non gender specific. Farm animals, a green ball, a cuddly dinosaur. But now in the corner by the window in the Ikea storage boxes were her new toys, My Little Pony, another Barbie or two. Presents from Hannah's parents no doubt. Alice would have had a lot to say about them. The pinkification of the world. That book she'd made him read after their first date, *The Society of the Spectacle* by that French guy from '68 – 'We live our lives aping images', 'We turn our children into copies of copies.' The hidden ideological meaning behind the word 'reproduction'.

Her hand dropped from his. Her eyes were closed. To have your child fall asleep beside you. It stopped all questions. Breath, touch, so painfully simple. You fool, you sad self-pitying fool. You walked out on her.

He got to his feet and tried not to look back. The corridor. He could navigate the place with his eyes closed. Would have preferred to do so. To not have to see the Victorian cornicing he and Hannah had repainted together, so like the one Alice had in her studio. The bookshelf they spent months looking for in antique dealers. The wooden floor he'd varnished himself although Hannah had insisted they get a professional in to do it. Five days it had taken him. The effort involved would convince him that he'd done the right thing in marrying her – was what he'd told himself as he'd scrubbed and sanded and varnished and revarnished. And so it was with the knocking down of the wall to make space for the redesigned kitchen and the hosting of dinner parties. Don't think, just do. Again and again. The Indian throw rugs she'd bid for at the auction. The 50s chairs she'd found on eBay. Everything a little mismatched. Eclectic. Unlike the sofa he was now sitting on which was regulation khaki Ikea. Everything else had been part of that attempt West End couples make to have original things. To reassure yourself that your home is different from everyone else's. The West End. A joke. A joke told twice. He might lose his job and then there would be no point in even unpacking. He and Alice would have to leave. Moving so close had been a mistake.

Staring at the Sony widescreen TV, not the programmes. Be honest though. Even back then what did you feel? Shame. Worse. He'd had it all, the West End home, the 4x4 with side-impact bars and the Mothercare car seat and sticker on the back windscreen that read 'Child on Board'. But even then he'd felt it was like drama school – a role called 'Father'. Walking round the block with Amy in her hi-tech stroller, past all the other West End fathers with their kids in hi-tech strollers. The sky is blue, the grass is green, the sun is yellow. Words he'd said to Amy, over and over, as much to try to drum it into his own head as to teach. A world like a child's drawing, where the sun was always yellow and everyone had a big red sandstone house and a green garden and a big silver car and two golden-haired kids. A world in which he'd felt a fake. And there he'd been instilling these values in his own child.

Another hour killed. He'd forced himself to watch fragments of TV shows so that his thoughts wouldn't take him through there, to where they always took him. To Amy's bedroom. To stand there silently watching her sleep.

Ten twenty-five and a half-hour of reality TV. He put his shoes on in readiness. Hannah would be back at ten thirty. Was always prompt. He'd have to be ready to leave quickly. The few awkward exchanges. But ten thirty had been and gone and he was pacing, forcing himself to just sit there in the living room. Look at it. Like some photo of a des res in an estate agent's window. Sit down. Stop thinking. Sit down in the photo of a room in an estate agent's window. This is no longer your life.

In Alice's paintings there were no cars. There were no people. The grass was red, the sky was green, the sun was black.

The sound of keys in the lock. Hannah. He was on his feet and at the door before she'd had time to close it. Her usual questions to fill the silences. 'What time did she go down?', 'Did she brush her teeth?', 'Was she good?', 'Saturday then. OK, call to confirm.' But then she'd said it. The thing he'd feared she might say for almost two years. The thing she said to him on that night when he ran from her.

'We need to talk.'

All he could do was nod, grunt, stare at his feet. 'Uh huh, OK, sure.' Then as usual he was away, out the door, pulse racing, feet catching up. We need to talk.

Past the big gardens, past the 4x4s. To talk, to talk about what? What was there to say? Money? Had she heard about the situation at work? If she had he'd have to tell her how there was this shadow, just this shadow, of a doubt, this fear he might lose his job. And if he did, could she just hold off for a month till he'd sorted out the childcare payments? No, it could be worse. The Talk. Were they finally going to sit down and analyse all the reasons he'd left? Posit blame, analyse incidents. Break the silence which had so far been covered over with details, dates – Thursdays not good, she has a party, Monday is better, can you pick her up from school? For a year and a half they'd both been postponing the Talk.

Step after step along the old street. Would he tell Alice that Hannah wanted to talk? It felt wrong. Another one of his rules with Alice was that they never talked about Hannah. So, the Talk, if it ever did take place, would be a secret he'd have to keep from her. It felt in some way like a betrayal. Perhaps it was why Hannah wanted it to happen. More than likely, she didn't want to find out why he left. Just wanted to subject him to a confessional and make him keep it secret from Alice. Almost two years since they separated and still there were these games.

Finally, he caught sight of a yellow light coming up the hill towards him. Unable to face the short walk, he stepped out into the street and hailed the taxi. No, he wouldn't tell Alice about this. They had enough to worry about, with him and work. He would keep this from Alice. Protect her from work, protect her from Hannah.

* * *

She'd waited for more than an hour. Could have used that time doing her art but it was dead time, waiting time and yes, she'd been a little scared of going back into that room again. She had it all planned, memorised, it was kind of routine now. The night after the evening of babysitting – David's story. But when David came back he was wasn't interested. Was even more morbidly silent than usual. He wanted to see her art, he said, and she told him no, not yet. He fell asleep in her arms, and she tried not to think about what he must have been through tonight, with his ex, and how she was the reason for all this. And she tried not to think about Sharon and her boyfriend, and the countless other stories she'd memorised about couples fucking. As she lay awake beside him she tried to focus on her art, and the room, and to tell herself as the textbooks said, that self-esteem was a powerful tool in dealing with impotence, and if she could just make it as an artist, it might be a beginning of the cure. If only she had one single idea. Not this overabundant confusion that would lead, as it always did, to nothing.

* * *

Nine thirty and he was back at his desk. Again he resisted the impulse to call Alice and tell her about the signs. No, the lack of signs, which in itself was a sign. He had just walked the corridor to the water cooler to find Alice's friend Pauline, the career soothsayer, but she wasn't there which was another sign.

More signs. Directly behind him there was a flurry of activity going on in the soundproofed offices of PR. Sheila, the head, was shouting silently down the phone to someone, as some new employee sat at her desk and read from her screen. Another sign. When PR brought in new people it was to do with spin, fear, problem solving, probably some leak about the merger. The unions, maybe.

Do something, anything. When you are anxious make a list. His marriage guidance counsellor had said this. Log the time.

10.15.   Emailed Tom, head of Corporate Affairs, to ask what is happening about the post of head of HR.
11.02.   The photocopier is jammed floor four.
11.49.   No reply from Tom, Corp. Affairs. Resend email. CC to Jackie, head of Accounts, to ask update on merger and redundancy packages. CC to PR.
12.07.   No replies.
13.02.   New message to Tom, Corp. Affairs. If there are new staff and new redundancies, then who is hiring and firing? We are not.
13.37.   The toilet roll in the Gents has run out and has not been replaced.
13.42.   Email to Facilities. Complaint about male employee sanitary provisions.
13.45.   Walk through floor three. Sarah, head of Facilities, is not at her desk.

Hours and minutes and fearful milliseconds with nothing to do. So he was back at his desk and it was swinging-paradise again and Pussy-galore. This was how it happened. How it started for Archie the gross misconductor. Anxiety about work. You sat at your desk and no one was telling you anything and so as you suffered in silence you wanted to see others suffer. Every time David had felt in any way threatened in his career it was the same. Sex and pornography. You feel like a pathetic inconsequential male so you read the spams for penis enlargement and miracle cures for impotence. You were exhausted having to sell yourself so you wanted to see other people sell themselves for your pleasure.

Pussy-galore. Seeking W/E men or couples for mutual fuk, suk + DIY. W/E, that was good, could mean West End but meant well endowed. VW/E being the natural extension of that. Very West End.

No point just looking. Why not reply for the hell of it? She was a Bond girl after all. If nothing else, passing the rest of the day in an online debate about Connery versus Moore would kill the anxiety. Which was the best Bond? Yesssh. My dear Pusshhhy.

13.52.   No email. Another new junior employee walked past carrying three boxes. Whose desk is being cleared? Who has hired these new employees?

14.15.   Walk to canteen. Not hungry. Detour through Studio Two. Empty.

14.48.   No one has fixed the photocopier. Email to Sarah, head of Facilities, asking for it to be repaired. Reminder about Gents sanitary provisions.

14.50.   New employee walks past with new paper shredder.

15.21.   Toilet roll has still not been replaced.

15.32.   Email. Sarah, Facilities, has resigned her post. We wish her luck with, etc.

16.20.   Still no reply from Tom, Corp Affairs.

16.32.   Email from the corporation. CC to all employees. Inviting staff to invest in the new employee share option. (Bastards trying to raise the stock value after the merger.)

16.45.   Tom, head of Corporate Affairs, just walked past carrying two boxes and yucca.

As soon as David saw him pass he got out of his seat, opened the glass door and ran after him, then slowed his steps. Looking at Tom from behind. He wanted to call out to him – 'Tom, you OK? What's going on?' But the sight of the man in his pinstriped shirt and chinos carrying his well-loved yucca. A gift when he got the job, four years' growth. One of the saddest things he'd ever seen. Like that movie with Michael Douglas. That line, 'What am I? I'm a corporate man without a corporation.' *Falling Down*. So he stopped and let Tom make his solitary exit along the corporate-coloured corridor. His yucca waving above his head like antennae.

Five past five. A shadow passed by his cubicle. He hit the button for the spreadsheet to hide the close-up on Pussy-galore's pussy. Anticipating the required smiley turn in his leather swivel chair, the hello David, the just-thought-I'd-pop-by-and-give-you-the-update. But the shadow passed and he was almost angry for being ignored. So he waited another five, ten, amazing, amazed at this first time ever he'd been in a job and had absolutely nothing to do. Silence. Apart from the distant rhythmic guzzling of the document shredder. Fuck it. If they came, he would hear their footsteps before they saw him, so why not. Reply to Pussy-galore.

Subject: Bond Girls.

He typed: Forget Dr No – Try Dr Yes. Delete. Would you like a Gold finger? Delete. *You Only Live Twice* could be turned into a gag about a foursome. *Octopussy*. Hands all over you like an octopus. Oh James you are such a cunning linguist. *From Russia with Lust. Thunderballs. The Man with the Golden Gun.* No need for a double entendre there. Sex and death. Death and survival. *Tomorrow Never Dies. Live and Let Die.*

Fuck, it was a silly waste of time. But a whole day had passed and no one had offered him promotion, or demotion, and there really was no one else left to ask what the hell was happening. So why not? Another little role to play. Give yourself a name, set up a fake Yahoo account so they can't trace it in IT. Another ten minutes and it was done. His new name was: James + Moneypenny. Password: Bondage.

He changed the title of the email from Bond Girls to The World is Not Enough. And added: thirties couple seeking same for action and adventure. He was about to delete it when he heard the shredder gagging on the quantity it had been fed. Fuck it, fuck them all. Click. Send.

He pulled his jacket slowly from the peg and aimed himself at the door. But just as his hand hit the handle, AOL told him that he had another message. There it was. Fourteen-point azure blue.

Sender: Direct Human Management

Dear David Mackay,

We have recently been given the contract for Human Resources at Scotia TV. We will be overseeing the merger with BMTC and look forward to . . .

He was well skilled in deciphering the corporate gobbledygook but this was a whole new level. Real professionals. The gist of it was they were a new company based in London and had been given the task of re-recruiting to see the company through 'the seamless transition into the merger period'. The corporation requested, and fully anticipated that, he send every single one of his employee files and profiles to them at HQ. ASAP. Accompanied by his own recommendations. Your co-operation in this matter will be, etc.

Clever. Machiavellian. No guarantee of tenure. The vague insinuated promise that if he helped he would be able to keep his job. But vague and insinuated. He could do it and then they could fire him. The fall guy. The sucker. The one thing they'd overlooked, these clever bastards, was the good old-fashioned hands-on approach. The contents of his desktop. Sure they could fire him and get some new employee in the IT department to download all his files and forward them, but they needed an insider guy to help. It would be so easy to go into the file management folder and select 'Delete all files' then hit return. Ah, how the powerless dream of power. But still, they'd asked for his recommendations. He'd make sure at least that Alice's job was safe. Go through the employee list and give her five stars.

It was five twenty and he was damned if he was going to work overtime for these fuckers. He'd email them tomorrow, at least that way he'd be guaranteed employment for another day.

Time to kill. A good Bond title. So he clicked back on swinging-paradise.com, looked over his reply to Pussy. Changed the title from The World is Not Enough to Die Another Day. Absolutely. Die Another Day. Click. Send.

*   *   *

A man standing alone naked in his kitchen at night seen in profile, staring out of a window, right of frame, his body barely lit from the neighbour's window he was looking out at. Vermeer, Hopper. She'd glimpsed David standing there like that on that third or fourth night, after she'd woken at three after three or four sleepless nights worrying about her stupid fucking art. Woken to find he wasn't beside her in bed and staggered sleepily to the bathroom and stumbled across him, there by the window, then turned before he could see her and went back to bed. And as she lay awake pretending to be asleep, because she was too worried about him even to start to discuss it, and he came back and cupped his hands round her breasts and kissed her head thinking she was asleep, she told herself that she shouldn't worry about him, that it was more than a little perverse for sure and that he'd been more than a little distant the last few days. But still. There were only a few days left to do her art.

Fuck, it was perfect. The image. A man looking out of a window. A woman maybe. It said everything she'd wanted to say. He'd done it again. That way he inspired her. She'd get up early the next day and start a fresh canvas. When she was sure he was asleep she lay beside him stroking his head and telling him that she was sorry for the horrible moody silences of the last few days because now he'd saved her, helped her find her thing and everything was going to be OK. 'I love you so much,' she whispered, because she knew he couldn't hear her and that was the only way, ever, that she could say those words. When she had completed her first painting then she would be worthy of love.

She was up early like she told herself she would be. Sitting there with her sketchpad, charcoals, pencils, eraser, trying again, at the kitchen window, doing sketches of the woman next door. Lowering her gaze, whenever the woman looked up, so as not to be seen staring. Trying to picture her as David must have seen her.

Look at her. Tall, pretty, busty. Every movement the woman made Alice sketched frantically. Page after page. Framed by my window frame in her frame, looking from my kitchen into hers, packing up her things, on the phone, washing the dishes, sipping coffee. Sketch after manic sketch. The woman, pacing about, staring into space. Staring at the Edward Hopper reproduction on her back wall in which a woman in a window stared at a man staring into space. Yes, it was fucking excellent. Frames within frames. The last few days had been a mess but now the idea was clear. The woman in the window. Good title. Window woman. We are all framed by how people see us but still we stare out – wanting more. So many possibilities. A canvas, the first canvas, the twenty-five colours of paint waiting. It was this radical mix of the abstract and the figurative. The flatness of the wall. Then the window. A square within a square. Two areas of solid colour, then the abstract movement of a human form. Francis Bacon. Beyond Bacon. Not people, women, a woman. She was beautiful. The neighbour. Not in a traditional sense but because the idea was. It was about. No, enough procrastinating. Just do it, Alice.

She was running, tripping over her feet to get back to the room she'd been so scared of for the last few days. 'What a fucking drama queen you are,' she said to herself as she stood there at the door. Twenty-five sketches in her hand. Deep breath. Why are you still standing there? Open the fucking door, Alice. Open it. She stepped in. But look at it. Jesus. The hole in the wallpaper. The sketches and paint and glue and charcoal all over the carpet. Shit. It would have to come up. The carpet. A hammer, tools, a what? A whatever. Get David to help. Fuck. No time left. Get started, Alice.

She laid out all the colours on the palette. Got the

turps, the charcoal. Fuck yeah. It was happening. She riffled through the sketches. Damn. Too many good ideas. Equally worthy of attention. There was nothing to do but try them all out. Four canvases, three, no four ideas. Start them all. Yes, yes. The first marks were just technical. The bold square of the window, the outline of the woman's body. As the charcoal moved almost independently of her she suddenly wanted to call David, to tell him he'd been right. It was going to be OK. It'd be like that first time, back in art school in California, in 1992 when she was top of her class, mastered every genre.

Paint now. The frustratingly slow process of mixing the oil paints with the turps and linseed oil. Her biggest, boldest brush blocking in the colours. Running from one canvas to the next. The one on the easel, the one propped up against the fireplace, the one on the window ledge. In each, a square within a square. Yes, women in frames. When she'd finished the first painting she'd sit David down and tell him the whole story. He'd only had it in fragments before. How all her life she'd thrown herself into one thing passionately, excelled, then abandoned it. The same way with people, lovers. People in frames, it was always about that. How she'd always run from being a this or a that, from feeling trapped. How now these pictures made sense of it all.

The problem. Really. The problem was that now that she'd painted these squares, these windows, what it needed was the human subject in the second window. But what would she be doing? This human, this woman, what do women do? Pottering about? No. Too vague. Standing still, but facing which way? Towards or away from the viewer. Alice painted the outline of the woman's back staring away, but it seemed too contrived. What was really needed was to see the expression on her face. But she hadn't done any sketches of her face.

A face. So it was this bright idea and running through to the bathroom to get David's shaving mirror. She would sketch her own face and superimpose it on the sketch of the neighbour's body. Perfect. She could choose the facial expression. You look into the neighbour's window and there is your own face staring back at you. Awesome.

So David's mirror on the easel and sketching her own face. Jesus. Such a dumb old-fashioned male sexist Renaissance thing to do, this self-portrait thing, but no way. No way was she going to give up on this portrait. Still the face didn't look like her at all. Either that or it must have been a long time since she'd actually looked at herself. She'd shaded in the cheekbones and started on the eyes. There were crow's-foot lines round them, her eyebrows were a mess and the roots of her dyed hair were showing. OK, it wasn't a pretty sight but it would make a good honest drawing. Keep on. But Jeez – the eyes weren't right. Just marks on the page. A sphere, highlight and shade, a touch of white reflected in the iris. Not her eyes at all. She stood back and examined it. There was no self in the self-portrait. Garbage, she'd got too distracted with the details. Doubts were starting. But no, keep on Alice, finish it, just to prove you can.

She went through to the kitchen, made herself another cup of coffee and stared at her phone sitting there on the unit. Maybe she'd turn it on. Be good to call David or Pauline, get the gossip from work. Maybe it had been a bad idea to force herself into solitary like this. You could go mad. If she could just hear his voice, he'd make her laugh, stop her drifting off. No, she had to do this for herself, couldn't depend on him for everything. Get back through there. Draw your own face directly onto the canvas. Start again.

As she headed back through the corridor she passed the boxes she still hadn't unpacked. All the textbooks she'd carried round for years. Peeking out from under Foucault and Freud was the old photo folder. It wasn't such a bad idea – to copy from photos instead. Other people's faces, her own, it might give her some ideas.

She sat on the floor and started leafing through them. The more recent ones were on the top, so she flipped them over and started at the bottom.

God, look at her. First year art school. 1990. The typical hippie kid with long tangled hair, woollen jumper and paint-spattered denims. So unfashionably serious-looking. Chubby too. Some photo a friend had taken in the student bar, a year or so later, her new indie haircut, her arm round her indie boyfriend, Tony, and some other girl.

The second year art school awards. First prize. No other students in shot. Stripy tights, Doc Marten boots and dreadlocks. Her tutor Steve Michaels hugging her in front of her canvases. She looked distant. Around the time of the first abortion probably.

The old contact sheets from the months when she'd become disillusioned with painting and found photography. The photos of her mum asleep on the sofa at Big Sur, ashtrays filled with joints, empty vodka bottles. Then photos of herself in the mirror, wearing her mother's clothes. The photos her tutor, Toby Schwartz, said were 'disturbing', 'subconscious', 'profound'. That would guarantee her a place on the PhD course.

A photo of her with Toby at the top of the Empire State Building, during their brief affair. 1994, when he told her he would leave his wife for her.

Tons of photos she'd snapped during the flight to Glasgow, after she'd given up on photography and temp jobs and her mother and America. So many photos of clouds, glimpses of the Scottish coastline. The land her father's family came from. Flying to this place where she hoped, finally, she'd find some roots. Views of the city from above.

Photo of her on her day of enrolment. Philosophy, Glasgow University. Skinny, dressed in black, the retro-goth phase. One of those first-day photos you paid a pound for. The Gothic spires of the building behind her. More photographs of Glasgow streets. Her hall of residence. People snapped at random in the street. Looking almost Soviet bloc. Fellow students, also in black, whose names she now couldn't recall.

Photos of her receiving the award for her essay 'The Fragmented Self'. Year two philosophy. Post-punk phase. Purple hair. Fishnets, ironic T-shirt and nose stud. She'd remembered thinking that philosophy gave her justifications for why she was the way she was. So restless, why she could never see anything through. It wasn't a personal failing, it was the spirit of the time, the postmodern condition.

Photos of her during her Madonna lipstick-lesbian phase. Peroxide blonde, boob tubes, heels. What, '98? On the verge of graduating with her MPhil. Pretending to kiss some girl in a nightclub. Always, with her friends, she seemed to be on the edge of the frame. So few lasting friends she'd made in Glasgow.

Then, the chronology was messed up. Older photos. The only photograph she had of her father, the one she'd picked out after her mother got moved into rehab, then care, that she'd found with maybe a hundred others in a box. All the same. His face cut out of each of them. Her mother had done it with scissors. A photo, with him, of her aged maybe four, in some park, on his knee, her smiling, his hand on her shoulder. His face missing.

Photos she'd taken from the spire of Glasgow University, looking down at the city. In those lonely months, so close to finishing her second thesis, when she was disillusioned with philosophy and was thinking of moving back to the States.

Photos of her in nightclubs. As many changes of hair colour as outfits. The trashy phase. The grunge phase. Make-up, no make-up, too much make-up. Drunk. Stoned.

Photos she'd taken of herself after she shaved off all her hair. 1999. After switching to psychology. Starting again. Bathroom mirror. Second abortion. Almost anorexic. The vegan phase. The anti-male phase. An image, then another, of a demonstration. Gay Pride. She'd been such a terrible dyke, no matter how hard she'd tried.

She was close to tears looking at the photos. She tried not to think about that first lecture on psychology, the one she'd snuck into, that had made her give up on philosophy, when the lecturer told the students that this thing, this inability to see things through, this distrust of long-term goals and commitments, was a condition. Page three hundred and four. Children of Alcoholics tend to over-invest in projects or people that will save them. Be highly motivated because they want to escape their pasts. Children of Alcoholics tend to abandon the things they believe in as quickly as they found them because they grew up seeing an endless cycle of hope and its destruction.

The self-portrait, on the easel, incomplete. And that other lecture, the final one. The Rorschach test. Year three. The lecturer was a Jungian, a hippie, like her mother had been, she talked about art and archetypes. How art was the purest expression of the subconscious. The panic she'd felt then. Having spent ten years running only to end back where she'd started.

She dried her eyes, chastised herself for getting distracted by the photos and forced herself to get back to the self-portrait. But, no matter how hard she tried, every mark seemed more and more random and she could feel panic starting to rush at her. She would never finish this picture, would never be an artist, be anything. Stop, stop Alice. Look at what you've done.

The face. Staring back at her. Some mistake. It wasn't hers. Was in so many ways her mother. She grabbed the eraser and rubbed frantically, but the marks were still there, the ghost image. Worse. You have done all these things to try to escape from her. You hated her. You wanted her to die and she did. But now she is back.

Then without warning it was six and David was back and she had to put on her brave face. And he was marching down the corridor, laughing, asking if he could see what she'd been doing in there and she'd stood in his way, pulled the door shut.

'C'mon baby, just a peek.'

'No. No way.'

'I'm sure it's fucking devastating, c'mon, lemme see.'

She'd had to lie and tell him that, yes, her art was great, really, that she just needed a bit more time, and would he mind if she skipped dinner and just kept on working, maybe through the night and then tomorrow, in the morning, she'd show him.

And she'd forced herself to believe her own lie. And gone back in there and taken a deep breath and attacked the canvases. Throwing paint around for hours. Collaging on the sketches of the neighbour, copying them

onto the canvas, with the fragments of the old photos.
Keep going, keep going. To do this. For David.

Then somehow it was two thirty a.m. and she was tired
and hungry and she'd drunk a whole bottle of wine to
keep her up, to keep her going, and David was in bed
and this new fear came to her as she tried to focus on
the three canvases. What had she done after psychology?
David. The only reason she took the job in TV? David.
She was on the verge of going back to California for
good, again, but then David. No, it was more, she needed
the money, she thought a real job might help her, any
job, commit to something, anything, stick it out. But
really the only reason was David. He'd thought getting
back to her art would be good for her. To go back to
that first thing she gave up on and see it through. But
the fear was drawing closer. Staring back at her from the
three unfinished pictures. Fight it. She told herself that
he would save her. David. He would break the cycle, stop
her running from one thing to the next. Even if it took
all night, she'd stay up, even if the paintings were crap
she'd keep working at them until they were good. She
had to because, if she failed, she knew everything would
repeat itself all over again. And she would have to run
again. Only this time it would be from David.

*   *   *

It was late like now. Three or four. We were walking
round Glasgow, holding hands, and he was pointing
things out to me, the old art deco building on Sauchiehall
Street, some bar someone had beat him up in. He joked
about it all, like it didn't quite touch him any more. Like
he lived here but wasn't quite here. Like the way he
talked. He'd been on my interview panel. This man. A
Thursday, oh, nearly two years ago.

Shhh, don't wake up. I'm done next door. It's so late.
I'm done. It's going to be OK. You're sleepy, Daddy. I'm
touching you. It's OK. It's OK. Shhh, Daddy. I'm telling
you a story. I'm touching you, Daddy. You feel that?
Shhh. Story time, Daddy.

He was different from everyone else, this man. This
kind of ironic attitude of his. He looked so square but I
could tell. The smart things he said no one in the room
noticed. I had no idea why I was even there. Just the last
of a whole bunch of interviews I'd gone to, random really,
but they offered me the job and I accepted it and I don't
know why now but it was a lot to do with him. So at the
door I invited him for a drink after work. He said OK,
maybe, and told me there was this place round the corner,
so I sat there all afternoon and waited for him because
I had to know.

You're hard in my hand, Daddy. You're hard now.
Shhh, don't wake up. I'm being so gentle. Stroking you.
Shhh, Daddy.

We got drunk in this bar and talked about Hitchcock
and Damien Hirst and Slint. He was the first guy I'd met
in the UK who'd ever heard of this stupid old post-rock
band, who everyone had forgotten, that I'd been crazy about
since, well, and he told me that there was this track on the
second album that always made him cry and I said, Fuck,
track four, yeah and then he took my hand. And outside
we were holding hands and trying to remember the words
and trying to sing at the same time and getting the words
all mixed up and laughing. And then he pulled away a little
and told me he'd just been separated and had a kid and I
told him it was OK. We walked, just walked for hours,
some industrial estate, the motorway, like he didn't want to
go home and then the sun was coming up and he said. 'It's
like a movie, like *Brief Encounter* or something.' And I told

him I was tired of brief encounters. And then we were at
his door, in this shitty part of the East End, and he said,
and I'll never forget this. He said I could come in if I really
wanted, but I should know 'I'm impotent. In so many ways.'
That was what he said. And I told him that it was absolutely
the best chat-up line I'd ever heard.

You can't hear me, Daddy, can you? You're sleeping,
Daddy. I'm as quiet as quiet can be. Sweet Daddy. I wish
I could make you hard like this all the time, Daddy. Shhh.
I have to tell you. Shhh. Shhh.

He showed me his Slint album and said sorry 'cos he
didn't have a stylus anymore, and did I mind if we listened
to it on tape instead, so we did and we got pissed and
goofed around for hours and I made him play the song
over and over so I could get the words right, but it was
impossible, 'cos it started so quiet, the lyrics whispered
like a lullaby, and gradually the guitars grew and grew
till the voice vanished beneath the wall of sound.

Then we got all cuddled up on his crummy little single
bed, and the window wouldn't shut and the place was
so close to the motorway and all night I couldn't sleep
for the cars, so I hugged him and he hugged me. And
I was thinking we were just like that song, track four,
just these little whispers against the noise of the world.

And there was no making out, not the usual fucking,
the stupid fucking fucking, just holding each other, half
our clothes still on, like I dunno, like refugees or something. And he fell asleep, and I stroked him, like I'm
doing to you now, Daddy, like I'm doing now, Daddy,
sweet Daddy. Shhh.

And I just knew that he was the best thing, really, the
best thing ever, that he was as fucked up as me. That line.
'Impotent, in so many ways.' It made so much sense. 'Cos
I felt like sick and tired of being so smart and not being

able to do anything about anything. It was like this phrase just summed me up and it was like perfect, was like, the answer to so many things. Like maybe I could just hug like this forever and it would be enough and I'd stop fucking around and falling in love then walking out and maybe learn how to stop trashing everything and just hug like this, forever, Daddy. Because this is perfect, Daddy. And I don't care if I can't make you come. Shhh. You're sleeping, Daddy. You're soft now, Daddy. Shhh. That's OK. Shhh.

Sorry, I don't want to cry, but I'm scared, Daddy. I don't want to be like this again, Daddy. I'm such a fuck-up, always. You say you know and it's OK but you don't know. And I could just walk, Daddy, that's what I do, when things get like this and I'm sorry, Daddy. And I think I might have fucked up again and you don't have to know about all that, but I'm a waste and you are my Daddy and I love you but it's too much, Daddy. And I get scared when I get needy like this. If I fuck up again I know what I'm going to do, Daddy. And I fucking hate myself for it. I'll have to walk, Daddy, you should know that. I told you but you wouldn't listen. I'm sorry, Daddy, I don't want to cry. There there, Daddy.

Shhh, you're sleeping. Sleepy Daddy. Sleepy Daddy. You're sleeping. Shhh, you're sleeping. Everything'll be fine. Shhh, Daddy, shhh.

*   *   *

Nine thirty. Two messages. The new HR company repeating their need for his employee list and stressing the importance of his immediate response. Bastards. He should have asked them straight out yesterday. What will you do for me if I give you the info you require? Do I have a contract? Bastards. The other one was on his secret Yahoo account.

Sender: Pussy-galore
Subject: Re Die Another Day

Dear Mr Bond. Sum new pics. FOR YOUR EYES
ONLY. LOL. Send us dik + puss pics in return. Hav to
prove UR legit. Free Fri's and W/ends. MWAA

Prioritise. OK. Within two hours he'd gone through his
entire employee folder, adding a star rating to the spreadsheet, and had made sure that Alice was the only person
with five stars. Downloaded it, emailed it to London,
then sent a supporting email asking in the most discreet
terms about his own position.

Then it was the silence again. A certain silence that
only those in the corporate world can know. The distant
tapping of fingers on keyboards. The sound of the air
conditioners. The sound of someone trying to unchoke
the paper shredder.

To hell with it. Pussy-galore wanted a pic of his dick
and in the absence of any other information it made
him feel wanted. It would be hours till the capitalists
replied. His dick. He didn't have a pic so it was Google
and a search for 'nude amateur male pics'. An hour later.
The details and difficulties of downloading had replaced
his anxieties. The fascinating practicalities. How to get
pics without paying for them. It was back to the
swinging sites again. Free and cheaply made. No
subscription rip-off. You could drag the pics straight
onto the desktop and open them in QuickTime. He
picked a website from New York because he didn't want
Pussy to do a search of Scottish sites and find the same
dick with another name attached. One was of a bigger
guy, one was hairier, the third was too skinny and too
well endowed, the fourth was almost right and was

thankfully out of focus. He cut and pasted it into a reply and sent it off to Pussy. By the time he was done it was about one-ish. He wished he'd called Alice but she would have heard the need in his voice. He sat back and waited for Pussy or the new HR company to reply and stared at the glass walls of his office. The Homer Simpson executive toy on the top of his PC was no longer funny.

In the last hours his fellow or about-to-be ex-colleagues passed him by, knocked on his door and invited him to the bar. But still he sat. He sat there alone because he couldn't face the bar and the intimacy of desperate people he might never see again. He sat there in front of his PC because he was furious at himself for not having been more prepared for the aggressiveness of the takeover. This time it was him that was on the desert island. There was no choice. Survive or die. If they offered him the job, he'd kill all the people they wanted just so he could survive.

Alice, he should call and tell her, but he worried. If he lost his job they'd both be sitting at home unemployed. Clawing at the walls. That horrible forced intimacy would start. It would be exactly the thing she didn't need right now. Her art had not been progressing as fast as he and probably she had hoped. What she needed was time, by herself, unsullied with jobs and earnings and all that shit. If he'd been fired, she'd gracefully take it all on and go and find new work. Why couldn't they just fucking tell him? He was too old, too weary to start looking for a new job. Better not to have to endure another night of this. There were no replies from HR, or PR, so he logged on again to swinging-paradise. Time to kill again. Pussy, thank God for Pussy.

YR DIC IS A KILLER! UR hired 2 thrill. Can we see
MONEYPENNY? Has she done this B4? Are you on
IM 2gether? Need to confirm UR legit. 2 many time
wasters. Men pretending 2B couples. RU free this
weekend?

The weekend. The weekend to get through. Two days
with Alice. Not telling her, anyone, what was really
happening. Killing time again, killing the weekend, till
Alice's contract was signed. Killing time till he found out
if he had a post or not. Killing time till the queue of
angry ex-employees hit his door.

Three twenty-five. An email from the new company.
Could he please draw up contracts for the recommended
employees? Alice's name was there on the list – exactly
the same list that he'd emailed them. That was promising. A contract for Alice.

Four. Alice's contract done. Sent, hard copy and email.
Then time again. Waiting. OK. So, Pussy-galore. She'd
asked for a photo of Alice. Websites. Random female geni-
talia. Amateur. Search for it. Took less time than he
thought. Some ass in New Jersey. Older than Alice but
fit. Lying on a bed. Face blacked out by Photoshop.
Obscure enough to pass. Save to domestic folder, pics, save
as A-ass. What the fuck was he doing? Fuck the corpor-
ations. Fuck the merger. Fuck fuck. Fuck me. Please.

He typed: Pussy-galore. U have made me SO hard.
Hav a secret mission 4U. Make sure UR not followed.
UB dressed in suspenders. Bar in centre. Saturday night.
8p.m. Confirm destination. You flash at me while yr
hubbie watches. Moneypenny will give further instructions. Confirm. This message will self-destruct in one
minute.

He had no intention of meeting them. Just wanted to

see if he got a reply. Fifteen more minutes and no more emails. Nothing. What the hell. He typed: I want your sweet pussy. Want to smear your juices over my face – Die between your thighs.

Delete. Too much. Not funny. No Bond gags. Delete. No, fuck it. Send.

Four fifty-five. It came through. A reply. You have mail.

He stared at it for ten minutes. Fifteen. The azure blue twenty-point Arial font, so informal, so friendly-looking.

They thanked him for his list of recommended employees and his commitment to the corporation and wished him good luck with his future endeavours.

*   *   *

She'd slept late. Had been painting till four a.m. and fluctuated between a kind of despair and a kind of euphoria and back again until she could barely focus her eyes any more but had managed to convince herself that the paintings she'd done last night must be good, were at least promising. That it would all be OK. She'd got up at twelve and spent another hour having breakfast, coffee after coffee. Throwing glances down the corridor to the door at the end. Too scared to admit that she was too scared to go back in there and see.

Now it was almost one and she was standing in the doorway. She closed her eyes as she pushed it open. Breathe. Breathe again. Look, Alice. Look again at your art. Paint everywhere, the canvases, the walls, the floor.

Shit, all of it, shit and mess and waste. It made her think of her mother. Her mother's failed suicide attempt. She'd only mentioned it in passing to David then changed the subject. She'd been twelve. Her mother had told her that the reason she'd survived was because of her love for her. But Alice had, even then, suspected it was just cowardice. The years after. Her mother's cloying concern for her every move. She'd promised herself she'd never do that to anyone else. But now, to think about it. What? Live for others or for yourself. To pass the burden of your lack onto someone else. That was what people did. That was how you survived. You filled yourself up with others.

She steadied herself on the door handle as she lowered her body to the floor. Then she was laughing. Howling with it as she choked on the tears. Jesus. Look at you, Alice. There are children dying in the desert, cities are being bombed and here you are, with your pathetic thirtysomething career crisis, crying over art. Look at you. You are thirty-five and you have a man who loves you and you're sitting in a child's bedroom in a big West End flat, in a foreign country, and you don't know what you're doing, do you, Alice.

A diazepam. David took them sometimes to help him sleep. They were in the drawer somewhere. Or some wine. Something. Tearing through the kitchen drawers looking for the pills, pouring the last of last night's wine into a cup.

Sitting then, at the breakfast bar, concentrating on breathing. Her hands were shaking as she forced down the wine. Breathe, breathe. You have failed. It's OK, it's OK. People fail. She looked out of the window and the neighbour was there again pacing round her kitchen on the phone. Oblivious to being watched. Oblivious to all this. How could she, how could she be so happy, so indifferent to all this? God, Alice hated her.

Sit, breathe. What was she going to do? Go back to work and try to take an interest in her career. All the office gossip. All those things she'd despised. She wasn't a TV researcher who was really an artist. No, not now. Now she was just. What was she? How could she survive like this? Did she even have a job to go back to anyway? How could she tell David? She should call him now. 'Come home please. Something has happened.' No. He'd see the room. How could she ever tell him? Whitewash. The room. Whitewash it all.

Look at her. The stupid bloody housewife in her window. And it had been such a fucking good idea for a painting. It wasn't fair. Was a curse, to have insight and no means to express it. To be always seeing pictures in things. To see the beauty of the world and the art it would make and then be unable to create anything out of it. To have to laugh at yourself. Again. At this talent which was talentless. To inevitably come to despise your vision. To give up on art, hate it all. From now on, to have to avoid these confrontations with beauty. Stop reading the culture section of the paper. Stop going to galleries and watching *Late Review*. Work, eat, drink, sleep, breathe. Admit that you are just like everyone else. Average, uninspired.

The woman next door was having some kind of argument on the phone, it seemed. Her husband, perhaps, or the telephone company or the gas. All those stupid calls you had to make when you moved flat. Alice. What the hell are you going to do? Help me please. David. God. Someone.

Then it happened. Alice must have been staring at her without seeing anything. This little movement in the corner of her eye, again and again. She focused her eyes, looked up and saw. The woman next door. She was smiling and waving at her.

*   *   *

There was usually a scene in old Hollywood movies. It was what they liked to call the flash of hope before the fall scene. What would happen would be something like this.

The protagonist, someone like James Stewart, was coming home late and drunk after the town hall meeting. No, there was that other film, but what the hell. They were all basically the same. The hero would return with a gift for his wife. The gift always signified something imminently tragic, Alice had said, during one of their deconstructing TV evenings. Like losing your job or something. The kind of tragedy that didn't make sense any more, she'd said, because people lost their jobs all the time.

So yeah, flowers. There would be flowers. As soon as she saw them, she'd get it, David thought as he bought a bunch of lilies for Alice in the deli and a bottle of bubbly just to ram it home.

Sometimes like that one with Burton, you'd get the double whammy. Flowers and a roast. She'd have made a roast and got all dressed up especially for him because she had some news for him too. A peck on the cheek, the flowers in a vase, what's for dinner, love, and by the way have you done something with your hair? Oh, darling I missed you all day. You expect all will be well. She is warm and affectionate. He has something to tell her but she gets in there first. Her eyes wet with happiness. The flash of hope before the fall.

'I've got something to tell you too.'

'What is it, darling?'

'Well, I didn't want to say till I was sure but . . .'

'What is it, sweet?'

'We're going to have a baby.'

Now in this kind of movie, you'd get the full impact

because the protagonist was double fucked. He now had
no job and a baby to feed. So he'd keep it secret about
having lost his job. He'd turn to borrowing, then petty
theft and vice to make a living. The most important thing
being that what fuelled the second act was he had this
burning secret he hadn't told her. But then one secret
led to many more until, finally, he was hauled away for
bank robbery, or murder, all because he hadn't had the
guts to tell his wife that he'd lost his job.

So that was exactly what David decided he wouldn't
do. Instead he'd walk in the front door. Hand Alice the
flowers. Put on his James Stewart voice and tell her. No
septic secret festering through the second act. No hope
before the fall. Just the fall. Tell her. I have been fired.
The End. Roll titles.

He expected to find her sitting in the studio, worrying
over her art. But instead she was rushing towards him.
Kissing him, helping him off with his jacket. Talking
excitedly. Seemed almost stoned. She'd met the neighbour. Joan. Joan next door. They were moving out, Joan
that was. They'd been invited to their going-away party.
Tonight.

She put the flowers in a pint glass. Opened the bubbly
and poured.

'So how was work?'

It was bizarre. The quotation marks were falling away
from the act. It was *It's a Wonderful Life*.

'Well, you know, just the usual,' he said. And already
he'd failed. Failed to tell her about his failure. He was
about to give it a second attempt when he smelled something resembling dinner. A roast, even. My God. Had
she seen the movie?

Silverside, she said and apologised for her lack of
talent. This was absurd. She was talking rapidly about

how wonderful it was to do something with your hands
for once. She even used the word wonderful. And how
Joan had gifted her some cookery books with all these
other things. Thai fish paste, a whole chicken, some
salmon, Häagen Dazs, the roasting beef. Her hubby had
turned the freezer off and it was all going to waste. Only
a quick hello. It would be a big help if you'd just take
them. The party tonight. See you then. She seemed so
nice. Nice was not a word Alice ever used.

She talked and talked, hardly letting him get a word
in. She seemed vaguely hysterical. OK, he told himself,
one more drink then hit her with it. It was absurd. This
roast, this bubbly, this bubbly almost manic energy of
hers. He tried to joke with her to lighten the mood. Let's
just stay in tonight, baby. Who needs a stupid bloody
West End party? 'I mean just think about it – all the
walking clichés,' he said, laughing. 'You can practically
tick them off on a score chart.' He nodded out of the
window, the party was starting to fill up.

'Look at them. Local busybodies, breastfeeding
mothers, Ikea versus Habitat, private versus public
school. I mean it's all so fucking . . .'

She was staring at him hard.

'It's not funny,' she said.

'What?'

'I'm sure they're lovely people if you just made the
effort to get to know them.'

'Lovely people.' He couldn't help but laugh. C'mon,
whatever happened to Alice the angry neo-Marxist
feminist who said bourgeois monogamy was a sickness of
capitalism? He stared at her.

'Since when did you use expressions like "lovely
people?"'

It couldn't have been more incredible if she'd started

dancing round in a 50s pinafore. He almost expected to
hear the strings start up and to see the first drops of
snow fall by the window illuminated by the full moon.
Perhaps women in flowery dresses would descend from
the ceiling on swings and there would be a musical
routine.

'OK. Look,' he said, 'I've got something to tell you.'

But she was off again. Actually she was getting pretty
tired of his ironic attitude, she said. OK, he might hate
his job and laugh at all this but actually having a home
and a job and raising a family, these were things that
mattered to some people. And she was tired of feeling
cut off from things and sneering at people because really,
were they so different? And maybe this neighbourhood
could be really great. And how she might like to grow
organic vegetables in the back yard.

He listened silently, nodding his head at the right
moments, thinking this was the kind of talk that won
actors awards. Like Brando talking about milking the
cow, what was it called? Dutchy. *Last Tango*. When all
he wanted to do was cry over his wife's suicide. Always
something from childhood. Mothers, her mother used to
grow her own vegetables she'd said. Maybe Alice was
pregnant.

'Baby, can we just calm down for a minute then you
can say what you're trying to say?'

He reached for her, but she shrugged away.

'Don't patronise me.'

He tried to hold her.

'No, you fuck, you're not listening to a word I'm
saying.'

But he had. He heard the clichés in her mouth and
the platitudes on his own tongue and swallowed them.
Best to encourage her. Ask careful questions and after

not so long she'd come to see the absurdity of what she was saying. The little movie would be over and it would be time for the news.

Minutes he sat quietly with his listening face on. She outlined the plan. She wasn't going to go back to work. Hated it. Was going to start a neighbourhood work exchange. Like they had in Partick. Like in some parts of Boston and New York. And how maybe she could do some art classes for kids and or maybe start a writers' group or something. Because really community had to be something you built with your own hands.

Running over the words in his head. But I've been fired, Alice, and all these plans of yours are pointless. Tell me what's up. Really. She was staring at him.

'You know this has been our problem all along,' she said.

'What?' That was it. Now he was angry. 'You know, Alice, I could engage with this if I hadn't heard the same damn things a hundred thousand times. I could listen if I didn't know that this whole thing is just some kind of front for what you're not telling me.'

Her lip started trembling.

'Like what the fuck has been going on, Alice?'

She couldn't speak. Was about to cry. He wanted to hold her there and tell her everything would be OK, even though he knew it wouldn't. He wanted to hold her at least for a few minutes and squeeze those tears from her. She got up and went through to the bathroom, making her apologies. She had to blow her nose, wash her face, get ready for the party.

He sat there by himself and listened as she moved round. He felt trapped again, stuck staring out the window. Didn't want to be seen staring. Look at it. In the last twenty minutes the place had filled up. Buffet on

the breakfast bar. Bubbly. Fifteen people he could see,
probably more in the front room. Busy. Busy bodies.

This was the scene where the hero and heroine had
to abandon all their dreams and face a cold hard world.
No. The scene in which they'd lost everything but found
each other. No, this was not a scene like anything else
he'd performed before. There was no joking it off. This
was one of those situations he'd witnessed other people
go through. Like those community actors he'd once tried
to direct. Who'd forgotten their lines and stood there
mute and twitching on the stage with no idea what they
were supposed to be doing. Two unknowns nervously
trying to make it up as they went along until he'd stepped
in with the script.

He looked out of the window at the hostess. Joan
Gordon, Alice had said. In the heart of it all. Dressed
down, but yes, still stunning. He worried that in some
way Alice must have known he'd been spying on her the
last few nights. She was glancing up and out, gesturing
to someone in the direction of his window. Talking about
us, he thought. He stepped swiftly past the window and
poured himself the final glass of bubbly. Threw it back
and stood there and looked round his own home. The
home he'd have to pay for with temp jobs and short
contracts for ever indefinitely. To be one of those sad
fuckers whose work didn't even pay the mortgage. Alice
would be upset, but he'd have to tell her tonight. Get
the party over and done with, then tell her.

She'd be a while changing. He walked over to the
computer and logged onto his email. Just to kill time.
Yes, no one could see, and Alice would be ten or fifteen.
And there they were. Some new pics from Pussy.

*   *   *

Fifteen minutes later and they were there. Autopilot. Joan air-kissing Alice and herding them through. Some brief introductions, then thankfully the drinks table. Some old lady wouldn't let them move. She was drinking water. Where were they from? What did they do? Were they married? Had they bought or rented? David looked at Alice. 'Score one,' he whispered. But Alice wasn't playing. Mrs Miller. Head of the local community council. Busybody. Not so much a council really, she explained, more just a get-together of like-minded people concerned about preserving the identity of the community. He'd toned down his one-liner about Auschwitz and said yes really it must be so good to know that everyone is exactly like you. He'd grinned at Alice but she was having none of it. She turned her back on him.

He walked through to the front room. Yes, the Gordons were moving out not in. The place was stripped bare. Boxes everywhere just like theirs. Heads turned as he passed. Charming smiles. The kind that could burst into a conversation if you didn't look like you were passing quickly to go and get something, as he did. He pulled out his Marlboros and made a mute show of displaying that he was nipping out for a fag. Chinos – check. Debate on private schools – check. Ikea conversation – check. No sign of the obligatory baby yet. Thankfully. No sign of any of the ex-wife's friends.

Out the door and lighting up. OK, what was to be done? Do the fake politeness routine. Get Alice out of here as soon as possible. This was not the right environment to break the news to her. Sugar the pill for her. No doubt after an hour or so of this she'd realise the people were contemptible and would be only too glad to hear that they'd have to move. He'd tell her quietly. They'd cry and hug. Then it would be done.

A cough behind him.

'Hey, you David?'

He turned and there he was. Mr Neighbour. Mr Doctor slash Lawyer slash whatever. David smiled. Mr slash was pulling out his fags.

'What's the fuckin' world comin' to, eh?'

David was about to reply that West End parties were indeed awful, but held back. What was that accent?

'Can't smoke in your own fuckin' house.'

Mancunian was what it was. Working-class man. Not what David expected at all. He offered him a light.

'Or drink in the street,' added David. He raised his glass and toasted the guy.

'Cheers . . .'

'Yeah, right, fuckin' cheers.' Mr slash neighbour put his fag in his mouth to free his hand.

'Neil, mate, good to meet ya.'

David cleared his throat and shook. The accent had thrown him but now it would start. The 'so what do you do for a living?' chat. Having to explain to this stranger about the merger and how he'd just lost his job. But after five minutes and a second cigarette each there was not one mention of work or house prices or private schools or Ikea or sport.

'The push-up bra, you see her?' Neil liked to joke about women.

'Can't say I did.'

'Peach. Sam's her name. Teacher. Yeah. Primary school.'

'Really?'

Neil leaned in, winked, whispered.

'To be honest, not much talent in this neighbourhood. Glad to be getting the fuck out of here.'

So what? Was Neil a serial adulterer, a player? Were he and his voluptuous wife swingers like on Archie's website? What was the deal? Man-to-man jokes. Should have had that one on his checklist. No, but this guy was truly, truly an unexpected event. Neil flicked his cigarette over the hedge, it bounced off the windscreen of someone's Golf GTI then hit the gutter.

'Right. Back in. Hell is other people, eh?'

Walking behind him, David couldn't help but smile to himself. He'd misjudged the guy completely. He was a lad, yes, a laugh, definitely, but somehow he'd read Sartre. College maybe. Wow. Ole Jean-Paul in the West End – who'd have thought. He reminded himself to try to reserve judgement more often and to check out the peach with the push-up bra on the way in.

Back in the kitchen. Alice beside the busybody. Her face so sincere. Hell is other people.

'There you are, darling,' she said touching his arm. 'Mrs Miller, sorry, Edith, was just telling me that she'd love to come to a painting group.'

'The old scout hall is free on Sundays,' beamed Mrs Edith Miller.

'Sunday painters?' He raised an eyebrow to Alice. But she wasn't responding.

'Your wife is quite exceptional,' said Mrs Miller. 'So wonderful to have such talented people in the neighbourhood.'

David nodded, smiled, gave Alice's arm a squeeze and made his way to the drinks table. The peach. It could only have been her. She was sitting there with Joan the hostess. The world cleavage competition. He leaned over the table under the alibi of reaching for another bottle and had a good look. Funny, the peach was still not quite as peachy as the hostess. But of course, that was what happened with married men. Neil would now, after what – five years of marriage, be blind to his wife's unique charms. She touched his arm. Joan.

'David, you have to meet Sam.'

'Sam, as in Fox,' he said.

The girls giggled, there was shaking of hands.

'David's an actor,' she pretended to whisper to the peach. 'Alice was telling me all about him.'

Laughter. What was happening? Was he actually blushing? And then they were all laughing together. David and the two peaches. But what the hell had Alice been saying to Joan about him? Right, fifteen more minutes of this existential tragedy then get Alice back next door. Tell her.

*   *   *

Alice pecked Mrs Edith Miller on the cheek and said bye-bye and see you soon. She scanned the room. David was busy pretending to flirt, so she wandered back through the flat. It was almost an exact mirror image of their own, the layout in reverse. There were people all round, trying to catch her eye, but instead she looked at the decor. The wallpaper was different of course. There was a border. B&Q, aisle five. Fake stained glass. Aisle ten. Jesus what was happening to her? You give up on art and you become obsessed with interior decor. David would have laughed. And what the fuck was wrong with him tonight? She couldn't tell him about the art. The room. Not yet. About how she had never felt so lost in her life. She picked up a half-full bottle of bubbly from the Ikea table, and headed through the flat to where she assumed the toilet would be.

Jesus, why did she always do this? In the midst of the real world she always had to find a little private space, run away and hide. David was better at this than her. He could perform. But every phoney smile she had to make on the way, as she passed the neighbours, drained her that little bit more.

The toilet was where she expected and thankfully no one was waiting outside. She stopped at the door and took a mouthful. As she lowered the bottle from her mouth she felt her head begin to spin. She'd been drinking solidly since the afternoon, had hoped she could drink herself sober again. Stop now. Make excuses. Go. A headache. Or keep going, drink more, reach indifference. Beyond indifference came lack of inhibition. Reckless hilarious abandon. No, sober up, make yourself sick, splash your face with water.

She opened the bathroom door and almost stepped inside but there was someone in there, two people in fact, a mother with a child at her breast. Alice muttered sorry and turned to walk away, but the woman called out.

'Could you help me please?'

Alice stood there, the bottle in her hand, staring at this woman seated on the toilet with the child to her breast.

'Could you shut the door behind and . . .' The woman stabilised the child's head as she moved slightly to get more comfortable. My God, thought Alice, look at that. She'd seen breastfeeding before, usually in public, and found it distasteful. No, traumatic.

'Oh sure, sure,' Alice stepped inside and locked the bathroom door. 'Sorry but I'm not really sure how I can help exactly.'

'I'd love some of that wine you have,' the woman said. 'I know I shouldn't, but. Nine months and then breastfeeding you know, but I'm trying to get him off the breast this week so I can get really drunk. The little bugger.'

Alice laughed. In spite of it all. It had been the way she said bugger with that accent of hers, what was she, French? Alice sat down on the edge of the bath and

poured the woman a tumblerful of the wine while the
baby sucked almost violently.

In ten minutes she'd had her whole story. Her name
was Sylvie, the baby Joshua. She'd moved from France
to start again. Had the same urgent restlessness, it
seemed, that Alice knew so well. Wore it on her face,
her body. The baggy eyes, the little deposits of baby sick
on her army trousers. Her hair was dyed black, long
before a woman would need to hide grey. Alice sat there
on the bath and couldn't help but imagine them both in
the toilet of some Parisian nightclub aged eighteen,
wearing black, and chain-smoking as they got drunk and
listened to the Cure and made plans together for escaping
to the UK. All of this was such an unexpected relief from
the party, from the failure of today.

Sylvie tried to pass the child to Alice, but he screamed
whenever his mother let go. Sylvie was insistent that this
was to be the next stage. Separation. She had to reclaim
her body, she said. The maternal bond was so intense. It
was hard but she had to let him feel how it was to be held
by someone else. Bowlby's Maternal Deprivation Theory,
thought Alice. Some class in first-year psychology. When
a child is left for more than a day it refuses to recognise
its mother. Her childhood had been a case study in Bowlby.

Alice accepted the child into her hands. Took its
weight. Awkward. Not knowing what to do. How to hold
it. It. Joshua. Think Joshua. Sylvie was not like a typical
West End mother. She chatted away like an old friend.
Didn't subject her to those appalling lines that new
mothers always did – when are you having one? Are you
trying for one right now? Like junkies trying to get you
to take a fix.

Alice tried to hold him still, but he kept wriggling then
started crying. Sylvie reached to take him back, cradling

the head and taking the tiny squirming body into her arms. As soon as he was clamped back on her breast he was content and falling asleep. Sylvie put one delicate finger into the side of his mouth and pushed him gently from her breast. Alice stared at Sylvie, her nipple dripping the last drop of milk. The contented expression on the baby's chubby face. His tiny fingers still gripping his mother's. Alice couldn't stop staring as Sylvie gently stood, supporting her child's head, and placed him gracefully in his carry-chair. It came to her that she herself had never been breastfed. That her grandmother must have breastfed her mother. Never in her life had she ever felt as secure and safe as that tiny baby must have. Head rolling back. Hands at his sides. Prone, vulnerable, but still infinitely confident in his mother's care. She felt an ache in her gut. Her heart. What was it? Had she really been moved by watching Sylvie with her baby? She was conscious of staring and lowered her eyes. This relative stranger and this feeling.

Or was it that. The memory of her first abortion? Aged nineteen. Or the fact that she'd terminated because she wanted to be an artist. A hand on hers. Sylvie touching.

'You OK? What's wrong?'

Alice lifted her eyes and looked into Sylvie's. What was wrong with her, had always been wrong with her? Was Sylvie being tactless, naive, or had she just cut through all the crap? What the hell was wrong with her? The look on Sylvie's face. She was being sincere. Whenever strangers were caring towards her she felt like crying. Crying from anger, then from a sense that they had no right to violate you with their sympathy. Then ultimately because it was so rare, this sympathy, that even as an intrusion it was welcome.

'I don't know. I'm sorry. I don't know.'

Sylvie squeezed her hand. 'You can tell me.'

Thoughts fought for dominance, like they always did before she spoke. Always making what she said seem overconsidered, calculated. She wanted to tell Sophie about today and art and failure. About how when she argued with David earlier she thought she might leave the country. Study again. Go back to the States. Take drugs. Start again. Again and again. The thoughts. Her mother. Her grandmother. The first generation struggles to survive. To give their kids the education and the chances they never had. The second generation goes to college, becomes middle class. The third generation is spoiled with choices and feels crippled by them. All this education and intellect, this impotent knowledge. Every choice became overanalysed. You were crippled by your inability to do something. So much so that you just wanted to stop thinking. Do something stupid, sensual, physical, something that would last a lifetime even if it took your life from you. To go back to that first state. To be like your own grandmother. Like Sylvie. To breast-feed four children and have no choice. To have no time to question. To be happy with that.

'I'm sorry,' she said. 'I'm being totally self-indulgent. I dunno, I guess I'm just a little drunk.'

'Sure, that's OK,' said Sylvie and lifted her hand. 'Lucky you, I've been waiting almost a year to get drunk.'

Alice felt guilty. Here she was, so full of self-pity, with this woman whose life was so limited yet so simple and honest. She looked down at the sleeping baby. His lips moving so slightly in some tiny dream of the very few things that he knew. His mother's breast, her face. Alice got to her feet, she didn't want to cry.

'Well thanks,' she said. 'I live just next door, pop round any time.'

'Really?'

'Yeah, David has a kid too, and David – sorry he's my—' She was going to say boyfriend, then partner, but then she interrupted herself. 'Both of you, just pop round any time, any time.'

Then Sophie was up and carrying baby Josh and shaking hands and joking and laughing and Alice was left alone in the toilet with the bottle. The gold taps. The jacuzzi slash bath unit.

Out in the corridor, people were getting their coats and the place was emptying. Vague mutterings, as they headed for the door, the couples. About not drinking too much, driving, babysitters, how hellish it was to have to work weekends. They shook her hand as they left, apologising for not having had a chance to speak. As soon as they were gone Alice raised the bottle to her mouth again. There was nothing for it but to get drunk, really fucking drunk.

Find David. She was walking around with the empty bottle in her hand. She made a play of pretending to tidy up. Picking up some empty glasses on the way down the corridor back to the kitchen dining room. Couples filed past her smiling. At the table, the busty girl was shaking David's hand and air-kissing him. Joan was upon her already.

'Oh sweetie, you didn't have to tidy up.'

She forced herself to smile back. 'What are neighbours for?'

David seemed drunk too. On her way past him to the kitchen with the empty glasses and bottle he whispered, 'Go?'

She shook her head. Wanted more than anything else to postpone that trip back home. The night of tears. Showing him the room. Her failed art. Clinging to him.

What am I going to do? Please, just tell me. She made it to the kitchen.

A noise from behind. The front door closing then Neil was back in, beaming.

'Gone,' he said. 'Thank fuck for that!'

He had this really thick accent. He was tearing off his shirt, to get down to his T-shirt.

'Peachy peach,' he called through. 'Leave that shit till tomorrow.'

Joan giggled. Peachy peach. What the hell kind of name was that to call your wife? Alice watched him drain a half-empty glass from the table. He was crazy, really.

'Why's there no fucking music in here?' He threw his shirt down. She noticed that he had a good body. 'By the way, you guys are fuckin' stayin',' he said, pointing at her, like a command, like a dare, grinning at her and David. They glanced at each other. 'Fuck it,' she thought. 'Why not? Better than going back there.' Neil went swiftly back through the corridor. Shouting back through. 'Peachy peach, loaded baby. Loaded.'

And there was Joan, giggling. Holding up a new bottle of vodka. Waving it at her.

There was a blast of music from the front room. First three notes. Some line about wanting to be free. That band from Manchester. What were they called? Primal Scream. The first sound a baby makes when it's born.

*   *   *

The empty bottle was in his hand and he was about to spin it. He looked up at them and grinned. Neil was bare-chested and sitting in his underpants. Joan like Alice was in her bra but still had her trousers on, and he, David, had done remarkably well so far at the game of truth or dare. There was no tomorrow anyway. There was a hard sleepless night ahead in which he'd have to tell Alice about the job. Fuck it all.

'Fuckin' spin it, man,' laughed Neil.

David's hand gripped the bottle and gave it a good hard twirl. Watching it spin somehow made him smile. To be this drunk for the first time in years. Spin, spin. Joan was laughing for no apparent reason, and the lack of a reason made him laugh more.

The bottle came to a stop at himself. Neil roared with laughter.

'Bout fuckin' time too, mate.'

'No, but it doesn't count. What do I do, I mean ask myself a question or what?'

'Get ya kit off,' shouted Neil as he opened a bottle of some kind of malt whisky.

'No, truth or dare.'

'I dare you to tell the truth,' said Alice. 'For once.'

'Get ya kit off,' shouted Neil as he passed round the bottle.

David took a swig. He was splendidly drunk. And Alice, look at her. He'd never seen her like this before.

'Truth or dare! Truth or dare!' shouted Neil, over the music, which was now the Stone Roses. Words flying round the room, everyone shouting. Neil and Alice singing along.

'I wanna be adored.'

'Wanna be yer dog.'

'Bollocks, get ya kit off.'

'No, no. What will the neighbours think?' joked David.

Alice rested her head on the table. Her whole body was jerking with laughter.

'We are . . .' she stammered out.

'What, what the fuck?'

'We are the fucking neighbours.' And then everyone

was in hysterics. David's eyes wet with tears of laughter. OK, OK, get a grip.

'Truth!' he said.

'Ohhh!' said Neil. 'Right, I got one for you.'

'No, me,' shouted Alice.

'Bloody hell,' said Neil, and leaned over to put his arm round Joan. What were they doing? He had his hand round her neck, his finger playing with her bra strap. Try not to look at her tits. What had they had so far? Bubbly, Smirnoff and now the whisky. What questions had they got through? Have you ever bought a sex toy? Have you ever been in therapy? Have you ever had same-sex sex? That question already to Joan and she'd said yes. Have you ever been aroused while looking at root vegetables in Sainsbury's. That question, his to Alice, and she'd laughed and said that she was always drawn to the courgettes.

'OK, OK, I've got it,' shouted Alice.

OK, he thought, she's merry. Not tonight, don't spoil her night. Tomorrow. Hungover, cold light of day. No, tonight, it would have to be tonight.

'OK, OK,' Alice shouted at him. 'Have you ever fantasised about having sex with more than one person?' Jesus. Why ask him this, in front of them, when she knew the answer. Jesus. The dares were safer. Stand on one leg. Take off your T-shirt. Sing a Beatles song. Joan had done that. Michelle ma belle. Couldn't sing for shit in French or English, but they'd all joined in. Fucking hilarious. Do fifty press-ups. Neil had done that and was still dripping with sweat. Dare. Dare. Wash up the dishes. He'd got that one and had gone to start but Neil had stopped him.

Alice. 'C'mon, answer the question.'

Suddenly he felt a foot moving against his leg. Footsie.

Alice. No maybe not. Neil probably, just doing it to wind him up. Couldn't look underneath to check.

'Tell the truth,' said Alice.

Or maybe it was Joan. God look at them. Neil was kissing her neck now. His hand was edging closer to her breasts. Joan let her head roll back and took Alice's hand in hers.

'No,' he said, 'I mean not fantasised or the other really.' And they all seemed disappointed by his answer. Alice particularly, given that that was all their bedtime stories had been about lately.

'C'mon, people, let's play!' shouted Alice. She spun the bottle, throwing him an angry sexy defiant kind of smile. He was still trying to work out what it meant when they all started shouting. The bottle had stopped at him again.

'OK, OK, dare,' he said.

'Get ya kit off!' shouted Neil, yet again, then started kissing Joan. She was still holding Alice's hand.

'OK, OK, I dare you to . . .' Alice leaned in and whispered, 'to kiss Joan.'

'C'mon.' He shot her a worried glance, then at Joan and Neil who were still kissing and seemed to have not even noticed Alice's dare.

'OK, forget it, forget it,' shouted Alice. 'Spin it, spin the goddamn muthafuckin' bottle.'

*   *   *

God she felt drunk, really. But still, it didn't explain this need she felt to push it as far as it could go and beyond. Just to see. What time was it anyway? Two maybe three. Drunk, medicated, drunk, no dinner, then drunk again. All the shit had gone. No more worries about what the fuck she was doing. Fuck it. Fuck art. Fuck the West

End, and Sunday painters and fucking interior decor. There was that line by Patti Smith about fucking with the past or was it the future? Fuck Patti Smith. I want to see them fuck. I want to tell them to fuck. How to fuck. On the breakfast bar. Me and David'll go back next door and spy on them through the window as they fuck. And he'll get hard.

Now she was getting that lucidity thing that happened. She knew her words were slurred and her brain was moving faster than her mouth, but she felt sublime. Sublimely detached. Yes, she had suspected that Joan had been playing footsie with David, but Joan was drunk too, and perhaps had thought it was her husband's leg. Fuck it all. Bring it on.

David took her hand. He was telling her that she'd had enough.

'Spin the bottle. Spin it, spin it.' she shouted again.

Joan laughed. Why was she shouting? It was her turn anyway. Another CD started up. Nirvana. 'Smells Like Teen Spirit.' She started singing along through her laughter. Oops, sorreeee. She lifted her left hand from Joan's and felt David's clench round her right. He wanted to go. He was being judgemental. Responsible. He was shifting round in his seat. Staring at her with some kind of worried expression. What the fuck had he been trying to tell her tonight anyway? Fuck it. Forget it. Later she'd. She'd try. Or maybe tomorrow – about the room. No, fuck it. Couldn't tell him, couldn't tell herself. Fuck him, fuck David. Being so caring and paternalistic and concerned for her. This was not about him, or them, not any more. This was about all the truths and dares she'd played on herself since she was sixteen. No, fuck all that. This was about now, some stranger's, some strange woman's hand in yours.

Just before she spun it David got up, slipped back on

his shoes and shirt and excused himself. Was just nipping next door, he said, to check his messages. Back in five minutes, take his turn for him.

*   *   *

He turned the key in the lock and flipped the light on. Stood there staring at the packing boxes but could only think of Alice. Fragments of stories she'd told about her wild years. Hints she'd made about her capacity for self-destruction. But nothing like this. How could he even speak to her when she was like this? If he told her she would freak out. Trash the place. Walk out on him in the middle of the night.

The damned flat. Every step felt false. He thought about the website again, that maybe he'd left it on the screen when he'd been checking it earlier. What the hell. He staggered inside and found himself balancing against the door frame of her studio. He was curious. Had she made some incredible artwork this week and not told him about it? Had she felt so pumped up with achievement that she'd come in the last day to see him for the mediocrity that he was?

He couldn't resist. He pushed the door open into the dark room and flicked the switch.

The carpet half rolled back. Torn wallpaper fragments and hundreds of sketches all over the floor, soaking up a spilled bottle of turpentine. A torn drawing of a woman in a window. Other pages scrunched up and lying on the floor. Frantic charcoal marks on the wall in the shadowy shape of a square. Pots of wall paint. A pasting table half assembled. A canvas sitting half stretched. A broken frame. Pages of writing strewn everywhere. A Home-world catalogue open, its pages slashed. Fragments of wallpaper scattered around in an aborted attempt at some

kind of collage, glue and paint everywhere. A wet canvas
face down on the carpet. On the facing wall a huge splash
of colour but no canvas. An image of a face painted then
half obliterated. On the floor by the window, an empty
bottle of wine.

As he turned off the light and closed the door he knew.

*   *   *

The lights were off. Alice used the wall to steady herself
as she felt her way along the corridor. She stumbled
giggling as she kicked off her shoes, feeling queasy as
she pulled her dress over her head letting it fall wherever. There would have to be tooth brushing and all that
self-respecting bullshit.

She fell onto the mattress and found him there. He
was silent, his back to her. Must have been asleep. She
had no idea how long she'd taken to come through. Half
an hour, an hour. Another two shots of whisky? As long
as she could to postpone it till she felt too drunk to postpone it any longer. The room was spinning. She couldn't
lie down. Sat upright. Tried to focus on him. Found his
head. Stroked his hair.

'You know what happened, Daddy?'

He said nothing. She pulled his head onto her lap.
Stroked his chin, his neck, his temples. He made a few
faint noises.

'I took the bottle, right. Spun it. Put my hand on her
leg. Hold-ups. Was wearing them. Her. Hmmm. You like
hold-ups. You asleep, Daddy?'

A grunt.

'Spin the bottle. Right. They're shouting and he's
fondling her and he takes my hand and puts it between
her legs. Panties. Tight over her pussy. He's kissing her.
Watching me. She's getting wet.'

Her hand stroked his back. His ass. His flaccid dick.

'You like that, Daddy? You wanna know?'

He moaned a little. Was waking.

'He's kissing her. He takes my hand, my finger, and puts it inside her. My finger. The bottle it stops at him. That good?'

'Uhhh huh.'

'My finger in her. I'm looking at them. They're waiting. It feels kinda good, them watching me, waiting for instructions. My finger in her. Moving. Yeah, Daddy?'

'Yeah.'

'So I say. I dare you, I say. To Neil, I say, "I dare you to go down on your wife." That's what I said. You like that, Daddy? You want to know what happens next?'

'OK.'

'You sure?'

'Tell me.'

'OK. So he gets down on his knees and he's got his head down there and she's leaning over and kissing me. And he's fucking her with his fingers. And then he's taking his fingers and sticking them in her mouth, and mine. Tasting her. And he's pushing them in and out of my mouth as my fingers move inside her pussy.'

'Uh huh.'

'You're hard, Daddy, you're getting hard.'

'Uh huh, keep going.'

'OK. So then we're kissing, me and her. And I'm finger-fucking her and he's got his hand in my panties and I pull away and whisper to them.'

'What did you say?'

'I say, "He's watching us right now. From the kitchen. Don't look." That's what I say. You're so hard, Daddy.'

'I am.'

'I want you inside me. I want that hard cock.'

'Oh baby.'

'God, you're so hard. I'm going to get on top, Daddy. OK. You're going to stay hard.'

'OK. Tell me. More.'

'So, I'm kissing her and he's finger-fucking me and he pushes her back and slides inside her. I reach out and feel his cock moving into her pussy. And all the time I'm thinking about you watching us.'

'Don't stop.'

'You're hard inside me, baby, you feel that. Oh my God. He's fucking her and his fingers are in me and then he pulls out and I have his dick, it's so hard. Like you, and he's teasing me with it, and my pussy is so wet and he's pushing it against my lips. And it's so big and hard like you, Daddy, and I can feel myself opening around him. This big cock, then he's inside me, like you are.'

'Fuck.'

'What's up, Daddy?'

'Sorry. Sorry, fuck.'

'It's OK. You were hard, Daddy, hard inside me.'

'I'm sorry.'

'It was beautiful.'

'Sorry.'

'Daddy, it's OK, it's OK.'

'Baby, please, just lie down and curl up beside me.'

'Would you like me to do that? Fuck them, so you can watch?'

'Shhh. Curl up. C'mon.'

'If you wanted me to I would, you know that.'

'Roll over.'

'If it made you hard.'

'You're hogging the quilt.'

'Sorry. Here.'

'It's OK.'

'I would, because you're my Daddy, you know that.'

'I know.'

'I would do that for you. Because I do. You know I do.'

Silence. His body was shaking. What was it? Was he jerking off? Crying? She rolled over and held him.

'Shhhh, shhhh, what is it? It's OK. It's OK.'

Crying. Never felt him cry like this.

'Shhh, shh, Daddy. What's wrong?'

'I . . . I.'

'It was beautiful, Daddy, really. You were inside me.'

Her touch made the tears come harder. Soon she was holding him tight, her body jerking with each spasm of his. Just when she thought her touch and her 'Shhh's had calmed him, a new spasm would start.

'Shhhh, shhh, Daddy.'

But each time she said Daddy, his tears came harder and then he was choking as he tried to talk, gulping back tears as the words stammered out. Poor Daddy. They made no sense. Some kind of confession. He'd known about the job for a week, he said, he tried to tell her. God, God.

'Shhh, shhh, it's OK.'

He'd been going crazy, he said. Drinking, surfing the net. These dating sites, this stupid obsession all week, he didn't know what he was doing, he'd never leave her.

'Shhh.' Stroking his head.

There was this reply he'd got from this couple. He was sorry, so sorry, such a pervert.

'It's OK, it's OK.'

'Fucking job, bastards, fucking bastards.'

He'd been going on for minutes and was still making no sense. And the rhythm of her stroking hand on his head reminded her of the many times she'd done this

with her mother. Stroking her head, saying, shhh, shhh
as her mother cried in her ten-year-old lap. And Sylvie
holding her child. Shhh. Shhh. When finally he could
breathe enough to speak he told her. All of it. How he'd
been fired. But saved her job. How he was so worried.
He didn't want to be like this, dependent on her. Shhh,
shhh, shhh, she told him. It would all be fine.

She felt it now. How she'd been so selfish. Too preoccupied with her own shit to notice what had been
happening to him. Poor Daddy. It'll all be fine.

'It's so unfair,' he said, 'so unfair. You were going to
do your art and now . . .'

She wanted to tell him that she'd never make art again.
That the thought of it terrified her. That she never even
wanted to see that room again. That in some strange way
she was even glad to be forced to go back to work, to
that job she despised. Anything, just to get away from
that room where she had fallen so hard.

But for real, what did she feel? She was trapped now.
Her and David struggling to make enough money to
support themselves. Working just to live. No escape.
They'd invested in this house together, signed the mortgage almost as a joke. They hadn't foreseen that there
were other traps. Poverty, for one. Now they were
trapped and she would have to run, run again, start again
and again, there would be other jobs and other Davids.

'Love you, Daddy,' she said as she held him.

'Oh my God.'

'I do, I love you.'

So overcome with it. The rule about never saying it,
broken. Those many long nights discussing how they
hated these words. Better to feel them and not say them.
To feel the burning need and still not to say them, as a
sign.

But now she was saying them and it was painful and the pain made her want to say them even more.

'I do. I do. I love you.'

'I do too, baby. Love you so much.'

'I love you, I love you,' she said, her hands stroking his head in rhythm with the words. Like it was a simple stupid song you'd sing to infants to lull them to sleep. To lull the infant inside yourself to sleep. Like those words you said at the altar, to convince yourself that for once you were doing something big and final. These stupid words. I love you, I love you. But when the rhythm of the words became a kind of song the meaninglessness of them no longer mattered. I love you. I love you. I love you. To embrace your own stupidity and weakness. To see the stupidity of a mother feeding her child. I love you I love you. To accept that after twenty years of trying and failing, that you were not as cynical as you thought, but scared and as innocent as a child on the breast. Feeding in the words. I love you I love you I love you.

At some point the tears, the rhythmic spasms of her chest, became the thrust and the pulse of his penis inside her. Crying, clutching each other, her pelvis moving against him. Rhythm. Words pouring out. A little story about being watched while they fucked. The neighbours. Everyone fucking everyone. Then the words breaking down into gasps. Breath. Tears. And he was coming. The first time ever he'd come inside her.

*   *   *

They were standing in a park before a huge oak tree. There was some kind of statue or fountain to his left. Covered in moss or lichen. Their bodies were touching but their hands weren't. She was leaning in, resting against him slightly.

He was a good foot taller than she was and was turned slightly towards her. Broad-chested in a well fitted charcoal grey suit. A flower attached to his lapel. He was slightly balding but had had his hair recently trimmed. He was wearing a white shirt and a pink and yellow striped tie.

She was on the right of frame in her white satin dress clutching her bouquet. Her long brown hair had been expensively interwoven with flowers. Ringlets falling over her shoulders. She had an almost sheer veil held in place by hairpins. Her arms were slightly chubby and suggested that she was at least five years older than he was. She had a digital watch on, which didn't match the rest of her outfit. She was wearing a gold necklace with a jewel hanging at the top of her cleavage which was tastefully presented by the tight-fitting yet understated corseted dress.

It was safe to assume that they were smiling. Although impossible to tell. Their faces were blanked out by two white squares. One each.

After they'd made love Alice couldn't sleep and had been looking round for sleeping tablets but found herself just wandering around by the breakfast bar. Tidying up a few things. Saucers. The bottle and glasses. The light was off in the Gordons' kitchen. Perhaps what had happened tonight was of no importance to them. The flirting, the touching. Perhaps it hadn't even happened at all. But whatever the Gordons felt about it, something had changed between her and David and it was all because of them. She found the tablets in the kitchen drawer and as she waited for the cup to fill with water, a different kind of tears came. Not the ones of anger that she'd felt before the party. Not the ones of compassion she'd felt when she found David in bed. But the tears that only came in the aftermath of gratification. The humility of intense interior satisfaction. Happiness. Brutal animal stupid happiness.

She must remember. This night, always. No, but she must also remember, one other thing, no two. She must remember to take her Pill and then try to find some image that would stay with her, that would imprint this night on her mind, to give her the courage to stay.

The room was lit by the blue light from David's computer and she felt drawn towards it. Sat before it and clicked the mouse. The last web page came up. David must have been looking at it before they'd gone out. Swinging-paradise.com. Beneath the picture were the ad details.

PUSSY-GALORE. Thirties. Looking for couples for Str8 full swap and mutual DIY. Age and race not an issue. Can travel or accom. Fulfil our fantasy.

After David's confession it wasn't a shock, and yes of course she was liberal, open-minded. It wasn't so shocking either that a married couple would be so dissatisfied that they were looking for something more. What was surprising though was that they'd post it, this, the most intimate of pictures, on a website.

She stared. Ignoring the site details, the flashing banners and other ads. Double clicked on it and blew it up to fill the screen. More detail. The flowers were lilies. The gem was a ruby. His suit had subtle grey stripes. But it wasn't the details that held her there. That had her staring at the image for another ten minutes.

All week she'd been struggling to create a picture that was at once an image and its negation. That expressed the desire for coherence and at the same time its wilful destruction. That was about history and her mother and David and his failed marriage. That was about the need for belief in something beyond the self. That was beyond irony. That was fucked up and angry but at the same time spoke of some kind of trust, some kind of commitment.

There it was. This thing David had found on the Internet. Probably by accident. This wedding photo with the faces erased. Disturbing. Beautiful.

As she stared at the image David's cold sperm ran down the inside of her leg. The image in front of her blurred as her eyes filled with tears. Tears which were laughable but still beyond judgement. The contradictions of modern life, the contradictions inside yourself. And all this in an image.

She closed her eyes but could still see it. It was perfect. This perfect artwork. This image discovered by accident on this perfect night after this day of hell. This perfect artwork that she could never have made by herself.

2
WHITE ROOM

The alarm clock. He turned it off and rolled over. Held her breast, kissed her neck as she snuggled against him. No idea what time it was. The warm mustiness of their breath and sweat. Turning over the pillow. Legs wrapped round each other. Sticking a foot out of the duvet to keep it cool. Holding each other. Spoons. Car doors slamming outside. The motorway. The odd weekend worker heading to the office.

But it was no good. He was awake, dry, hungover and troubled with fears of that first hour when she woke and they'd have to face the day. He pulled his arm from under her neck. Asked in whispers if she wanted breakfast. But she turned over and he was alone. His feet took him back to the front room.

Look at it.

To focus his mind. To help her. He thought it was for the best. A coffee then a quick trip to Homeworld. To put lining paper over it all. Cover over the mess she'd made, paint the whole thing. Two coats. An hour between to dry. Not the studio or the children's room now, or the old room or the front room. The white room. That was what they'd call it.

And the effort involved. The mall and back. Running back and forward as she slept. Stripping up the rest of the carpet. Dumping it out the back. Assembling the wallpaper table, stirring the whitewash. It was for the best. It took his mind off everything. She'd sleep all day and all night, like she always did when she was down. He'd show it to her tomorrow. Whitewash. The white room. A fresh start.

After the lining paper was up there were still marks and textural differences. But when the first coat of white had dried they were almost invisible. By six p.m. it was done. Alice had only got up once to take a pee and was back in bed again. He'd put two cups of coffee beside the bed and tried to wake her, but she'd decided that the day was best lost and rolled over. Forcing herself to sleep. Seven p.m. He tidied up the brushes then put some water by her bed and two Ibuprofen. Went back through to the white room and watched the last coat drying. Yes, it was done.

Late evening. As Alice slept on he made himself a sandwich, turned on the PC. He would find work in the next few days. Any work. Put in a nine to five tomorrow on the net contacting companies with his CV and a letter. Finding work is a job in itself. He'd said those words himself to employees that he'd had to fire. As Google opened up he paused before typing 'Jobs Glasgow', he felt the draw of the sex site. Just to log in to see if there had been any replies. No. There would be no more of that. He turned off the PC. There would be no more of that.

*   *   *

It began. This time of carelessness and almost wilful provocation. To throw yourself at the world without a thought and see what the world thought, if anything, in return. To put the weight of history with all its heavy hurt on one scale, your fear of an empty future on the other and set the balance swaying. Afterwards Alice couldn't remember how long it lasted. The weekend vanished in a hungover blur of hugs and plans and long silent kisses, and then it was Monday morning and she was back at work learning what life looked like, as they said, in the cold light of day. Looking back months later, after all the impossible things that were to happen to them, the only moment she could recall from that time was that very first one. The sight of her new office.

Flashing her ID badge at security. The elevator to floor three. David had joked about it, told her she'd laugh, but it was still a shock. The doors opened and it was like a moment from one of those home-makeover shows where someone else decorates your apartment for a week then you come back and WHAM. Uplights and coloured desks and flat-screen monitors and new college-kid employees, lounging about on sofas with clipboards. And where was everyone? The people she'd worked with. The first thing to do was find Pauline. Assuming of course that Pauline was still there. Shit, she should have called her last week, she'd been so selfish, and Pauline was probably the only real friend she had.

As she walked through the newly carpeted space, it was impossible not to smile, this wasn't an office. No more fluorescent yellow grey monotony. Gone was the lingering smell of deodorant and sweat and dust that had sat on warm monitors for years. But gone too, it seemed, was everyone she'd ever worked with. Then it became clear to her exactly what David had been hiding from her all last week. He'd been a good Daddy and she'd been so selfish. The new faces, the new desks. A pile of boxes by the fire exit with names of people she used to work with written in marker pen: Sarah. Steve J. Wendy.

She stopped at roughly the space where her old desk used to be. In its place was a semi-circular bright red hi-tech computer desk with a brand new twenty-inch flat-screen monitor. On the desk was a piece of paper with her name printed out in a huge bright pink font. Underneath was an envelope. She looked at the other desks and was relieved to find that Pauline's name was there too. But where the hell was she? There were a bunch of new kids over by what must have been the new printer-copier. They were joking and one of them waved over to her. Funky-looking girl, surfboard gear, must have been twenty max. Feeling chirpy and surprised at how chirpy she felt, out of habit her eyes moved over to the desk where her boss, Angela McIvor, sat. The old glass-walled surveillance booth was still there but she was gone. The bitch. How many ideas had she thrown back in her face? Too out-there. Too Channel 4. Maybe she'd been fired. Yes, Alice was feeling ridiculously happy.

But it was short-lived. Sitting down and opening her contract it all became clear to her. Twelve pages. Forcing herself to read the new jaunty version of corporate speak. Non-union buyout – two months, available 24/7 – in all media known and not yet known, forever in perpetuity, in this universe and all those not yet known. Amen. The funky bright font, the stylish new notepaper.

Out of some allegiance to David she wanted to tear it to shreds, and feel the little kick of empowerment that the act of destruction would give. But instead she sat and forced herself to finish reading it. As she finally set it down she thought of David at home, alone. That he'd done this for her. This was an act of love and had to be honoured. Because she had to teach herself to stick things out, to endure the trails of commitment. It was something you had to work at, they said, so what better place to start than work. Temp contract or not. She would really fucking give it a try. Suspend judgement. Sign it.

'Jesus, where the fuck you been, I was fuckin' callin' you all last week.'

Pauline. Alice jumped to her feet and then they stared at each other. Pauline had had a makeover too, it seemed, new haircut anyway. Moments of silence as they took each other in. Then that uncontrollable laughter bursting from her. Pauline infected too. Her big full frame convulsing. David's air crash all over again. Two old friends finding each other on the desert island. Hugging. Pauline's thick East End accent.

'Stop it, it's no' fuckin' funny.'

Pauline doubled over. Alice wanted to hug her. Pauline looking round to see if anyone was watching. Which was even more funny. Pauline's Scottish reserve, her fear of being touched, whatever. Pauline backed away.

'Honestly,' she said. 'You've no fuckin' idea.'

'Hit me. Debbie and Sylvia?'

'Gone, died, but I think Debbie's gonnae reapply.'

'No! And Angela? I mean.'

Pauline nodded her head. A smirk there for sure. It said miserable old cunt deserved it. Shite boss. But Pauline said nothing, kept smirking.

'Jesus. So who's running the show now?'

'No fucking idea, just you and me, babe.'

'I got you, babe.'

Then they were at it again, this laughter thing that Alice did at moments like this. When everything was too much.

'Fuckin' stop it,' Pauline kept looking over her shoulder. 'C'mon, the bogs.'

In the toilets Pauline said 'Right, right,' how many times, maybe five, then tried to get Alice to stop laughing. A slap, Alice thought. Slap me then tell me. Get a grip Alice. So Pauline told her about how, and she wasn't sure about this but, about how. Basically what had happened.

'What, what?'

There was no one to hear them but Pauline was whispering. Well basically, they'd fired maybe eighty maybe a hundred people and it was only the ole whingeing cunts anyway and those sexist bastards that worked in the studio that sat on their arses all day and played cards and pinched yer arse, so fuck them, and how they'd all been given a, you know, a no-bad severance package anyway and arrivaderci to them and had she no been reading the papers? But well, anyway, the whole channel was going to be run with about a third of the staff and they'd all be multitasking now and how that meant that she'd get to do a bit of editing now, 'cos they'd got rid of the edit suites and you could do it on your own PC and isn't that fab. And how they were going through a whaddaya call it, a skeletal staff right now as they started bringing in new freelancers from London and that, and how it was a kind of a test really, 'cos it was all performance related-rated-whatever, but easier to get promotion. And to be honest all the other lassies on the floor had just been sittin' round twiddling their thumbs till they got pregnant and doing fuck all really and some of the new guys were really cute. And how there was this new head of department from New York or wherever, forget her name. But she'd given this big speech last week about how she was going to turn this shitey wee local channel round. And everyplace was no place now, and they'd be making programmes to sell to like fucking HBO and the ITV network and Channel 4 and so they had to come up with these ideas for a new series that was. What was it? Trans. Aye. Whaddaya call it? Trans somethin'.

'Transcendental?'

'No, no.'

'Transglobal?'

'Aye, sort of, but no.'

'Transgressive?'

'Aye, that's it.'

Transgressive. Fine. Three years spent diluting her material to make it acceptable to a mainstream audience.

Back at their new desks, Pauline showed her how to download her old desktop from the new shared server, and they sat giggling while it came through mega fast on the new broadband connection. So then she told herself to be serious for a moment and looked at all the files. Really it was amazing that she'd managed to hold on to this job at all. The number of projects she'd been paid to research but had never had commissioned.

Abandoned Mothers. Adultery for Beginners. Suicide Fathers. Failure. That had been a good one. A damning indictment of the 'cult of success'. Eight stories, ranging from a junkie in Easterhouse to a corporate executive in Manhattan. All of them victims of an ideology that placed the individual before anything else. Not heavy theorising like she could have done, liked she'd learned not to. The whole Marxist-feminist take had been carefully embedded in the choice of interviewees. Compare and contrast. Dialectics. Perhaps, if she got the right vibe from the new head, she could pitch it at her.

'Mince, all my ideas are mince,' joked Pauline. 'By the way,' she said without looking up, 'how'd it go with the art?'

'OK,' said Alice. 'Fine.'

She couldn't help but notice that this made Pauline smile a little to herself. Probably Pauline was just glad to see her back at work but there was that other darker thing. Maybe she was being paranoid but she sensed that Pauline had guessed and had been glad, in fact, that she'd failed.

Art. For people like Pauline, the word made their
stomachs turn. Although they both worked in Arts and
Ents it was clear to Alice that Pauline hated artists. Saw
them as pretentious. Got a slightly sadistic pleasure in
dumbing them down. Artists were only too glad of a little
media spotlight and Pauline always made sure that she
asked them the dumbest questions she could in her
programmes. 'So what is art anyway?' 'Do you think
Madonna is an artist?' Watching them squirm. It was
almost like Pauline had taken it upon herself to teach
artists the ways of the world. Teach them they only existed
because of her. Drag them from their ivory towers. Alice
recalled a pitch Pauline had given a year ago. The history
of twentieth-century art presented by pop celebrities.
Pauline had insisted that it was ironic, of course. But
Alice knew better. It was motivated by pure hatred. That
these artists had the freedom to express who they were
when she was stuck in a shit TV job. Posh Spice
explaining why she had her entire kitchen designed to
look like Mondrian. Robbie Williams telling everyone
how he loved Duchamp's urinal because 'We're all fuckin'
pissheads, man.'

Pauline leaned over. 'Lesbian lap dancers. Whaddaya
think? A series?'

Alice smiled a little and got back to her old files:
Depression for Beginners, a semi-witty series of five-minute
slots with useful tips; *The A to Z of Scotland*. A is for alco-
holism. X is for xenophobia.

Amazing really. It had taken these two weeks away
from work to show her what she'd been doing. For three
years she'd been peddling her private obsessions as TV
programmes. And what had she ended up doing? That
interminable series on immigrants. The usual tiresome
wishy-washy liberal fodder in which they'd had to edit

out the more salient points from the bigots in favour of a 'balanced argument'. Make everyone nice, yeah. Liberalism in action. Put out pictures of the world you want to see and everyone will copy them.

Life Without Parents. Suicide for Beginners. How the Hippies became Yuppies.

* * *

Guardianjobs.com. Idealjob. BBCemployment. Heraldjobs. Tempwork.co.uk. Six hours sitting in the kitchen trying to resist the pull of the site.

CV. Make lists. Things I have done.

Acting
Edinburgh Festival fringe
Moved to London
Tried to get agent
Hotel domestic
Failed to get agent
Signed on
Auditions and no work
Call centres
More auditions – no work
Moved back to Glasgow
Call centres
Applied for work as an extra
Tree planting
Call centres
Acting in corporate training videos
HR
Marriage
Child

Pension plan
Separation
HR

If God existed he would work in HR. If you were God
would you give this person a job?

List two. 'What I will do.' Thirty minutes web
searching then typing then deleting, then trying to resist
the urge to peek at the swinging site then making himself
write the list and forcing himself to believe it might just
be possible. Call centre, cleaner, security guard, supermarket, retail, bar work. Then giving up. Being weak,
just a click of the mouse. Nothing to it. Just a minute or
two. Goodbye world. Hello swinging-paradise. Oh Pussy,
oh Pussy, oh Pussy my love, what a wonderful pussy you
are, you are, what a wonderful pussy you are.

*   *   *

The conference room hadn't been given the makeover yet,
and so Alice sat there with her list of old programme
ideas, feeling ancient and fearing that her list of worn-out
radical concepts wouldn't wash with the new researchers,
who were ten years younger and who Pauline had introduced her to already and whose names she wished she'd
tried harder to memorise. The new head of department
had had the chairs arranged in the new non-hierarchical
way that they liked, to give everyone a feeling of equality.
She was pretty stunning. The head. Thirty-three maybe.
New York accent with a hint of something almost
Australian. Single – definitely. No suit, but expensive low
slung designer denims and a 70s shirt. Her *Sex in the City*
haircut probably cost more than Alice's weekly wages.

She'd been trying to find a gap in the pitch to throw
in her own ideas, but as Pauline held court, and the

younger, more ambitious researchers pitched their out-there programme ideas, she found herself striking the old ones off her list.

By the time the third new girl had finished Alice had crossed off everything and started scribbling angrily just to kill time. Crazy ideas, off the top of her head. At this rate she wouldn't last long under the new regime so what the hell. David was right. How could you compete with the young, the naive?

Silence in the room. Pauline cleared her throat. Nodded at her. She looked up and sensed it was her turn.

'OK, well they're kind of nuts,' she started. 'Like first up. There's *Life Swap*. Like you get a lawyer and a homeless guy and you make them swap lives for a week. It's kind of sociological. Yeah, well I mean it's probably all too worthy and been done before but . . .'

The head raised an eyebrow and rested her chin on her hand.

'So, well this sounds a bit sick, but *Ikea Crush*. You know like after all those riots and people getting squashed in all these new Ikeas all over the world. Well, it's like *Supermarket Sweep* but well, just more violent, I guess. Sorry, that wasn't funny.'

Nobody laughed and the new girls looked bored in a way that she used to do with women who were ten years older than her. Pauline threw her an anxious look. She was losing it. The head, however, clicked her pen and was making a few notes. 'Go on,' she said, pausing, 'Alice.'

'Right so, there's great failed psychological experiments of the last century. Like *Big Brother* but with this serious scientific backbone, like uh, the Stanford prison experiment. The one which went so wrong they had to bring in the army to stop it. So we redo the experiments again and film everything. But it needs a catchy title.'

'Channel 4. Last year,' said one of the new girls, avoiding her gaze.

Fuck. Fuck, she hated TV, never watched it. In Stanford the prisoners smeared their shit on the walls. What she knew, what she wasn't telling them, was that the way to stop the riots and the excrement was to give the prisoners a TV. To let them watch others suffer.

'Sooooo,' said Pauline, before anyone else could jump in. Alice looked up and Pauline was nodding at her. Go on.

Her scribbled list was done but another idea came to her, right there. Who knows, something about David's swinging site, about the neighbours, whatever.

'*Swinging*. It's like four couples swap partners. Not like *Wife Swap* – the American family version, which is basically just mommy swap. I mean really swap. Like you get these four houses together, and there's surveillance in every room and every week the couples have to swap partners, and I mean like, totally, sleeping with each other and everything. It's like *Big Brother* meets key parties meets I dunno, the 60s.'

Silence. Pauline interjected trying to express some enthusiasm.

'Aye, yeah . . . and we could have a marriage counsellor on board, doing the voice-overs and giving advice and . . .' Then Pauline was losing it. Going back to the old routine. 'I mean, it would make for, you know, a more balanced programme.'

No idea where it came from. Alice just blurted it out. Her fingers quoting the air.

'But surely "unbalanced programming" is more fun.'

Pauline blushed. A new girl giggled. The head suppressed a laugh and crossed something out.

OK. She'd gone too far. Everyone could tell all of her

ideas were a piss-take and she'd embarrassed Pauline in front of the new boss. Alice dried up, put away her folder and waited as the new researchers shook hands with the head and handed her their brightly coloured printouts of ideas. Alice was just going to slip away but then. The head's voice.

'Alice. A word please.'

Pauline gave her a look. She was for it. A reprimand on day one.

An hour later and she and the head were sitting together in some new Asian fusion place Alice didn't know existed, on their third Mojito each. The head had introduced herself properly now as Linda, although Alice couldn't stop thinking of her as the head. The head had just bought her first pack of cigarettes in three weeks, she said, and they were laughing together, smoking. Alice was off again.

'A thousand years ago, marriage was a contract to ensure the continuation of the blood line, DNA, right? To pass on the property to the legitimate male heirs. Adultery was punishable by death. Am I talking too much?'

'Go on.'

'Then in the eighteenth century you had Romanticism, right? Poetry, painting, music. The idea of falling in love. It was antisocial. Usually adulterous. Against convention. This dangerous force that could destroy a culture. I swear. I did Foucault. Before the nineteenth century no one married for love. So anyway. Then love got co-opted by the Church and the love of Christ was extended to include the sanctity of marriage. Think about it. The word marriage was still the same but its meaning had changed so many times. Like, like a church that got converted into a nightclub. I'm sorry, I dunno, I've just been thinking about this for so long. It's not even to do with the series or . . .'

The head exhaled, coughed a little. 'God that feels better,' she said and passed the cigarette to Alice like it was a spliff. Alice did a play act of toking on it, and the head was laughing.

'OK, OK. So in the twentieth century, the death of God right? He was replaced with psychoanalysis. You confessed to your shrink. Then in the 60s the Pill, free love. Again it was co-opted into marriage. Free love became honesty, became the confessional. You confessed to your partner, because the Church was dead.'

The head lowered her head and nodded. Alice knew she had to bring this to an end soon.

'Right. So. Well, the problem is, the way I see it is. That marriage has picked up all this baggage along the way. We expect our partner to be "everything for us". Like in women's magazines, on TV. We're still confessing even after the death of God, of psychoanalysis. And . . . we've built a whole genre around this. Jerry. Oprah. It's no wonder the magazines tell us that the divorce rate is through the roof. That most couples have a crisis after two years. Then a break before seven. Seriously, it's like that movie.'

The head threw her glass back and circled her hand from the wrist with a kind of implied yada yada, go on, hurry up meaning.

'Yeah, yeah. Bergman.' She paused, summoning it. 'I need one man to feed me, one to fuck me and one to look after my soul. Yeah?'

The head laughed out loud. 'You're right. You're so right.'

'I am?'

'Yeah, but I don't know what the hell this has got to do with our new crazy-assed swinging show.'

'Well, it's . . . Sorry, what was that?'

'Alice, I dunno what planet you came from but . . . you're . . . you're so. Jesus we should just point the camera at you.'

Alice was blushing. The head raised her fingers to do that quoting thing that Alice did.

'The mad voice of the masses.'

'Oh Jesus. Yeah. Like what's it called. That movie . . . with uh . . .'

'Faye Dunaway.'

'Yeah, yeah. *Network*. Fuck yeah. I used to sneak into media studies classes and they were mad for it.'

'Right, what's that line?'

Then they both said it together. 'I'm mad as hell and I'm not going to take it any more.'

And roared with laughter. Came up with a few more lines from the movie. Laughed all the way through dessert. All the way into the taxi and back to the office. The head talked about how hard it was to be an American in Glasgow. How she was hoping Alice would show her the city. And then, suddenly, back in the building it was over. Alice was left standing there in the head's office, which used to be her boss's, lowering her voice so the others couldn't hear. This one stupid question.

'So, uh. Swinging?'

The head was already on her email. Without looking up she said, 'Did I put six Mojitos on the company card?'

'Well yeah.'

'So I'm assigning you five junior researchers. I want a full outline with budget for end of play tomorrow. Location and participant list to follow in three weeks. Contracts on my desk in four.'

'Sorry, four houses, surveillance, four couples fucking?'

'Yeah, *Big Brother* meets key parties meets the 60s. I'll put the call in to HBO soon as I get the budget.'

The head got up and offered Alice her seat. She was going back on the six o'clock shuttle, she said. This would be her desk till the job was done. Then she left. Alice stood there staring at the leather executive-style chair. The glass-walled partition. The flat-screen monitor. Like Bush said. Shock, shock and awe.

She sat down and logged on and already the other researchers were emailing her and vying for position as her lead assistant. Pauline wasn't at her desk but had sent her a two-pager telling her how much she'd been inspired by her ideas and how she'd always believed in her. Jesus. No, she'd never really believed in this job but from now on she'd try to try. In the absence of belief in anything else she'd do that impossible thing, which was what all of America believed in, which was to believe in yourself. She'd be a union breaker and a scab. She'd walk past the picket lines if they even existed and stop whingeing about bosses. She'd make it what she wanted. Become indispensable. Take control. It was like that joke David had made. On the desert island, only the team leader will survive. Was this the way the world worked now? You said something as a joke. Then it got taken seriously. Then the joke became real.

* * *

He'd tried to keep himself busy over the first week. Finally assembled the bed and the wardrobe. Unpacked most of the boxes. Put another coat of white in the white room. Tried to tell himself to stop worrying about the mortgage, as he sat by the window and watched the estate agents show couple after couple round the Gordons' flat.

He surfed for jobs, for loans, to see him through till he was back on his feet, because the redundancy package would only last for twelve weeks and he'd wasted one already and knew that it would take at least the time he had left to find a decent job and he'd be damned if he was going to go to the job centre in the meantime. He went to the supermarket, put it all on the credit card and cooked each night for them both. Marinated salmon. Roast lamb with caramelised Mediterranean vegetables. Like nothing had happened. Decided it was best to detox from all the alcohol he'd had last week. Went for a walk each day at around one to stretch his legs, to take a look at the world, and work it all out of his system. The only human contact he had, sitting at home in those first three or four days, were the neighbours. The old busybody from the West End Society inviting him and Alice to a coffee morning. Some woman with a kid and a French accent who claimed Alice had asked her to pop round any time. Neil Gordon, next door, when he dropped off a spare set of keys on the day the removal van came. Neil asked him if he'd be so good as to forward their mail and if he didn't mind being spare key holder in case the estate agents screwed up. No mention of their riotous party last week. No embarrassment either. The rest of the time he was alone. Hour after hour. His footsteps echoing round the flat as he paced in his slippers, looking for ways to make himself useful. Checking the email for any replies to job applications whenever he became conscious of pacing. Checking the time. Compiling lists of job websites. Trying so hard not to check in with Pussy.

A week gone already and he still had no sign of work. Alice's promotion should have made him happy. Yes, they'd celebrated and he told her how wonderful it was. And she'd been so downbeat about it all so as not to rub it in. But still there were those hours in the day, after he'd signed the agreement for his pitiful severance package and hadn't the energy to argue for more, when the future stared back as blank as the computer screen before him. Eleven weeks, ten, to find work. Any kind of work, to eat, to sleep, to pay the mortgage. The new economy, the thing he and Alice had joked about. To be thirty-eight, forty, starting again. A generation of men like him. All the people he'd fired. Tom, Steve, Archie. Temp typing and call centres. Unqualified for anything else. PC skills, sixty words per minute. Forty-five-second telephone reply times. Welcome to the blue team. We're twenty points behind the reds and greens but if we just believe in ourselves we can be winners.

Those hours in those long days, when he was on the net and he found himself doing the very thing he'd told himself he wouldn't do. It was on the Friday of the second week that David tried to give it up, that he realised he had a problem.

He'd lost sleep worrying about it. The day before he'd spent six hours on swinging-paradise, the day before that it had been about four and the one before that. Lying awake as Alice snored, staring into the dark. Running over lists in his mind of things to do to keep himself from the site. Worrying again that this might be part of the same addictive trait that led him to cheat on Hannah. And Alice, he'd have to get her to stop these stories of hers, these stories about couples. Too easy to put it all together into some erotic fantasy fuelled by anger and this nagging sense that he was in so many ways redundant.

Ten thirty-five in the morning he tried to give it up. He was craving a cigarette, a drink. He forced himself to go back to job searching. Sixty-two job applications sent out with his CV in the last few weeks and nothing in the inbox. Perhaps he shouldn't have tried to be so witty and upbeat on the application forms. A sign of desperation for sure. One more at least, give it a try. Type in 'Jobs Glasgow' on Google. Bar staff required, security guard, long-distance lorry driver. His father had started off with small jobs and ended up with a salary and a pension. His position growing daily in respect and stature. His career was the opposite. He'd started off with the safest salaried job he could find and was now faced with a future of nothing but short-term temp work, increasingly lacking in dignity.

Moments like that on the net and a blind rage came over him. He thought, Fuck it, only be a minute, it'll be a laugh. Pussy-galore.

Hello James. Pussy luvs Moneypenny. Please send FACE PICS. 2 confirm UR legit. We R free Fri/Sat evening. Chat first – If all OK 2 meet. XXX.

End it all. Apologise to Pussy-galore. Tell her all about his redundancy. About how it was just him, his partner didn't know about this. He was sorry for being a time-waster. But as he deliberated on what to write he started looking through the other ads.

Joiedevivre67 (39). Divorcee. Keen to try to have fun again. Had taken the photo herself. Arm outstretched, face filling the frame. Naked at night. In the background a cremation urn sitting on the mantel. A Dyson vacuum cleaner on the edge of frame. A teddy bear on a floral pillow. Clothes on the floor and falling out of drawers. Safeway bags on the sideboard. Looking for big-tit lovers. M, F and couples.

It was OK, he told himself. Just a laugh. And in the absence of any appreciation from the outside world it did reassure him that he actually existed and that other people were as fucked up as he was.

Cumslut (42). A photo of her spread wide on an Ikea bed. Her Caesarean scar visible beneath her lingerie and her smile. 'No Jordan, small in that dept.' Married woman wants 4 good-looking men 4 good seeing to. Husband + Video 2 be present. Face and dick pics essential.

Those seconds waiting for the next ad to download, that turned into minutes, hours, as he clicked from one to the next.

Johnny (45). 'Not hung but happy.' Hairy chest. Beer belly. Photo in garage. Naked, standing proudly next to a new silver Lexus. Looking for couples.

It was almost time for Alice to come home and he'd done it again, three hours on and off swinging-paradise and he was still sitting there in his underpants. He had just enough time to think up a reply to Pussy. This stranger on the net. This person who wanted him even though she'd never met him. In some strange way he felt some kind of obligation to her. Guilt. Leading her on then disappointing her. It wasn't like he was cheating on Alice. Not really. He typed.

Luv 2 Meet @ W/end. Will discuss w/partner. For real. Chat on phone 2 Confirm. Our mobile is 07976 605 334.

Fucking stupid. Delete all. Log off, never log on again. Delete history, delete cookies.

*   *   *

It had haunted her. That image of the newly-wed couple with their faces blanked out. Free weekends.

Bodies without faces that wanted faces.

It had been lunchtime, Friday, the end of her second week back at work. She'd told herself to stop working so hard, to take a break. Forced herself to eat something. Some cold soggy sandwich from the new vending machine where the staff canteen used to be. She'd printed out the picture and sat staring at it as she nibbled the cold wet thing that was called a chicken salad baguette.

The two white squares on their faces. Like the photos of her dad her mum had cut his face out of. About an inch square. The same size as a passport photo. She went through her bag and found one of her old work IDs. Scissors and a minute of focused purposeful endeavour then the photo-booth pic of herself landed on the desk.

Just to see. For a laugh or whatever. To put the old image of her own face aged thirty-one over the blank white square. To see what she looked like in a wedding dress. Of course it didn't match but if you screwed up your eyes and made it all soft focus, as she did, it did sort of work. The way her face was turned slightly to the left just like the woman's must have been. The way the pictures were almost the same size.

Alice married. Just look at it. Jesus.

If she had a photo of David. For a laugh. To stick both their faces on. Photocopy it. Make a gift of it to him tonight. Look at us. Me and you married. Nice bouquet. I didn't realise you had such broad shoulders!

Really, it was art. But she must stop thinking like that. There was no going back to that. So maybe even. The image for the TV series. Posters. Really. Swinging. Two passport-photo faces stuck onto the bodies of people in a wedding photo. Po-mo, clever, and a little shocking. All the things required for the kind of out-there programme they were looking for. She might suggest it to the head next week.

But as the processed chicken sat there cold and clammy in her mouth and she felt the inclination to spit the damn thing out, she stared at the image of her face on the bride's body and the whole thing became a bit like the sandwich. Sickening.

Alice in bridal gown next to a man without a face. The image floating before her. Her mother's third wedding. Her mother's smile, so forced. Husband number three. The hypocrisy of the woman. This woman who had hated convention, who'd dragged her from commune to commune, rock festival to rock festival, who had let her be brought up by strangers. Who, in her cowardice, had recoiled back into the thing she had so failed at and despised. Men, marriage. The smile frozen on her face. Number three. Yet another man who was little more than a blank face, a blank cheque to subsidise her despair. Lover number forty-five. A man whom she predicted her mother would betray and who within a year was betrayed. A face Alice could not even recall. Like her real father. Men without faces.

She sat there in her glass-walled office looking out at the other researchers. She really should have made more of an effort to get to know them. As David would have said, 'to build the team'. The budget had been done, approved. The swinging series was a potential reality, her first commission. Maybe she should have the researchers in for a meeting, get them on her side. Pep talk. Jesus, it was weird being a boss. Every time she looked out at them, they turned away. Giving her the side of the face. The polite face.

And wasn't that exactly what David had been doing the last two weeks? Hiding what he felt? Wasn't he really in some kind of trouble? Those last few nights with him so distant. Every night she'd tried to arouse him with talk of the neighbours. But even that had now become forced. They'd never repeated the success of that first night. Perhaps it was her fault. Like the manuals said. Putting pressure on him.

A married man without a face.

*   *   *

Six forty-five. He was sitting straight ahead of her on the subway home. Staring right through her. It pissed her off the way men could do that. So she did as she always did. After a few brief glances she raised her head and stared right at him. Mid thirties, tired-looking, in an old suit and dirty sneakers. Playing with his wedding ring. His dark eyes sunk in his skeletal head and staring out. Desire and need. Staring through her. As the subway stopped at Kelvinhall, she got to her feet, and on the way out noticed what he'd been looking at. Just above where she'd been sitting there was some kind of shampoo advert: a model displaying ample cleavage. An unemployed man lost in some sad sexual fantasy.

She didn't like to think about it but knew exactly what David would be doing right now at home. Sitting at the PC surfing the swinging site again. His face tired, humourless, after another day failing to find work. His subservience. Dinner on the table. Having to appreciate the effort he'd gone to to make it. David and his wounded pride and his recipe books. Trying so hard. It would be no good confronting him about it all. Being judgemental. He would become defensive as he no doubt had done with his ex. Retreating into himself.

As she walked the eight blocks to home she worked out the plan. It would have to be like what had happened at work. You take the thing you fear and you turn it into a game. Take this perversion of his and get him to laugh with her about it. Couldn't confront him. Couldn't watch as he went more and more into himself. Like that man on the subway. Couldn't lose him to a fantasy.

Oddbins. Two for the price of one. Merlot.

She opened the door and called his name but there was no reply. She walked into the kitchen and he was at the computer. He tried to hide it from her but she saw it. Just before his finger clicked on the mouse – the swinging site.

Say nothing.

Dinner. And it was lovely but even complimenting him on his cooking skills seemed like a wall building between her and what really had to be said. So hard to say anything to him like this. Relegating him to this position. These words unsaid between them, this picture of him that was developing, the typical unemployed man. To talk about her day at work. To express enthusiasm about it, now that she was a boss. Impossible. So these polite clichés.

'The lamb, was it marinated?'

'Aha.'

'Lovely. Really.'

'A bit overdone.'

'No really, it was perfect, just right.'

'Daddy, maybe we should talk.' That was what she wanted to say.

To get drunk then for courage. To face it head on and stop it. To stop the urge to pity him. Pity someone and your love dies. You become a carer, you listen, you hold them. In time come to resent them.

Joke about it all. Take his obsession and make it hers. Stop it before it became silence. So she fed him phoney lines about how she'd been doing research into swinging, for the new show, and did he still have the name of that site that Archie had looked at because she could do with interviewing some of these people and could they look at it together?

An hour they sat there at the PC. Her laughing. And she told him about how the faceless picture he found was really an incredible artwork and how she'd been thinking about it all week. And it said so much about life today. And so, for the first time in two weeks, he was there laughing with her, relieved almost at showing her the swinging site, sharing it with her.

2-4-U. Mid thirties couple. Bi-curious. Looking for W/E black males.

AC/DC. Early forties. Rock'n'roll Bi-fem looking for a Whole Lotta Rosie.

Trust, it was all about trust. And she was winning it back. And he confessed that he'd been more than just looking, that since he'd lost his job, he'd been messing around, just for a laugh, emailing this Pussy-galore couple and that he'd got a lot of replies. A joke of course, but she, Pussy-galore, her, them, whatever, had asked for some real face pics. And they wanted to meet this weekend.

'What? The couple in the wedding photo?'

And it was them. The picture. The white-squared faces.

'Jesus!'

'What?'

'They look just like, well, I mean sort of, no, they really do.'

'Who?'

'The Gordons.'

That these people without faces could have been the

neighbours. That their first real sexual experience in so long had happened after that night with the Gordons.

Send Face Pics pleeez. ASAP! Mwaa.

The last glass of Merlot. Laughing again. Her in the computer seat. Forcing enthusiasm, finding fun in the details. Jesus! The language of swinging. Look at it. She tried to laugh through the mounting fear. It wasn't Pussy's replies that were scaring her. It was this theme that was now running through her life. That life-changing decisions hung on so little. A joke, a whim, curiosity. A month later and she could not recall that moment. That moment of choice, if there ever was one, that changed everything. Call it the murmurings of the subconscious if you dared. Or insecurity. A hard day at work. A momentary fuck-it-all attitude. Hormones. Guilt. Two bottles of Merlot.

Whatever it was, after the second bottle was finished they found themselves, just for a laugh, getting the digital camera out. Face pics for Pussy. And fuck it. She did want to see what they were really like when you removed the white boxes from their faces. To meet them even. Maybe. For a laugh.

All the ridiculous porno poses. Things she never even knew she knew. Two shots of vodka after the wine and one finger in her pussy and one in her mouth. Laughing and waiting for the laughter to subside before he took the pic in which she looked so serious that it made her laugh for another ten minutes. Are we really going to send this to them? Laughing, fuck, why not? To be a real porno star for a night. Fuck, why not?

And the photo of David lying back on the bed. She had to suck him for ten minutes to get it to look presentable. Him in her mouth, her looking up at the lens. Those big porno eyes. Crouching, giggling between his legs to shoot it. They'd joked afterwards about how the perspective had made it look so much bigger then it really was.

Then it was their ad, because Pussy wasn't the only pussy out there and it would be fun to see how many replies they got, if any, and maybe someone would see the joke. She sat and typed as he looked over her shoulder. Laughing together about the weird terminology. W/E at W/E in W/E, she'd said. What? Well-endowed at weekend in West End. Coming up for a name for themselves. Checking the site to see what was the done thing. A funny name or the letters of your name. David and Alice. D+A, DnA, DOA. Anno Domini. No, she had a better idea. She didn't care if anyone knew it was her. A classic double bluff. Who'd be stupid enough to use their own name? After half an hour of hysteria it was done.

WONDERLAND

Alice + White Rabbit – Bi-curious couple – seek W/E Kings + Queens to join us 4 adventures in Wonderland – Full swaps, Parties, Orgies, Role playing O and A. Can travel or accom. W/End Glasgow. Week nights only. Age and size not important. No one-offs. Looking to develop long-term friendship w/like-minded people. No Timewasters / Pic collectors. Step through the mirror w/us. Face/ nude pics + phone # guarantee reply.

That was how it happened. A drunken night of fooling around. A moment fuelled by booze and some desire to be distracted from a future that seemed all too predictable. Cutting and pasting the pics into the advert and still laughing. The almost accidental choice which was little more than a click on the mouse. The laughter then dying after half an hour and the silent acknowledgement that this meant something. That it had been sent. Posted into the world. That they'd wait and see. Like work. A joke about the absurdity of it all. A joke that became absurdly real.

*   *   *

Sender: Pussy-galore
Hi Wonderland. Loved yr pics. Got us hot. Luv to meet 4 Blind date. We will B @ La Revolution. 7.30/ 20 Aug. Confirm. If OK – our place or Yrs? Luv 2 Watch mayB2 swap. Toys and role-play poss. Call/text 2 confirm. 07965 563 443. S+ S. XXX

Role-play. He had to laugh. Like the old instruction manual at work:

Role-playing games, exercises and activities help build teams, develop employee motivation, improve communications and are fun – for corporate organisations, groups of all sorts, and even child development. They help improve training, learning, and liven up conferences and workshops. They can also enhance business projects, giving specific business outputs and organisational benefits.

To make a room full of potential employees strip bare and get blindfolded. Easy. You're on the desert island. All of your clothes have been washed away. To shout instructions at them. Them so soft and malleable, wanting to survive. How far would you go to hold down a job? What are we talking here? Your desert island is the last remaining mile of human life in the whole world. Apocalypse. Forget the flares, and the mirror and the hundred-yard-wide sign made out of sticks on the beach that reads SOS. No one is coming to save you. Forget teamwork. You are going to starve to death. How do you want to spend your last days? Crawl on your hands and knees. You are in darkness. Crawl and find an ass and kiss it. I want to see a chain of blindfolded bodies kissing corporate ass. Yes, in his last week at work, he should have tried it.

We cannot accept responsibility for any liability which arises from the use of any of these free role-playing ideas or games – please see the disclaimer notice below. Always ensure that you exercise caution and sensitivity when using any role-playing games or activities which might disturb or upset people.

Seven thirty. La Revolution. The new Stalin-era communist theme bar in the centre. One drink, maybe two. The chat. Two couples discussing how they would fuck each other. Assessing if they would. David couldn't help laughing about it. He'd decided to write down a list of questions. It was in his pocket and he'd run over it in the bathroom before they came out. It could be some incredible parody of a human resources interview.

What qualities do you think you could bring to this position?
Are you a leader or a follower?
Do you prefer to initiate or participate?
How do you feel about role playing?
Are you looking for something short or long term?

He hadn't bothered to get dressed up, just pulled on another shirt, decided that his attitude was enough in itself. Alice meanwhile had stripped, bathed, perfumed and was now trying on her new lingerie again. She was about as comfortable with it as the old fish out of water, speared on a desert island by one of the blindfolded survivors with a stick that could have otherwise been used for the SOS sign on the beach. What the fuck. They were supposed to meet them in twenty minutes in some trendy bar on Sauchiehall Street and at this rate they would be late. To try to calm her down and ensure that she was buying into it all he ran over the details. Useful tips from the swinging website. Always pick a public space. Don't drink too much. Location: ideally a hotel for a first encounter. Do not invite strangers into your home. Discuss dos and don'ts in advance. Agree on whether using protection or not. Have a secret safety word or words you can say to each other if you don't want to go through with it. Don't forget to have fun. But his little list, as he said it, was if anything making her feel more nervous.

'I'm dressed like a fucking Thanksgiving turkey!' she said, staring at herself in the bedroom mirror he still hadn't got round to hanging. She'd bought suspenders for the hold-ups even though they didn't need to be held up. She was fumbling with the clasps. They kept coming undone as she straightened her back to look at herself in the mirror. Calm her down. Strategy one. Old one. Flattery.

'You look stunning. Horny housewife.'

'Fucking fuck!'

No, Alice was too intelligent to fall for that one. Her clasps were coming undone again and again as if they were some kind of embodiment of her own doubt. It was amazing that they'd even got this far. Hard to remember how he'd managed to turn things around and get her to go along with it, or even why. It had been almost two weeks of three strategies, constantly varying them. Slowly leading her towards this moment. It had been something to do.

Strategy two. Touch. He moved closer and went down on his knees, taking the clasps from her hand and fastening them for her. Kissing her thigh. Strategy three. Play devil's advocate, make a suggestion to Alice and she'll always want to do the opposite.

'We don't have to do this if you don't want. I mean, we could just not turn up.'

'Well, I'm bloody well dressed now.'

'Yeah, but we could do something else, a meal, the pictures.'

As soon as he said it he knew what her reply would be. 'We can't afford to go out for a meal.' Thankfully he was wrong.

'They'll be sitting there waiting.'

'So we don't show, turn the mobile off. Half an hour, they'll get the message.'

Alice was fussing with her bra now. Trying to get her breasts to sit right. He moved back onto the bed and watched. His post-feminist intellectual wearing Ann Summers. If playing devil's advocate had been successful in getting her to dress like this then a little more gentle use of the same strategy would get her to the bar. One drink and Alice wouldn't be able to resist having another. Nervousness always made her drink more. Then her natural empathy for people would take over. He'd hit her with all the tricks at once. A little flattery, some ironic commentary, a gentle touch on her shoulder, neck or knee that the strangers could see. She'd be aroused by being watched being touched. It would be daring, rebellious, and all the time he'd keep on playing it like he wanted to go home soon.

'Anyway,' he said, 'it's their first time too. Chances are they won't show up either.'

She exhaled in her on-the-verge-of-an-Audrey-Hepburn sort of tantrum way. 'You don't want to go, is that what you're telling me?'

Shit, his little strategy was close to backfiring. 'No, not at all. I thought . . . you. This is all about you, baby.'

'No, you started it.'

She was slipping away. She was uncomfortable in the gear that she'd first bought as a joke for him but which was now going to be worn in public. She was getting self-conscious and when she got self-conscious she would always back down and talk instead. There would be rationalisations, arguments and counter-arguments. Not only would they miss the date but the whole evening would be spent in cross-examination. He had a few seconds to turn it around.

'OK, so let's just see it as a dare. I'll bet they won't show. So we go just to see if they do. We get a look at them, if they're monsters we turn round and leave, don't even say a word. If they're OK, we have a chat. We'll say our safety word and then it'll be over. Think of it as research for your series.'

Good. Her work. Give her a get-out.

'Babysitter, right?' he said. 'You say babysitter, or I do, then you go to the toilet and I tell them, we'll see them another night, but we won't ever call them back.'

'Still think it's weird.'

'Of course it is.'

'No, our word.'

'OK, so we use some other, like, like . . . what? Like banana or car or butterfly or . . .'

She mumbled something. Sounded maybe like something about kids. So we have kids. I got kids. Something like that. She grunted a little, stared at her stockinged feet then looked up at him.

'OK. But what if we like them?'

'We'll just talk, then come home, another time maybe. C'mon. One drink, then we'll see. It'll be a laugh if nothing else.'

She slipped on her shoes. Pulled her jacket on. Pouted at her reflection.

'What the fuck. C'mon we're gonna be late.'

He kissed her cheek gently. He'd done it. Made Alice feel she was conservative, that she was conforming and so she'd have to take the bold leap forward. Classic HR crisis-management technique. Allow the participant to feel that they have made the decision themselves. He pulled on his jacket, and checked to make sure he had his mobile.

He didn't want to ask himself why. Why this need to have Alice have sex with someone else. But as they walked closer to the taxi rank the possible reasons rushed at him.

He wanted to see if it turned him on.

He wanted her to be satisfied by another man. For once – because he couldn't satisfy her.

To feel empowered by manipulating her because she had a job and he didn't.

To just do something, anything, out of sheer boredom.

To set off a chain of events that when started would get out of control.

To live through the heady intoxication of losing control – with her.

To develop a new deeper shared intimacy.

To make her strong. Strong enough to deal with his weakness.

To help her find the real her.

Her hand was suddenly in his as they turned the corner. The bar was there ahead of them.

'You crazy fuck,' she said, laughing. 'I do love you.'

*   *   *

So many clichés you could come up with for why you should do this. Life is short. You only live once – the grass is always greener – nothing ventured nothing gained. To be honest, though, her desire for this, if she could even call it that, was purely theoretical. Call it therapy for David. Call it research for the new swinging series. She had her questions.

Over and above the purely theoretical, she wanted to see if David could get hard with another woman. This problem of his with intimacy. An anonymous female form might be what was required. She made a mental note to remind herself not to be jealous if he got an erection with Pussy-galore. This was just an experiment. She would be taking notes.

In the door. Wall of sound. The Chemical Brothers. Then the decor. Soviet kitsch. Busts of Stalin. Red walls and agitprop posters everywhere. Her mother had called herself a communist, and at university Alice had studied the sad decline of the Left. Now it was a theme bar. There were flavoured vodkas, strawberry, vanilla. It was a fair guess that no one who drank here was old enough to remember the Cold War, the fear of nuclear holocaust, or to know that Marx had said that history repeats itself, first as tragedy, then as farce.

She scanned the place trying to imagine what kind of couple would choose this as a place to meet another couple. Perhaps Pussy-galore were Scottish socialists, perhaps they took this seriously and were wearing Red Army fatigues, perhaps it was part of their James Bond routine. Her eyes scanned the twenty or so people there, singles mostly, all wearing the latest hippie chic. Bo-ho or faux-ho. Part gypsy, part 60s heroine, part Woodstock libertine. The kind of things her mother would have picked up for a buck. The girl by the bar, big belt and semi-transparent cheesecloth skirt, the guy beside her in designer denims with sewn-on patches, dreadlocks and a 'Make Poverty History' T-shirt. *Roberto Cavalli or Ungaro are the designers to look for this season if this is the kind of hippie you see yourself as.*

She couldn't help but wonder how many people here knew what happened when you put communism and hippies together. It created terror. Her mother and her obsessions with the Symbionese Liberation Army and the Weather Underground. Her mother and her radical friends. The many men she's grown up with whom she called uncle. The men from U.N.C.L.E. *Essential pieces include the long skirt. Brown leather accessories. Big belts. Sheer tops with embellishments. Barely there blouses.* One bottle. Three parts gasoline, one part fertiliser, one part sand, one part sugar, one wick made of lint soaked in gas. Cocktail? Lovely. A Molotov please. Light and throw.

They took a seat by the window. She was convinced that none of the fashionistas and Aparachicks there could possibly be swingers. David was scanning the bar, twitching. The place was supposed to be fun but it made her sad. That history was worth so little, that it had become nothing more than a backdrop to pose beside as you got drunk on vanilla vodka. Swinging and the end of communism. Some connection there. Something to do with the collapse of belief in alternatives.

David's phone beeped. Message.

'Cool,' he said, clicking his phone shut. 'That's them at the end of the bar.'

She looked up. The woman waved. The faces were not the ones she'd imagined hiding behind the white squares.

Her – some shop-assistant type, thirties definitely, in the kind of trendy hipster denims that only made your age more apparent. Him – younger, army fatigues, some kind of mad clubber. He looked like he'd been out all night and had just woken up. Quick profile. Working class. Him – white van driver. Dodgy dealer. Her – house-wife. Older. Slightly forced in her manner. Wearing a big hippie pendant, very unlike the one in the wedding photo. Alice would probe with her questions. Get a complete picture of the kind of people who did this and why.

'C'mon. It'll be a laugh if nothing else,' he said. 'They look wild.'

She could tell he was acting. He underestimated the power of her perception sometimes. Never mind, let him think he was running the show. She had her curiosity and she wanted to hear the voices that lived behind the white squares.

David led the way. Did the introductions.

'Pussy-galore I presume, how ya doing?'

'Steve, mate, and this is ma wee darlin', Shona.' He had a thick East End accent.

'Wonderland,' said David, shaking hands. 'Well, David and Alice actually.'

Already he'd given their real names. The site suggested that you didn't do that straight away. They had planned to say that Alice was a fake name, and give a fake real one. Alice smiled at the woman, Shona. Her face had a tired look about it.

David made some lame joke about being secret agents in a Russian bar, but the James Bond thing didn't wash.

Alice worked out that all of the emails they'd received had been from the guy. The woman didn't look like she liked Bond.

'Sho, vodka tonic? Shaken not shtirred,' said David.

It was funny but not funny. The Sean Connery thing. She was just grateful that he hadn't done a caricature of Steve's Glasgow accent. Seen him do it so many times before. Picking up on people's accents then mimicking them. Deeply patronising of course but not nasty. He was barely conscious of doing it so it was kind of amusing. His Connery was pretty good. But not as good as his Southern hick. Let David do that all he liked. Her focus was on Shona. She couldn't stop picturing her in her wedding dress. She made a quick choice and decided it would be best to speak to her as if none of this was happening, as if they were just meeting some friends.

'Hiya,' she said in a chirpy voice.

'Hi.'

One word and already she could tell that the woman's Glasgow accent was as thick as her partner's. And she seemed down. Compellingly so. Alice looked over at David and Steve. They were giving it the best-mates routine already. A pair of actors both of them. Leave them to it. The important thing was to get Shona alone then start the questions. The clichéd profile of swingers was suburban nouveau riche. They were more proley. Why? Why would you do this?

Steve was buying the drinks. Insisting she tried a flavoured vodka. A closer look established that he was wearing a Cavalli shirt, and had an expensive haircut with highlights. Had three big gold rings and was probably more than the four years younger Shona had said on the website. Ten years ago, guys like this would have worn a medallion and been called Steve. Shit, but he was called

Steve. Maybe not his real name at all. OK so this was someone who aspired to the condition of being a Steve.

'Vodka peach for Alice and a straight Stolly for Pussy. Wee cosy nook in the back, lassies.'

David and Steve led the way. In the eight beats of the Chemical Brothers it took to get to the back, Alice had the guy all worked out. He thought he was funny but his patter was now well worn on his partner. A player and serial adulterer. She seemed more than tired. Depressed. This was his game then. But what held them together? A kid of course. Unwanted pregnancy. Poor Catholic family. East End. Pro-life, lo-life. The kid had been an accident and now this was the deal. They'd struck it after the last time he got caught. Stay together for the sake of the kid. He could fuck around as long as he told her the truth. She'd do anything to hold onto him, he was a catch of sorts, good-looking, new money. Didn't want to let him go so she agreed to his deal. Poor woman. No doubt concerned about her sex appeal after the child. Felt unattractive so this was some self-esteem kick. So the theory went. That the whole scene was run by men who wanted more pussy and subservient women who complied. Months of gentle persuasion. Bedtime whisperings. 'You'd love a woman to go down on you wouldn't, ya, love?', 'Suck ma finger, yeah, bet you wish it was some guy's cock.' Hadn't it in some way been like this with David? But it all seemed too pat, some undergraduate feminist thesis. Men exploit women. No. Speak to them, find out. Ask the questions.

They were seated boy-girl facing girl-boy. Although she was facing Steve and David was facing Shona, she sensed that the boys were only really comfortable doing their male bonding routine. David. Appalling really all this fake enthusiasm. Pretending that he was interested in football. The act would be over pretty soon, when Steve asked him what he thought of this or that player and David's blank face would give him away. Best not to worry. But it was hard to talk to Shona, although she could tell the woman desperately wanted to talk. A few awkward minutes of platitudes half heard.

'Nice bar.'

'Sorry, wos that?'

'Shit, this music.'

'I canna hear ya.'

Shona seemed to give up. Lit a cigarette, Kensitas Club, and sat back. It was slipping away. Think about the series. Potential interviewee/participant. Alice leaned in.

'I know you're not supposed to do this, give it away I mean, but what's your safety word?'

Shona coughed, laughed. Went to say something, stopped herself, then blurted out, 'It's fuckin' stupit.'

'No go on. I'll tell you ours.'

'Naw.'

'Go on.'

'Parkin.' She stopped, trying not to laugh. 'Parkin' meter.'

Laughter. Alice roaring with it. 'Jeez! Parking meter. Like . . . like I'll just go check the parking meter.'

'It's fuckin stupit.'

Alice noticed Steve shooting Shona a recriminatory glance.

'No, no. It's brilliant! So much easier to drop into conversation. Like, I'll just nip out, love, and put some money in the meter. Brilliant.'

But Steve's eyes had unsettled Shona. The joke suddenly wasn't funny. Alice worried that her laughter had been too loud.

'So, Shona, why did you get into this?'

'Ahm goantae the bogs. You cumin'?'

Alice had never done that girls-talkin'-in-the-bogs thing before. She worried that it would confuse David. The trip to the toilet meant they'd leave. Safety word: babysitter, then go to the toilet. But she hadn't said the word and David was too busy to notice. She smiled at Shona.

'Sure. OK.'

*   *   *

The toilet was decorated with pictures of communist women in red neck scarves with scythes and fists in the air. Alice didn't need to pee and rather surprisingly neither did Shona. Alice was waiting for it. The confessional. The poor woman would break down and tell her all about her life with the swinging moron. Alice was tired now of being able to guess someone's entire life from a quick glance.

'Ahm, sorry,' Shona said, as they stood by the sinks. 'Ah should huv telt ye.'

Women came and went, pissing and fixing their make-up in that clichéd way they did, pouting in the mirrors, trying to imagine how they looked for their men. Shona lit another cigarette and talked and talked. She felt sorry for her man, she said. This was the fourth time they'd tried and each time when she told folks the truth they bolted. The truth, the truth, thought Alice. That some people still believe there is a truth. The look in Shona's eyes. Got to find out the truth, a truth, even if it was only one person's partial little truth. She touched Shona's shoulder.

'It's OK,' she said. 'I understand.'

The first few points she'd got right. Shona was older,

yes, did have a kid, yes, but not with Steve. Simone aged three. Shona, Steve, Simone, she thought. Don't judge.

Alice tried to interject, tell her about how hard it must be. How she felt for her. She really did, felt almost moved for the woman and it felt good to feel something other than indifference for a change. But Shona kept on.

'So this is the deal.' She had this all planned. Must have said it to others before. Shona told her about her divorce three years ago, about how she'd decided that being with someone was out of the question now. Just wanted to date casually. 'You know, no strings attached. A man to shag every now and again. Ah mean we've got wir needs right?' But how she'd met Steve online a year back, wouldn't let him move in, but he'd kept pushing it. Really wanted to be part of her life. Bought presents for Simone. Presents for her, proposing to her, said he couldn't live without her. He had this fucked-up past she said.

How finally a year ago she'd given in and let him meet Simone. Simone loved him and then it all took off from there. The wedding. But still, it was a pain. They'd be having sex and she couldn't come. So like her first marriage, so many things. He was a sexy guy and needed more sex than she felt like. She didn't want to be dumped again, go through all that shite, so she'd had this idea. To let him have his fun. Teach him people didn't own each other. That was the reason for the name. Pussy-galore. Let him have his pussy. She'd been talking him into it for months. Give him space so he would leave her some space. Give him a wee bit of encouragement. To keep the marriage together. He wasn't really into it but was doing it for her. So this swinging thing.

'My God, but I thought . . .'

'Aye everyone does.'

Nothing more said but they understood each other. Alice had been wrong, so wrong. This man, this Steve, his energy and enthusiasm, nothing but nervousness. He wanted to be with Shona but she was holding him at bay, this was her plan. All hers.

'Ahm sorry,' said Shona as she stubbed her fag out in the sink. 'S'OK, if you don't want tae. Ah mean I understand where you're coming from yersel.'

Shona touched Alice's hand. 'Ah mean, we've all got wir problems.'

The act was over. Touched by this woman who touched her hand. This woman who she'd got so wrong. This woman who had seen her problems with David, problems she hadn't even begun to grasp. Alice leaned forward and hugged her.

*   *   *

'This is the kitchen.'

Bizarre. He felt like the estate agent in the next-door neighbours' flat. Giving Shona and Steve the guided tour of the rooms as if they were potential buyers. Who knew, in a month, maybe they'd have to do this for real. Sell up, move out.

'Bedroom. Victoriana rather than real Victorian. They call it the West End but it's not really.'

He was worried that he sounded too middle class. Doing some caricature of the Hyndland husband. Being judgemental. These poor proles with their cheesy wedding photo online. He couldn't help but feel that Shona was excited just being there. Seeing a place that was so big, so West End. Alice made herself busy in the kitchen. He stopped before the white room, knew better than to show them in.

'Same size as the bedroom. Only bits and pieces in there, junk really. You know, just having moved in and to be honest we're not really sure quite what to do with it yet.'

'It's lovely. Really nice,' said Shona.

'So where do you guys live?' he asked. Forgetting that he'd already asked them that on the way there in the taxi. God he was such a snob, had totally blanked it with his phoney smile when they said they came from Yoker. The other side of the tracks. Poverty and Ann Summers parties. Robbie Williams and high-rise flats.

'Just down the road,' said Shona.

Music started up from the next room. The Velvet Underground. What was Alice playing at? These people would never have heard of the Velvets. It would freak them out.

But then the guy started singing along, even putting on a Lou Reed voice.

'I'm Waiting For The Man'.

He was curious indeed. Probably got into the Velvets in his drug-crazed days. David took a mental note on drugs. No swap. Just watching, some touching maybe. Didn't want to catch anything. God he was nervous.

Shona walked into the kitchen and Steve stuck with him. They were still both staring at the bedroom. So weird to have strangers in your home like this. Strangers who would soon be undressed and fucking on your bed. How could you actually relax enough to go through with it? How did you segue from chit-chat to 'OK, let's see you fuck.' Like those awful scenes in B-movies where a plot point rested on a single line of dialogue.

David stared at Steve as Steve stared at the bedroom.

'Aye. Bet that bed's seen a bit o' action.'

'Well actually, it's new. Just put it up last week. Habitat.'

'Right, aye.'

The one thing he hadn't foreseen in this cunning plan

of his was his own internal resistance. This almost bourgeois fear of strangers in your home.

'So, your lassie,' said Steve. 'Whit dis she like?'

My lassie, thought David. You mean my daughter? Oh
Jesus, no, sorry. Silence. They both just stood there. This
is one of those awkward silence things. Speak, think.
Anything.

'Oh, you know,' David said, feeling himself blush, not
exactly playing for time, working out exactly what mode
of address, what degree of calculated Glaswegian accent to
apply. 'A bit of this, bit of that. Really quite open to anything
really, I mean depending. You know because it has to be
about chemistry, as they say.' Already he was running over
the strategies in his head. If he could just stop this inane
chit-chat. If he asked the man to undress or. Ask the man
to get his partner to undress or. In all the pornos people
started tearing the clothes off each other as soon as the
door was shut. Please God no, let's not keep talking. What's
next? 'So you've got a girl too. Sorry, wee girl. Sorry, lassie.
Where does, sorry dis she go to, sorry go tae school? Sorry,
skool. Like wir dis she go tae skool?' Jesus. The silence.

The song from the next room. OK, that was it. Talk
about the music. Did you know that Lou Reed based this
song upon the novel *Venus in Furs* by Sacher-Masoch,
the nineteenth-century Austrian writer whose name
Krafft-Ebing, the eminent psychologist, used as part of
the expression sadomasochism, masochism being named
after Sacher-Masoch and sadism being, of course as we
all know, being based upon the Marquis de . . . sorry am
I boring you? No, wrong, wrong, wrong.

But the guy was singing along to it.

Word perfect. David hoped 'Heroin' wouldn't come
on in case the guy started on some story about shooting
up. Or maybe even pulled out some gear.

David just stared. Blurted out, 'Fancy a drink?' This man. Name. Name. Call him Steve. 'Steve.'

'Aye, was wonderin' when you'd ask.'

David took the lead and walked Steve back through to the kitchen. The music was loud. This thing was going to be impossible. Just some ridiculous fantasy that was humiliating if you ever tried to act it out. He pushed the door open.

'Alice.' But she wasn't there. 'Alice?'

He backtracked. They must have slipped past him when he and Steve were in the bedroom, they must be, could only be in the white room.

He pushed the door open slightly.

The bare floorboards. The packing boxes. The edge of the spare bed. A shoe. Alice's. Alice on her tippy-toes kissing Shona against the wall.

He stood there in the doorway. Steve behind him, peering over his shoulder.

'Fuckin' A,' whispered Steve.

What to do. To clear his throat. To say 'Hi girls'.

He had wanted this, but now all he wanted to do was turn and leave. Steve was behind him. The girls, suddenly aware that they were being watched, stopped and started giggling.

To get away. Anything. Any excuse. What? The keys for the Gordons' flat.

Steve had made his way into the room. Kissed Alice and Shona. They kissed him back in turn. Alice looked up at him as Steve nibbled her neck and Shona put her hand on her breast. What was that look on her face? Defiance? Anger? Did those eyes say 'Fuck off'? Did they say 'Go away'? Or 'Watch me be a whore. This is what you wanted. Live with it or run'? Alice closed her eyes as both of them, these two people, kissed and touched her.

'Sorry,' he said. 'Just need to . . . have to go next door for a minute and check the mail.'

'Parking meter, eh mate?'

The woman laughed. Alice threw him that glance again but he was out. Keys in hand. Almost running. Fingers fumbling with the keys. Remember. What did he say? Bronze Yale – front door. Silver Yale – inner door. One Chubb – three other keys.

He'd tried every option and was finally in. A few letters caught under the draught excluder. The bare boards and empty space. Minutes he stood there. Trying to get his breath back. The entire space was the mirror of theirs. Everything in negative. He walked through the hall into the first bedroom, the second. The dimensions the same. Not sure what he was doing. Just pacing. But then he wanted to see. Walked through the corridor. Pushed open the door identical to theirs. Into the kitchen diner, better than theirs, and stood by the edge of the window, too anxious to look out. Seconds, then he couldn't resist. If he squeezed himself up against the window frame he could probably just see.

He forced himself to do it. A fragment, a thin section just visible, the white room, through the window. The white walls. The edge of the spare bed. Alice's shoulder just visible. But then Alice seemed to lean in, glance out, then move the woman into view, as if she was framing a picture for him. She motioned for the man to move closer. They both kissed her, touching her breasts, her neck, then Alice stepped back, seemed to speak to them as if directing them. She stood there and watched the couple as the man pulled down his wife's jeans and undid his fly.

Alice suddenly looked up. Across the space. Through the windows. Her eyes to his. A smile on her face, like a secret. She leaned forward and touched the man's cock. Working it in her hand. David found himself reaching into his own pants. Taking his cock out there in someone else's kitchen. Looking at Alice as she looked out at him. Seeing her work the cock as he worked his. Like an out of body experience. You see her hand on his dick, you imagine what it feels like as you feel yourself. Like a story. Like Alice's stories to him about the neighbours. The story alive.

The man was hard, he was hard. The man turned his partner round, she rested her hands on the bed and he started fucking her from behind.

Her eyes. Alice in the background, not even watching these people fuck in her white room, just staring out. Through her window, through his. Staring at him.

This is for you her eyes said. She put her hand inside her pants. Two panes of glass and a couple fucking and thirty feet of garden between them. It felt right. That distance, finally acknowledged. Alice. He'd never felt so close to anyone in his life.

*   *   *

JOHN_DOE (49). His photo cut off at his shoulder, a woman's painted fingernails still there, cut off from her arm. What? Divorce? Ex? A kilt, some Burns supper party photo he'd posted. Looking for M2M, M2F, MMF, MFF or MMFF. No pain please.

John Doe. His name had the right degree of tele-visual irony. She emailed him. Had set up a new web address and advised the other researchers do the same to find participants. Fake names so they couldn't be traced back to the company. So some tabloid didn't get hold of it. Every site, every interesting couple or swinging single. Email them. Start the dialogue. Four couples is all we

need. Five days ago she'd sent a memo to IT asking them
to give her access to forbidden sites. Explaining that it
was for her new series. She'd been in constant touch with
David. Picking up on his tips. Accessing his sites. No
doubt the guys in IT were having a good laugh right
now hacking into her research. Joking in the pub about
the kinky new boss in Research.

The web pics. Flash photographs on domestic digital
cameras. Anyone who said that technology hadn't changed
the world had better read some Marx. Flash. The brutal
materialism of the images. The way that everything in
the photos was treated with the same importance. A
Subaru, a wicker chair from Bed, Bath and Beyond, labia
spread by fingers, an Ikea dining table, an erect penis.
Material circumstances determine consciousness. The little tell-
tale domestic details: a holiday chalet; a dado rail; a stack
of books; videos; *Bridget Jones*; the *Star Wars* trilogy. *The
consciousness of the mass is inherent in the material of their
lives.* A Mothercare stroller in a Homeworld kitchen
behind an ass in Ann Summers. The revolution will be
televised – if we can get enough participants.

It was week four. The budget had been approved
twelve days before. Cut back by ten per cent but still it
was twenty thousand per half-hour programme. Twelve
programmes. HBO were interested. C5, and CANAL+.
Confirm location, the head had said in her last email.
ASAP. List of participants – imperative. Four swappable
couples. Numbers, names. 'Innovative,' the head had said.
'Out there.' Not sure just yet whether this should be a
competition with viewer votes or VoyeurVision. Please
comment. Audience bored with titillation factor in *Big
Brother*. New series will give instant gratification. Pre-
press is amazing. Controversial. Hoping for Christian
Right to get leak. Hope they try to ban it. Twenty-four-

hour webcams definitely. Live website confirmed. Should we award cash prize to couple who survive this? Comment. WE NEED PARTICIPANT LIST. Like yesterday.

But the list of names was proving difficult. Pauline's team were working on it right then. She'd sent the memo out asking them to hurry up, then another reminding them that the series depended upon it. To find couples in Scotland who were willing to swap partners. For cash. Couldn't be so hard. Try wider, try whole UK. CC to all researchers.

Yesterday, Pauline had knocked on her new office door. Had wanted a word, in that way that was no longer friendly. A word, and that word, no matter how many words it took, involved resistance. As soon as Pauline had started speaking Alice had been hit by a wave of nausea, the new responsibility she'd taken on, no doubt. She wanted to apologise to Pauline. Crack a joke. But Pauline's face didn't say friend, now it said 'You are the boss'.

'It's just, I don't think we'll find any people who'll do this, I mean . . .'

Pauline's tone, resentful. It would take a lot to win her back.

'Well, where have you looked?'

Pauline had fumbled for words. Alice knew full well what the new researchers were doing. Going through Pauline's old Rolodex, contacting people who'd been filmed before in the six years Pauline had been there. On makeover shows, on fashion shows. The Hogmanay special. Yes, this was Scotland.

'I think we have to go a little further than rehashing old contacts.'

'But how do we find them?'

'I emailed everyone a list of websites last Wednesday.'

'Yes, but they're . . . I'm not doing that. We're not.'

She'd looked hard at Pauline. Her new *Sex and the City* bob trying to look like the head of department. Her new FCUK outfit, even though she was ten years too old to be wearing FCUK. Her face frozen with resentment at so many things so much bigger than Alice which had found symbolic representation in her person. Alice had lowered her gaze. She wanted to apologise for this boss thing she had to do. This boss voice. But when the boss voice came out it sounded like she really meant it.

'We're researchers, aren't we. We do research.'

'Tut.' Definitely, she had definitely heard Pauline tut as she left her office.

After Pauline had gone she felt that wave of nausea again. It had started just a few days before. Sickening, yes it was, to have to talk like this to an old friend. Two years of working together. But there was bitching going on about her on the floor. Her name was shit and she knew that Pauline was behind all of it. 'How come she gets promoted when she's never done anything?' 'She's not even from here.' Pauline had changed. Marx was right. The bourgeoisie might talk radical but when it comes down to real change they are counter-revolutionary.

Back to the PC. The world on there seemed to make more sense now than the one on the other side of her glass partitions.

Easyrider (34). Looking for first F2F experience. Husband older – 2 watch only. Standing in a country lane in a biker jacket, lifting up her incongruously out-of-place Laura Ashley floral dress to reveal her shaved pussy. Edge of a car. BMW. Replies without pics will not be responded to.

The honesty of it all. These people naked on their cars, in their living rooms, who let you into their homes that were so horribly similar. The same ornaments, furniture. Ikea, Dyson, Mr Muscle. The generic ornaments on the sideboard. You started to look for variations in class background, education, income. Their email names gave you clues. You could tell whether someone was educated or not by the varying degrees to which they used cliché or irony. This with their interior decor and domestic possessions gave you a pretty good idea. These people weren't stupid.

Zeus (37) W/E. Aphrodite (43) W/E, which for a woman must have meant busty. Seeking couples and large women only for first time bi-fem. Double E or bigger. The photo of his nine-inch dick. Large dog bowl right of frame. Copies of *House and Garden* magazine on the table beyond. Pic 2: naked, standing together in their kitchen, faces covered with black squares. Christmas decorations. Greying hair. Plates hanging from wall. No oven. A microwave and a toaster. Almost gynaecological close-up of her with a cucumber. Can travel or accom.

And David had given this to her, it was in some way an answer to all the questions she'd ever had. Or a question, a million questions that would inevitably lead her closer. To him.

The Couples folder was filling up. She had to create sub-folders, file and order. After almost a month of intensive research and planning she'd worked out the pattern. Word document. The six basic facts:

1. Most women on sites claim to be 'bi-curious' and seeking threesomes with another woman and their partner. Explicit pics. Why so many beautiful, sexually adventurous women? Assume (a) lots of lesbians

trapped in marriages, (b) women are naturally more openly bi than men, or (c) horny husbands have talked them into acting out the every-man's-dream scenario of fucking two women at the same time.

2. Over sixty ads from couples say: 'No single men'. No doubt most swinging couples are inundated with replies from single men. Probably men think it's easier to score a swinging couple than spending all night in a bar trying to chat up a female.

3. Only a few ads from single women looking for sex with single men. Fifteen a day. At most. All of them except one looking for W/E or VW/E men. Five were for VW/E black men (note: and so few black men in Scotland). Remaining one looking for man with small penis 'to try anal for the first time'. Three were in relationships but said 'Husband not 2 B present'.

4. Half of all ads are placed by first-timers. Either (a) the scene is growing quickly – is a new trend, or (b) a lot of people try this once then never do it again. Their ads generally long and rambling. 'I don't know why we're doing this' and 'Give anything a try once – LOL'. They always write LOL. Doubtful that people who write LOL ever laugh out loud.

5. Most of the ads say 'No time wasters'. Implies that either (a) a lot of people set up dates then fail to show, or (b) that people are lying online about being part of a couple and through extended emailing are revealed as being single men trying to get lucky. Had a few replies like this: 'Usually swing with Liz but she's out of town this weekend. You up 4 a 3?'

6. Fifteen per cent of ads are from experienced swingers. Almost professional. Lots of photos. Almost encyclopaedic lists of things they're into and not. Pics at orgies. Circle jerks. They show their faces. NB Dolly.

Looking at it all like this. Not sexy but radical. A new subculture. Just one website and 137 couples in Scotland looking for sex. At least seven other sites in Scotland and over fifty in the UK. She did the maths. Multiply. In England, fifty times the population. A whole culture living secretly beneath the one we walked about in daily. Thirty-three thousand couples doing this all the time.

UP4IT (40s). Two couples. All fully clothed. Men, thickset, sitting on sofa arms. Women in middle. Smirnoff, Coke, Kensitas Club, lighter and remote control on B&Q table before them. Man on left, balding, beer belly, Guinness T-shirt. Tattoo on arm. Touches arm of woman to his right. She rests her hand on his knee. Behind him a picture of an angel hanging on the wall. Raphael. Catholics. East End. The two women, huddled closely together, laughing. Party dresses on. Two sisters. Both girls – bi. Men – str8. Looking 4 couples, for 6, 8 sessions. No supermodels. Face pics please. Balloons, dolphin ornaments. Frilly curtains. Fake brick fireplace. Photos of family members. Frame right, cropped, a hand-painted sign reads HAPPY BIR MAG.

Of course there were those who were just after more. More sex, with more people, with bigger tits and cocks, in different positions, more exotic places. But there were the others whose needs were either bizarre, laughable or actually quite touching.

Ted (49). Been gay all of my life. Want to lose my virginity with a woman. Boyfriend approves.

Warts and weaknesses and all paraded with a candour that was almost confessional. It took her back to her year in psychology. You could grasp it. People's reasons. And they made jokes about their looks. Their backgrounds. They lived in Hull and Milton Keynes and Cumbernauld. They didn't want to buy or sell anything. Fucking was hard to objectify. There was always some kind of human contact. Not just two adverts rubbing against each other. Mr Calvin Klein meets Miss Ann Summers. There was negotiation. Empathy. Humour.

Mr + Mrs Robinson (late 40s). Mid-range hotel room. Her: nurse's outfit. Blonde. Leaning out of the window. Him spanking her with one of his shoes, laughing. Him: balding, Levi's denims and Gap T-shirt. Into BDSM. Role play. Looking for: parties. No single men. Weekdays only. Can't accom.

Must have meant they were married to other people. A hotel or a stay with another couple. Weekdays only. Both adulterers. Definitely. That's what 'Can't accom' meant.

Perverse as it was, she found herself in some way moved. Something to do with her mother, with David and his divorce. About all the mistakes that had been made over so many years. How we spend our lives trying to possess someone, so they won't leave, to own them. We turn them into objects and then we tire of our objects. This culture of boredom and this endless desire for the new. These swingers were different. They weren't for sale. Gave themselves away for free. It was about sharing. No financial transaction, no ownership. It was in some way a kind of rebellion, a kind of utopia. The answer maybe, to their problems. Hers and David's.

Yes, the pictures touched her. Like that one of the slim delicate woman. Fiona (24) Boyfriend Ian (23). Seeking bi-curious females. Holiday snaps. Nothing sexual about them at all. Him in sunglasses on the beach somewhere with three male friends. Her laughing with another couple at some family do. The way they looked at each other in that photo at the top of some mountain. Husband not to be present. Her arm round his shoulder. Fiona and Ian. Newly-weds. He took her on lots of holidays to make her happy but she's gay. Ian tried to incorporate that. That look on his face. His love for her has grown since they started this.

She sent replies to all of them. The same pseudonym. Wonderland. Hi, we have an unusual proposition for you both.

Couples RUs. Steve (53) and Joan (51). Sitting naked at a white plastic garden table. Lattices. Suburbia. A lawn-mower behind them. A black bin bag. Bearsden or Newton Mearns probably. Sunlight in their hair. Remnants of breakfast. Croissants, orange juice, cafetière. Toasting each other with fluted glasses of champagne. Holiday w/us in Barcelona. All expenses paid. Share chalet and each other. Help us celebrate our second honeymoon. Age no issue. Let's have sum fun before we kick the bucket.

You could imagine it. Retirement with David. Some holiday together, holiday snaps, faces obscured by squares. It all made sense. Your wedding picture as a swinging advert. For richer, for poorer. It was almost like a second marriage. A reaffirmation of your vows. In sick-ness and in health. To do this with David. To bring him lovers.

So sad but so true. So easy to forget that this was about making a television programme. So easy to lose yourself in this. Hard to log off. Just one more. Another. It was already five thirty and the rest of the staff were packing up to go home but she was still online. Her mother. The things her mother used to read to her. Dr Seuss and the importance of communality. Anti-capitalist children's stories. Monogamy is a sickness. Men exploit and rape the world. Never forget that, Alice. We must be free. Sweet dreams, Alice. Fifteen, twenty years and she'd hated all that, but now staring at the screen, she saw that there was a certain truth to it. We. We are women. We are not for sale. We cannot be owned. We must learn how to exchange love freely, no matter how terrifying that prospect is. Never forget that, Alice.

The staff had left, it was six thirty and God, look at you Alice, sitting alone in your glass-walled cubicle in an empty office, so close to tears, dreaming of the 60s. Of that time before you were born, that great utopia, because it's easier isn't it, than dealing with the present, to imagine that lost time, that time of hope, that was dying before you even arrived. That was killed by your birth.

*   *   *

He'd been postponing it for yet another week. Thinking about the stinking nicotine-stained walls and the lines of grey-faced third-generation urban poor swearing at the faceless government officials cowering behind their security glass that he'd last seen a lifetime ago. But when he got there they'd changed the decor in a way that wasn't unpleasant. Everything fresh primrose yellow. Gentle concealed lighting. No overhead strip lights. Large pictures hanging everywhere of smiling people in overalls sitting at PCs. Real smiling social security employees sitting at open desks without security glass. Lovely.

And the unemployed didn't look so bad. There was a queue to the left. A security guard to his right. He approached him – where to go, what to do, hello my name is David and I haven't been here for a long time. The guard interrupted and nodded at the queue.

'Yes, but I was just wondering, to save everyone time, if I could just pick up a form and . . .'

The nod again.

So the queue. About ten people. He considered trying

to make conversation with the mother and child in front of him. Asian.

'Ten months is he? What's his name?' But decided against it. So he just stood there. Waiting in line and trying not to feel guilty about being a middle-class man in a job centre. You were laid off in a huge corporate merger. Not your fault. You've paid your National Insurance. No shame in signing on. OK. This is not the scene in *Falling Down* where Michael Douglas freaks out and shoots the ceiling.

One man, three ahead, swearing. Nipping out for a fag. 'Keep ma place, mate.'

Another, face ashen. Maybe fifty. Posture rigid. Old suit jacket. Heels worn down to nothing. Ex-army or police, thought David. Knows how to stand in line without twitching.

Fifteen, twenty minutes and still the queue. David had worked out that the security guards knew nothing, were of no help. Bouncers basically. He didn't like to think about the instances when their skills would be required. It was the other people who could really help. They had name badges on, must have been supervisors. They came up every ten minutes or so with a clipboard, took the details of the person at the front and either asked them to sit in the open-plan area or go into the room. The room to his left where people vanished and kept coming out again to smoke. Room 101 obviously. The wait after the wait.

He resisted the urge to do what others had done and go for a cigarette. Didn't have a pack anyway. Understood why it was that so many of the un-working class smoked.

Only three people ahead of him. But as the man who'd just been summoned to the desk insisted on giving his whole life story and people behind started swearing, he had this sudden desire to leave. I mean what was it anyway? Fifty-five quid a week, sixty? Was it really worth it? This huge effort to do nothing but stand. He used to be paid twenty-one pounds an hour.

Finally he made it to the front and a supervisor – name badge, Susan – was there in front of him with her clipboard. Name. National Insurance number.

'I'd just like to get a form, if you could just get one for me then I can fill it in at home and—'

'Unemployment benefit? Income support? Contribution or earnings-based jobseekers' allowance?'

'Well, actually I don't really—'

'Take a seat.'

The seated waiting area. Some kind of bubble-shaped friendly-looking Ikea-type chair thingies like the TV company. The whole world was turning into practical solutions for modern living. He noticed for the first time as he sat there with four others that they were playing music. Definitely something they never used to do. What was it? Queen? 'Another One Bites the Dust'. How gloriously inappropriate for a job centre. The Asian mother and child were seated across from him. A security guard kept leaning over and coochee-cooing with the kid. The mother seemed embarrassed. Next to her was a very tall young man wearing a tracksuit and expensive-looking but well-worn trainers. He had a scar running from his mouth to his cheek. Classic central casting Glasgow Ned. An extra in that old film called signing on. A Ken Loach maybe. Really, he was pretty good, the make-up department had done a great job on that scar. David tried not to stare so he let his eyes drift over to the big woman to his right. Something not quite right about her. Her huge hands. Feet immense for a female. Her skin was bad too and she was wearing tons of foundation. Was dressed

almost like a grandmother, like Bette Davis in whatever it
was called, something to do with Baby Jane. Bette Davis
sensed him staring. Crossed her massive legs and ran her
hand through her hair in an incredibly delicate way. Then
he worked it out. Queen's greatest hits and a drag queen
signing on. He slash she, he thought and giggled to himself.
Could you imagine the job interview? 'I've been finding it
hard to find work as a man so I thought I'd . . .' Yes, something strange had happened to the world since he'd last
looked at it. Ten years ago and you'd have been lynched
for being a trannie. Maybe no one else had noticed. Or
cared. He hoped that 'Fat Bottomed Girls' didn't start up.
A supervisor walked over to the table at the side, picked
up some list and called out, 'Steven McAlpine.'
    No reply.
    'Andrew Craigie.'
    Central casting scar-face got to his feet. So it was
waiting again. Another person joined them. A woman,
looked foreign. Central casting asylum seeker. You could
tell by the clothes. The song had changed again. 'I Want
to Break Free'. Freddie Mercury in a plastic miniskirt
and fishnets with a vacuum cleaner. Really, Jesus, was this
someone's idea of a joke?
    Impossible not to look at him, sorry her. She was
twitching under his gaze. He almost felt like saying sorry.
Checked his watch and looked over at the desks with
people being interviewed. Central casting scar-face was
making a fuss. One of the security men walked over and
stood behind him. The man was pointing, on the edge
of shouting. The security man's hand on his shoulder.
David looked away. The trannie seemed to be getting
very nervous now with all this noise. The security man
led the man away. He staggered. Was he drunk? Jesus.
Drunks and trannies.

God, could it be possible, that after Queen they'd play Lou Reed's 'Walk on the Wild Side'?

No, it made a kind of sense. They may have changed the decor and the music, but this was still a job centre. Unemployment, drugs and booze and sex. Easy to work out really. All ways of escaping. And he wasn't so different with his swinging thing.

He wanted to call Alice and tell her that the world had come into sync with Queen's greatest hits. He'd been sitting there maybe half an hour and still no one had called his name. The CD had gone round and started again. The poor fuckers that worked here having to listen to 'Bohemian Rhapsody' all day every day. Was Queen government issue now? Was it playing in every dole office in the country? Did it have the Royal Seal? David tried to focus the music away by reading all the posters. Customer care. You left HR and the doublespeak followed you to the dole office. 'Welcome to our new customers.' 'We believe in you.' Job Centre Plus. Super-size me. Even newer. Bigger. Better. New Labour.

'Another One Bites the Dust' again and he was sure someone had turned up the volume. He was just on the point of leaving, of deciding to come back another day when they'd got a new CD maybe – *Anarchy in the UK* perhaps, or *Loser* by Beck – when he heard his name being called behind him.

Desk four. A young man behind it with a plaster on his eyebrow and long dreadlocks. His shirt slightly open at the neck. Looked like he'd just walked out of some anarchist commune. Name badge, Jed. Jeddie Mercury. As Jed took his details David couldn't stop staring at the plaster. There was something underneath it. What? A boil? There was some kind of metal edge. A piercing then. The guy smelled slightly of patchouli. A rebel who worked for the State. What was this – inverted reality day? David asked for a form. The young man worked out what kind of benefit he would be applying for and got the form for him. Could he just fill it in now? David pulled out a pen and started. The young man cleared his throat and told him that it would take fifteen minutes or so. They had a customer quota to get through. If he wouldn't mind just taking a seat, someone would see him shortly.

My God. It had actually started. 'Fat Bottomed Girls'. David did as he was told and sat back down in the waiting area. Don't stare.

'Brigitte McGilvery.'

Fucking hell. Brigitte. En Français bien sûr. C'est vrai. C'est moi, Brigitte. Don't laugh. The trannie passed by him. Doing her slash his best not to walk like a bulldog in heels, syncing with the rhythm of the Queen track. Wow, amazing performance. No one else noticing. Think about it. Those short painted fingernails. Bitten down to the stumps. That awkward wiggle of the hips where there were no hips. That actually rather clever way of turning yourself into an unattractive woman so you could just about pass. Genius really. For a second David wondered whether he could claim twice as many benefits by signing on as a man on Tuesday and as a woman on Thursday. Alice had always said he had good legs and a pert bottom. Jesus.

Back to the form. Section 2B. Did you leave your job voluntarily? Have you recently lost your job through redundancy? We will need documentation to confirm this from your previous employer. OK, it would be impossible to get his redundancy notice since they'd long since stopped his access to his work email. There would be a P45, somewhere, no doubt in the office. The problem being that he would have been the person who issued the P45s and since he'd been fired – well. Could he sign his own P45, even though he didn't work there any more? Catch 22. He'd have to ask about that. Section 3A. How many hours are you available for work? Tick the boxes. All the hours every day. Most people at the TV company had twenty-four-hour buyouts, but that couldn't be right. Not here. You tick 'Available all hours' and they take you up on it. Find you some work as an overnight security guard and you'd be forced to take it or lose your benefit. So there must be a certain amount of hours you were supposed to put down. What was the minimum, forty-eight? He'd have to ask.

It was like one of those tables-have-turned scenes in so many movies. The former HR employee being subjected to a job questionnaire. The millionaire who becomes homeless. The judge who ends up in jail. The cop on the run from the police. The psychiatrist who goes mad.

Twenty minutes and Queen's 'We Are the Champions' now seemed so loud that he could barely concentrate. Tell us about the house you live in. Do you have a mortgage? Well, yes I pay towards the mortgage on the old house but I don't live there. And yes, there's a new mortgage for the new place but I don't think we'll be there much longer. He couldn't find any boxes to tick that fitted his situation. We will need evidence of your mortgage. Jesus. He didn't have a copy, he'd have to ask Hannah for that but then he'd have to tell her he'd lost his job. Your partner. Tell us about your partner. Was that Alice or Hannah? Did they mean who he lived with or who he paid child support to? He ticked a box then crossed it out and started again. If he could just get a fresh form, get the patchouli guy to explain the whole thing to him.

He looked up and another man was just leaving the anarchist's desk. He strode up. If he could just get a bit of help with the questions. Wait in the queue. Just a minute or two. Sorry sir but we have a customer quota. Just this question here about evidence of redundancy. You can take the form away and mail it in, sir. Yes, no, I know, but if I get something wrong. I mean I'll have to start again, and this whole thing could just go round and round in circles, for months, I mean if I make a mistake and then.

Take a seat sir. It was no use. Enough. Enough. David walked back to his seat, took a beat to stare at it, then in time with the drum solo on 'Bicycle Race' he kept on walking, past the seated area and the queue to the front door.

Block after block. The only soundtrack now his feet and his breath. A certain kind of clarity. Step after step and reality seemed to be returning. It was only two o'clock and there were hours to kill till Alice came home. Dumbarton Road. Charity shops and chip shops. So many people unemployed and unemployable.

A couple arguing in the street. A group of students in goth gear. Not so different from what he once wore in drama school. A drunk begging for spare change. Two single mothers pushing strollers who could have been no more than fourteen. A woman standing in the doorway of a bar, smoking, checking her messages. Two small geriatric women blocking the way, like the street was theirs. A queue inside the chip shop. Women shopping. People on lunch. Some working, some not. Those in jobs not so different from those without. A hundred pounds a week. No more. A few more things to buy. What was the point?

Two male voices behind him. 'Fucking cunts.' 'Fucking

right.' 'Fuck.' The word over and over again. Laughing
as they said it. He turned. These guys in workers' overalls. This was their street. They walked it every day and
said fuck a lot. They said fuck about their bosses, their
jobs, their homes, their wives. But still they were here,
happy to be here. This eternally negative take on life. It
was what you did in Glasgow if you wanted to fit in. You
complained, whinged, swore, you said fuck all the time,
but you never did anything to change anything. Why
should you? Nothing would ever change, fuck that, and
so you said fuck. Three, four generations of being unemployed or, if you were lucky, minimum wage and you'd
grow to love complaining, even split words up to put
fuck in the middle – im-fuckin-possible. Fuck, fuck, fuck.
It was a badge of identity, and being the shit of the world
was not so bad because you had a place. And there were
hundreds of thousands of you, and being angry every day
and saying fuck a lot meant you belonged.

Fuck Glasgow. But still he was here, signing on in
Glasgow. He'd walked out on his wife and child and tried
to leave all this behind, but still he was here. Tonight
was childminding. He was unemployed. He was an unemployed father. Yes. He was still here. Fuck. Fuck.

*   *   *

While Amy brushed her teeth, 'All by herself', David
went through the things yet to do. Pyjamas, read a story
till she falls asleep, a fly fag out in the close, put the lock
on the snib so as not to lock yourself out, then two hours
to kill, a glass of wine from Hannah's bottle, small, so
she wouldn't notice, a video maybe, or *Late Review*. Then
she'd be back. Then it would be the Talk. Yes, tonight
was the night for the Talk.

He picked out a book as Amy got under the covers

and he lay on top of the bed. Amy was too young for the stories he really wanted to read with her. Stories from his own childhood. She was just learning to read now so *The Lion the Witch and the Wardrobe*, *The Hobbit* and *Alice in Wonderland* would have to wait.

Instead it was *Wendy and Tommy's Big Adventure*. He stretched his arm out over Amy's pillow and she snuggled against him. 'I love you, Daddy.' He worried that she was saying this too much now. That even though she was only five she'd worked out what had happened to them.

No time to let these things upset him. Proceed with the reading. Hannah had let slip recently that she was worried Amy had been falling behind at school with reading skills. This worried him too. If he'd still been with Hannah then he could have calmed her anxiety and between them they could have helped Amy catch up before it became an issue. The whole thing had been blown out of all proportion. Amy yawned.

'OK, sleepyhead. Homework.'

Three weeks ago Amy would have moaned and whimpered, 'No, read me the story Daddy, read it.' But in those three weeks some incredible change had occurred. Amy had gone from being a child who hated lessons to being hungry to learn how to read. How had he missed that turning point? Had it happened at school? Or with Hannah or her parents? One of the biggest turning points in her life and he'd missed it.

So now it was strange, helping her learn to read in six hours a week. It made him feel guilty. Better maybe just to play with her, have fun together, make time with Daddy special, make the bond stronger. But still, in some way, even though he knew he was no longer a responsible parent, he felt the need to instil some discipline in his daughter. Best not to question that. Press on. Turn the page.

His fingers pointed at word after word.

'Wendy and . . .'

'Wendy and Tommy go, good, very good.'

'To . . . the.'

'Aha.'

Then Amy was stuck. David's finger floated below the word. He readjusted his arm just to make sure that his hand wasn't obscuring the page.

'Spell it out. "Ef."' He wasn't sure whether they taught kids phonetically or not any more. 'Fuh. Little fuh.'

'Fuh, ah, ih.'

'Great, you're so clever. Put it all together.'

'Fuh, ay, ih, rrrr.'

'Fay, you say fay.'

'Fay, rrrr.'

'All together, faster.'

'Fay, fay . . . ur, fair.'

'Yeah, yeah, whole sentence. Wendy and Tommy . . . go to the fay . . . to the fay . . .'

'To the fair, Daddy.'

'Brilliant, brilliant.'

The joy on Amy's face. Imagine discovering that all those marks on the page meant something. All those pages, all those books. The libraries, the street and shop signs. That everything in the whole world had a word. To stare and stare at a big long word and work out it was the sign for something you already knew about.

'Daddy, do all books have the same words?'

To think that every book had a different language. That you'd have to learn to read each book separately. Like that line in *Alice in Wonderland*. 'Every word means

exactly what I want it to mean.' The Cheshire Cat. Was
that what children thought?

'Well, once you've learned enough words you can read
anything.'

'Wow. How many words are there? A hundred?'

'More.'

'A million?'

'Maybe.'

'A gazillion?'

'A what?'

'Granddad said the biggest number in the world was
a gazillion.' Amy started laughing.

'Really?'

'But then I said a gazillion and one.'

He couldn't help but laugh. Good old know-it-all
Granddad. The lah-de-dah Edinburgh lawyer. A gazillion and one. But still the old man had raised a family.
Spent more time with Amy than he did. Jesus, to have
values. Good on the old man.

'You're so clever, Amy, so clever.'

Amy nuzzled into his shoulder. For an instant he closed
his eyes and breathed in the smell of his daughter's hair.
Sweet. That smell you could never forget. Newborn baby's
head. My child. My child. Weeping as he held her in the
postnatal ward, wrapped in the towel, blood and vernix,
the pungent smell of a new life. A life held so closely in
the balance. They thought they'd lost her. Fourteen-hour
labour. Last-minute emergency Caesarean. My beautiful
child.

'Daddy, come on! Keep reading.'

And so word by word, they worked through four more
lines. David's finger hovering on the page. Another word.
Ball. 'That was too easy, Daddy.' Candy. Tree. Amy's joy
was so great at learning words that David wondered if

she could remember what the stories were about. Did it matter? Stupid stories about going somewhere and trying hard to do something and succeeding and making friends on the way. Predictable stories of achievement like the ones adults lived by, day by day. Better to marvel at one simple word.

Words though. The Talk tonight with Hannah. To have to pick through it all.

'What did you mean when you said that?'

'Well perhaps that doesn't mean the same thing to both of us.'

'Commitment. I thought the meaning of that was pretty clear to everyone.'

Words you learn by rote, even though you distrust them. What did it mean to distrust a word?

'Daddy. Daddy! What does that word say?'

He'd been drifting off again. His daughter's finger on the page. 'Tomorrow.'

'It's a big one.'

He encouraged Amy to work it out phonetically, repeating each letter again and again, trying to say it faster. Tom, tom, tomo, row, row row your boat gently down the stream. Tomo. Tomorrow is a new word.

But the truth is, every tomorrow looks very much like every today. Every night seems like the same night, when you're an adult. A tired adult. Face it. Tomorrow would be a dark day, darker than today, as it always was the day after he'd been with Amy. And he'd have to hide that from Alice too. Because this was his problem not hers. Save her from that. Tom-row. Row, row row. Yes, row, like in a boat. To – more – row. Row not row. There could be a row with Hannah tonight. Jesus. He'd have to stay sober after Amy went to sleep. Merrily, merrily, merrily, merrily. A fight was the last thing he wanted to

have. Down the stream. Already he felt anger, about
having to have the Talk. Life is but a dream.

The book dropped by his side and he woke abruptly.
Amy was asleep beside him. Those eyes, even when
closed, so like his mother's. Granny Mackay. Amy.
Stroking her hair. Listening to the sound of her breath.
He could stay there all night. Listening to that breath.
Feeling that tiny chest rising and falling against his arm.
The warmth between them. To hold your mother in your
daughter. To fall asleep together breathing each other's
breath.

No.

He gently removed his arm from beneath Amy's head.
Pulled his feet slowly from the bed and climbed out. He
stretched and set the book down on the pile on the
bedside table. What to do now? Sit next door. Try not
to think about the Talk.

Almost two years of separation and he'd told himself
it would get easier. Over a year now with Alice. Why
this sudden increase in anxiety? Why had seeing Amy
only become more difficult? Was it that in some way he
sensed that he could go, leave, just go, not come back?
Leave with Alice. Forget the apologies. Forget explaining
to Hannah how he'd lost his job and couldn't give her
the usual alimony. Just go.

He leaned over and kissed Amy's head. Go now, don't
stand there staring. Go now. Four footsteps out of the
room. Don't look back. Shut the door quietly. Tippy-
toes.

He was standing in the corridor, momentarily thrown,
thinking he was in their new flat. Almost expecting to
see Alice.

Total silence. No sound of the thermostat and the radiators creaking and the motorway. Look at it. The decor.

The prints on the walls. Copies of Victorian originals. Copies. Like everything else in the house. The reproduction 50s chairs, the pseudo-Victorian stained glass above the front door. Perhaps that had been the problem. All of this. More than anything said or done. The fake authenticity of everything. Maybe that was why he'd left and then found Alice in her squalid bedsit. With her Godard posters and her crap 70s carpet and her ability to laugh at all this. They should have stayed in her bedsit in Woodlands.

Eight o'clock. Still in the corridor. Two hours to kill till the Talk. Time, like this, like no other. Babysitter for your own daughter. Waiting in the house you left. Waiting for your ex-wife to return. Not really able to do anything. Too anxious to read. Too distracted to watch TV. Not sure whether it would be acceptable to make a sandwich with the things she bought from Sainsbury's which are in the fridge you bought together. The bottle of wine. She used to only drink a third and now it's two thirds. A glass. She wouldn't notice.

Half a glass then.

Walking back through to the sitting room with the half glass. The light was still on in Hannah's room. Things lying around. Changed quickly, no doubt, while he was feeding Amy her dinner. Yes, she'd changed. Had started wearing make-up again for the first time since they'd been engaged. Out on a date tonight maybe. Yes, she was due a man. A date at least. No, many. Better to think she was playing the field than bringing one man home.

Hannah's clothes were scattered on the floor of their old bedroom. A blouse over the back of a chair. A bra on the bed. The bed they'd bought together. 'I don't want you going through my things when you're here,' she'd said. 'Of course, of course not.'

But he stepped in, couldn't resist. Lifted the bra, rubbed the silk between his fingers. A new bra, not one he had seen when they were married. The label. 32 D. Hannah's breasts had grown to an E with Amy. She was now a D again. As her ex-husband it didn't seem improper. He lifted the bra to his face. Closed his eyes and inhaled. New perfume. Still the faint trace of her body. Something tickled his face. One of her hairs. Her long red hairs.

He opened his eyes and saw his own reflection in the window. It was dark outside, the curtains had not been drawn. The window was like a mirror. There he was reflected, illuminated, by the bedside lamp. The neighbours. Imagine if they saw him there. Standing in his ex-wife's bedroom, sniffing her bra. 'Is it him?' 'Is that him?' 'What's he doing?'

He set the bra back down, taking care to make it look like he'd never touched it and walked through to the living room. Two hours to wait in here. Look at it. The Habitat slash Bauhaus sofa, a copy of a copy. Less than two hours now. The phone was on the side unit, also from Habitat, next to the remote controls for the Sony TV and DVD.

Same problem. The front room. The nosy neighbours. He drew the curtains. But as he did his feet hit something. A Barbie. The ideological discussion they'd had about children's toys and their influence. So pointless now, such debates. Maybe tidy up Amy's toys. Hannah would notice. A few points scored. Helpful ex-father doing domestic chores. Or not. I told you not to touch anything. Leave the toys where they are.

Just over an hour and a half to go till Hannah and the Talk. 'We have to talk.' The whole week, he'd been trying to pre-empt what she would say. Struggled to try to find answers. He told himself, only last week, that he would never do this. But every spare moment, at the computer and before sleep, he examined and cross-examined the details of what had gone wrong with Hannah. How did he even meet her to start with? Why had he thrown it all away for ten minutes with a hooker? He'd even come to start questioning his reasons for being with Alice. Did he really know anything about her past? Did anyone really know anyone? Damn. His mind was racing again.

He went into his jacket pockets and pulled out his notepad. OK, it was a typical HR thing to do. Make a list of problems. Annotate. Compare. Order and reorder them in a hierarchy, reduce the list, as he'd done last week. Decide which are your primary action items and act upon them.

Things she wants to talk about.

1. Unemployment and money/child support.
2. She's had legal advice and is going to sue me for abandonment.
3. She wants us to try again.
4. She wants me to see more/less of Amy.
5. She wants me to tell her why I left.
6. She wants to prove to me that she's managing even better without me.
7. She wants to sell the house and for me to give her all the rights.
8. Public or private school for Amy.
9. She wants to move to another city, and I'll have to move too, if I want to stay in touch with Amy.

Through the week, he'd honed it down from about thirty-five topics. He'd arranged and rearranged them maybe fifteen times. As he looked back over it now, and finished off the half glass of wine, it troubled him that the more emotional numbers were making it higher up the list.

To hell with it. No point pussyfooting around. Finish off the bottle. After tonight the recriminations would be worse than some squabble over how much wine he'd drunk. Have a drink. A good half bottle. To get the guts to have the Talk. But first a cigarette.

He went out into the close and took great care putting the door on the snib. Imagine, locking yourself out for the sake of a fly fag. Your child home alone. You on the other side of the doors. Locked out. Abandonment. Wilful abandonment. The lock on the snib, and leaving it open just in case, but not open enough to let the smell of the cigarette enter the house. There was an hour till she got back. By then hopefully the smell of the cigarette would have gone from the close.

The living room again. He tried the TV. Two channels of home-makeover shows. Two with celebrity interviews. One with some cheap crime story. He wanted to call Alice, but it would be the third time that day and she would be freaked out again, at hearing his voice coming from Hannah's home.

The central heating maybe, the wine, or just emotional exhaustion. Whatever it was, he found himself jolted awake on the sofa when the front door clicked open.

It took seconds to adjust. Where am I? Home? Am I decent? Put your shoes on quick. Get ready to go. No, the Talk. Sit up, prepare yourself. You have to tell her that you have lost your job. That the alimony payments may be a bit slow for a while. But still this was her Talk. What she wanted to say.

Then she was there standing in the doorway, looking at him. He fastened his shoes, threw her a quick glance. Was she smiling? Yes, so she was drunk. Maybe the Talk had made her anxious too. One more for Dutch courage then home to confront him. But first, thankfully, the ritual conversation.

'What time did she go down?'

''Bout eight thirty. She was great, just great.'

'Brush her teeth?'

'Of course, all by herself this time.'

'Good.'

David got to his feet, scanned the room for his coat. With any luck she was too drunk to bother with the Talk tonight. She seemed much more drunk than usual. Was she smiling or smirking? Just staring. Staring at him getting ready to go. That jacket she bought him that he was still wearing, and smiling. Smiling. Was she really so drunk that she was enjoying looking at him, or did she get some tiny sadistic pleasure in watching him squirm nervously before her?

'So uh, next time, Monday?'

'Tuesday's better,' she said. 'Monday she's got a party.'

'OK, I'll email to confirm.'

He pulled his coat on and made for the door. The Talk. She was postponing the Talk. And she was still leaning in the doorway. There would have to be more eye contact. Physical proximity. Moving closer to her, she would naturally recoil. This urge he felt at times like this. To reach out, God knows why, and touch her. Kiss her cheek. But her standing there, drunk and smiling, he got the impression that it was her that wanted to reach out and kiss him. It could start like this so easily. The goodbye kiss at the door. Lingering. Then tongues. Hands groping. Imagine. He'd heard of this before. Ex-partners having these clinging sexual encounters. So many betrayals all at once. Betraying their past, betraying Alice. Fucking your ex-wife. It would fuck everything.

He moved towards the door. Maybe this was her plan. To unsettle him with talk of the Talk but to never actually have it. To dress in sexy clothes and lead him on. For him to make a pass at her, for her to brush it off. Yes, there was more revenge in that. This whole thing had only lasted a matter of seconds, but the building tension. He had to break it.

'You wanted to talk?' he said.

'Oh, right, yeah.' And she walked past him into the living room. He was stuck there, just hovering. From where he was standing he could glimpse her rummaging through the bookshelves.

She came back out with a folder full of papers.

'The agreement,' she said.

'What?'

The agreement, what agreement? So little agreement in so long. Then she explained. This week was the end of the two years' statutory separation period. Sign it and the divorce would be final.

'I'd appreciate if you . . .'

'Of course, yeah.'

'Thursday, my lawyer on Byres Road, you've been there before.'

'Sure, yeah, OK. Good.'

At the door. A peck on the cheek. Her to him. He turned back to look at her as he crossed the threshold, to look at her face, to try to read what the peck on the cheek had meant, but already she was closing the door.

The walk home. What the hell had happened? He should feel happy, elated. Should go back to Alice and tell her that finally he was free. Hannah would no longer be an issue. But as he reached the turn-off to his street, he walked past it and his feet took him meandering back through the neighbourhood. He couldn't go home just yet. Things had suddenly got so much more complicated. The doorway, her lips on his cheek. These feelings.

Block after block. By the time he'd walked all the way to the edge of the motorway then round the corner he was shivering. He reached for his door keys and again wanted to turn away. Postpone speaking to Alice about any of this. If she got him started it would all come pouring out. And it made no sense. Two years he'd been dreaming about being free from Hannah. Running away. That thing he and Alice had talked about so many times, going to the States together. Looking at it now the whole thing with Alice had been a kind of escape fantasy. But when the divorce was final, the fantasy would vanish. If he ran, what was he running from? If he stayed, Alice would become the focus of his life and they'd finally be forced to face exactly what it was they were both running from.

He made sure the divorce papers were hidden inside his jacket before he turned the key in the lock. Planned to hide them somewhere inside and take time, as much time as it took, to think about them. His desk maybe. No, better, on the bookshelf behind the TV. Try not to think about them till next week. Hide them from Alice. He'd have to work this out all by himself.

*   *   *

'She went down on her knees, and took him in her mouth. Right there in the white room. You saw them. I watched you watching them.'

But he wasn't listening. Was falling asleep beside her on the bed, his dick in her hand. He'd become so distant, so morbidly preoccupied in the last few days. She pumped his dick harder to try to get him to respond.

Maybe it was her fault. This tired story of hers, ten

days old now, about the encounter in their flat. Every night, telling, retelling, expanding on it, so that now, surely, he was even beginning to doubt the reality on which it had been based. Maybe it had even come to bore him now. That very real thing which she'd done for him which he'd only watched through a window. The smell, the sight of these people. These people she didn't even like, in her home, in her room. Fucking on her spare bed.

His breath was slowing. He pulled the covers round his face but still she struggled to finish the story. Struggling with what? Words, names. Give it a name. Yes. Anger.

It is important not to let yourself become angry about the situation. Let it go. Anger may trigger the **domino effect** of **performance-related psychological impotence.** The more pressure you put on him the worse the condition will become. Try to relax with him in a comfortable domestic scenario. Let him choose a movie and enjoy it together. You love his movies. Tell him that. At all costs do not threaten him with judgements or ultimatums. Relax. Have a quiet night in with wine and candles. Cook him a steak, don't up the stakes.

Yes, he was asleep and she was angry now. Because she'd tried so hard. Because she'd done it for him, to try to close the space between them. But now as he rolled over and put his back to her, she realised that no matter whether they did it again or not with some other couple, there would always be, from now on, this image of two other people filling the six inches of cold bed between them.

An image. On either side of the couple, just watching.

Her against the back wall looking out at him through the window. The same problem of hers again and again. To be always on the outside looking in.

It was all too predictable, this one-off voyeuristic transgression, that they could recount at drunken dinner parties. 'But of course we never tried it again.'

No. The picture had to come to life. They had to go one further, she decided as she rolled over and turned off the bedside lamp. Like it had said in their ad. Step through the mirror w/us.

*   *   *

How long have you been doing this? Did one person initiate it? How do you manage it with a child? Are you both bi? Does it create or dissipate conflicts in your relationship? They were called Marcia and Tony. Glaswegian. Mid thirties. Married with a kid. They had Saturdays off. Daytime only. Babysitter. Interested in same-room fun. Str8. Full swap. First-timers welcome. Alice had all the questions worked out like a standard TV interview. But as she ran over them in her head she realised they were all rhetorical and it would seem a shame to interrupt the flow of their chat. Events would soon overtake and speak louder than any consciously formulated reply. Do you feel this is in some way part of a growing movement? Is it, for you, something to do with opposing the concept of sexual ownership? No. It was all happening so naturally as, in the bar, they joked together about fake personas and all the funny names they'd seen on the net.

'"RU 4-sum 2nite?" I mean really.'

'Elvis fans you think?'

'I don't think the fan club would approve.'

'Maybe it *is* the fan club!'

Only five weeks since it had all started, that drunken

night with the Gordons, and only two since their first encounter with a real swinging couple and they were together in this new bar like old pros already. Laughing together. Tony and Marcia and David and herself. Alice felt none of the anxiety that had threatened to eclipse the first encounter. Hadn't felt David pressing her on. He seemed relaxed in their company. Good. 'Relaxation is the first step in dealing with your problem together.'

And they had taste, these people. Had picked an out-of-the-way working-man's pub with leather seats and old adverts on the mirrors, an interesting mix of students, professionals and old folks. Tony had a quick turn of phrase. Worked in advertising and was in many ways like David. Witty, middle class, slightly balding, tiny well trimmed goatee beard, looked rather like an ageing pop star or music producer. Marcia had the cheekbones of Dietrich, jet black dyed cropped hair and a badge on her designer jacket which read 'FUCK FCUK'. She worked in PR. This lovely couple, so comfortably, not boastfully, well read, who joked about work and selling yourself to Satan and who couldn't stop touching each other. They'd tried this a few times before but had never really felt such a strong connection with anyone else before, Marcia had said, as she and Tony held hands. And really, these people, they could be your friends, she and David had so few friends, he had none in fact, after his separation. So when, two glasses later, they asked her and David back to theirs she had to remind herself that they were in fact going back for sex.

As they sat joking in the taxi, getting closer and closer to the West End, she realised they hadn't mentioned that they lived there too. Hyndland Road, Queen's Drive. His ex lived in Bellevue Gardens. Five blocks or so away. David had become understandably agitated. Had dropped out of the conversation and was staring out at the sand-stone tenements. The very few things David had said about his ex. It was possible that Marcia was just like her.

She took his hand discreetly, squeezed his fingers and whispered, 'You OK?'

He nodded. She could feel the tension in his grip diminish as the taxi took a turn south and headed away towards Broomhill. Shit, yes.

Inside, they were given the whole tour by Marcia as Tony uncorked the bubbly. The kitchen needed a bit of work, she said. They'd been there a year and somehow hadn't got round to it yet. They were going to strip it all down, knock through the partition wall and create an open-plan kitchen with a range. They liked throwing parties, not dinner parties of course, not that whole West End dinner-party thing. Get a huge rustic hardwood table and maybe some old church pews for seats. What did she think?

'Perfect,' Alice said. 'Sounds just perfect.'

She felt David drifting silently behind her. He was staring at the newly sanded original floorboards. She let Marcia's words carry her round.

'Whole thing was carpeted when we got in here. Should have seen it. Pizza-coloured, we called it. Brown, red, yellow. Swirly 70s stuff, totally obscene. Tore the lot up and thank God the floorboards were good. Got one of those sanders, did it all ourselves. Hell of a job, but worth it.'

Stained-glass window by the bathroom. Art deco, authentic it seemed, not like the reproductions they had in their own flat. Marcia leading her onwards. Front room. Tony had excavated the cornicing. Was so nice to see the craftsmanship of the original features, Marcia said. A large antique sofa and a chaise longue. Ikea-free.

Alice had this strange sense of déjà vu. This woman's values were a subtle variation on her own.

'It's cool, really,' she said, and found herself asking about the colour of the wallpaper, was it matched to the original Victorian decor? Yes, how did she guess? Was she an artist? Well, she'd done some training in art school she said, but she was no specialist. And as Alice talked she couldn't help but feel that this kind of déjà vu would happen again and again and that this would be the future. That maybe all over the West End, all these people in their five hundred or so desirable residences were still desiring something else. That maybe she and David were not so different. Not so different from David and his ex.

He had said before in passing that he had sanded the floor in his ex's house. That they had original art deco. This was all a horrible mistake.

She turned round to seek his reassurance but he'd slipped away. Marcia led her back into the corridor and Tony approached them with a cheeky grin and two fluted glasses of bubbly.

'Thanks. Sorry, where's David?'

'Nipped out to the garden. Fly fag. Told him he could smoke in here, but he said he'd rather not.'

'Sure. Of course.'

Suddenly they all seemed lost for words. Alice sipped the bubbly and felt she had to speak before things got awkward.

'So this is the bedroom?'

Tony and Marcia exchanged a glance.

'Well, no actually. That's Sean's room.'

'Sean? Right. Sorry, of course.'

And as her eyes ran over the door, slightly ajar, she glimpsed the toys inside. The edge of a Spiderman mattress cover. A child's drawing board. Yes. They'd said weekends only. Babysitter.

She sipped the bubbly and smiled as Marcia and David cuddled and teased each other. Look at them. You did this to escape from who you feared you were. You fled down halls, through doors and mirrors until ultimately you were led back to where you had started. Tony, Marcia. She tried not to think of them as Hannah and David, had to say something to kill the picture.

'So. You have any original features in your own bedroom?'

It wasn't intended as a joke but Marcia started laughing. Tony grabbed Marcia by the waist and kissed her neck. Marcia reached out, took Alice's hand, and led her towards the bedroom door.

*   *   *

After trying to kill himself, James Stewart is saved by Clarence the angel who forces him to revisit the world as it would have been had he never been born. He walks through his house, his garden, past his friends, his wife, and no one knows who he is.

The red yellow blue plastic Toys Я Us slide and matching swing. The football. The perfectly proportioned, neatly trimmed privet hedge, the childproof safety-locked garden gate exactly the same as the one he'd bought with Hannah. David had long since finished his cigarette.

You'd think it would make you turn and leave. Jump the gate and keep walking. Past the 4x4s and the recycling bins. But instead he stayed and stood and considered the possibility that Alice had become Clarence and that with her help he could finally have an afterlife.

Alice would be worrying that he'd been upset by this

little accident, he'd seen it in her face, that she knew. But he'd firmly reassure her that seeing this through was totally necessary. A stroke of God knows what kind of accidental genius. Clarence was a ghost and Marcia was the ghost of Hannah. If he could fuck Marcia then he'd be cured. His feet were falling over each other as he made the back steps, up to the door. All there was to worry about now was if he could.

As he paused at their door he told himself it was just like the bits Alice read him from textbooks – performance anxiety, like stuttering. Worry about it and you do it. Give up on what people think and the pressure is off. James Stewart had a stutter. It could be, really, a Wonderful Life.

He'd get himself hard in their bathroom. Then walk through with it still hard. Kiss Alice. Get the whole thing started before he had a chance of losing it.

He turned the handle and stepped over the threshold. There was no one in the corridor or kitchen. No sign of them anywhere. Had Alice taken his departure as a cue and left? How long had he been out there? A noise behind him. A giggle. Movement beyond a door. He listened, ear to the door. Felt like a fool. The door was open an inch. He counted to ten, twenty, tried to calm his breathing. To thirty, fifty. Then moved closer and peered in. The woman sat on the bed, pulling her top over her head, her breasts bouncing in her bra. The man, jumping around like some kind of *Fawlty Towers* sketch, pulling off his trousers. Jesus. The bedroom was an off-white colour. Lovely crisp linen sheets. But where was Alice? Out looking for him? Said her goodbyes and now he was there spying on this perfectly innocent domestic scenario? Should he knock, cough? Apologise? He just stood there silently spying through the gap between the door and the frame. Watching the couple moving onto the bed. Her lying down. Black frilly bra and panties. Him climbing between her legs. Then he saw her. A slight movement by the back wall. She was undoing her bra, standing there in nothing more than her knickers. Alice. Standing there. One hand straying over her neck to her nipple. Watching them. Her, the woman, arching her back as he, the man, went down on her, his wife, and slowly pulled off her panties. Alice standing there, her hand moving back down from her nipple to her stomach and finally to her crotch. Her lips moving, silently. Whispering to herself. It seemed, in some way, she was talking to him. 'He's going down on her, you see that, Daddy? He's circling her clit, you like that, Daddy? Like you do to me. Huh? You see them, Daddy? You're so hard, so hard.'

Standing there spying on them. As he stroked himself he couldn't help but wonder if Alice had set this whole thing up, like a precise repeat of last time. Then it happened. She looked up. Looked up as though she'd known he was there all along. Finding his eyes through the gap in the door, her fingers finding the edge of her panties and slipping inside. This couple between them on the bed. Him bringing his mouth to her nipples. Alice watching him watching them. From either side of the bed, through the doorway.

He was hard. Took it out as he watched her touch herself. Her eyes moving from his eyes to his crotch and back again. Their little secret. This couple. Turned on by being watched fucking. Eating each other, feeding him and Alice. Alice's lips still moving. Talking to him across the bodies. Telling him his bedtime story. And this couple. Look at him. Lifting up her ass and pushing inside her, on that bed so like their own. He could hear Alice's voice in his head. 'Come closer. They're fucking on the bed. Look at her. The way she moves her hips. He's pushing inside her. You hear her?'

Through the gap he watched Alice close her eyes. Her mouth shut. The story was over. Her fingers moving inside her panties. Suddenly, he wanted to feel what she was feeling. To hear what she'd been whispering. A door and a couple between them. The sounds of their breath. His dick in his hand. He entered the room.

*   *   *

David was hard, he really was. There were these seconds when they just stood there staring at each other. If he was hard now, like this, then soon she would know. One or two things, possibly contradictory. That they needed these people, people like these, to give them a love life or that he found other women more attractive. She would, she would let him fuck other women if that was what it took. But still she was worried that if he couldn't stay hard, she'd be pleased by his failure. It would save her from jealousy. Whatever happened, the experiment had started, had its own momentum and soon she would know. He was standing there and they were watching him, as he worked his dick in his hand by the edge of their bed, watching them, his eyes shooting up to her, as if looking for permission. Her eyes telling him yes, telling him to watch. Watch them, this couple, writhing on the bed. This couple. No longer Marcia and Tony. Just a couple. The man had a good back. Strong arms. But she felt no desire for him. David was hard, he was smiling, and that was all that mattered.

Look at him. Looking at her looking at him. There they were again, the impasse. How much longer could they stand on either side of a bed just watching? The self-consciousness would start and he would lose it. Alice held David's gaze, tried to imagine his dick in her hand as she touched herself. Their eyes, secretly talking. Yes, go on, go on. You want me to, don't you? Go on.

Alice bent forward and stepped out of her panties, watching David. She felt some kind of surge of power as she watched him undress at the same time, mimicking her. Her eyes darting towards him as his gaze fixed on the couple who were now fucking hard, her legs round his back. Then finding each other again. 'You like this. Want me too, Daddy? You're so hard.'

Look at us, she thought. Naked together. On either side of them. Eyes locked, as we touch ourselves, as they groan and grind and start to come, turned on by being watched. Look at us, looking at each other. How can we make the first move? Who should do it? To stop looking. To feel something more than ourselves. Just watching.

'How Do You Think It Feels'. Da de dah de dah. Fuck you, Alice. Lou Reed. Fuck Lou Reed. Times like this you always think of a fucking song. Don't you. Shit, fuck. Touching yourself but feeling nothing. Look at David. How long could they keep this up? Already he seemed to be losing it. That song. Stop it. She should never have put on the Velvets with that first couple. Lou's second solo album. That fucking song her mother used to play. All about fucking on speed and being lonely and taking more speed to fight the loneliness and fucking more.

It seemed wrong. Not ethically or anything, just physically, musically. The bed, in the way. The couple. The song. Fucking each other frantically, so turned on by being watched but really, these people were like the song, an obstacle. Alice stepped to her left and walked round the bed towards David. Reached out to him, her fingers reaching for his dick. He was semi-hard. What to say? Have to say something. Daddy, you're so hard. You. Hard. These words the manuals told her not to say. Say 'we', say 'together'. Best to say nothing. To block out words. She went down on her knees and took him in her mouth. Another bloody song in her head now. Jangling tambourines – 'All Tomorrow's Parties'.

Fuck! It was as if he'd heard the song too. He was losing it. She didn't want to stare up at him, those eyes with questions which he would interpret as recrimination. So she kept on going even though she knew, by now, it was pointless. Taking his flaccid length into her mouth, sucking harder as the couple behind her gasped and groaned. How long could this last, before he placed his hand gently on her neck like usual and said, 'Sorry, sorry. Please. Alice. Sorry. No.'

So she turned and watched. Watching. Always just watching. Damn and fuck it. The fucking song still there. Louder than the sounds of the fucking. Nico moaning about how dull and pointless everything was.

To just find out. If David could get hard with another woman, then she would know. To close your eyes and take that leap. To drown out the stupid theme tune. Close your eyes. Close the gap in darkness. She kissed David gently on his inner thigh. Looked up at him. She could feel his anxiety, crackling like static in his muscles.

The man's hard cock, pulsing in and out of the woman. David seemed to be staring at it. Was he envious? Turned on by it?

She smiled at him to tell him it was OK. Whatever it took. Yes, if it meant being fucked by this cock. She would let it happen so that David could get hard. And then before it was done she'd slip off him and they would sit watching David fuck this man's wife. And David would feel good like that. Performing, no performance fear, no domino effect. But David's face told a different story. A story. He needed her to talk him through it. His bedtime story. So the story again.

'He's fucking her hard. You see the muscles in his ass tighten as he thrusts into her?'

'Aha.'

'Her hips rising to meet him. Her breasts so swollen. Her face flushing. You see?'

The woman turned to look at them, curious.

'Sorry,' said Alice. 'We like stories. Shhh,' she whispered to David, 'we do, don't we, don't we, Daddy?'

As she stared up at David, and heard the woman's little embarrassed laugh, she sensed by the look on his face that something had happened. The couple had become self-conscious and were struggling to get back into rhythm. It could all just end, just now. Close your eyes, Alice. Take the leap.

She turned from David, leaned forward onto the bed and whispered into Marcia's ear. 'Swap?'

'Sure,' turning to her partner, 'OK love?'

'Fine,' the man said as he dismounted.

'OK, Daddy?' said Alice, looking back at him. Poor Daddy, his semi in his hand. He nodded.

Standing before her then, as she knelt on the bed, the man, erect. Parading it in a way that she knew David would find threatening. She looked back at David again. 'You OK?'

He was nodding. Wanted this. 'Yeah, baby,' he said.

To do this for David.

She was on all fours then, like all the porno shots on David's sites. The man was touching her but she wanted to slow him down. She asked him to get a condom and he was distracted for a few minutes as he searched through the pockets of his jeans on the floor. Alice stayed there, doggy style, waiting, watching as the woman got to her knees in front of David and played with his cock. David kept shooting anxious glances at her. She tried to calm him. It's OK, her eyes said, or at least that was what she wanted them to say. You can do it, Daddy, just try to concentrate. She nodded at him. Go on. It's OK. I love you so much. The woman took David in her mouth and he closed his eyes. Good. God!

The man was back beside her tearing the wrapper open with his teeth. He was telling her how beautiful she was, what a great tight ass. She smiled back at him. Hoped he couldn't sense that she was trying so hard. She watched David instead. His eyes were darting from her face to the man's hard dick as he rolled the condom on. The woman's head bobbed on David's dick. She couldn't see whether he was hard.

'Such a sweet fucking ass,' the man said, parading his condomed cock. It was bright red, gave off a faint aroma of synthetic strawberries. It wasn't right. Something was missing. Like the magazines said. Not David's but the ones at work, the ones Pauline and the researchers read, *Hello! Marie Claire*. Emotion and sex. Meaningless without emotion. She had to try to remind herself that this was all an experiment. But still, her heart was racing. Could be on the point of breaking. Emotion but not the right one. In a few minutes she'd find out if David needed another woman. It surged through her. Looking up at his eyes as the woman sucked him off. His eyes urging her on. The man ready with his hard cock. Yes, I will do this for you. My love. I will.

'*Love Me Tender.*'

Fuck it. Every fucking time, Alice.

'*Love Me Do.*'

She tried to focus on the here, the now, but she was back at the start of this.

Aged ten with a stutter. Sitting alone in one of many front rooms while her mother was in the back with one of her uncles. Alone with their record collections, putting a song on to drown out the sounds of their fucking. This irritating habit she'd developed. Whenever her mother said something serious, she'd pick out a word and sing a line from a song with the same words.

'Alice. Can you STOP doing this!'

'Stop, In the Name of Love.'

'Please, you're driving me crazy.'

'Crazy Horses. Eweeh- EWEEH!'

'Alice, please!'

'Please Please Me.'

To just kill those voices. To let go of that cowardly irony. To just be able to reach out, touch. Feel something. For once, for real. Focus on the now. Some woman is sucking the cock of the man you love. How much more real do you need, you stupid fuck. Fuck it. Feel, you coward, feel!

Seconds had gone by. The poor man just standing there, parading his penis politely before her, waiting for her go-ahead. David still staring at her, waiting.

Just do it. Pull it towards you. The man, the cock he is dangling in your face. Close your eyes. Open for him. Pull him in. This is what David wants. For him. Please.

But then. The strawberry-flavoured scented condom.

'Strawberry Fields Forever.'

Wagging it in her face. This large penis wrapped in synthetic strawberry-flavoured plastic. Women liked dessert. No meat flavours. Did it come in dark and milk chocolate? Chocolate for anal. Fruit salad with real pineapple chunks for extra stimulation. Jesus. And the head of his penis did look like a strawberry.

She was in grave danger of bursting out laughing. Think of another song.

'*I Am the Walrus.*'

A sadder one.

'*Eleanor Rigby.*'

Better. Poor Eleanor, waiting by her window. Enough of waiting, of windows. She was ready. She was going to take that strawberry-flavoured dick inside her. She looked up at David and he nodded.

* * *

And then he heard it. Her gasp.

The cock. A real cock. The man holding her waist, pulling her back onto it.

A gasp. Like he'd never made her gasp.

Watching her like that. Seeing her close her eyes. Seeing her pelvis buck. While this woman struggled with his cock, which was lifeless now, beyond feeling. Hearing Alice respond to each thrust. At some point later, when they had gone home, they would struggle to try to repeat her success. But he would go soft inside her. Her words then: 'Yes, yes, c'mon, Daddy, you can do it.' His words: 'Sorry Alice, sorry.'

The woman pumping his cock, sucking it frantically. Licking his balls. He tried to think of her as Hannah but it only made matters worse. She gave up on it, smiled at him politely, then turned, put her hands on the edge of the bed, bent forward and put her ass in the air. She reached back and started touching herself, her fingers, between her legs, motioning for him to come closer.

A lovely ass, no doubt. The curvature from her hips to waist was quite exquisite. He rubbed his flaccid cock against her ass but still his eyes were drawn to Alice being fucked. Her head was thrown back, her eyes closed. Oh

Alice. If only I could do this forever. Bring you men. Hold your hand as they stroke your thighs in the bar. Feed them lines. Plant words in their mouths that will make you laugh. Encourage them and you as I bring them to our home. Relax you with my witty one-liners. Pour you that third glass of bubbly. Lead you and them through to the bedroom. Kiss your forehead as they cup your tiny breasts in their hands. Kiss you on the mouth as their lips wander down your body. Tell you that they are so big and so hard. Suck in your gasps as they enter you. Whisper to you that it's OK, it's beautiful as they push inside you. Whispering, telling you what they are doing to you as I bite your ear. Feeling your nails digging into my skin as they make you come.

But she was gone. No longer there. Three feet away and she was inside herself. Lost to him.

He grabbed the woman's hips firmly, brought his body close to hers, stroked her back and neck, bit her ear. Then whispered. 'Sorry, I've lost it.'

*   *   *

There were polite goodbyes. He apologised for having had too much to drink and maybe next time, but there could be no next time.

Alice had been pleased by another man. She said she hadn't come, no one had, but the only thing that stopped her from really letting go, it was clear, was him. If he hadn't been there she would have come.

It wasn't far so they walked home, through the West End proper back to their little place by the motorway. All the way he told her enthusiastically about how great it had been, but once they were inside and she slipped into the bath it came back to him. The guy's face when he was inside her, that moment when the guy turned and stared at him. The eyes on his flaccid dick and then the look in those eyes. The man grasping in a second why it was they were swinging. The look, definitely it had been. Face it. It had been pity.

Alice was singing in the bath again. Some Beatles song. And once again he was in the corridor. Caught between rooms. He couldn't take another second of it. Snuck out silently putting the door on the snib. Alice would understand that he needed to be alone. Maybe.

He walked twice round the block, then away. Down Dumbarton Road and past so many people that he lost track of his thoughts and found himself just following them. They were all dressed up. Of course, it was Friday night and this was Glasgow.

Walking towards him. Three girls, early to mid twenties. Long legs, short skirts, strappy heels. Belts slung low over their hips. The girl in the middle, midriff showing, belly-button piercing. The girl on the left, her breasts squeezed into a T-shirt which read 'BABE'. Laughing together as the two guys behind made lewd comments. Young. No kids yet. Tight little pussies.

He moved to the edge of the pavement and felt the energy drain from him as they passed by. He resisted the temptation to turn and look at the girls' asses. Fought the predictable impulse to mull over his failure tonight. He kept moving uphill. Twenty or so bars. Six, seven hundred people, maybe more. Watching them would stop him from thinking. But it was everywhere – sex. The whole street buzzing with it, making him weak. Dark eyeshadow. Bleached blondes and brunettes and bobs and long hair and short hair. And bracelets that flattered the wrists and pink painted toenails and necklaces that hung round slender necks. And laughing and huffing and strutting and pouting and falling about. In threes or fours with or without men on their arms. The blonde in the stilettos. She likes to hold a hard cock against her face, making you read her assessment in her eyes, those eyes that critique or laugh, that measure a man. That push your head down, that make you eat her, that say, no not there, that hold your head just there, till you satisfy her, because you can't in any other way. Because you can't really share, just do it one at a time. Me then you. This world of wankers.

The chip shop. A group of young males dressed up in that way Glasgow guys think is smart. Number two haircuts and gel. White trainers. Football tops on with no jackets. Twitching with testosterone, cracking jokes, pushing each other around as they waited for the chip suppers that would soak up the ten pints they'd have later to give them the guts to chat up the girls at the dancing. Those little whores who flirt with you all night then dance with other guys, checking out the competition, then end up with you later, at the end of the night, when the options run out and the bar closes, sucking your cock in a back alley because they need to feel needed.

Further. The noise of the throng ahead. The estate agent's window. West-Wise. Three couples, mid thirties, by the illuminated window. One man in a suit holding hands with a woman in a little black dress. Pointing at the pictures. He stopped behind them and looked over their shoulders, trying to see the photo of the flat they were looking at. Hyndland Road. Three bedrooms, rear garden, recent conversion with mezzanine. Offers over two sixty. The woman turned and noticed him leering. She whispered something to her man and pulled him away. David looked at their hands. Sapphire engagement ring. The kind of bitch who never comes, who says maybe next time. Who's holding back, who makes you think maybe you're not big enough, that maybe if you get some property you could be, who jerks off just fine by herself, who gives you the show but not the ending. Who makes you try harder. Next time. Who's so beautiful. Spreading herself for you. Who's promising, like property.

Stop it.

The click of heels passing. Two women and so he followed them. The way the heels made the calf muscles taut. Exaggerated the swing of the hips. The one on the right wearing a red thong, just visible above the line of her skirt. The other a gold ankle bracelet. The slenderness of her legs contrasting with the fullness of her thighs. Silk skirt swishing just above the knee, stretched tight round the curves of her buttocks.

So easy to leave Alice tonight. To start the whole game again. The power play. The grand denial. To seduce some slut, get a hotel.

The bitch. The whore of Babylon. There she was, tempting us all. The by now nauseating play of appearance and disappearance which was once called seductive. Revealed intermittently as she passed the street lights. Her body toned, her skin smooth. Wearing nothing more than a black silk bra and matching panties. Standing with her feet provocatively apart playing with her hair. Thirty foot tall. He stood there watching her gradually wind her way up Byres Road till she assumed almost human proportions. She may have been only an advert for some brand of lingerie on the back of a double-decker bus, but she seemed to David like some kind of image of the way things were and would be for ever. This aggressive culture of desire in which the impotent were the new proletariat. Banners in procession. Mao Tse Tung, Stalin, the American flag.

The noise, louder, as he passed the bars. Music,

hundreds of voices, talking, laughing, shouting, glasses slamming, laughter released, ringtones beeping past him. He let himself be pulled along by other people's desire.

The line for the cash machine. Bank of Scotland. He must not think about money and unemployment. He must just watch. Twenty or more of them in a line. Students mostly. Three goth girls. The one in the middle wearing a corset. Her breasts E-cups at least, held rigid like a shelf on which her crucifix necklace sat. The girl next to her, fishnets and filigree. Blood red lips. Vamps and vampires. The third, thigh-high leather boots. Tattoo at the base of her spine. Texting on a mobile. Some date no doubt, some infinite choice of dates. These poor kids, so new to all this. They think they are so dark, seductive, above it all. See them in fifteen years' time. Partner number fifty-five, still wearing fishnets and blood red lipstick, temp jobs and one-night stands. Thinking that they've found a real connection with a man when they find out they loved the same CD from the 90s.

And the others before them. Those things, those love handles, those perfect quantities of calculated feminine flesh that diminished and turned to taut slender muscle as your eye roamed from the thigh to the waist. The low-slung denims and the miniskirts and the push-up bras and the deliberately visible frilly black shoulder straps and the deep straight line of the cleavage and earrings that swung when they laughed and low-cut dresses that revealed the curvature of the spine. And when they were lost in some activity – slipping a foot out of a high heel as they waited in line, playing with their hair as they texted their friends, making you wonder if they knew what they were doing to you.

Impotence. Like being in a land where you couldn't speak the language. Like being in a shopping mall with a maxed-out credit card. An impotent man could easily be the perfect addict. The perfect consumer. A desire which could never be fulfilled. Which left you wanting. More. More of anything. More. Begging the bastards to increase the limit on your credit. Your impotence multiplied by the number of women you desired. Your desire infinite and your ability to perform horribly finite. Infinitely impossible. Your desire to fuck, hostile, angry, coming in the face of reality.

Sound of glass smashing. Laughter and shouts. David turned. A woman in stilettos trying to run after someone. Her breasts jiggling, feet stumbling in the four-inch heels. Domestic row. No one bothering to look.

He moved towards them. A man ran past and some other man was chasing after him. Another mate was holding the girl. Their bodies silhouetted against the bright lights of a mortgage broker's. The mate's hands lingering just too long on her slender shoulders. Bringing her head to his chest so she could cry. His hand slowly drifting down her back to her arse. And she will go with him tonight. The one who holds her. Not her boyfriend who fought over her. The one who is playing her, whispering words in her ear, and she has to, doesn't she, be with someone tonight, because she got all dressed up. And the effort involved becomes ever more of an effort. And she will cry tonight as he fucks her and he will think it was because he was so good, making her moan. He will think she is crying because he did this to her. Because she can't do this to herself. Because she needs him to feel alive and she will sense that and cry more because the reason she is crying is she is tired of all this and he is not the answer to anything and she knows that she has exhausted another man and all of his friends and she will have to start again.

He had been standing staring for too long. They would notice. Ashton Lane then, by the subway. The noise deafening. Heels on cobblestones, a busker, voices of a thousand drinkers. The Ubiquitous Chip, Jinty McGinty's, Bar Brel, the Attic.

He needed a drink. Kept moving. He stepped into some big new bar he hadn't seen before. Up the steps. Vast inside. Blue light. Neon. Three hundred people. Chat like static, crackling. Energy trapped. Eyes flashing across the room, heads turning. He ordered a double Scotch and threw it back without looking at anyone, as if he suspected the danger. He found his mind wandering again, to his failure tonight, every night. The reasons. Hannah. Alice. To be an actor and be unable to perform. This whole thing. Men. Women. This performance. Extras overdressed for their audition. Then he made the mistake of looking round. It only took a few seconds. A woman, with two men. Blonde. Her T-shirt read 'FUCK ME' in diamante. Bored of her friends. Her eyes catching David's for a second. The desperation he sensed in her eyes. The mirror of his own. Useless.

He had to get out. Walked out, away, back down the lane, round the back, through the car park. A hundred feet away a man was puking as he supported himself on the bonnet of a Lexus. A woman standing over him, stroking his head, holding him.

Alice would have done the same. Would have stroked his head, told him it was OK. Face it if you could, Alice. She had actually grown to love his problem, and that was the new problem. As the woman held the man's head, she was looking out as if to find a new man. Smoothing her dress over her hips. Lifting one foot to check her heels. He could have wept. To be a woman, to be this walking cliché of sexuality. Heels that imitated the image of a woman's pointed toes when she was about to come and lipstick which aped the flush of blood to the lips during orgasm.

It had been a mistake. All of it. The walk. The car park, lit like a stage. The sickeningly cinematic flashback of that incident in the car park with the whore two years ago. All of it. He stood there, just waiting for someone to pass. So he could have some excuse to leave this spot where the lights threw four shadows of himself around him.

A car door slamming. He turned. A young couple were climbing out of an SUV. Late twenties early thirties. His hand resting on her hip. They breezed past him, pulled him along in their wake. Lovers. Not a first date. But not married yet. Still showing each other off in public. As they made it onto Byres Road he followed, at a decent distance, watching the rhythmic swing of their hips. Slightly out of sync with each other. Every five steps or so the man would take a half step to get back in time again.

To just follow them. Feel the hope in their touch. Safe distance, getting closer to see the details. Watching her knuckles squeezing into the back pocket of the guy's denims, the long line of her arm leading to the soft curve of her neck. Then backing off, so they wouldn't notice him. Listening to the language of their bodies. He could follow them all night. Into bars and nightclubs. Like he'd done that first night when he left Hannah. Following people. Trying to decode the signs. Who they were. Where they came from. Whether they would kiss in public or not. How long they'd been in love.

They stopped. He almost bumped into them. They turned and went up some steps. He lifted his eyes from their backs and saw it. Immense and spotlit. The old church at the top of Byres Road. Alice had said it was some kind of restaurant-bar-nightclub now. An irreligious conversion, she'd called it.

All of this was stupid. He should call Alice, tell her he was OK, before she got the cops out looking for him. But no, he had to defy to her, to see how far he could go.

The couple headed up past the bouncers. Men in Black. Their arms crossed at their crotches as if someone was about to aim a kick at them. Walkie-talkies hissing. David followed. Nodded at one of the bouncers, hoping they wouldn't ask him where he'd been tonight, how much he'd had to drink.

He was in. The couple drifted past the bar to the restaurant section. As they talked to the waiter and he fixed them a table behind the velvet drapes, David took time to look around. Low ceiling. No enclaves, eaves or vaults. Not like a church at all apart from the stained-glass windows with neon strip lights behind them. The clientele. More than a hundred. Upmarket. Must be the trendiest place in the West End. All mid thirties. Too expensive for the riff-raff down the road.

Groups of men and women in booths and tables. The women even more shocking than the ones in the street. More voluptuous, but dressed like teenagers. Cleavages and split skirts. Older. So many groups of women, threes and fours without men. Back on the pull again after five or more failed long-term relationships. Trying harder.

The couple had long since vanished so David walked to the bar and waited in line to order a whisky because that now seemed like the only thing to do.

As his second double whisky was being poured his eyes came to rest on the three women sat in front of him. One seemed almost familiar. She kept staring at him then turning her head away. Big-breasted blonde. Slender neck. Turning and talking to her friends. Then shooting glances up at him. Then she was up at the bar ordering a drink beside him. Flicking her hair back and smiling.

'Hi.'

'Hello.'

Thirty-nine was his guess. Her breasts bulging where the push-up bra dug in too deep. There was this thing Alice had read him from a book by some French guy. Women over thirty-five were incapable of love. Too many ghosts.

'You know how to get into the nightclub downstairs?' she asked. 'Is there a guest list or . . . 'cos I'm fucked if I'm going to queue.' She had a thick Glaswegian accent.

'No idea,' he said. Turning away.

'I'm buyin' a round for ma mates, you want another one?'

Yes, she was really trying to chat him up. She talked about how she was from the South Side and didn't know the West End very well and she'd heard the club was fab and was he here with his mates? And he could chat her up. He could go dancing with her. He could leave Alice and go back to the bars again. The endless cycle of seductions and failures. But he wanted to cut her off, just tell her. Tell her that there was no point in this, any of this. But still she talked. She liked the West End 'cos people were more arty she said. She was still talking. She was a nurse and what did he do for a living? She was moving closer, doing that almost pornographic thing that only women over thirty-five do. Leaning over the counter and displaying cleavage in a way that you are supposed to notice but not notice.

'So you come here a lot?'

The cliché, like a dare. I'd like to make you get down

on your knees and hold your ass cheeks apart so I can see. Make you go on top and pinch your nipples as your pelvis gyrates and spasms on my cock. He said nothing.

'What you do for a living?' she asked, trying again.

'I live,' he said, and she laughed.

'So where do you live?'

It would be so easy. He'd done it so many times before in that first six months after Hannah. To feed this poor stereotype the clichés, get her laughing about human resources and how he hated humans, sit with her and her friends, entertain them all with his cynical one-liners from all the movies he'd seen. Play Cagney, De Niro and James Stewart. The old routine. Have them all in hysterics, go clubbing with them, get them all chasing him, ignore her for a bit then make sure at around two that they were dancing together. Get kissing in the back corner. The well worn word-perfect act. Tell her he was from out of town and staying with friends so she wouldn't want to go back to his. Get a taxi to her place. For him to open the bottle of wine he found in her fridge. For the kissing to resume again on the sofa, for it to take them to bed where they would tear off each other's clothes, and she would lie back for him and he would be standing there yet again, with his flaccid dick in his hand saying sorry, it was probably the drink, and she would play with him, and suck him and put on a show for him and he'd have to interrupt and say that maybe if they had a snooze then they could try again when he'd sobered up in an hour or two. Then in the morning he'd have to slip away before she woke, so he wouldn't have to face the humiliation yet again.

She was still waiting for him to speak. He couldn't even remember the last thing he'd said to her. She'd no doubt interpreted his silence as something broody, sexy and interesting. Even the silence was a cliché. He set down his glass.

Alice was the only woman he'd ever told straight up. First date. I'm impotent. She whispered to him in his sleep, she told him stories. And what no one realised, what this girl didn't grasp, was that every day we told ourselves little stories, just so we could get through the day.

The blonde. The words. He didn't know where they came from, and as he walked past her, out of the bar, after saying them, leaving her stunned, he wondered, worried. Why those word, those particular words?

'Sorry, I'm married,' was what he'd said.

*   *   *

For instance you might say: 'You remember a couple of days ago when we were making love and we had that wonderful foreplay where your touch was perfect. Then I noticed you lost your erection for some reason. Being a woman I have no idea what that must feel like, but I would like us, together, as a couple, to find a way of talking about this.'

She'd been on the Internet since she'd stopped trying to call him on his mobile, after the first hour he'd been gone. Mens-health.org. Relate.com. His-health.com. The sites she'd visited after their first date.

Failing this the urologist may request that a nocturnal penile tumescence test be done. A recent study at the New York School of Research found that impotence was common among smokers. Don't dwell on the negative. Recent studies show that twenty-five per cent of alcoholics become impotent. A symptom of prostate cancer.

May also be the result of deep-seated emotional trauma, such as having been sexually abused as a child. At the same time the artery to the penis dilates to twice its diameter, increasing the blood flow sixteen-fold. If you stop touching each other, your chances of making love successfully decline. He then attaches the pump to draw air out of the cylinder, creating a vacuum that draws blood into the penis. Reducing anxiety prior to the sexual act is vital. PAPAVERINE, PHENTOLAMINE, PROSTA-GLANDIN-E. Falling out of love can be a trigger. It is a good idea to sit close to one another, don't worry too much about maintaining eye contact. Two long rods (also referred to as semi-rigid prostheses) can be inserted into the outer channels of the penis through a small incision in the lower abdomen or scrotum. Most of all don't panic or allocate blame. VIAGRA, XENICAL, CELEBREX. On the downside there have been reports of deaths and severe side effects in some men. Other adverse effects may include headache, flushing, indigestion and temporary changes in vision including seeing a 'blue haze'. Ordering these medications online has never been easier. It is also important to ask for his help in coping with the emotions you may be experiencing. Start by saying something like 'I know this sounds silly but . . .' Impotence affects one in ten men. Act as a team to solve this problem. Recommend that your partner sees his GP, as erection problems can often be an indicator of heart disease, diabetes or spinal cord injury. Create a stress-free, intimate and stimulating environment. Scented candles and relaxing music. A herbal bath followed by a gentle massage. Increase the frequency of hand holding, kissing and hugging when you meet each other. If you are worried about whether your partner still finds you attractive, try improving your own sense of self-esteem. Eat regularly, exercise regularly, have a makeover and make time to relax. If your partner has been working hard and trying to meet deadlines, tiredness and worry can cause problems in focusing on lovemaking. Vacuum pumps. Hormone treatment. Counselling. Snuggle up on the sofa while you watch a DVD together and always cuddle before you drift off to sleep at night. ALPROSTADIL – to be injected into the penis using a special applicator just before intercourse. You will need to keep up this kind of touching for several weeks if you are to see positive results in your relationship.

Then it was going through the old books in the boxes in the corridor, tearing through her texts on psychotherapy. The ones she'd kept with her for years because she knew they meant something. Codependence and her mother. Facilitators and codependents. Some as yet undiagnosed problem. Women who feed their partners alcohol and men who make their partners fat so no one else will find them attractive. Women who criticise their men for drinking, like women who attack their men for erectile dysfunction, who feed the problem, who live with it, who love it. Page 307. Because they need the intimacy of a dependent man, because they need to feel needed, because if they make themselves part of the problem they will not be rejected.

She had made herself part of the problem. She had fallen in love with his problem.

But still there had been that moment, when he'd been watching the couple and his eyes had fixed on the man's cock. Page 427. The chapter on impotence and repressed homosexuality.

It was no use, was her usual. Struggling to find reason and words, denying how she felt. And he was out there,

wandering somewhere, nowhere, lost. You will have to
do what you fear, Alice. Close your eyes and stop reading,
close your eyes and take that leap again. Stop intellectu-
alising. Do something.

Suddenly she was reaching for her jeans. Fumbling
with her socks and shoes. She would walk the streets all
night looking for him. Go in and out of bars till she
found him. As she made it out the front door, she had
worked out what she had to do. It was nothing new. It
was textbook, but the fact was they had been wrong.
They were no smarter than the textbooks.

> It is also important to explain your feelings about what
> has happened and to ask for his help in coping with the
> emotions you may be experiencing. Try explaining that
> you are worried it may be connected to your relation-
> ship.

She broke into a run and reached the end of the street.
Which way to go? Down to Partick or up to Hyndland?
The rain pounding on her head.

Street after street. The wet and the dark. And then a
hunched human form approached her slowly. Dark and
sullen. Shoulders tensed, hands in pockets. She slowed
to a stop and waited for him to look up and face her.

*   *   *

'We have to talk' she said just like Hannah had said and
just like with Hannah he could feel himself shrinking
away from her touch as, just inside the door, she helped
him off with his jacket. Alice didn't know. That first time
Hannah said 'We have to talk' was the night he walked
out.

She went through to the kitchen and poured them

both some red wine. He was still standing by the door. She seemed unsure how to get him to come in, sit down; she was hovering around, twitching nervously.

'I mean not like Talk talk, like 'the Talking Cure', like 'Oprah'. I mean, just if we can just, you know. Like we used to.'

He was silent, and she was becoming almost frantic.

'"Like we used to", Jesus listen to me, like "The way we were", like "You don't bring me flowers any more", like I'm fucking Barbra Streisand and you're . . .'

Her fingers flying up and down to the sides of her head, quoting the air, like she was trying to protect her face. Seeing her like this, so self-conscious, so vulnerable, was what made him take those steps towards her. Take a seat. Lift the glass she'd poured.

She was sorry, she said, that they hadn't had a chance recently, it had been her work but also she had to admit she'd been a bit weirded out by the change in him since he'd lost his job, but how all this was her fault. This was Alice-talk, so unlike Hannah-talk, which was silence waiting for him to talk. But for all the words Alice threw in the air it came to the same thing. Enough.

'And this whole swinging thing was a kind of experiment and maybe some kind of self-therapy.'

Enough.

'Not that I believe in therapy anyway, well not in the traditional—'

'Enough!' he said.

He had never raised his voice to her before. She looked like she'd been slapped. He lowered his voice.

'Enough, Alice.'

The silence again. He felt it was his duty to break it. Words again, coming from nowhere.

'You can't . . . OK. You can't cure me.'

'Well, I don't think I was even—'

'I know you'd like to, I know you'd like us to be like a normal couple and—'

She put on that contemptuous laugh thing she did. 'Jesus, that's the last thing in the world I—'

'Give up on it, OK! OK?'

He was raising his voice again. She took a big gulp from her wine.

'Daddy,' she said as she reached across the breakfast bar to touch his hand. He pulled away.

'And stop calling me that, OK?'

He'd done it. Gone too far. Wanted to. He took a sip of the wine and could feel her eyes blazing at him. Could tell she was about to cry. She hated being made to cry. Hated this. Every time in the past, when they'd been close to an argument, she'd called him Daddy and taken him to bed and told him his bedtime story. But not tonight. He was no longer her Daddy. The whole thing had been a childish game and now she knew it. He couldn't raise his eyes to look at her. She'd cry and leave the room. He'd sit here and drink this bottle and when it was done he would put his jacket back on and leave as he'd done with Hannah.

'You're such a fuck,' she said, her voice crackling with contempt. 'Such a fucking self-pitying sonofabitch.'

He set down his glass, still couldn't look at her. She was raising her voice now.

'You think I want to cure you. Jesus, well let me tell you, Daddy, that I studied psychology, OK. And the only person that can cure you is you, and you know I don't have a problem with your problem but you seem to. In fact no, let's be honest here. Fucking is just not such a big deal for me, not that I'm not good at it, 'cos I fucking am.'

'OK.'

'I'm multiorgasmic. Did you know that? And I've done a lot of fucking in my time. Big cocks, fat cocks, I've fucked and fucked and come and come and—'

He set down his glass. What the hell was she doing? Trying to make him angry? If that was it, she'd succeeded.

'You're such a selfish fuck. You know, you actually quite like being impotent, don't you, 'cos it makes you different from everyone else and that's what you're so fucking scared of.'

'Oh really?'

'And if you can't talk about it, if you can't be honest with me, then you know what, you're going to be doing this for the rest of your life and never get it up. You're going to just walk out on me and try again with someone new, then they'll dump you and you'll start again with someone new until you're too old to even—'

He got to his feet. Pointing at her. 'Shut the fuck up.'

'And hell knows how you conceived a fucking child anyway but maybe you didn't, hey maybe she isn't even yours.'

That was it, she'd done it. A flash. Brando. *Streetcar*. He did it. Sweeping the contents of the table onto the floor. Glasses smashing.

Then like a fool, staring at the glasses and the wine, and feeling not like Brando at all, who'd walked out straight after, but like a little West End house husband who was worried about the carpet and had to clear up the glass and say sorry. That was what he did. Down on his hands and knees saying sorry, sorry. Her hand on his shoulder. That was when the tears came.

She took the shards of broken glass from his hand. Kissed his forehead.

'Sorry. Undergrad psychology. "Drive 'em nuts, they spill their guts."'

Impossible. To be laughing now. To be holding her legs, crying and laughing all at once. There was no escaping Alice, no way he could leave her. Even thinking about it was as dumb as Brando. Theatrics. The truth, which was harder to bear, was that they were stuck like this, indefinitely, always.

'Baby,' he said, 'baby.' Burying his head in her.

'And I'll call you Daddy if I fucking want to. You fucking fuck!'

Then they were both laughing there together hunched down on the floor. Tears on their faces. The words stammering out of him.

'God, I hate you.'

'I hate you too, Daddy.'

'Fucked-up bitch.'

'Fuckin' sleepy sausage, fuckin' floppy-dicked fuck.'

Hugging till the laughter stopped and the hiccupping breath slowed to normal. She got him a tea towel to blow his nose on and helped him to his feet and walked him arm in arm through the corridor, leading him to bed.

*   *   *

Snuggled up together. She held his head in her lap and stroked his hair as he talked and talked. She'd heard most of it before in fragments, in little asides, but now he felt it was his duty to her, to himself, to put the whole story together. How it started, how he thought it had started.

'It's OK. Tell me, Daddy.'

When Hannah was pregnant, then breastfeeding. Months and months of no sex and then sleep deprivation and she'd felt so awkward about her body. He'd wanted to touch her but she'd been lactating and she had Caesarean scars and didn't want to be touched down there. And so he'd developed this secret pornography habit on the net.

'Shhh, Daddy, I know.'

And how one day she'd caught him jerking off at the PC and she'd said that maybe he should get a whore because then he wouldn't keep pressuring her into sex.

'Shhh, it's good, it's all good.'

Or how maybe it was work and this fear, this fear he had of being a father, and being stuck in this shit job. And how he'd started coming home late. Drifting round bars, checking out the lap-dancing clubs, finally getting up the guts to go in. Then driving round the red-light district before home. Because home had become this place where he felt guilty. Where there was this child in bed between them, who woke three times a night. Who woke both of them, and how he could never sleep when she was breastfeeding in bed.

'It's OK, it's OK. Tell me.'

And there was this one time, this hooker. Just this blowjob, in his car before home, and he could never forget the sight of her, how she was wearing fishnets over a pair of tights, and how she said it would be ten more to fuck her, but that she never did kissing. And all the time when she worked away at him, there in his car in this multi-storey car park, all he could think about was the fishnets over the stockings, and then he'd worked it out. It was winter and was cold outside and she still had to look sexy because this was her job. And he'd failed to get it up, and how he thought that maybe that was the first time.

'It's OK, it's OK, Daddy.'

Whispering he was. So quietly, like talking to himself, but holding onto her so tight.

Then how it was impossible, home, the guilt, and how

he was sure he'd caught something, HIV, hepatitis B, and went for a secret test, and he was OK, but the day when he was waiting for the results he broke down and confessed to Hannah.

'Shhh, there, there, shhh.' He was whimpering like a child now, the words jerking out of him with a force that seemed all of its own, and she had to move down and bring her face close to his so she could hear what he was saying. Stroking his hair.

How it wasn't her fault, Hannah's, it was his and every day Hannah reminded him of that. And he shouldn't hate her but she'd seemed almost pleased, because then sex was something dirty and the pressure was off, and every day she'd say these things, these loving, caring things and maybe she said them to him just to remind him of what a filthy beast he'd been and he'd started drinking, and then they barely spoke and he'd moved onto the sofa for two weeks, because the guilt was too much lying beside his wife and daughter and how then one day she'd said those words: 'We need to talk.'

'Shhh. It's OK. It's OK.'

'We need to talk.'

'I know, I know, I'm sorry. It's OK.'

And how he'd left in the middle of the night, when she was asleep. Picked up a bottle of wine and left and wandered the streets drinking, just hoping someone would pick him up, the police, a whore, anybody, and how he'd managed to check into a hotel and spent the next month drunk, fucking, trying to fuck anybody, and failing, too drunk, too fucked up. How he'd got himself this bedsit in the East End. Again and again, picking up women and trying again, hoping that with each one it would be different. This kind of obsession. As if with each new one he'd have a chance to overcome his failing. But it was always the same, Sheryl, Charlotte, Fiona, Debbie, Sarah, Liz, Beckie, Sophie. And how, how if he'd only.

'Shhh, it's OK. It's all OK.'

If he'd only stayed that night and had that talk.

'Shhh, shhh, no more talking.' But still he had to get it out.

And how when he heard her, Alice, her, you, say those words tonight. He'd almost gone. And how he could never go. Because she was his Alice. His Alice. Alice.

As the rhythmic jerking of his chest finally calmed, he murmured little things she couldn't quite hear. That no, maybe the thing had started earlier. He didn't know.

'Shhh, go to sleep.'

That even with Hannah, before, there were times when he couldn't perform.

'Sleepy Daddy.'

That he was a bad actor.

'Go to sleep, it's OK now. You're sleeping now. Shhh.'

She lay awake for another half an hour, holding him as he slept. Her mind racing. A burden, some people would have called it. A burden, to mother a man, to make his problems yours. But it made her happy in ways she could never explain or justify. You can't cure me, he'd said, with such anger, and then begged her to help him with such tenderness. Yes, ambition and a career, his and hers, all these things, they were worthless, they meant nothing when you were alone. So she held him, held him so tight she thought she might wake him. She would cure him. That was the big project that would make her stay. She wouldn't give up on him like her mother had with her father. Like she had done with so many things before. She would cure him and through doing so she would cure herself. She had to because he was. He was her Daddy.

*   *   *

It happened in the little corporate mini-kitchen when she was helping herself to her third coffee. Pauline passed by, ignoring her, and she was a hit by a sudden wave of nausea. She just managed to make it to the sink, with her hand over her mouth, ran the tap to try to mask the sound of puking, then looked over her shoulder to see if any of the junior researchers had noticed. There was no one near but even from a distance they would have heard her retching. She told herself it was the stress of work, of her new responsibilities and that she really should try to cut back on the coffee and actually attempt to have breakfast. Yes, the tension in the office had been growing steadily since she stood up to Pauline last week.

She cleaned up the mess, washed her face, dried it with a disposable hand towel, then braved the open-plan office. The five new researchers, three local girls, two from London and Pauline, all talking in hushed tones. They fell silent as she passed and turned their heads to their PCs. Alice stoically walked the steps to her glass-walled office.

Inside, she collapsed into her seat. Five weeks of difficult research and in all that time Pauline had created a coven, turning the researchers into duplicates of herself. Teaching them the fine arts of gossip, backstabbing and bitching about the boss. Pauline called herself a feminist but, for sure, didn't see any value in having a female boss. Fact was she'd bitch about any boss, male or female, but would never want to take on the responsibility of being a boss herself. It was still strange for Alice to face the fact that she was in charge.

She opened the desktop again and stared at the screen. Three ads from swinging-paradise. HOLLYGO-HEAVY (51), FUKMYHOLE (49), DOLLY (56). Dolly described herself as an experienced swinger. Was looking for men and women, couples and parties, for multiples, anal and oral.

There was a picture of her surrounded by erect penises. One in each hand, one in her mouth and another obscuring her eyes. Although it was hard to see her face something told Alice that this woman was in control and that behind the dicks she was smiling. Someone like Dolly could be exactly what they were looking for to partici-pate in the series, or at least to establish connections with others who would. Dolly said she welcomed all cummers, that she was experienced in helping men with 'problems'.

Alice looked up from her PC and caught Pauline turning away swiftly, then going back to her gossip. One of the other researchers turned and looked over her shoulder at Alice then Pauline covered her mouth to hide a laugh. It was clear. Pauline didn't want to research this series. Would probably do everything she could to sink it.

They didn't know. These new researchers. The sad career trajectory Pauline had and that was waiting for them too: get a job aged twenty-three – work freelance for a decade – lead the single life – dedicated to your work – the nice but tiny one-bedroom flat in the West End – no long-term partners – no long-term contracts – fighting for the right to make your forty-fifth programme on B-list celebrities and the uniqueness of their interior decor – no ladder to climb – not moving to London or New York or Channel 4 or HBO – stuck here – going nowhere – after years of it, boredom and cynicism set in – the minimum effort spent to get through

a day – surfing the net for holidays to go on alone –
going to dinner parties – the only single woman in a
room full of couples – your friends' attempts to set you
up with Mr Right – settling finally for some less than
satisfactory any-man with a pension plan because time
was running out – because you wanted to give up your
job and have a baby – because having a baby was the
only thing of value you could find – because that was
what women did – women who worked in lifestyle
programming and lived in the West End. The other
researchers would end up just like Pauline if she didn't
warn them.

Through the glass partition she saw that one of the
guys from IT had joined Pauline's gang and they were
all joking with him. Yes, everyone was laughing at her
now.

If only they realised how much was at stake here. If
they fucked up on the swinging series, they'd all lose
their jobs. And it was hard for Alice to work out why it
was that they didn't share her passion for the programme.
It was pure research. Untapped. Sociological and histor-
ical. There were things that the world had to know about
sexuality today. This new series would be a benchmark.
An examination of the contradictions of our time, the
crisis in marriage. In years to come people would write
PhDs about it.

Alice typed a quick email to Pauline to ask her to keep
her informed on how the participant list was shaping up.
They were, after all, behind schedule. Sent it off. But
Pauline was not even looking at her computer.

Alice's eyes moved back and forth from the picture of
Dolly and the dicks, to Pauline flirting with the IT guy.
Polar opposites, she thought. Pauline thinks she's a liber-
ated modern woman but buys *Sex and the City* shoes –

she says she doesn't buy into the whole celebrity culture thing but wastes hours every day poring over the pages on celebrities and their breaks-ups and adulteries – she thinks that pornography is a demeaning objectification of women but that getting a boob lift might be empowering – she looks at people like Dolly and sees them as sad old victims – she read Germaine Greer fifteen years ago and thinks that swingers are an affront to feminism.

But Dolly has probably been married, had three or four kids, divorced. Had a home, a car, a life, lost them all, started again and now, aged fifty-six, finally found some kind of freedom. She doesn't need Germaine Greer to tell her what to think or *Cosmo* to tell her what to buy. She cuts through all that crap and goes straight for gratification. Dolly. Overweight and oversexed. Phone number in return for dick pic. Like some old advert from the 50s. It is what it says on the packet. No irony. No spin. Fuck me now. Have experience in helping men with problems.

Half the day gone and Pauline had still not replied to the email. Alice didn't like to, but had to admit it. Before, she would never have considered it plausible. That an old friend could be standing in the way of a series on the empowerment of women. But just because Pauline was a woman didn't mean she understood. She was also a bourgeois. As that old poster had said in art school: Paris 1968 – 'Let the last bourgeois be hung from the entrails of the last capitalist.' She made up her mind. Two things had to be done. One, she would contact Dolly herself. Two, Pauline had to be fired.

She'd worked late again. Sent out over forty emails to swingers, inviting them to take part. Introduced herself to Dolly. Watched as all the researchers left en masse at five twenty-five. Still no reply from Pauline and no emails from any of the other staff. She was going to have to do the whole thing herself.

Out of the subway and on the way home she passed the usual houses and gardens and thought about how maybe the reason she was working such long hours was that she was anxious about going home to David. To see him yet again putting on a brave face, over dinner, in front of the TV, but really struggling. After his last failure, the incredible intimacy of their shared tears. But still she could do nothing with it. Hugging, cuddling. Days later, not crying any more. How could she keep him close? To make him cry every night? As David had said on that first date: 'I am impotent in so many ways.' She felt impotent, the impotent intellectual. The dictionary definition of impotence. To know you have to act, but to be unable to do anything. Wasn't that the way she was, the way everyone was now? Politically, everything. All her theories on helping him, all her theories about the series, but still she couldn't get started, couldn't make that change come about.

The awkward nights they'd spent in the last week. Her trying to reassure him. When she was dying to tell him about her work, about the philosophical radicality of swinging, but felt it was inappropriate because he was still unemployed and signing on. The exhausted polite smile on his face. Their lack of touching in bed. She must thank him tonight for starting all this all those weeks ago. Reassure him that it was a great thing, that they shouldn't stop now. Dolly had to be the answer.

Suddenly the nausea was there again. She stopped as her head spun and a hot flush of panic came over her. It was not the nausea she'd had every day at work for the last week, but the horror of realising what that nausea had been. Over a month it had been since they'd started swinging, more than five weeks in fact. What with the move and all this stress she'd forgotten the dates, been careless with her Pill. She had definitely missed her period.

*   *   *

This silence in front of the TV. He couldn't tell her that he'd been sitting there every minute since he woke up around one. That he'd made himself watch daytime TV today after finding, for the fourth week, that he had no replies to the one hundred and forty-seven CVs he'd sent out. That it was the only thing he could think of doing, to keep himself from trying to jerk off all day to porno websites, like the three million or so long-term unemployed men just like him must have been doing. He made himself watch, minute after painful minute. To see how bad the world really was. To just see what his future might be as someone without a future. In five hours he'd been taught how to make a painting out of macaroni; how to make your sagging breasts sit up and look appealing with the help of Scotch tape. He'd been sold discount liposuction and discount holidays in Spain and over thirty domestic cleaning products. Twelve different types of life slash personal injury slash car insurance that confirmed the world was dangerous and the sofa was the safest place to be. He'd watched children's programmes that promoted toys that were advertised in the commercial break and chat shows that discussed the problem of supermodels with drug addictions and anorexia, that had discreet product placement and made him want to discreetly jack off to supermodels online and shoot smack into the biggest vein in his dick.

Now it was his third and her first home-makeover show and he was still in his dressing gown and slippers.

They were waiting for the Chinese takeaway again, because he'd given up cooking. Sitting beside her on the sofa. He no longer had a future in TV and she had. He'd lied to her earlier, told her the reason he was like this was that he'd had a bath.

The adverts. Not commenting on them or laughing at them like they used to. Just watching. The words on the screen.

Sofas SLASHED.

Beds SLASHED.

Kitchens SLASHED.

A graphic tear across each image revealing the new discount price. Usually he would have wanted to make her laugh, to joke about the wildly inappropriate use of a violent metaphor in a furniture ad. To comment on the self-loathing inherent in consumerism and the thinly veiled contempt of advertising agencies towards their product and the consumer. But tonight he wanted to make her watch crap TV. The Homeworld autumn sale.

SLASHED.

This was her world now. TV. This was how the mortgage was to be paid. How she would support him. Advertising was contemptible but it underwrote the programmes. So there was no laughter, no critiques, not any more. If he told her what he felt, she'd be forced into a defence of this thing that she had to do, which she used to despise but which was now putting food on their table. So he was silent. Watching the ads.

*   *   *

She was being quiet for once, not her usual babbling self. She could sense that he found her silence difficult. But her silence was not about what he might have thought it was. Not about Amy or Hannah or his negative attitude to finding work or even the things he didn't even know, like how he'd hidden his divorce papers from her and she'd found them accidentally, or any of the other things they'd lacked the courage to argue about that week. She sat there beside him on the sofa, staring into the space where the TV was. Half an hour and she'd hardly noticed a thing. She was thinking about the growth of a foetus. About how it was in the second trimester that limbs developed and fingers and fingerprints. She was thinking about the last abortion. Aged twenty-two. The natural thing to do. You didn't throw your life away at such a young age to raise another life. To plunge you both into poverty. To do as your mother had done. To grow up resenting your own child. To bring a child into a world that was so much worse than the world you grew up in. She was thinking about the abortion before that, aged nineteen. She was thinking about how her mother had told her she'd been an accident.

Easy flight, get away for half the price.

The twenty-four-hour chemist. The detour there on the way home from work. Colour Plus. Home pregnancy test. Then having to find somewhere to do it. Going to Safeway and having to wait outside the public toilet while some old bitch took her time. Sitting there then with the old woman's stench and the neon lights and the cubicle door locked and the piped music. The theme from *The Bodyguard.*

To have to piss to Whitney even though she didn't need a piss. Reading the instructions over and over and watching. Not a dramatic or noble scene at all, like in *The Bodyguard.* More like some schlock horror movie. Forcing the piss out as Whitney sang through the toilet speakers about how she would always love Kevin Costner. Watching as the little plastic window revealed at first one then two blue lines. Re-reading the instructions again and again in case there was some mistake and then walking out, past the shoppers, through the car park, holding the object in her jacket pocket, not caring any more if the shoppers saw her crying.

Royal Life Insurance. Because life is change and you change too.

The sofa in front of the TV. His feet almost touching hers. It was his. Could only have been. It must have been that night after the neighbours' party. That only time. No one else other than the last couple had been inside her. No one had come inside her. It had to be David's.

I am carrying your child. Was what she needed to say but couldn't.

Incredible to hear these words in her own head. 'Carrying'. Like you could carry a tune. God. If your head could be filled with these thoughts that weren't even yours, what did that say about you? Saying something to yourself that you didn't, couldn't believe. These words echoing round inside you. Like what? Like Whitney. And I will always love you. This stupid song that you heard in a supermarket toilet at the most important moment in your life. That made you want to defy it all. Abort. Just because of Whitney.

They were showing Bob Dylan in some advert. '"The times they are a changin"'

She was thirty-five. More than anything the thought turned her stomach – that this could be her last chance. The sickening idea that you just accepted a pregnancy because time was running out. The selfish gene. No thought for David and how it would ruin his life. To be unemployed and to have to raise a second family.

'Classic rock. The real sound of the 60s. The whole eight-CD box set. Yours for only £18.99.'

She would abort, as she had done twice before. But she wouldn't tell him. If she did he'd insist she keep it. She'd have an early vacuum extraction, in two weeks, week seven like before, never tell him. It only took an hour or two. Lunch break. While they were at it, get the coil installed so this would never happen again.

There has never been a better time to plan for your future.

Face it, Alice. You bring a child into the world and you give them nothing but your fears and your insecurities. Your anger. You bring a child up with your anger, your anger at what? This fucking rage against what? Against everything. You bring a child up with questions. Happy birthday. Your whole history hanging like a dead-weight over the life of your child. This abortion would be final. The final decision. The full stop. I will not have children ever. I am the end of our family line. We were all a mistake. The longer she postponed the decision the greater the chances she'd be unable to conceive anyway after the operation.

'Medicare. Because we care about you.'

Abort. In the name of what? Some greater goal. What? Her career? Have a child in the name of what? Family? Love? It would have to be for something. You couldn't, shouldn't, bring a child into this world of vague, random, freelance futures, of endless restarts and murmured half-commitments. It would be hard, but if she did it, it would have to be in the name of something. There had to be a real choice. A reason. If you kept it, the last thing you wanted to do was make your child your reason to live.

'Kalpogen. It's your life to live.'

To tell David then. Ask him what he thought.

'Freedom at your fingertips.'

She hated to admit it. Was pro-choice, but still the experience was always horrific. Had been before. You could try to deny it. But so few relationships survived an abortion. Fact.

'Because you deserve it.'

No. This was her choice. Hers alone.

'Available without prescription, at all chemists.'

She felt his eyes on her face. An hour of makeover shows, *Big Brother* and almost forty ads. She could have cried but instead she spoke, to fight the tears.

'Don't you just hate these fucking ads?'

'Yeah, they're so fuckin'—'

'Like that fuckin' one for life insurance, c'mon.'

'Like anyone has a life these days.'

'Yeah, like, exactly.'

'Exactly.'

'Daddy, you OK?'

'Fine, sure.'

'Can I? You wanna? You wanna bedtime story, Daddy?'

*   *   *

There was a man and a woman and they met at a party. Italy or somewhere, somewhere warm. They went for a walk together and held hands. He was tall and handsome and she was smaller, with long red hair. She laughed at all of his jokes and their hands found each other's as they walked. They turned the edge of a hill, a dune, and found a vast beach stretching before them. Deserted. Moonlight on the water. She ran down the dune, stripped and dived in. He watched her from the edge for a few minutes then laughed, undressed and followed. His arms were strong and within a few strokes he was there beside her. Holding her in the water. Treading water together, holding each other as her legs wrapped round his and she felt his hardness. She opened for him as her entered her. Closed her eyes and felt and listened. The sounds of the waves and the deep thrust of the man. And so quickly they came together. Her screaming and digging her nails into his skin. Him shooting his seed deep inside her. And as their eyes finally opened and she felt her muscles contracting round him in that perfectly synchronised spasm, they saw that all around them the water was sparkling. Little stars in the water. Algae, he said. She reached out her hand and drew it through the water. Flashy sparkles splashing in the air.

David was falling asleep. The story had not made him hard, and now she felt that terrible self-consciousness of hers that she hated so much. OK, the story hadn't been sexy enough. It was different from her usual. Usually they were watching or someone was watching them. But this time they were alone, together. Typical Mills & Boon crap. Prince Mark and Princess Daphne on the beach at his estate in Tuscany. 'Flashy sparkles splashing in the air.' Fucking hell. Her head was full of so much crap now. This cloying weepy hormonal sentimentality. Had she read it somewhere before, some pulp novel, some short story in *Cosmo*? Wasn't there something even worse than that? That deep down she had some kind of romantic ideal, planted by God knows which weeping old relative or what B-movie. Or even worse than that. She had to face up to this thing. It was not part of her usually cynical repertoire but had come from somewhere deeper. This was an almost natural idea. Was maybe how she really felt. To make love to a man in nature. To feel his virility. To have his seed inside you.

Lying beside him as he fell asleep. He slept for so long now. He denied it of course, but she was sure he spent most of the day sleeping. Was depressed, clinically. She would abort. It was definite now. Abort and after that she would swing. Swing till they had reached the limit of the arc. Just to prove to herself that sex was sex and nothing more and that there was nothing more. Just to get all this out of her system. This Mills & Boon sparkly seawater. As he drifted off to sleep she whispered in a voice she was sure he couldn't hear that she was sorry. She didn't have a problem with the divorce papers, or work or anything. She kissed his neck. Stroked his shoulders. She wasn't ready to give up on swinging just yet she said. She had to find her own limits she said. She was not willing to admit that they were just this couple in the West End who were going to have a child. There had to be something more. Could he help her please. Do it, just for her. She had something she had to work out she said. A big question for her, for them both, and they had to answer it together. Tomorrow she would hear back from this woman called Dolly, this old woman, who could be the answer.

David was fast asleep, and so she held him and told him that she wished she was already an old woman like Dolly, so that she could curl up with him like this every night, the best years of life behind them, like an old retired couple, impotent together, only a few years left to live. Desire spent. Just cuddling. She held his dick in her hand and its softness reassured her as sleep finally came.

*   *   *

He could tell by her face that she wasn't happy. Hannah, as she left. There was no talk about why he'd failed to show at the solicitors. Why he'd put off signing the papers. And he felt cheap for having done that. Cancelling at the last minute, last Thursday, with a text message. V BUSY. SORRY. DO THIS NEXT WEEK? But of course he hadn't been busy. Had spent the whole day in bed instead. Couldn't face the solicitors. His signature on the page.

Sitting beside Amy on her bed now. Words. Aeroplane, friends, house. Tonight David could barely hold his concentration, felt he wasn't giving his child enough. He'd been losing sleep over the papers all week. Anxious. So much so that on the way here tonight he'd stopped off at the corner shop to buy a half of vodka. Taken a slug of it even before he'd arrived at the house. Hannah had left quickly with hardly a word. Dressed up again. Stunning. While Amy had been in the bath, he'd poured another shot into a teacup. Filled it up with Ribena and a little water and ran over what he would say to Hannah later about the papers. He didn't even know why he was so scared of signing them.

As he kissed Amy goodnight he hoped she wouldn't smell the alcohol on his breath.

'Another story, a story!'

'No.' His strong, responsible voice that made him feel weaker with every word. 'Sleepy time, sleep.'

Back in the kitchen after she'd drifted off. The kitchen-sink drama. Struggling to think of a movie that had a scene like this. Devotion, adultery, reconciliation without punishment. Couldn't think of a single one. Too implausible even for Hollywood. A double shot, no more Ribena. Orange juice instead. The vodka wasn't calming him like he'd hoped. And after three more shots, when it was finished, he started in on some of the sherry she kept for cooking. He anticipated that she would be late again tonight, and probably a little drunk, like last time, so it was a shock when he heard her keys in the front door. Two hours early. He got to his feet. She was walking towards him quickly. Fragments of ritual small talk. God, look at her, in that dress. Talk to her.

'She went down at about eight, was really tired!'

She seemed to have no patience for talking. Her hand was in her bag and she was trying to pull something out. The effort unbalanced her and she went over on her heels. Automatically his hands shot out to catch her. But she stabilised herself on the table and his hands were left hovering awkwardly in space. She set something down on the table with a thud. Stolichnaya. Before he could meet her eye she was in the kitchen tinkling around with glasses. A glimpse of her legs.

'Look, I'm sorry about last week. I was really busy and . . .'

But there she was. Two large glasses with ice and a drunken smile.

'Could you?' she said. 'You mind?'

He stared at her. 'Could I . . . could I what?'

She laughed and indicated the bottle. 'You know I'm no good with lids.'

So they were to get drunk together and she would cross-examine him about the divorce papers. She'd had a few already, but had this lucid clarity in her eyes, as she was watching him. So like Alice when drunk. It scared him. But her gaze, like a touch, unlike Alice's touch. On his hands, his arms, his shoulders. Measuring him, reassessing, it seemed. She started undoing her heels. This power, this game of looks. He couldn't help but engage. The heels, so different from the flat-soled shoes she wore during pregnancy and after. Her cleavage as she leaned over. A little moan as she massaged her feet. She had clumsy feet, she'd always said, for a woman, but look at her. She was smiling to herself. She must have known he was watching. Teasing him perhaps, giving him a glimpse of what he'd thrown away.

The seal cracked open in his hand. He was about to

say 'The papers', but she spoke first. 'Sorry, there're no mixers,' and nodded for him to pour. He felt like a teenager with an older woman. Dustin Hoffman. Mrs Robinson. Yes, she had aged since he'd left her but had become even more beautiful. And he, he'd become like a kid, in so many ways, regressing.

He poured two small shots.

'Cheers,' she said.

Cheers to what? To his abandonment of his family? To separation and antidepressants and counselling and nights crying yourself to sleep like a child: To what? Jesus. Had she some solicitor hiding somewhere? Was the door-bell going to ring and he'd walk in with a witness? Sign here and here. She was holding up her glass to toast him. He couldn't lift his, but she clinked it anyway.

'So, yes, I was going to sign them, and I mean I will, if we could arrange another time in the week and—'

'Can't you just chill?'

Not the kind of words she usually used. She started giggling. Some joke. Chilled vodka perhaps. Look at her. Drunk, flirtatious, angry. Sexy when angry. He'd never seen that in her before. Ran away before her anger came. Almost two years postponing this night.

Sipping her vodka. Look at her. My old wife in our old kitchen, my ex-wife, my dull ex-wife, my ex-dull wife who is now beautiful. Yes, if she wants, I will touch her. We'll go to bed. Or fuck right here on the table. And I will be hard for her. I won't have a problem getting hard, because it was her, the aftermath of her, that was to blame. I'll be hard for her, because of her anger and mine. We'll fuck and not talk, and we won't sign the papers. Just keep seeing each other. I'll babysit twice a week and instead she'll stay in, and we'll fuck behind Alice's back. Fuck like strangers. Because now we are strangers. Utterly strange to each other.

He set down his glass and thought about reaching for
her knee. His hand starting to enact the movement
towards.

'I heard about your job,' she said. He pulled his hand
back. Relieved in some way. She'd want to know what
guarantees of income he could give her. Part of the
divorce would be a financial settlement. No more discre-
tionary amounts. It would all be in writing.

'Well, I'm looking for work. To be honest I don't really
care what I do. I thought maybe consultancy or any old
nine-to-five really. Just to make some money. There's a
little in the severance package but I need to get a loan
probably, just to make sure you get something once a
month till—'

'Alice isn't worried?'

'No, no . . . we've talked about the whole thing, in
fact.' But why was she talking about Alice? It was the
first time she'd ever mentioned her. By name. He'd never
said her name. She'd heard about Alice through her
friends, no doubt. They'd been spotted together around
town and Hannah had done her research.

Clever. Get him talking about Alice, get him finally
to confess. OK. So what would he have to say? It was
clear now. All week pussyfooting around it but what he'd
say – to be honest I think we need more time. I do. I
mean everything's in the air right now and if we could
just wait till I get a job and take a long hard look at
whether this is best for you and me and for Amy. Because
we could. If you think it's possible. Consider at least the
possibility of some kind of reconciliation. I mean an
agreement at least because divorce seems so final and . . .

'As long as you're both happy,' she said.

'Yes, actually, I suppose we are.'

So she was looking for the evidence, not of what went

wrong with them, but of what was going wrong with Alice. Looking for the crack. Just to let him know that she knew he'd given her up for something unstable. The look on her face now, it made him angry. She wanted him to tell her about Alice.

'Look, I don't know what Alice has got to do with this.'

His anger. She knew how to play it. Those clever tricks of hers. Provoking it. Knowing that as soon as it had abated he'd say sorry. Sorry. Feel so guilty that he'd do or say anything to make it up to her. Sign here please.

'I'm just . . . sorry if I'm intruding,' she said and stared at him over the top of her glass as she sipped.

How wonderfully civilised of her. One of the reasons he left her in the first place. Along with the hundred others he'd written down on some list that he'd long since lost. Slowly, she poured another shot for herself, nodded in his direction. Refill?

Fuck, just go now. Go and don't explain. Stand up. Enough is enough. Stand up. Shout – Shut up. Shout – Damn you, fuck you. Walk out on her again. Show her that she had no monopoly on anger, that she was to blame too. Walk out now. No matter what the repercussions. Access denied to child. Fine. Restraining order. Fine. Fuck it. Anything better than this. Suffering these self-righteous questions of hers. Bring out your solicitor right now. I'll sign. Forget the small print. Sign over every-thing if it makes you happy. He got to his feet but then he noticed. A slight repeated twitch of her shoulder. Her head lowered. Was she laughing at him? At these well-worn routines. Laughing at how horribly predictable it was to play games with each other. No, not laughter. She was crying.

Oh baby, please, don't cry please, not now, please.

Nearly two years and we've hidden our tears, please don't cry. Jesus, please. These things thought not said.

Four and a half feet away on the other side of the Habitat table. Her head lowered. Her hand reaching across. A shiver through him.

Trapped there, sitting, staring. Her hand is on mine he said to himself. Nearly two years without feeling that hand. Her fingers curling round his and squeezing. She still couldn't show her face. He lowered his head, not to hide tears because there were none. How could she be like this and still he felt so little, felt nothing but confusion. To have the clarity of an uncompromised emotion for once. She needed him to cry. So he tried, tried to think back to that time just before he left, to force the tears on, but even then it had been the same. The actor, the bad actor, in the crying scene, trying to feel something other than the self-conscious barrier between him and his emotions.

There they were, heads bowed, unable to look at each other, her tears shaking her body, him gripping her hand trying to force the tears to come, thumbs circling each other's thumbs. Suddenly her whole body started jerking. He'd have to get up and go to her side of the table, hold her. Damn her, look at her, she's crying and you can't. You have to. You do. Get up and hold her tight. Sink so deep into the moment that the tears will finally come. Make yourself cry, that is what she needs you to do, to cry like you never could together. Remember, remember how it's done. Stanislavski. Recall an image of childhood trauma or loss. A dead pet, a grandparent. A more recent trauma. The point of the break. Put yourself there. She still loves me, she's still holding out for me. Sorry, sorry, sorry. No. Guilt was no good for tears. Further back then. Picture how much you once loved her, and you did, you really did. Recall that trip to Sweden, in the boat together, the fjords, remember that day you made love on the beach, remember that night you conceived Amy.

He was up on his feet and holding her as her body shook in his arms. If they had been able to cry together, back then, then maybe he would never have left. Tears with Alice came so easily, were thoughtless, wordless. You must cry. Push it further. Picture the end of Alice. The scenario, that Alice had just been some kind of way of postponing all this, this end, and now that it was about to happen. Admit it, you want to come back. Be a real father again. Please, please take me back. Everything, everything else, failure, ego, anger, it was all exhausted now. Just please, take me back.

'David,' she said. 'I'm sorry.'

He was so close. The idea was there. Tragic. That he still loved her.

'Look at us,' she said. 'God, look at us.'

Then she was laughing and he was thrown. Damn. Her laughing through the tears, as if she felt there was, for once, a real connection.

'David,' she said. 'David. This is hard but . . .'

He squeezed her hand, lowered his head. Let us cry together. Please God, please and maybe I will believe the things I tell myself. Maybe I do love her, just help me here, please, make me cry.

'I hope you're happy with Alice because . . . because I've been seeing someone too.'

He let go of her hand. Seconds of not knowing what to do. That salt taste rising in his mouth that was not tears.

'God,' he said. 'Good,' he said. 'Great.' He wanted to pull his hand away but she was still gripping it.

'Yes, it is. Really. But I want you to be happy too.'

'I am though. Really. I am really. Fine. We are.'

Then she explained how this man, she'd known him at university, before, what – maybe five years before she'd ever met him, this shy guy and he'd been obsessed with her for so long, and she'd always found that kind of unattractive. But how now he'd become this different person. And he'd always said she was special. And how she'd told him she was scared of any kind of commitment now and she wasn't sure how she felt and told him that too. But love was . . . She wasn't sure that she loved him but she thought now that maybe it was something you had to learn to do and. And how she'd married him, you, David, without ever really thinking about love and how she felt in so many ways that it had all just been an act and was sorry for that now, so sorry. And how they had been dating now, her and the other guy, three months and it really felt like something and she was so sorry for keeping it a secret from him. And how he'd been divorced too, and they'd lost a child, and how just being with him had helped her put it all in perspective and she'd finally learned how to forgive.

But he was not ready to be forgiven, still didn't know what he was supposed to be forgiven for, and it would take so much longer, so much longer and this was so final.

And his name was Tom and he was an architect and she hoped that things would work out for him and Alice because she just wanted them both to be happy with other people, because Amy could tell when they weren't happy and.

And then her tears started again and he was conscious of the fact that he was still standing there. Sorry sorry, he kept saying. His hand hovering over her head.

And he did feel something now. Now that she had talked of this other man. And he wanted to lean down and kiss her. For that kiss to lead them to their feet, through the corridor they'd painted together, past the old prints they'd bought together, to the bedroom and the antique bed they'd bought together. To make love, still kissing each other like they'd long since forgotten how to, and for him to be hard for her and for them to laugh and cry and hold each other. And to be woken in the morning so early and exhausted, after a night of waking and making love again and again, by their daughter pulling at the covers. Shouting, Daddy, Daddy play with me. And for them to have breakfast with Amy and to find a discreet moment for the kiss to start again. But the longer he held her the more distant she seemed. He couldn't stop picturing it, her happy with this other man. This Tom. Seeing this Tom in the play park with Amy. Teaching her how to ride her bike. Tucking her in at night. Teaching her new words. See-saw, family, Christmas. The meaning of words.

Tears were close. He could force them out. But then it came to him. That the reason he wanted to cry now was nothing to do with love. This feeling, this hot hard needy feeling. It had a name – jealousy. Amy will have a new man she calls Daddy. Yes it was. Furious, murderous jealousy.

He kissed Hannah gently on the forehead, told her he'd see Amy on Monday between three and five and walked silently to the door.

*   *   *

She was just as she was before he left. Still on swinging-paradise. She wanted to show him this message she'd got from this woman called Dolly.

Experienced Big Beautiful Bi-fem. Choice of partners avail. Face + dick-pics essential. No age/race limits. Love cock, all shapes + sizes. Men with problems welcome. No timewasters pleez. Hotels + weekdays only.

'Come on,' he said. 'Really.'

'Really, what?'

'I thought we were done with this shit.'

'Are we? We haven't talked about it.'

'C'mon. It's sick. Hotels. Weekdays. It's pretty clear.'

'What?'

'It's an affair. You spend the weekend with your kids. It's pretty fucking clear. Hotels. Weekdays. Fuck. They're both committing adultery.'

'Oh, so that's suddenly an issue?'

'Yes, actually. It is.'

'You're being weird. In fact recently.'

'Recently what?'

'Seriously. Don't think I haven't thought about it. It's so obvious, that you do.'

'What?'

'That you do still have feelings for . . .'

'What? What the fuck?'

'Forget it, all of it.'

'No, what the fuck is this?'

'Your ex.'

'You can't even say her name.'

'Hannah. Ha-fucking-Nah.'

'Christ.'

'You could at least be honest with me.'

'Fuck! I can't believe you're even looking at all this shit again. Can't you just turn it off and—'

'You're avoiding the question.'

'I mean, after last time, fucking Jesus.'

'If you do, it's understandable. You just have to be honest with me.'

'So now all of a sudden you're actually interested in my marriage?'

'Why did you hide them from me?'

'Like it's some kind of sick revenge of yours, because of your mother or whatever. You know this whole swinging thing, it's—'

'I found them.'

'I mean look at you. Fuck, I mean. Hotels and swingers and fuck!'

'Your divorce papers.'

'What? So now you're going through my things?'

'Two weeks ago. She asked you to sign them. That was the date.'

'Come on, fuck, really!'

'No, fuck you, and why the fuck haven't you signed them?'

'Will you stop swearing?'

'Oh so now swearing is offensive. You make me laugh. Ha ha ha ha.'

'So what? This big interest in my family suddenly. Like, like, you've never even met them. Never even expressed any kind of interest in—'

'I do, I have.'

'No, no. You barely even know what Amy looks like, you don't even want to see photos. And she's my daughter for fuck's sake. She is my daughter. My family.'

*   *   *

After six weeks the spinal cord connects with the cerebral cortex. The foetus develops limbs, after eight weeks, fingers and toes. There is no possible measurement of the development of consciousness, but after ten weeks,

discernible human characteristics appear. Thumb
sucking, eye motion, independent limb movement.

It varied across cultures. That was what the net research
told her at her PC at work. There were different times,
timings, on when it was acceptable to abort. Ten, twelve
weeks. She should have seen a doctor, got the scan. She
reckoned the date of conception was that night with the
Gordons. So she was just over six weeks in. 'Distinct
genetically determined facial characteristics develop after
eight weeks.'

To have an early scan, to see the ghost imprint of the
foetal face. David's high forehead, her long fingers. She
couldn't do it.

From Google at work she got the name and number
of the clinic. From her desk overlooking the researchers,
in a private moment, she dialled the number. She set
the date. No, there was no need for an interview or
counselling, yes, sorry, she'd made up her mind already.
Yes, she was aware of how traumatic this could be, no
she wasn't in a relationship and no partner would be
present. A mistake, that was all it was. Her and David.
How could they progress without undoing the mistake?
A woman's right to choose but there was no choice.
Choose to have a choice. After this she would never be
able to have a child again. She would be as impotent as
him. It made some kind of sense. They could free sex
from its biological imperative. She would have the time
required to help him. She was not going to become his
ex-wife. Not going to have a child he would abandon.
Better to abandon the possibility of having a child than
lose him. Better to cure him than to pass your sickness
onto another generation.

Tuesday 29 September. Vacuum extraction. Fifteen

days' time. Until then, every possibility would have to be explored. Every single fucking one.

*   *   *

It was revenge. That was all it could have been. He'd been letting it slide, these past few weeks. Letting her decide on everything, but when it came to this. This old woman, this monster, this Dolly. He'd begged her to stop but she'd insisted.

'So what have you been doing all week?' Alice had said.

She'd printed out all of Dolly's pics and pinned them up in the kitchen. Dolly was in a garden, in the back seat of a car, on a hotel-room floor and a kitchen table. Her tits, pussy, ass, with fingers, tongues, dildos, butt plugs and dicks, but in the only shot of her face she had been wearing some kind of Venetian party mask, so there was no real way of identifying her in the bar. What the fuck was he even doing there? Dolly. What was that about? Dolly Parton? Dolly the sheep. Some genetic accident. Blow-up Dolly. Probably all of the above. David reckoned her real name was something like Maggie and that she came from some pox-ridden housing scheme. Hoped to hell she did in fact. Hoped she would be so utterly repulsive that Alice would call it off.

Sitting next to Alice on the window seats for the last fifteen minutes. Sipping his cheap wine, reluctantly scanning the passers-by struggling to find a way of ending this without ending what little was left with Alice. Five minutes ago a BMW had stopped at the lights. A woman in her fifties looked up at them and when the lights changed she drove off. Must have been her. She'd taken one look at them and decided against it. Probably noticed how agitated they seemed. And they were. David noticed that Alice kept fiddling with her suspender belt through her skirt. She was trying to force a smile. God, this whole thing was a ridiculous inversion of their first encounter. She was doing this to spite him. All he wanted to say was 'I want this to stop. We're taking this no further.' But as he knew, Alice always took opposition as provocation.

They wouldn't show, that would be ideal. He and Alice would leave after twenty. No, better in fact to stretch the time out. Sit there and force it home to Alice that they'd been played for fools. Tell her how this whole thing was just an escape from the sad lives people led, and they should go home and confront what little they had left of a life.

'Safety word "babysitting",' she said, like he'd said it to her. 'You say it, go to the toilet and I tell them it's not for us. OK, Daddy? OK.' He checked his mobile and confirmed that Dolly was twenty minutes late and had not sent a message. Alice had just finished her drink. He'd hardly touched his.

He scanned the bar again, yes they had been stood up. No one else had entered since they'd come in. Horrible place. Fake teak, wrought iron in the Mackintosh style and leather sofas. Three lads at the bar, one of them with a Rangers top. A grim-looking thirties couple at a table holding hands, some old hippie with her bored-looking son, something that looked like an all-girl office party in need of a man, two twentysomething couples, reclining on the leather sofa at the back, doing some poor Glaswegian imitation of an episode of *Friends*. Thankfully no one who looked like them could ever have had gang bangs and double penetration. He looked over at Alice again. She was becoming restless. Checking her mobile. Losing confidence. Good.

Her mobile rang. She hello'd, nodded, covered the mouthpiece, whispered.

'It's her.'

David tried to read her face as she listened. Aha. Aha. She burst into laughter. Something flashed across her face as she leaned out to gaze over his shoulder. She placed a hand on his knee, then waved into the back. He turned just in time to see the old hippie and her son lowering their hands. Jesus Christ! Alice shut the phone.

'That's her. Says you're cute.' Alice got to her feet with her empty glass.

'Fuck, not them,' he said.

'Cute, but nervous-looking, she said.' Alice kissed his cheek. 'C'mon, be a laugh if nothing else.' Just like he'd said to her on their first encounter.

Then Alice was off, walking towards them. God, look at the old hippie. Long hair tied in a bun, glasses on top of her head, some kind of Palestinian-looking pashmina thing, heavy knit Arran cardigan with pendulous no doubt bra-less breasts dangling to her knees beneath it all. There was no way, absolutely no way, anything sexual could happen with this relic and the young man who, it was now certain, was not her son.

He tried to make eye contact with Alice, to say 'No, c'mon, I'm going' but she was already on her way. He called out after her.

'A fag, two minutes.'

As he turned the corner and looked back inside he glimpsed Alice shaking hands with them. Head thrown back in what could only be laughter.

Outside. Jesus. Why would an old hippie be into this? What had fist-fucking got to do with love and peace? Drugs maybe, head frazzled by LSD. Some weird corruption of the concept of free love. Trying to relive

Woodstock in her menopause in the suburbs. Sad, sad. Probably on a couple of big alimony settlements to top up her pension. Is into nine-hour tantric sex sessions and calls her clit a chakra. Feels the need to convert others to her own causeless cause. Mother Earth. Yup. Sad. OK, they'd do the chit-chat, get away ASAP. In a way it was the perfect end to all this. The whole thing would be so awful Alice would never want to do it again.

The counter at the corner shop – Marlboro Lights, please. What the hell was Alice thinking? Why deliberately pick an older woman in the first place? She'd said it was because the ad had the word 'experienced' and they needed to learn more, but he had a sneaking suspicion that this whole thing for Alice was some weird psychotherapy game. She'd said that she was well aware that he'd coerced her into doing this the first time, and so he owed her one. Clever that, how she'd used his guilt to push on further. But why the hell did she want this? With them.

He headed back inside, fully intending to cut this as short as possible. They were sitting together now. Alice, Mother Earth and Toyboy. He really did look young enough to be her son. But something about him. His bleached blond number-two haircut, distressed designer denims and tight T-shirt suggested he'd been hired for the day. Think, think. You are on a desert island, four of you. Tarpaulin, flares, a mirror, vodka. Pick the vodka. David headed for the bar. Stopped short. No, it would be rude to buy a drink only for himself and Alice. And Alice would take it as a sign that he wanted to leave and then make him stay just to spite him. OK, so best to do the hellos, buy a round. Get the whole thing over and done with.

He headed to their sofa. Suddenly the old hippie was up. Arms out and reaching to hug him. He leaned in so as not to embarrass Alice. He could feel his shoulders tensing under the old woman's touch.

'David, how are you?'

She'd called him David. Jesus, Alice had given their real names.

'Drinks?' he muttered.

The young stud was on his feet. Shake. 'Darren, pint of Stella.'

Another Sauvignon Blanc for Alice. A Lagavulin for Mother Earth. At the bar he ran over things to say. He'd have to do some minimal small talk then throw in the safety word for Alice. Some story about how he's just had a call from the ex-wife and had to do some babysitting. I repeat, 'Babysitting, Alice.' Then she'd take his cue and he'd apologise and promise to meet them again some other time.

Carrying the drinks back to their sofa. Old Mother Earth was holding Alice's hand. The toyboy was leafing through *GQ*.

'Just got a text from Hannah,' he said, setting down the drinks.

But Mother Earth and Alice were deeply engrossed in some debate on modern culture. Mother Earth turned to him suddenly. 'David. Alice has been telling me all about you.'

'Really?'

'I used to be a performer myself.'

That the old dear could imagine they had something in common. She'd been one of the three witches in *Macbeth* no doubt.

'Karaoke,' she said.

'Well, you know what they say, all the world's a—'

'A stage,' she interrupted, laughing and turning to Alice. 'Oh he's trouble, I can see that already.'

Mother Earth had placed one hand on his knee. He felt like gagging. Tried to deflect attention from himself by turning to the toyboy. Conversation. Anything. What? Music? Sport? The guy, thankfully, seemed to have little interest in talking. Obviously a rent boy. David sat and watched as Alice and Mother Earth laughed and whispered and touched each other's hands and knees. Waiting for a gap in the conversation so he could finish his little lie about Hannah and babysitting. But the old witch was jabbering.

'Folk who go to nightclubs. I mean, it's so sad. All that drunken messing about. Join a swingers' site and everyone knows what they want.'

Why were they even here? Hadn't Alice learned after last time? What would it take for her to accept? To give up. Thankfully they'd hit rock bottom with Dolly. Hallelujah. After a drink, Alice would, could only give all this up.

But my God the old witch could talk. Like she'd just been released after thirty years in solitary. David leaned back and looked round the bar. They must have looked like two average couples having an average chat. Weirder still. They probably looked like a family. Granny, daughter, her husband and their nephew. Dolly's voice was just that little bit too loud though. David noticed that the couple at the next table were eavesdropping. Every time he looked over at them they turned their heads away and started whispering. Mother Earth was still jabbering on. Maybe she'd offend someone and they'd have to leave. Good.

'Really, it's a wonderful thing. People my age get so twisted and cynical. Think they've seen it all. But last week. You wouldn't have believed it.'

Alice was engrossed. Give the witch enough rope,

thought David. Sit back and wait. Dolly turned to the toyboy.

'What did they call themselves, sweetie?'

Without lifting his head from *GQ* Toyboy said, 'Trekkies.'

'As in *Star Trek*?' giggled Alice. Trekkies, this was pathetic.

'Aha, he was a, what do you call them?' asked Dolly. 'Big foreheads.'

'Klingon,' said the toyboy.

Jesus, thought David, the old crow has fucked all of humanity and is now having to start in on aliens. In a matter of nanoseconds Alice will see how sad this is.

'Masks and everything, and she was that gorgeous black girl, the one with the thing in her ear and the beautiful figure.'

'Uhuru, Lieutenant Uhuru. First on-screen interracial kiss. Her and Kirk. James T.' said the toy.

Alice had started that big uncontrollable laugh of her. Wait for it, wait for it David told himself. So Uhuru and the Klingons smeared each other with shit, they stuck laser guns in each other's mouths.

Dolly leaned in and lowered her voice. 'They had costumes for us and everything. A whole scene worked out. It was hard not to laugh but they took it all very seriously and it was really, quite surprisingly exciting.'

Alice's laugh was drawing attention to their table. She could barely get the words out. David tried to come up with his most sarcastic line.

'So what did they have? Phasers on stun?'

It had backfired, the old hag had thought he was interested and Alice had reached to touch his knee.

'Oh yes, the whole thing,' laughed Dolly. 'She'd turned her thingy into some kind of vibrator. Yes, stunning, really.'

Alice gripped his hand tight. In spite of himself David couldn't help but laugh a little. Fuck, it was laughable. And Dolly was off. Her voice so loud in such a public place.

'First the Klingon tied up Uhuru and tortured her and then we had to come in and set her free and we took turns torturing him. It was quite literally out of this world.'

David shook his head. OK, the old hag was repulsive but it had been a good punchline. 'And this was where, in their living room?'

'Oh no, no they had this basement all kitted out with silver paper and lights and everything. The whole thing was highly creative.'

David told himself he wouldn't respond, but he was always a sucker for a gag. 'To boldly. To boldly go where no man has gone before.'

Dolly exploded in laughter. Her huge breasts jiggling about. Even the toyboy set down his magazine and started snorting. Alice was doubled over. Squeezing his hand, almost thanking him it seemed.

'Oh, I think he'd had a few bold men in there before,' said Dolly.

David heard his own laughter fill the room, chastened himself and decided it was time to burst the bubble and say something so they could get away. But Alice was still laughing. She'd needed a good laugh for a long time. Let her have her laugh. Then whisper the safety word to her and go.

David looked at their faces. Dolly smiling at them with almost maternal warmth. The toyboy putting his hand on the old woman's knee. Disgusting. He was about to whisper to Alice, but Dolly got there before him.

'What's your safety word?'

'Well, it's kind of babysitter,' said Alice.

'Do you have kids?'

'No,' said Alice.

'Yes,' David interjected.

'Not together. David does.'

'Well,' said Dolly, 'why don't we just leave it here for today? I think you're both lovely and we'd love to see you again, but why don't you just take your time and have a wee think about it all.'

Thank fuck, he thought and was already nodding and reaching for his coat, but Alice leaned forward and whispered to Dolly. Dolly beamed a huge smile. She had lipstick on her teeth, the way his grandmother used to.

'Well, if it's OK with David. David?'

'What?'

'The Marriott, if that's OK with you.'

*   *   *

In the event of an emergency landing on water, ladies please remove your heels before making your way to the nearest emergency exit. There had to be an exit before the cab arrived at the hotel. He was sitting with his back to the driver while Alice was squashed between the other two in the back seat. He could now see that under her baggy hippie trousers Dolly was wearing fishnets. Like that whore in the car park. God she could talk the hind legs off a . . . probably had the hind legs of a donkey – in fishnets.

'Questions, questions. I know, but it's best if we get this out of the way. If we don't know the limits we can't have trust and if we don't have trust . . . well, you can imagine.'

The taxi rolled down Great Western Road.

'Are either of you jealous types?'

Yes, thought David. You have no idea. Alice shook her head.

'Good, because, newbies often think they can cope with this but when it comes down to it and they see their partner getting spit-roasted they get jealous and it can turn nasty.'

'Spit-roasted?' laughed Alice, reaching for his hand.

'You know.' And Dolly made some crude hand sign to represent a piece of meat being skewered from both ends. God, she was obscene. Obese. Obstetric.

'Really? So you've . . .' asked Alice, curling her fingers through his.

'Oh darling, you wouldn't believe. I'd say that a lot of couples fantasise about this but never make it past their first experience. It can either make your love stronger or bring out conflicts in your relationship. If you have problems, this'll only make them worse.'

How right you are, you walking corpse. If he could only get Alice to really listen to what Dolly was saying. There could be an out there. He looked straight at her, willing her to turn. Please Alice, just look at me.

'We have a strong relationship,' said Alice. Circling his thumb with hers.

'Good,' said Dolly. 'I could tell.'

The old woman's hand on his, her other on Alice's, on top of his. The old corpse must have sensed his tension. The toyboy was sitting silently smiling to himself. He'd done this before. How much did he charge? One, two hundred an hour?

'OK, next question,' said Dolly.

David stared at the old fossil's hand as she lifted it from Alice's and placed it on the toyboy's crotch. He looked up at Alice. This change in her. Like Hannah, she'd become stronger. He tried to make his eyes tell her

no, please, stop now! But she seemed to be almost deliberately ignoring him.

'Condoms?' the old hippie asked Alice.

'Of course.'

'Bondage?'

'No, I don't think so. Not yet anyway.'

'Girl on girl?'

'Well . . .'

'First time?'

'Well, in college, a bit, so no, I guess. OK. Yeah, whatever.'

David stared out of the window. They were heading
towards Cowcaddens, the flyover, the high-rise housing
schemes of Maryhill. Look at it. The greyness of
Glasgow. Two teenage girls pushing prams, an old lady,
stooped over with Tesco bags. The grey people, heads
bowed staring at the grey beneath their feet. Going home
to their grey tower blocks. The ones the council put little
red Japanese roofs on to make them look more cheery.
The old hippie. Colourful at least. But weren't people
like her just a temporary distraction in a city like this?
All this exoticism which only made the grey greyer. How
far was Alice willing to go to test his impotence? He
should have moved with her to America last year. But
Alice would never have done it. She found the multi-
colours of America artificial. Preferred the greyness of
Glasgow because it was more real. But was this real?
Sitting in this taxi with an old hippie and a toyboy, going
to fuck in some global chain hotel. Escape. If you are
seated next to the escape hatch please read the instructions on what to do in case of an emergency.

'David?' Dolly.

'Sorry?'

'Man on man?'

David looked at Alice. She was blushing. Dolly smiled. 'Sweetie. Are you bi, orally, anally or just a little curious?'

'No, neither. Not at all, no.'

'OK,' she said, turning back to Alice, 'We'll start. You watch and then we'll see where it goes. OK?'

There was a slight pause, enough for him to interject, but he still hadn't worked out what to say. Nothing left but his pathetic strategies. Alice, please, I have a headache. They were approaching the TV station, the hotel was just beyond it. He wanted to say Alice, Alice. Just to say her name to try to bring her round. But Dolly spoke first.

'Toys?'

'Dunno,' said Alice.

'I love toys, got lots in my bag.'

'OK then.'

'Two girls one man?'

'Uh. OK.'

'Great. Eat or be eaten? You prefer which?'

The taxi passed by the TV station and headed towards the hotel. Alice. Just say her name, force her to turn. She was really going to make him do this. Confrontation never worked with Alice but it was all that was left. Enough. Enough.

'Alice,' David blurted out, 'seriously.' He leaned in and whispered. 'I have a real problem with this.'

'What is it, darlings?' Dolly took Alice's hand and placed it on the toyboy's bulge. Her hand on top holding it in place. 'Speak now or forever hold your piece.'

Not funny. The toyboy sniggered. Alice lowered her voice. 'Well, David sometimes has this problem with . . .'

No, no that was not what he meant at all.

'Oh, you just leave that to me,' said Dolly, as she went into her bag.

She pulled out a small plastic bag with blue diamond-shaped pills.

'Mother's little helper,' said Dolly and passed one to the toyboy and one to David.

He sensed that Alice and Dolly had some secret that they weren't letting him in on. Maybe it was just paranoia. They turned off and entered the darkness of the hotel's underground car park.

* * *

He looked so nervous. She'd picked Dolly precisely because she had claimed she was experienced in men's problems, and they had very discreetly discussed David's problem when David popped out for a fag. Dolly's conclusion had only confirmed what she'd suspected now for a while.

If they survived today, then she would tell him about the pregnancy. If this broke them, then it would be final. The appointment at the family-planning clinic was set.

The reception desk. She felt like taking David to one side and having a private moment with him. Just to reassure him, tell him this had to be done. The whole thing would be unbearable if he was going to be moody like this. If only he knew how much was resting on it.

The smiling receptionist. Alice went into her wallet to pull out her credit card but Dolly insisted that this was her treat. It was funny, the staff seemed to have no problem with the idea that four people were about to share a hotel room.

'Pardon the pun,' Dolly giggled to Alice. 'But I do come here a lot.'

Why did this woman do this to her? She made her crease with laughter but then there would be these seconds just after, looking at her, when Alice didn't like

to admit what she felt. That there was actually something about the old woman that reminded her of her
mother. The raucous humour maybe. The big buxom
body. Or maybe the fact that she had a younger lover.
She'd have to stop thinking like that. The whole thing
would be impossible if she couldn't get her mother's
image out of her head.

As Dolly marched them off towards the elevator Alice
took David's hand and gave it a big squeeze. 'We need
to do this. OK, Daddy? Trust me.'

Crammed into the tiny space together. Awkward. An
elevator and four people who knew they were all about
to have sex together. Dolly was French kissing the guy
and pawing at his crotch and only making things worse.
Alice felt like clearing her throat. Dolly must have sensed
her anxiety. She pulled away, laughing.

'Well,' she giggled, 'pardon the pun, but you're only
as old as the man you feel.'

Alice found herself laughing again. She put her hand
behind her and stroked David's inner thigh. He was tense.
She watched the numbers going up.

'Must admit I feel a lot younger than I did in my
forties,' said Dolly. 'You know, the whole wifey thing.
Cooking, cleaning, shopping, going back to work knackered all the time. My husband, sorry my third, is really
happy that I'm doing this now. His name's Leo by the
way, you have to meet him sometime.'

'Yeah, no,' said Alice. She was thinking about David
and his marriage and his blockage, but instead she said,
'I know what you mean, my mother was . . .' She shouldn't
have said that, comparing Dolly to her mother. But Dolly
just smiled. 'I mean, she had lots of different men, but
she was never happy. No, she was never happy.' She
worried that David would take it the wrong way.

Dolly took her hand. 'Women don't know the power they have. A woman can be satisfied ten times over. We're polyamorous by nature. We have simply too much love to give to keep it all to one man. You ever ejaculate?'

Alice laughed. 'Well, can't say I've noticed.' Floor three. She was worried that the closer they got, the more anxious David was becoming.

'If you had, you would have known. Men try to say it's just urine, but, pardon the pun, you can taste the difference. When it happens there's this incredible release of energy and everyone in the room feels it. Isn't that right, sweetie?'

The guy nodded his head. Funny, thought Alice, he's exactly the kind of man I've always despised. A male bimbo. A bimboy. But, as me and Dolly agreed earlier when David left the bar – he's for David, not for me.

The doors were opening and Dolly was leading the bimboy out by the hand. David wasn't moving. Alice reached back for his hand. The door started closing. She stuck her foot in it and turned to him. The pressure in his hand, the look in his eyes, holding her back, like a question to which there could only be one answer.

'I do,' she said. 'I mean, not just think that we should do this, but I mean, we should because I do.' She went up on her tippy-toes and kissed his cheek. 'I do love you, Daddy.'

There was something there, between them, small and sticking in his hand.

'Viagra,' was all he said as she watched him put the pill on his tongue.

*   *   *

Damn, it was so weird. Staring at the dado rail and having an erection. Staring at the TV and having an erection. Staring at little pots of UHT milk and having an erection. Staring at your erection and wondering why the hell you had an erection. Viagra. The old woman was in the bathroom with her bag and was singing. Some Billie Holiday number. He wanted to turn to Alice and tell her. Look I'm really sorry but I hate Billie Holiday and I hate UHT milk and this erection that I have no reason for having. It was weird, to feel hard but not aroused. To be staring at the floor and think, I am aroused by the carpet. Alice and the toy boy looked at his erection and Alice started some critique of Western culture and the way in which it made you feel turned on by things you despised. Give them all a pill before they voted. Get them turned on to voting. Massive turnout. Six million in the UK on Viagra. Same as the population of Scotland. Independence, yeah. Go to war, fucking right. Pathetic. OK, converse. Ignore the damn thing alive in your pants. The thing that was chemically engineered to make you engage with life. Make chit-chat. Speak to Toyboy. He'd had one too. Where do you work? How long you been doing this? About eight inches. Pardon the pun. Jesus it was hard to admit, pardon the pun he thought again, but he was excited. Alice's feminist theory said men were led by their dicks. She was right. For the first time in so many years he had an inexplicably beautiful erection. But yet. The thing was an embarrassment to your intelligence. To be erect but not aroused. To be this stimulated without a single thought or feeling.

Everything slo-mo. Portentous. Someone is going to burst in and kill us all. It would end here. The man with the gun comes in and you beat him to death with your dick. Schwarzenegger. He wondered how many people knew about Mr Schwarz. What his name meant. Negger.

Black nigger. California Über Alles. Big black dick on a white Republican. Fuck the world.

He was watching the toyboy undress and he still had an erection watching this man's erection. The clouds were passing by the window and he had an erection. He looked over at Alice and wished he could have had this erection for her without the clouds and the carpet and the UHT milk and the toyboy. She was sitting on the edge of the bed, unsure whether to undress or not. They exchanged quick glances. The kind of glances people shot each other to say 'What are we doing here?' Viagra. Viagra is what's doing here. His top was off. Toyboy. He had a Celtic tattoo across his chest. He was so quiet, self-absorbed, must have done this a hundred times before. This was the lull before the storm. The man with the gun would come in soon. David's dick was uncomfortable in his pants. He was aroused because of a little blue pill. Jesus. Think about it. Global peace, piece, like Dolly would have said, pardon the pun, through medication. Hard to admit, pardon the pun, but he would have fucked anything at that point just to test out the mechanism. And the award for the hardest dick goes to. This dick was brought to you by the makers of Prozac.

'You think you can smoke in here?' was all he said.

'I dunno,' said Alice. 'Are there any signs?'

'It's smoking,' said the toyboy as he folded his jeans and stood there in his white boxers and white socks and an erection that he seemed surprisingly indifferent to. He picked up the remote.

'Radio Clyde, Classic FM or you wanna watch porn?'

Gimme the news channel, thought David. Let's see if I'm still hard. Gimme the weather.

Suddenly he felt vaguely nauseous. No doubt some

side effect. Light-headedness. The pill directs blood to
your dick and away from your head. Like the feminists
said. He needed some water. Headed for the toilet door,
but she was in there, the old hippie. The door opened
before him.

Astounding. The transformation. The drug surely. Head
to toe in lingerie. A huge pair of heels. Beautiful long legs.
Her breasts pushed up into some kind of corset. They
appeared immense. Does Viagra make people seem more
attractive? She registered his bulge. Smiled at him. Picked
up her bag. Set it on the bed and started to unload all
manner of toys. A huge white number with a semi-circular
head about the size of a tennis ball.

'We'll just start and you can watch,' she said.

Somehow all the resistance had gone. There was this
thing, this alien, cyber-pharmaceutical phenomenon
alive in his pants. Nothing to do now but show Alice
this ridiculous dildo that was somehow attached to him.
And she, Dolly had picked up her dildo and laid back
on the bed. Without prompting, the toyboy put a pillow
under her pelvis then crouched between her legs as she
began to touch herself with it. His head down there
watching her. Their movements seemed, in some way,
co-ordinated.

Alice moved closer. Took his hand and led him to the
front of the bed. Squeezed his hand tight and nestled
against his neck. Bizarre. They were fully clothed, just
standing there. It was like watching a natural history
programme. Dolly took the toy and turned it on, then
ran it over the crotch of her panties. The toyboy climbed
up beside her, and started kissing and fondling her
breasts. With her free hand she reached over and ran
her fingers over his body. David tried to laugh it off,
but couldn't take his eyes off what was happening. The

young male body. The abdominal muscles so defined,
the broad, strong chest. The bulge in his boxers. With
one graceful movement Dolly freed the toyboy's dick
from his shorts. It was impossible not to look. Impressive.
Maybe an inch longer than his and much thicker. A wrist,
he thought, as thick as a wrist. David felt Alice's hand
on his crotch.

'Isn't he beautiful,' said Dolly. 'My Adonis.'

And with that she pulled the toyboy closer and opened
her mouth for his cock. Her eyes kept staring up at David,
as she took it inside. David felt a bolt shudder through
him. Alice tightened her grip.

'Look at her sucking his cock,' she said.

'Tell me about the cock,' he whispered.

'It's big and hard, see the way she's taking it in, she
loves it. She's doing deep throat. You see that?'

'Aha.'

Dolly looked over at them, then took it from her
mouth. 'You like stories, that's good.'

Dolly worked her way up the toyboy's chest then whispered something in his ear.

The toyboy moved slowly back down Dolly's body.
Alice undid David's fly and took his cock out. Smiling as
she stroked him.

'You want me to tell you what he's doing now?'

'Aha.'

'He's pulling her panties to one side. He's licking her
clit. It's pierced, can you see that?'

'Aha.'

'Up and down he's licking it. Circling it. He's putting
his fingers inside her. She's wet, can you see that?'

'Yeah.'

'He's crouching over her pussy now. Look at his dick,
the way it stands out like that.'

'Aha.'

Now this was strange. Could they talk their way through the whole thing? Would Alice describe some fantasy of what it would be like to be fucked by this guy, while they both stood there, fully clothed? She'd make him come and they'd leave, without any contact with the other couple. Like the first time. Just watching.

*   *   *

She didn't really want to touch that cock. It was merely secondary. She hadn't told David but she'd had this theory. Dolly suspected the same. David's inability to sustain an erection was due to the fact that he was repressing homo or bisexual urges. He was an actor after all. He'd been acting straight for too long. Perhaps if he'd admitted it to himself long ago, long before he'd got married, he would have become a good actor, a committed actor, proud of who he was.

She wouldn't love him any less. More in fact. He'd come out. They'd still live together. They'd be closer than ever and he'd have lovers. He'd be fulfilled for once. He could bring men home. They could fuck in the spare room. At least then she would know for sure, and he would be grateful for her having helped him find his true nature. And she would abort and all his lovers would be their family and they would be this strange couple that nobody understood with their secret life and their stories of his adventures.

'You're really hard,' she said as she undressed him. 'It's amazing.'

'Yeah,' he said, 'but it's not me.'

'Maybe it's the new you.'

'Yeah right.'

Alice stroked it. 'Your beautiful dick.'

But he was almost embarrassed at having an erection. And she had been right, he was staring over there to the bed, to the toyboy, as they undressed. She couldn't let the moment go. If David was gay she had to let him know it was OK.

'He has a beautiful cock, doesn't he?'

David said nothing. He reached out his hand, was scared, and so she took it.

She could see Dolly looking over at them both. Their plan for David. Dolly was going to help David. She nodded to Dolly, discreetly so David couldn't see.

'Touch his cock,' said Dolly.

Alice turned and looked at David, her hand stroking his hard cock.

'You do, don't you, you really want me to touch it, don't you?'

David nodded.

'You touch yourself while I do it. OK?'

Alice let go of him. Pulled off her jumper and skirt and crouched before the man's legs. She reached out and cupped his balls in her hand. She turned and looked at David. He was hard and jerking off behind her. His eyes darting from her eyes to the balls in her hand.

Dolly got up and rolled the man onto his back, then straddled his face. Alice crawled beside the man and ran her hands over his chest and abs, down to his cock. She stroked its length and kept looking back at David. She hoped that David wasn't anxious about the fact that the man's dick was bigger than his. Alice pulled the fore-skin back and brought her face closer. The man didn't smell like a man at all. He was washed, scrubbed, perfumed with odourless scent. The feeling of the dick in her hand wasn't unpleasant, but it wasn't what was important either. This was all for David. She brought her lips to the base of the man's cock and looked up at David.

'Come closer,' she said.

As David got down on his knees in front of her, she ran her lips up and down the length. Yes, he couldn't take his eyes off the cock. She was right.

'Beautiful, isn't it.'

'Aha.'

David's eyes were flashing. She hoped he wouldn't come, because if he did the whole thing would be over.

'Touch my face,' she said. 'Please, Daddy.'

David did as she said. Ran his fingers over her cheeks, neck, hair. She kissed his fingers, sucked on one. Alice the slut. A role she'd experimented with before. But now the experiment had a purpose.

'You want me to, Daddy?'

'Aha.'

She closed her eyes, and opened her mouth to take the cock. It was big, too big, almost. Her lips felt stretched, sore. It wasn't sexy, but this wasn't for her, it was for David. The man gasped, but he was of little consequence, he was just a means. Alice opened her eyes and looked into David's. There was something there, something painful and beautiful. His eyes. So full of love, but also suffering. Angelic even. The tragic beauty of the martyr. Renaissance paintings. Had she got this whole thing wrong? Was it all just simply that David wanted to see her with another man? That he thought he was sacrificing himself to please her? If that was the case then she'd miscalculated horribly. The man gave her no pleasure at all. Looking at David's eyes. It seemed he was on the verge of tears. Oh, David. She suddenly felt very guilty. She just wanted to hold him, kiss him. Forget Dolly and her man. To hold David and kiss that look from his face.

'Kiss me. Please, Daddy,' she whispered, and could feel tears rising in her throat.

David leaned in and their lips met.

* * *

Her mouth on his. No words for it. This feeling. They were in this room with this couple, but it was like they'd never been more alone. More alone together. Like the whole world had disappeared, and he was clinging to life through the suction of her lips. Breathing through her lungs, alone together in the warm dark closed-eye intimacy of their kiss. He wanted to cry. He wanted to curl up in a corner, hug his knees and weep. He wanted her to hold him tight and stroke his hair and kiss his forehead and tell him that everything was going to be OK. He wanted to tell her about how he'd been bullied as a kid, about how he'd been a lonely only child, about how he'd realised five years ago that he was a failure, about how he'd taken it out on his wife and destroyed his marriage. About the year of fucking strangers. About what it felt like to hold your newborn child. The taste of dried blood on that newborn head when you kiss it. And how you make promises to your child then break them. About how every day for moments he felt utterly lost and full of self-hatred, and how he feared falling in love with her, because he was scared of making her the reason for him to go on living, and how he had contemplated suicide many times, in that first year of separation, until he met her, about how he'd felt himself clinging to her and had forced himself to resist. But her kisses. He was lost but for the first time happily lost, lost with her. And he would never leave her. He would make promises to her but never tell her. He felt movement on the bed. Dolly getting up perhaps. No matter.

He could feel her eyes on him. Alice. Alice. He always
could tell when she was looking at him. He'd wake from
sleep sometimes and find her staring at his face. He
opened his eyes and hers were pouring into his. Her
eyes were wet but smiling. She rolled the hard cock over
her cheek. She kissed him again. Bringing the cock closer
to touch his own cheek. Looking into each other's eyes,
she took her lips from his and kissed the cock. He did
the same. Kissed the cock, looking into her eyes. Like
it was her cock. His cock. Like they were sharing it.
Like it didn't matter any more that he hadn't been hard
for her. Their tongues met each other, both touching
the cock. Then he lost himself. Her tongue, her cock,
kissing it, kissing each other. A hand between his legs.
A mouth. It was Dolly. Her mouth around his dick. Alice
put her mouth round the head of the dick, looking into
his eyes, then kissed him. Her eyes seemed to say 'You
too.' He closed his eyes and opened his mouth, taking
the dick inside. His mouth, stretched wide. He opened
his eyes and looked into Alice's. Such love there, her
open mouth smeared his cheek, then slid down, till they
were both kissing, licking, sucking the dick together,
eyes locked. All the time he could feel Dolly's mouth
round his dick, going deep, to the root, he could hear
her gagging. It pushed him on. He took the dick again,
deep this time, pushing it into the back of his throat.
Alice was holding his head, gently pushing it down onto
the dick. He gagged, and felt bile and saliva rising. But
her eyes, leading him on, saying yes, yes, it's good, it's
beautiful. He kept on going, forcing himself past the
point of nausea. He was choking, choking on life, sucking
it in. Something desperate, hungry, primal, animal. The
cock so deep inside him. Wanting more. Deeper. His
eyes were watering. The dick in his mouth, his dick in

another mouth, his eyes looking deep into Alice's. A huge surge. He was moaning, Alice was moaning, the man moaning, Dolly. Alice's eyes, deeper, deeper. He pulled away and their lips found each other, hands clinging. Alice moaned, gasped. Hot wetness shot over their faces.

Five minutes later and he found himself sitting in the corner of the hotel room clutching his knees. Spasming with tears and laughter and laughter at having tears. Saying 'I'm sorry I don't know what's going on here.' And Alice and Dolly were holding him. Dolly trying to explain what had happened. Remarkable, she said. Only seen it once before, for four people to come at the same time. Explaining how sex was a force of good in the world, how sometimes, at times like now, this spirit overwhelmed us and made us self-less and that was what the Buddhists called spontaneous enlightenment, and how the dissolution of the self was the highest spiritual goal, undoing centuries of patriarchal repression.

'I love you,' said Dolly. And her eyes were so sincere. 'Both of you. You are so beautiful.'

Tears and laughter, and him not sure whether he was laughing with or at her. His eyes on Alice and the tears in her eyes. All he wanted to do was tell her about this line he had going through his head. Which wasn't spiritual or anything. About how he was just laughing, crying, and how if it hadn't been for the stupid little pill and the story Dolly had told, *Star Trek* and Klingons, none of this would have happened.

'Oh my loves, my lovely loves,' Dolly said, taking both their hands. 'The voyage has just begun.'

That was it. The words jerking out as he looked into Alice's eyes.

'Yes,' he said. 'To boldly go where no man has gone before.'

*   *   *

They had made love again and again for a whole week with the help of Dolly's little blue pills, but no matter how much happiness it brought them she knew she was distracting herself from the real question, the one growing inside her. And she could only answer it for herself.

Before she made up her mind she told herself there was one thing she had to do.

There were the details. So many hours spent bashing them out till they were in total agreement. She was to go to the park at three twenty, ten minutes before he got there. She was to sit alone on the bench furthest away from the gate. She was to be dressed down and not drawing attention to herself in any way. She was not to strike up a conversation with any of the other women. She could not tell anyone her name. She should keep herself occupied with something. A newspaper or book. When he arrived she was not to make eye contact with him. She was not to phone or text him. Under no circumstances should she speak to him. She was just to watch, for fifteen minutes, then leave discreetly, without even a goodbye. The urgency in his voice told her that no matter what happened, she was not to speak to Amy.

David had already left to pick up his daughter. Alice was fussing around. To wear a scarf or a hood? Sunglasses? It was like she was a spy or something. How to draw attention to yourself by trying to look inconspicuous. She'd memorised the street name and double-checked the time. As she put the keys in the door she ran over the little mental reminders she'd worked out to keep herself from panicking: you are only going to watch him playing

with his child, that's all. It's natural that you should take
an interest. But it did disturb her that it had taken her so
long to do this. She told herself that all of this was in no
way connected with the fact that in less than two weeks
the spinal cord would connect with the cerebral cortex.

Alexander Street. Across from the old folks' home with
the lavender bushes, he'd said. It was about twenty blocks
away. Uphill into the real West End. As she made it street
by street and the gardens got bigger and the privet hedges
became more freshly trimmed and the ceilings got higher
and the cars turned from VWs to SUVs, she ran over
the reasons why she'd always avoided seeing where David
had lived before. Perhaps because he'd always been so
scathing about it. Or that in some way she'd always been
a little threatened by the idea of this woman, this Hannah.
Who was, as David had described her, a typical aspir-
ational bourgeois, but who she sensed must have been a
bit more than that for David to have lived with her for
eight years. It was that bit more that bothered her. Easier
to keep her framed as a cliché. Easier than meeting or
even seeing her. That bit more that David could never
explain. That bit more that would have turned her into
a real woman with reasons of her own, who he had loved
enough to have a child with.

Queen's Drive. Doune Street. Two big churches. A
tennis court. A private sports club. There was something
else bothering her. Why had she made such a deal of
moving to the West End? Had it not been even a little
sadistic of her to make him live so close to where it had
all gone so wrong for him? The sudden scent of lavender.
She looked up and she was passing the old folks' home.
Barely any grass in the garden. Fifty or so lavender
bushes. Just like he'd said. She looked across the street
and there it was. Large and grassy, framed by oak trees

in a triangle surrounded by beautiful old Victorian tenements that were now no doubt yuppie conversions.

She was perfectly on time. Ten minutes and then David
would be there with Amy. David had been right. This
whole thing would stress her out, but not in the ways
he'd predicted. As she opened the park gate and stepped
inside and the voices of the children surrounded her she
felt her self-consciousness grow. Were they staring at her
unfamiliar face? It was a tight-knit community, safely
guarded. Was it a private park? The mothers thinking
she was one of those baby-snatchers they'd read about
in magazines they wouldn't admit to having read. Stick
to the plan. Don't talk to anyone. Sit, read your book.
Last bench, furthest from the fence. But there were two
mothers sitting there already. Some child who kept crying
and pulling this little yellow bike from some other child's
hands. It couldn't be that bench. The middle one then.
David would know. She wasn't to meet his eye but he'd
be looking out for her. Seven minutes.

She took her seat and looked up at the children's play
area. So many of them. She always found it hard to work
out their ages but the biggest was just over waist height.
Six, seven? Look around. Tyre swing. Slide. Roundabout.
Not the typical government issue. Made of wood. It was
a private park then. So, really, she had no right to be
here. Any moment now one of those women could, ever
so politely, ask her to leave.

Five minutes. She decided the sunglasses were too
much, but was too anxious to take them off. And the scarf.
Jesus. The other women were looking over at her, smiling.
Another unforeseen thing. That to pass unnoticed you
had to go through some of the rituals of politeness. She
forced a smiling nod in their direction and fumbled
around for her book. From the corner of her eye she

could sense they were talking about her. She glanced back up and the smile the woman gave her was what? Almost compassionate. They were talking about how sad it was that single women in their late thirties sat in parks just to be close to children. Stop it, Alice. Four minutes to go. She tried to force herself to relax. Little mind game. Think of the last time you were in a park. Must have been a child. But no memories from that time. David always found it strange that she could remember so little of her childhood. Aged nineteen then, drunk, a student on a swing in a park in California, at night, that first time she gave up art, swinging, singing alone in the dark.

Three minutes. Maybe they would be late. Kids probably slowed things down. No doubt not putting on their shoes, wanting to bring one toy then another, then you having to shout at them with a 'No' and them crying and in a huff and not moving and.

The gate creaked open, she turned. David and his exwife. My God. Why had she never asked to see a photo? Why had she, in fact, refused on so many occasions to see any and all photos? This woman, this Hannah, this wife. This long red-haired – this child with red hair like her own.

Time seemed to slow. The details immense. She feels what she sees.

Looking at them but trying not to look. Glimpsing those little things. The way they stood, her, this ex, crouching down and kissing the child goodbye. Him standing there behind, waiting with the Batman ball. The way he looked at his ex. An awkward kind of intimacy but still. Like he didn't know what to do with it. To touch her, to kiss her goodbye, to shake her hand. Waiting there at the gate for her to get it over with. Alice had prepared herself for seeing Amy but not Hannah. Was not ready for the first thought that came to her. That they were separated but still a couple. Was not prepared for this feeling of being betrayed.

She watches as this woman, this ex-wife, kisses David's child, and turns to leave. No handshake. He moves aside to let her pass.

This female called Hannah was not supposed to be here. Not supposed to linger like that. This red, this fucking redhead who was so beautiful, and in many ways so much more of a natural beauty than she was. It was beyond betrayal, was ritual humiliation. David had a thing for redheads. That was all she was to him then. A redhead. The dyed-red version of his ex-wife.

Stop it, Alice. Fucking stop it. Mental management techniques. Rationalise. Release the voices. And the voices said: this was not the plan, but things get out of control. He can't control his ex-wife. Can't determine whether or not she turned up. She didn't know about the plan. It was not his fault. It was just a trip to the park for her. Once, twice a week. Many couples were separated these days. Forty-eight per cent. And parks were the most neutral ground to meet.

But then the sight of David walking hand in hand with his daughter, her skipping and jumping. He was not looking up at her. She was invisible. Had he even forgotten that she was supposed to be there?

She turned away and watched Hannah climbing back into her SUV. You hate her. You don't hate her. Try to feel for her. Feel for Hannah. Those painful moments at the gate handing over your child. She is a woman. Try to feel for the woman. And really Hannah's situation was not so different from her mother's. The broken home. To raise a child by yourself. To have this ghost of a father appear now and then.

For a second she sees David as the bad actor she fears he always has been. The liar and cheat. And really, maybe she'd romanticised her own father, the bastard, the man who'd left. Too easy to sentimentalise the one who had gone, so easy to hate the one who was left in all the complicated self-loathing that must go on with surviving for the sake of a child. Put yourself in her position. Hers. The single mother. Name her. Hannah. Yes, you would have anger. You would hate the father who left and that hatred would give you strength. And maybe. No, to even think of it for a second. That she was with David, because like her father, he had walked away. Her nickname for him, after all, was Daddy.

But then seconds later watching him lifting up his daughter and swinging her round. He is still a father. She is alarmed that she'd never thought of this before. That she'd always seen him as a separated man. Not a father. Amy won't let him set her down. He makes a dumb show of pretending he has a sore back and indicating for her to run off and play. Look at Amy. Playing with her father, playing with his emotions. Look at Amy.

She is not classically beautiful like her mother. Runs like a boy. No matter how much her mother has dressed her in matching pinks and whites and put her hair in lovingly made braids, there is still something about her. Precocious. Almost aggressive, dragging her father around, and he follows her, letting her lead him anywhere she wants. Spoiled child. Both parents giving her everything she wants in the aftermath of the separation. The swings, Daddy, no the roundabout. And he does everything she says, but still she is not satisfied. She changes her mind for the fourth time and David has just done what he promised he wouldn't do.

He looks round the park for her. Looks worried at not

seeing her. She is no longer angry because there is something she can see on his face. A kind of pain he's never
let her see before. A desperate need to see her. Then
their eyes lock. And his eyes say thank God, there you
are. They say I want you to see this now, to see what
this means to me and I am sorry for keeping this from
you. And she is glad when it's interrupted by his daughter
because if they kept looking at each other, across those
hundred yards, him standing there with the Batman ball
in his hand as his child tries to grab it, standing there
like a man, frozen, she knows that it would just make it
harder to be carrying his second child, that she will abort
next week at the appointed time.

Somehow, beyond any capability she knew she had, she
composes herself. Goes back to her book. The first book
her hands found on the way out. Some secondary text on
psychotherapy. Out of the corner of her eye she follows
them as they walk past the roundabout and the slide to the
swings. She tells herself again and again not to look up.

David lifts Amy onto the swing. He pushes her again
and again. And Alice sees that it is not an act. That he
is a good father. A father who cannot hold back his joy
at doing something so simple. This cynical man whose
cynicism she has loved, laughing like a child as he pushes
his child on a swing. And listen to them, he calls her
Ame, not Amy. The French to love, je t'aime. Aims in
life. Aimless Amy. She tries to block out what she hears
which can only be the sound of his child's laughter. She
tries to go back to her book but feels the pull of the
swings. To have another look at David and Amy. She
glances up but they are gone. She looks around the park.
Finds them finally. Amy running after the ball with some
little boy. Giggling together.

Amy kicks the ball close to David. Suddenly he jumps

up. Has a goofy face on and is dribbling with the ball. Gently moving it from one foot to the other as the kids try to grab and kick it. With each manoeuvre they shriek and try harder. He's dribbling it round his back, turning round, not letting them have it, pulling more funny faces. C'mon you want it, come and get it.

She never knew he could play football and she can't help but laugh. So unlike him. This perfect comic timing and physical skill. His usual twisted negativity, his clumsy hunch-shouldered stiffness gone. He is electric, snapping, jumping, circling, taunting and teasing, attentive to the nuances of their laughter. The other women in the park are laughing too. Yes, performance or not, he is good at being a father.

But then Amy stops. He must sense something is wrong because he stops goofing around and picks up the ball. She's in a huff. He holds the ball out to her and she reaches for it. Just then he snatches it away and bounces it off her head, then catches it again. He has a look on his face. His confidence is crumbling. He's overstepped maybe. He tries to bounce it off her head again but she doesn't find it funny at all.

Alice tries not to look, but can't help herself. There is no harm in just watching. A certain safety in just watching. Like you were in a glass box. But still the things she sees cause her pain. Even though they aren't touching her. Because, because maybe she wants to touch them.

Amy turns and walks away. Leaving the game. And David, he is standing there, ball in hand. He follows her, but she is having a tantrum. A big grumpy face. He takes her hand, not quite grabbing her, but turning her. He goes down on his knees trying to hug her. But she is pushing him away and stomping her feet. Shaking her head and staring at the ground.

She is five and already she knows how to twist him round her tiny fingers. And he's doing all he can to hold her and make her laugh again, giving her the ball. He whispers something in her ear and suddenly her mood changes and with a big smile she takes the ball and runs off with it, the little boy chasing her. But the effort of it seems to have left him exhausted. He sits down on the grass and watches the children run off. David, sitting on the grass in his long black overcoat. Sitting there where none of the other adults are sitting, like a collapsed thing. A mound of black. His eyes shoot out at her again. No, he was not supposed to do that. They had agreed. They were his rules.

It's no good. She cannot keep holding the book in front of her face pretending to read and the mothers beside her are definitely talking about her. And Amy is running around, chasing the ball with the other kid.

They are moving towards Alice in a haphazard sort of way. Five-year-olds trying to kick a ball. She is downhill from them. No matter what they try to do the ball is coming closer. She feels David's eyes on her again but can't look at him. He should get up now, shout or come and get the ball and make them play in some other part of the park. It is getting close, too close. They are. Now she sees it, that David is powerless. As a parent, as a separated parent. He is scared of shouting out. Drawing attention to himself. It must be like this for him always, playing with his child but no longer feeling it correct to shout commands at her. Because he is a guest, a visitor in his child's life. So these times like this, watching him, as the ball approaches and he does nothing, these moments, her eyes on his as he does nothing as the ball gets closer.

Amy kicks the ball with her toe and it hits the edge

of the slide, rebounding back towards her. David gets to his feet. The two kids run at it, hiccupping with laughter, falling over each other. The little boy hits the ball with his heel by accident and it's spinning towards her again. Right towards her. David just stands there.

It happens as if in slo-mo. The Batman ball turning over and over, the children chasing it, running, laughing, oblivious, straight towards her. She gets to her feet. Takes a step away. Eyes shooting out to David for help.

The ball. The ball rolls underneath her bench. Her bench. And sticks there. And they are standing there, the little people, right in front of her. Amy and her friend waiting for her to do something because she is a grown-up and because she is in charge. And she is stuck, as stuck as the ball. To move away now when their faces say get the ball for us please. Please. And the faces of the other mothers looking at her.

So she does it. She bends down and reaches underneath and as she does her sunglasses hit the ground and her scarf falls off, and as she stands up she feels the eyes of the whole park upon her. And she's just there holding this ball. Holding it out, trying to give it to the other kid so she won't have to look at Amy. But Amy is in there first and, although Alice tries not to, she sees it. That she has the mouth of her mother and the eyes, the dark nervous eyes of her father. The eyes. Not just physically, but in some other way. A precociousness but also a need. That look that David gives her sometimes. Daring her. Higher, higher, as if on a swing, push me higher. She has his eyes. Which could look through you and make you feel the need which was yours but also his. That look that scared you, that had such bottomless depth to it, that made you stay.

They speak. The eyes. The child. Speaks.

'I'm five.' Children speak to strangers she tells herself, it's OK.

'My daddy's going to get me a real Barbie horse for Christmas.'

Silence. So many things she could have said. About how she never had a Barbie when she grew up but loved horses and how her mother had let her ride on a real one when she was maybe her age and how it would be good to get to know you better one day and maybe give you a baby half-sister or -brother to play with, but how impossible it all was. All of it. Impossible.

She stumbled for words. Fingers fumbling the ball. Somehow passing it to Amy without a word. Rummaged for her sunglasses. By the time she'd picked them up the children were already away, laughing and kicking the ball. As she got up to go she sensed David approaching. As fast as she could she was on her feet and walking away.

Somehow the effort required to walk the gravel path helped her keep it together. She walked past the kids and the swings and through the gate. Round the corner. Out of sight. Outside the old folks' home by the lavender bushes she took out her mobile. To text him to say sorry. But scrolling through the numbers the alphabetic log listed the clinic just before his name and she hit Call. She walked slowly back and forwards as the number rang. Waiting. The sweet pungent smell of the lavender. She gazed up at the old folks in their home. Twenty of them in one room all watching the television. All old women. Their men had died. Women live longer than men. She ran the words over in her head – I'd like to confirm my appointment for the vacuum extraction. But as she stared at them sitting there, all alone, together, watching the TV, an old woman caught her eye. Thinning hair and a dressing gown, staring out at her through the double glazing. She would have been about the same age as her mother if she had still been alive. The voice on her phone said, 'Hello, Sinclair Clinic, how can I help you?' Her mother loved lavender oil, used to put it on her pillow to help her sleep. 'Hello, hello, can I help you?' The old woman staring out, wanting out. 'Hello, sorry who is this?' The smell of the lavender, the sight of the old woman. Weeks later she would realise that these were the things that made her click her phone shut.

*　*　*

Today was the day when it would be final. The divorce papers were to be signed. He was up early and couldn't face breakfast. Was almost glad that his interview at the job centre would take up most of the morning and leave him no time to worry.

There was no Queen any more. Tom Jones instead. 'It's Not Unusual' but really there was no end to how unusual this place had become. David joined the queue for the front desk and decided that next time he came he would bring his iPod and some Nine Inch Nails.

He'd got there half an hour early so went over to the computers to do a quick job search. It would be good if he had a few credible prospective job titles to throw into the interview. But as he logged on and discovered that it was open Internet access he couldn't help but type in the site address, the intention being to send Dolly a thank you. Almost immediately a dialogue box came up saying that access was denied because of pornographic content. He checked over his shoulder to see if anyone had been watching.

In the queue. He didn't try to make conversation with anyone this time. Went through the now customary

process of waiting and shuffling forward. Worrying that
some surveillance camera, somewhere, had been trained
on him when he'd been on the net.

He'd shaved that morning and put on a suit. Had done
everything they'd not even asked for. In the neat bound
folder by his side he had his P45 and the application for
benefits. In addition he had a nicely laid out CV that
he'd spent most of yesterday arranging. He started
running over what he'd say to the interviewer. He'd not
be defensive or impatient. Be polite and efficient. Get it
done and get out. The queue was moving more swiftly
today and in fifteen minutes he had got to the front and
given his name and was told to take a seat upstairs. Booth
twelve.

He sat before a jovial fifty-year-old man with bad teeth
and large thick spectacles. His name tag said Jeff. Some
terrible 80s music had started. Bon Jovi. T'Pau.
Something like that. Jeff took the form and the CV from
him as he logged on and skimmed over the papers then
started humming along to the music. This man, this Jeff.
'Heaven is a Place on Earth'. The dole office. Jesus.

David started to snigger. Jeff looked up.

'What was that?'

'Nothing. Sorry. I mean the music in here. It's just I've
noticed a few times that . . .'

The man called Jeff smiled and told him that yes it
was quite funny sometimes. Like last week. Abba's
greatest hits came on and he'd been serving this single
mother whose claim had been rejected and he couldn't
help himself. Singing along, quite the thing. 'Money
Money Money.' And you know it was no laughing matter
but you couldn't help but laugh sometimes. And how it
was probably because he was a wee bit too close to the
speakers and anyway, back to work. Jeff looked over his

CV and smiled again, with what seemed like even more enthusiasm.

'Actor?'

'Well I used to be.'

'Trampled the boards myself,' said Jeff.

Treaded surely, or trod, not trampled. David just wanted it over and done with but Jeff was off, trampling again.

'Student stuff mostly. Lots of pantos.'

David couldn't help but feel this was some kind of complex psychological test. Try to get you to admit that you were an artist and had no intention of finding work and planned to live off the State indefinitely. That kind of thing. But Jeff was still talking.

'Citizens Theatre, the Kings, the Pavilion.'

'Really,' said David, clearing his throat and trying to force a smile. 'Wow.'

'You ever play Oedipus?'

'No. You?'

'No.'

My God, here we are wandering blind through the wilderness in a rich man's world. Get on with it. Jeff's smile turned itself off and he seemed to click back into some kind of work mode.

'Right.'

'OK.'

Jeff took a few minutes to leaf through David's application form. He played with his pen and shook his head and hummed and hawed. Then lowered his voice almost to a whisper and leaned forward. 'Between you and me you don't want to say that.'

'What? Sorry, say what?'

'Available for any kind of work. No.'

'Really?'

''Cos then I'll be forced to find you any kind of work at all and we can't have you wasting your talents on some horrible . . . well, you know. I'm sure you can imagine.'

OK, so this really was some kind of psychological test. Either that or Jeff was genuine, caring, some possibly lonely sort who'd found his first real potential friend all day and was offering discreet, nay secret advice.

'So let me just change that for you and we'll put theatre and HR.' He seemed very pleased with himself. 'And do a little search for you.'

David couldn't help picturing him in greasepaint swigging back vodka in the changing room and wondered if he'd been an Ugly Sister or a Widow Twankey. The tears of the clown.

'Hmm. Didn't think we'd find anything,' Jeff whispered again. Conspiratorially, fraternally. 'To be honest our resources are really pretty crap, but there's a few here.'

Drama therapy teacher in a small charity school in a housing scheme. Jeff gave him the printout and told him with a degree of excitement which could only have been fuelled by alcohol or perhaps even sexual attraction that, even though the location left a lot to be desired, this could be a real opportunity. But if he preferred they could just overlook that one right now and give him some time to find work by himself.

This was a play by Ionesco. An absurdist masterpiece. To find an employee of the job centre who was teaching you how to buck the system. Who wanted to be your friend.

'And believe it or not there's actually another job going here.'

'Really?'

'But you wouldn't want to do that.'

David was glad to get away without a lingering handshake and an exchange of telephone numbers. On the way out he couldn't help but reflect that it would have been so much easier if the guy had been a faceless monosyllabic bureaucrat.

He'd felt moved almost to compassion. This poor man who wanted to be on the stage. Trampling. All these people who did what they did but dreamed they were something else. He was not so different himself. Like those people in lunatic asylums who thought they were Napoleon or Churchill. Like those people in prison who did push-ups every day and read Nietzsche and dreamed of being the Übermensch.

He stopped on the corner and checked his watch. Just over half an hour till the meeting with Hannah at the solicitor's. He took out the printout Jeff had given him. If Jeff had not been Jeff, if the events of the last week had not in every way been conspiring against his cynicism and given him a sense of hope, he would have scrunched it up and dropped it in the first rubbish bin he came across. But instead he stood there and read it.

Job Title: Drama teacher
Job ref: Mav/27766
Location: Easterhouse
Employer: Social Development Fund
Description: Must be qualified in literacy and discipline, possessing excellent verbal communication skills. Successful applicants must possess a degree in drama and the ability to deal empathetically with clients and have experience of working in a position demanding confidentiality, tolerance and impartiality. Teacher training qualifications non-essential. We are looking for a creative open-minded individual who has an ability to confront problems in an imaginative way. Working as

part of a progressive team building our new drama therapy social inclusion programme.

He felt neither creative nor imaginative, nor particularly progressive or team orientated. And he felt as excluded from anything social as anyone ever could. But nonetheless he folded it carefully, put it back in his pocket and headed down the road to the solicitor's.

*   *   *

It was over so quickly. None of the anxiety he'd anticipated earlier. He felt like a fool for having been so stressed out about the whole thing for so long. It had taken no longer than ten minutes. The polite shake of hands with the solicitor. Hannah sitting there on the other comfy leather chair, calm and dressed in her business suit. Taking the pen in her hand. Sign here. And here and here. Then his turn. Sign here and here and here.

He was still standing on Byres Road, only a few feet from the solicitor's door. He should move on. No point standing there when Hannah came out. No point in the chat. What to say anyway.

'Thanks. Good luck.'

'That wasn't so bad.'

'See you Tuesday.'

He walked to the end of the street and was about to cross the road to head for home, but the sun was warm on his cheek and there was no rush, nothing really to get back to, so he found himself walking.

Funny word. Silly really. What did it mean now anyway? But still it was there. 'Free'. These ridiculous clichés. 'I am free.' 'A free man.' 'I'm free now.'

He walked away from home, along Dumbarton Road. Yes, it was a silly thing to be thinking. Materially speaking he was no more free than he had been fifteen minutes ago. There was still alimony and childcare. But the shadow had vanished. Gone too was this desire he'd always felt after seeing Hannah, to get away as fast as possible. To a pub usually.

No, he wasn't running; his feet were slowly enjoying the feeling of walking. People were passing by, shopping, chatting. As he passed the park on the corner there was the sound of kids playing football. Old women were queuing at the fish van. Two old drunks were sitting on the benches deep in some discussion while sharing a can of cider. The solicitor's office, behind him, was now just another shop. He stood there at the bottom of the street and noticed that there were people everywhere. Strange that he'd walked here every day for years and never really taken any notice.

Look at them all. Negotiating, arguing, playing. 'I'm no paying that for herring.' 'The goal was offside.' 'If you gimme a fag I'll gie you a drop.' It struck him that his divorce was not so different from the kind of exchanges people made every day. Social contracts being drawn up every second. Tacit verbal agreements. That the whole world rested on these minute-by-minute negotiations.

Nothing for it but to walk and keep on walking. To turn around and head back into the midst of it. To look at things and people. He was heading away from home. But this moment felt so ridiculously fucking good. The park. The Kelvingrove. Be good to keep on going. To indulge in a little of that sunlight-through-the-trees stuff.

Dumbarton Road. The Lis Mohr. One of the many bars he'd picked up women in after he left. Now it was just another bar. Quaint, old-fashioned. One of the staff was opening up. A man was cleaning the windows. No desire to go in, not any more. To drown the moment. This phrase going through his head. 'I am drunk on the air itself.'

He was laughing at himself. The sun, warm on the back of his neck, pushing him forward. Past the charity shop from which he bought the second-hand futon for Alice's bedsit. So many charity shops on Dumbarton Road. Glasgow was a poor city. No matter how much they told you otherwise. These were his usual thoughts. But now, the charity shops didn't remind him of poverty. Didn't make him feel trapped. Instead he smiled to himself. Hell, there might be no venture capital here. Massive unemployment. The charities had to step in to fill the huge gaps in the welfare system. But still, to think of people exchanging their possessions, almost like a barter system. To stop criticising this place and just accept it for what it was. People passed on things and other people bought them again. There was a certain solace in that.

Past the foot of Byres Road again, heading to the park. The trendy new bars on the corners. They would come and go. Be fashionable, then out of fashion. And he would see them all come and go as he headed into his forties, his fifties.

For so long he'd been living with this desire to run and never come back. Yes, he was going nowhere but now that the papers had been signed, for the first time in years he was almost happy to be where he was.

Even the sewage works to his right. That shitty stench across from the hospital that always reminded him of death. He took in a good lungful of the crap and couldn't stop laughing. The hospital too. That horrible 70s monstrosity. So many sick people in the city. The only real careers anyone had were in hospitals. These were old thoughts now. Keep walking.

The Kelvingrove Museum. Still shut after two years of renovation. He didn't think about the stupidity of the planners who closed it. He thought about the joy he might have with Amy when it reopened. He hoped they still had those old papier-mâché dinosaurs with the incorrect anatomical proportions and vicious outsized teeth that had terrified him, but drawn him back again and again when he himself was a child. Probably they'd have some new huge 3D animatronics mechanism with realistic sound effects. Pity. But still this was change. These were the limits of things.

He walked through the park gate. The university up on the hill. The huge Gothic tower, that his parents had wanted him to go to, to study law. Their disappointment when he picked acting.

The path in the park broke in two. You take the high road and I'll take the low road. They both ended in the same place. He chose the low road, just because he once had before. The night he walked out on Hannah. Staggering through the dark, clutching his bottle of wine. The men walking round like shadows among the trees. Smoking. Whispering to each other as they passed. That night, standing, drinking, watching a young man sucking off an old guy by the edge of the rhododendrons.

But today they were in full bloom. Pink, purple, white. And even though there might have been men fumbling in there amongst the tangled branches, all he saw were the bright colours and how much the bushes had grown since he last bothered to look. The smell of the flowers. Pungent, rich. Downright bloody lovely.

He finally came to a stop at the old outdoor theatre off University Avenue. It had been locked up for nearly a decade now. Covered in graffiti. The stage was fenced off with metal spikes and barbed wire.

Beautiful thing it had been. Semicircle. A little Greek Athenaeum in the heart of the city. Seen bands there when he was a student. Never saw a play. He stepped up to the gate. The padlock was rusted. Rubbish strewn everywhere. The wheel of a pram. Bin bags thrown in, burst and rotting. Then it caught his eye. Spray-painted on the gate walls. 'The Hole'. Jesus. His old friend Tony. That had been his band in what, '92, '93. Pretty good. Sounded like the Clash. Guess it had been unfashionable to sound like the Clash then. Last he heard Tony had had a kid, became a psychiatric nurse then left his partner. He'd seen him on the street a couple of years ago but they'd both done that head-lowered-pretending-not-to-notice-each-other thing. Too many things to say.

David peered deeper inside. Twenty rows. The first eight had wooden benches. For mothers and tiny kids no doubt. The wood was rotten now. He had this sudden need. Childish and stupid as it was. He looked over his shoulder. Just a few cars passing. No one around. His hands found a gap in the rusty railings and he hoisted himself up, laughing to himself about being so naughty. His feet landed amongst the rubbish and he went over on his ankle, shit and fuck. He hopped about for a bit, then ducked behind the gate walls. Laughing like some hysterical kid.

He limped down the centre of the auditorium and felt its dimensions opening up around him. They could catch him. Do him for trespassing. But surely. He looked respectable enough. They wouldn't arrest him, just a little warning maybe. Let them anyway, what the hell.

Just look at this place though. A few weeks ago he would have found it a metaphor for this and that, failed ambitions, the end of his acting career, the limitations of this city. This city of commerce that had no commerce.

The way everything slid into ruin. But today he couldn't help but think that the place was somehow perfect. That it was just the way that things were. Always had been. That it was OK that nobody gave a shit about art or theatre. They would live and die, come and go as the culture around them changed. Glasgow had started off as an industrial city anyway. He would be here to see it change again. He was going nowhere and that was just fine. Another thirteen years and Amy would be old enough to leave. Until then he would stay. Would not run. Would see her twice a week and maybe even push it to three times. Maybe even have some kind of enduring influence on his daughter's life. Not just be the fraught wannabe escapee. Thirteen years, then maybe move away with Alice.

He sat down in the middle of the middle row. The concrete was broken. Grass and weeds pushing up through the cracks. He stared out at the stage. Graffiti. HYT – POSSO posse – Fuck the Polis. Behind the building, on the path to the right, he glimpsed a middle-aged man with two bags. He was throwing something to the pigeons. Bread? Nuts? Smiling to himself. He watched as the man bent down and picked up some rubbish. An empty bottle. A crisp packet. What? Was he a tramp or. No, too well dressed. And that bag was nuts. Not cheap, a big bag of nuts like that. So what the hell was he doing? David watched as the man hopped over the fence and picked up some empty beer cans and stuffed them into his second bag. The man glanced up slightly, smiled at David, nodded, then was on his way. That was it. He was tidying up the park. All by himself. Not a council employee, just some local guy. Decided it was his park too and he'd make the best of it in his own small way. But don't judge. David sat back and surrendered to the possibility of a moment of uncorrupted joy.

Maybe someone in those years ahead. Maybe someone with courage and initiative would bring the theatre in the park back to life. He would come with Amy. Puppet shows and pantomimes. *Hamlet* maybe when Amy was twelve or thirteen. Come here and tell his child all about Shakespeare and how he'd once believed that theatre could change lives. No point being melancholic about it all. Tell Amy about his passion for theatre and not let her know about his failure.

Thirteen years was not so long. Three thousand since the Greeks. For the last two years he'd had to fight with himself every minute or so. Had developed all these clever techniques to keep his anger at bay. People thought he was witty, ironic. This kind of fatalism he'd adopted. Day after day telling himself that everything was shit. That those who had faith and conviction, who set positive goals were naive and stupid. Embrace failure, predict it. Wait and watch it happen to all those around you. Laugh to yourself with that smug 'told you so' mentality. Yes, he'd been laughing at the world and expecting it to laugh right back. But the world was even more indifferent than that. Silent. So all this time he'd been laughing at himself.

He got to his feet and walked down the concrete steps to the stage. There was a hole in the fence. He put his hands out, took his weight and pushed up, grasping the metal bars. He could be arrested, but still. This feeling of strength in his arms. It was good. He was up. Through the hole and standing on the stage.

He had to laugh. On the stage for the first time in over fifteen years. Look at it now. A fence all the way round it. Me – like a man in prison. Fifteen years and I've built myself a prison. But I'm here at least. Here now. On the stage. Indeed. ''Tis an unweeded garden that grows to seed.' I will be an actor again. Hard to believe, standing there on the derelict stage, but he felt something he hadn't felt since he'd been a student. It was something to do with the future. Possibility. Damn it, even hope.

In so many ways hope was the hardest path. So much easier to sneer and judge. So much braver to try and fail. To have tried.

It didn't last long, this euphoria. In fact he felt ridiculous being up there, staring out at the auditorium through the bars. What the fuck was he thinking? Getting all metaphorical about the weeds growing through concrete, about the old man picking up the crap. C'mon, realistically what movie was this? Cynic finds hope. Corny as fuck, not credible. It had felt like what – like surrender. What did that mean? To surrender to hope. The atheist who finds God on his deathbed. Total cop-out.

It was all pretty pathetic really. He climbed back down carefully, anxious now about being caught. Almost running to get out. Head darting from side to side.

Heading back through the park. Checking over his shoulder to see if he was being followed. OK, the feeling had only lasted for a few seconds. Of course he'd never act again. But still he had to admit he'd felt positive for those few seconds. It wasn't just about himself or acting. It was about Amy. To turn a corner with his child and communicate the joy he'd once felt.

As he walked back past the university and the museum with the dinosaurs and the bushes where men fucked it was all coming together. An image, a phrase. Acting. Thirteen years. Amy. The man picking up rubbish. Work. Children. Home. Here. They all came together in a single idea. To teach acting.

Of course those who can do, and those who can't teach. But to hell with that. Yes, he'd failed as an actor, but damn it, there had been that vacancy in the job centre to do just that. That job in the shitty housing scheme. That might be just what he needed. To take on all the shit of the world.

To teach acting to children.

Who cared if they laughed at him. All those ex-colleagues of his. Fuck it. He hadn't seen any of them in ten years anyway.

That one kid, that one kid who made you appreciate what it was that you once felt as a kid. To inspire that kid to surpass you and your own ambitions. Sure, you were living vicariously through someone else, but wasn't that better. Better than wanting everyone else to fail because you'd failed. Fuck it.

You are thirty-seven. You will be fifty when your daughter leaves home. Thirteen years you've wasted, but you have thirteen more. Accept past failures and face up to them. He was here now. This was the place. Glasgow. He would be here till he was fifty, then maybe longer. He had to make the best of it. No more sitting around all day killing time. Seething with resentment. Daydreaming of escape. No more pretending to be something you weren't. No more toying with other people's lives as if you were directing a play.

As he approached the edge of the motorway he made up his mind. He might have to do a training course or two. He might have to apply for job after job, but he would do it. There were two things he had to discuss with her. Alice. No, two things he had to tell her. No. One thing to tell her and one to ask her. He knew it was crazy. They both were. But put together they became some kind of plan.

He was going to teach acting to children.

And by the way, Alice, or maybe not by the way at all. Not a joke or an apology at all but just the words. Those words which she would laugh at. Alice, I'm going to stay here and I want to stay here with you. No, but what I really want to say is. No, sorry to ask. Those next few words which seemed to flow so effortlessly from the other ones, but which were so hard to say. No, to ask.

Alice please, I know this sounds like a joke.

No, no jokes any more. Tell her about the park, and the old man with the bags, and your legal divorce. Stupid and pathetic as it may sound. Tell her about the old auditorium and the dinosaurs in the museum.

Alice.

No, don't tell her. Fucking ask her.

Alice, will you marry me?

But as he got closer to home he saw it. The flat, the interior decor, the neighbourhood, the glossy advert of newly-weds that had been his last thought. Stupid. Only half an hour since he'd signed the divorce papers and already he was wanting to get hitched again. What was he so scared of? Of free-floating with Alice indefinitely. Of everything flying around them, always, unfixed. Fear at his own freedom then. Yes. It was pathetic, but he was weak, he knew that now. Beyond hope. Alice, marry me. The only hope he had left now was to have hope. To at least try.

*   *   *

'Their names are Wilf, Summer, Jon, Jezebel, Tigerbee and Lysander,' said Alice with an urgency that betrayed her enthusiasm. One of the new junior researchers choked on a laugh.

This was it, the final pitch. Two weeks behind schedule, and still no participant list. The head had flown up on the red-eye shuttle just to be there sharp. Everyone had assumed the series was fucked. Pauline shifted in her plastic chair, sucked in her cheeks and pretended to stare at the corporate-coloured wallpaper of room 5C. It was Pauline's last day and today Alice would make her realise it had been a mistake to try to sink the series.

The head leaned towards Alice with an encouraging smile and clicked her pen. Alice forced herself to calm down, slow down. She had the material now and it would make sense of everything.

'Interesting,' said the head.

Yes, work had taken on a manic edge in the weeks of working late and the days spent not even attempting to speak to the research team who had abandoned her. Not wanting to go home and face David and the question of her pregnancy. But now after all the hundreds of hours spent researching swinging and alternative living, after having secured the location, the camera equipment and crew and having finalised the shooting schedule and after three hundred pages of transcribed telephone interviews, of having re-read Foucault's entire three-volume *History of Sexuality*, after having excavated a critique of marriage that ran back from the 60s communes to the manifesto of the communist Alexandra Kollontai, further back to Wollstonecraft and the rights of women, after locking herself away from the bitching and back-stabbing and deciding to go it alone, she'd finally found an answer to all her questions. Right there at eight thirty this morning, that word Dolly had said. Poly.

Polyamory. Polyfidelity. A quick net search and it was there. All questions answered. Sex and couples. A new way to live without repeating the problems of the past.

'Two heterosexual males, one bi, two bi females, one straight. They are non- or anti-monogamous, polyamorous, and share sexual partners with each other in every way every day.'

The head couldn't hold back her smile. Alice looked down at her notes and continued reading.

'They live by what they call a "balanced rotational sleeping schedule". On Monday Jezebel sleeps with Wilf. Tuesday with Summer. Wednesday with Jon and Tigerbee. Thursday, well there's Wilf again. He seems to do rather well out of the deal. Jezebel said that her first time in a threesome with Wilf and Lysander was a life-changing experience.'

The smile stretching across the head's face. Alice read on.

'Jezebel said. Having two men fuck me. It had only ever been a fantasy. One in my mouth and one in my pussy. One in my ass and one in my pussy. Two in my pussy.'

She could feel the researchers all around twitching. Pauline exhaling dramatically. Pussy. Fuck. These words being said in a corporate conference suite. She had to admit she felt a rush of power. Moving on.

'When it happened I felt guiltlessly fulfilled. Full and filled. I realised this was the meaning of fulfilled.'

The gag was lost on everyone. She flicked through more pages.

'OK, Wilf. He looks like the young Bob Dylan, but is VW/E as they say, according to Jezebel. Not that Bob Dylan wasn't similarly endowed but I haven't had time to research that.'

The head was laughing. Even the researchers, everyone, apart from Pauline. Yes, she'd done her research. Fuck Pauline.

'You get the picture. Friday they have what they call "joy time". Basically a jacuzzi and a free-for-all, and on Saturday they have the option of personal time, in respect of Jon's faith. It being the Jewish Sabbath. Interestingly

he came from a kibbutz. Summer sees this as an extension of her involvement in the women's movement.'

The head started writing, shaking her head, laughing.
Pauline tried to interject but the head held up her hand
and nodded for Alice to continue reading.

'They believe that monogamy is a Western male
construct. Only two per cent of animals do it. Only
sixteen per cent of all known human cultures have ever
practised it. It was unknown in ancient Greece and in
what we know of matriarchal societies where the fertility
of women was worshipped and the matriarch could take
her pick of lovers even when pregnant.'

There was silence again and time was ticking and she
had got too academic. She flipped from page fifty to page
ninety-five. Past Wilhelm Reich's critique of repressed
sexual energy as a tool of fascism, past Melanie Klein's
diagnosis of monogamy as a sickness of capitalism,
looking for a conclusion they would grasp. Tigerbee and
Wilf's big cock.

'OK, OK, these people. These six people who fuck
each other. They believe that polyfidelity cures the social
problems of loneliness, jealousy, adultery, possessiveness,
social fragmentation, housing shortages, single parenting,
economic strain and emotional boredom.'

She kept on talking, justifications and counter-
justifications on many levels. But while she talked she
sensed the silence growing around her which only made
her talk faster.

'They find this the ideal situation in which to bring
up their six children who receive constant attention and
affection and who participate fully in the day-to-day
running of the commune.'

The head lifted her head.

'Sorry? They live in a house? Together? With kids?'

'Yeah, yeah. They're part of this new movement. There's like one in San Francisco. Three in Seattle. Two in Germany.'

'These aren't contacts who you know then?'

'They're part of this movement, and there is this growing network of thousands of others online all across the world who are watching them like . . . like live "test tubes" and studying the polyfidelity alternative with the idea they may want to try it for themselves. This entire history that runs back a hundred years, more, to the birth of feminism and . . .'

Silence and in that silence Pauline spoke.

'Freaks!' she said. 'Judging by the ones we've found so far, I thought we could call the series *Freak Show*.'

Bitch. But the fucking stupid bitch had made the head smile. Speak now.

'No, no. This isn't a freak show. This is not some piss-take. We're not trying to ridicule these people for our own entertainment. The whole purpose of this is to try to engage sympathetically with a group of out-siders, to try to see the world from their perspective. They don't see sex as titillation, objectification. This whole consumerist sex-object bullshit. They're anti-consumerist. They're not selling themselves or anything else. They actually fuck, OK? Sex for them is a gift, given freely.'

The head stroked her temples.

'Free love,' said Pauline and the others laughed.

Ha ha ha, thought Alice. She said it. 'Funny isn't it. Ha ha ha ha ha.' Repeated it till there was silence again.

'OK, fine, another freak show. Fine, done, predictable. But you should know why you're doing that. Because you're scared of what these people represent. You're scared of your own freedom. So much easier isn't it, sitting here all day reading *Cosmo* and articles on how to catch Mr Right. Right?'

'Alice!' the head said.

'Let me tell you about why people fuck. OK? You wanna know why people fuck?'

'Alice, please.'

'They fuck because fucking is still fucking, is still two people touching and sharing and entering each other and these people know that.'

'Alice, can we just—'

'And yes, I know, it's sad. Not freaky, just sad, that our freedoms have been chased so far that all that's left, the only place you can touch another person is that little tiny private space, and so these freaks as you call them, they stick butt plugs up their arses because of the war, they fuck three people at once because the world tells them they are ugly. They fuck because they're angry, because this stupid fucking culture wants to turn everything you think or feel into an advert and now you're trying to take these people and make a freak show, so you can sell more fucking advertising space.'

'Alice, a minute, please.'

'So we can sit back in our televisual smugness and laugh it all off. And we can thank God, or whatever fucking godless thing we worship, that we're not like them so we can go back to our TV tips on how to be sexy and what colours are radical this season. It makes me sick. You, you make me.'

'Alice!'

Alice. It took her seconds to realise she was being spoken to.

'Let me put this clearly, Alice. Have you contacted these people? Will they take part in our swinging series?'

'But this is so much bigger than our original idea.'

'Have you made contact with them?'

Alice stared at the corporate-coloured carpet.

'Where do they live, Alice? Glasgow, Edinburgh?'

'Seattle.'

'Seattle. And you've spoken to them?'

'Not yet but—'

'All we need is four couples who are accessible.'

Pauline interrupted. 'Tommy Carlisle and Stella Becker. You know, the celebrity sports couple?'

The head turned away from Alice to face Pauline. 'The whole cocaine slash separation scandal?'

'Aha. Well, I met Stella at this party and she thought it would be cool for them to do a swap with their friends. Have you heard of Patty McGowan?

The head shook her head.

'Celtic midfielder. Well anyway. More like a lifestyle thing. Not like swinging, not like *Wife Swap*, but like life swap. *Celebrity Life Swap*.'

Pauline's eyes. Smiling, smug. Every word of Alice's would count. Survival.

Alice couldn't hold it back. Page 307.

'"We're all here because we've chosen to be here," says Tigerbee. "We've made a commitment to each other. We love commitment," says Lysander. "The hard thing is finding other people who are brave enough to commit to us. Love is selfless. There is no greater love than losing oneself in feelings independent of the individual. To love humanity through the body of another."'

'Really. I've no idea what this has to do with the programme,' said the head as she got to her feet. 'Alice, a word. Now!'

Within fifteen minutes she'd had the talk. Big ideas were all very well, but everything rested on achievability. Pauline's contacts were the only tangible thing that the team had come up with and they were long overdue and the company needed deliverables. TV was about selling air time. Nothing more. She should know this by now. Her research had not been relevant. She was giving control of the series to Pauline.

Alice cleared her desk. She knew it now, this thing she'd always known but tried to ignore. As if the world cared. She'd been asking a TV channel to justify this whole swinging thing. The pregnancy. Some manifesto that would answer all of her questions.

'Your research is not relevant.'

Packing her files away. If only she'd had some evidence, some contacts. Dolly. If she'd interviewed Dolly then they would all see. But it would have felt like a betrayal. Dolly had to be kept secret. Maybe some things were just like that.

Swingers didn't feel they had to justify themselves. Didn't need their values broadcast. They lived a secret. And maybe at a certain point in life, after a divorce or an abortion, you came to realise that you had survived and that how you did it, how you pulled yourself through was a totally private matter. The opinions of others were no longer important.

So that was it. This job was fucked. Her contract was only for another week or so anyway, and after today they wouldn't want her back. A week. Do the minimum amount of work and search for something else to do with her life. And what would she do? For the first time it would be something that couldn't be justified. Not to anyone, not even herself. Become a herbalist, a massage therapist, open a café, bake cakes. She'd have the abortion or keep the child and her reasons for either would be a secret. She'd swing with David and that would be a secret too and she'd do some quiet inconsequential job and her reasons for that too would be a secret.

'Your research is not relevant.'

Pauline marched past her desk grinning to herself.

'Your research is not relevant.'

This is not research, this is my life, you fuck. My fucking life. And all my life has been research. Soon, so soon, it will be done and I will decide how to live. 'Your research is not relevant.' Fuck you and your celebrity decor makeovers and your death-breath cynicism which you tell yourself is irony. I am sick of it, all of it. I will make my life relevant. I will. You fucks. All of you. One day you will come with your TV crew and your researchers and ask me why I am happy and what happiness is. And I will turn you away. Because it is a secret I am carrying, right now, inside myself.

3
BLACK ROOM

Sender: Dolly55@hotmail.com
RE: SSS
Dear David and Alice
After an exhaustive (and exhausting) selection process we
are pleased to announce that you are one of the ten
couples selected to attend the biannual Scottish Swingers
Soiree. The event will take place at the Rob Roy Chalets,
Swan Bay, Loch Lomond from 26–29 Sept. Please see
enclosure for our list of events, games and accommoda-
tion arrangements. A fee of £75.00 will cover all costs.
Please confirm your attendance by return.
Love and kisses Dolly XXX
PS So excited that you made it to the top ten.

They had more than enough time, she said. They nipped
into the mall to get some petrol and while they were
there, since it was just across the forecourt, Alice decided
it would be an idea to pop into the new Marks & Spencer
to get a little something for Dolly. Flowers maybe, a
bottle of bubbly. They walked up and down the flower
and vegetable aisle. Roses, carnations or lilies? She was
talking excitedly about the things they could try out
tonight. Dolly had helped her draw up the list.
    Spit-roasting.
    Anal penetration.
    Double penetration.
    How had he even let her talk him into this? He worried

that she was talking too loudly, as people passed by with
their runner beans and iceberg lettuces. Her behaviour
had been strange this last week after seeing Amy in the
park. Long periods of morbid silence followed by these
moments of intense activity, making lists, plans, but
almost randomly it seemed. He had begun to suspect that
she had already guessed the question he was going to ask
her. That if he didn't play along with her game then her
silences would grow until finally they became the greater
silence of her departure.

Sixty-nine F2F.

Sucking two cocks at once.

Female ejaculation.

Chill out. No one could hear them, she said. She was
doing her high-on-life routine, joking and laughing about
it all. And no doubt the irony of the context had even
been intended. Bigger, better, longer, stronger. Buy one
get one free. Now available in different colours. Get into
S&M at M&S. Her enthusiasm for all this was disturbing.

As she sniffed the lilies and complained about how
they added synthetic perfume, he ran over his plans for
cutting this whole adventure short. How far he'd have
to go before he could realistically put a stop to it, for
ever. Was she really serious in her suggestion that he
should try to take a cock up his ass? Would he have to
endure that just so he could get her to see sense? She
had done her research. Last night. She told him that it
would have to be the right size. No more than seven
inches, slender and with a small head was ideal, she'd
said. The opposite of vaginal, in which width was more
important than length. Details and plans: that was when
he began to worry that she'd already guessed that he was
going to propose to her. And all this manic energy of
hers was a kind of postponement panic.

He reminded her quietly that it had probably been the Viagra last time rather than any desire on his part and he wasn't sure he'd be up for it.

'What? Not sure about what?'

C'mon, do I really have to be fucked up the arse before you'll marry me, he thought, but said. 'The lilies don't look fresh . . .'

In the end, a bunch of pink carnations. Because they looked camp, she said. As they walked through the aisles she was joking about the sexy toys she'd bought from Ann Summers that week. There was a reproduction of an authentic Indian dildo and a copy of the *Kama Sutra* that she'd bought, for some reason, for him. There was a Japanese vibrating egg thing she could put inside herself and operate with a remote control. Get your partner to flick the switch. She'd joked that she might wear it into work. That maybe the TV remote in the conference suite would set it off. Even though she'd let slip that she might have lost her job too. Perhaps that was why. 'We're being fucked by the corporation anyway,' she said, 'so why not?' As they stood at the checkout he worried that she was beginning to sound like Dolly. New Age mysticism and old-fashioned perversion. The thought of Alice, years down the line, like Dolly. Fuck.

To just tell her that all the things that had been fuelling this madness – Hannah, unemployment – were now, in some way, resolved. To apologise for not explaining this to her sooner. That now it was over, the divorce papers signed, and he had his first job interview, and so this was utterly futile. What he wanted now was an end to wanting. To kill all desire and the anger that fuelled it. He wanted to curl up beside her, in bed, at home and ask her the question. As stupid and pathetic and crazy as it seemed, especially now, in this context. To say that thing. To say it not even as a question but as an expression. She might say no but still he'd have to ask it. These words in his head all week.

'Alice, marry me.'

He looked at her standing there by the checkout counter. Her energy and enthusiasm. She really was going to make him go through with this. But for all her insistence he knew she feared what they'd find there. She had to do it for herself, she said, over and over, until he finally relented. She had a big question that needed to be answered. For all his cross-examining and guessing she wouldn't tell him what the big question was.

He feared that the answer she found would be a no to everything.

Standing there in the queue, his anxiety came to a head. He'd assumed that the orgy would be a complete failure, that in its aftermath, in the tears and disappointment, he would hold her, calm her and tell her that even though the last time with Dolly had been a success of sorts this had to stop. Then he would gently, quietly, propose the solution. But what if it wasn't a failure, what if Alice wanted them to keep on going? Orgies, fist-fucking, shit, blood. What if this was just the beginning and not the end?

'Do you have a loyalty card?' asked the girl at the counter.

*   *   *

Speeding through the winding country lanes. It was early evening and the sunlight was throwing long shadows over the slopes of the Kilpatricks. A band of golden light across the treeline. It reminded him of being ten or so. Holiday with the parents. And like his parents Alice had not spoken to him for the last twenty miles.

Dolly had just called on the mobile to make sure that

they were on their way and Alice was chatting with her. David tried to control his speed but what with the fading light and the thrill of the question he found himself accelerating round the bends, playing a game of hide and seek with the sun. Chasing it as it slid over the hills. Like he used to do as a child in the back seat. On each corner it would vanish momentarily, hidden by trees or hills, and he would will himself round the next bend so he could glimpse it again. He was smiling to himself. He wanted to arrive at the chalets just as the sun finally set. To sit there in the car park and to take a moment alone with her, watching the gold sink over the hills, the loch, as the final fires flickered over the water. To hold hands then. As if. As if they were witnessing the passing of an old life and the birth of a new one.

For richer and for poorer.

Their little romantic rite of passage then, sitting there holding hands watching the sunset. The kind of romantic stuff you found in movies. But corny as it was, this thing did require some kind of poetic symbolism. Some music even on the stereo. Mahler maybe or better Bach. A moment together listening to Bach blessed by the sun. The only tape they had in the car was the Happy Mondays, but it was Bach month on Radio 3. To make their bond, promise each other that there was no going back and that they were doing this for each other out of love. To give her the clue. Plant the seed in her mind. And when it was over he would say the words. Johann Sebastian. Radio 3.

Do you take this man?

If they could get a signal among the hills.

Alice was laughing with Dolly on the mobile, unselfconsciously, in a way she hadn't laughed since that last time with Dolly.

Loch Lomond. It had been bothering him all week. It was an unfortunate coincidence that he'd got married there. But, he told himself, even more symbolic. To return to the source and erase it. It did worry him that he'd come up with this idea of marrying Alice within less than an hour of having signed his divorce papers. Alice might laugh in his face.

As he'd been mulling it over he'd been accelerating again. And the bends were tight. The drop on the left steep. He took his foot off the accelerator as they hit an S-bend and got stuck behind a tractor. Funny, farmers. Real people doing real jobs. Living with the land, totally oblivious to the activities of a group of twenty cosmopolitan swingers eight miles away, tainting their rural idyll with rubberwear and sex toys and Viagra. The farmer was taking his time and a line of cars was forming behind him. Perhaps some other swingers, impatient to get there too. In the rear-view mirror a large black BMW. An older man with a girl beside him who could have been his daughter. Black hair. Goth chick. Eighteen at most. Him, Sugar Daddy, or maybe even just Daddy. Maybe not swingers at all. He was so caught up in staring into his mirror that he almost failed to notice the tractor slowing down and turning. He hit the brakes. They jolted back and Alice looked at him sternly.

'Sorry, baby.'

Then she was back onto Dolly again.

'Yeah, sure. I'll tell him.'

Tell me what? He just wanted to get there, get it over with, forget the car park and the sunset and the music. Get Alice there, let her see how sad it all was. Propose to her then come back home no matter what her reply.

The BMW was riding his bumper, wanting past. He

waited for a gap in the oncoming traffic then indicated
for them to pass. As they accelerated past him, he checked
the side window. The girl was definitely only about
eighteen. Facial piercings. He'd never had sex with an
eighteen-year-old before, not even in his teens; he wasn't
too sure that he wanted to now. Jesus, they were going
to the biggest orgy in the country and the last thing he
was interested in now was sex.

*   *   *

The line was breaking up as they drove through the hills,
but after getting Dolly to repeat herself a few times it
was pretty clear. She said that threes were better because
in fours one person was generally left out. What were
the chances of four people all fancying each other? So
yes, note for tonight. Foursomes were problematic.
Threes were fine, said Dolly, but really to be able to
achieve the level of ecstasy required the Black Room was
the best.

Then Dolly started talking about how sometimes it
was difficult to concentrate when you had a dick in your
mouth and one in your pussy. There was a danger that
you'd bite down when you came. She had a story about
some guy whom she'd almost castrated in a gang bang,
and another about how she'd once broken a tooth by
biting a table. Ideally, for a woman double penetration,
ass and pussy, were better because at least the two men
could get into some kind of rhythm together. But she'd
have to insist, when she tried it, she recommended to
Alice, that the smaller penis went in her ass.

'How is David anyway?' she'd asked.

'Fine,' was all Alice could say because she didn't want
David to hear. Two weeks since their last experience
and Alice had it all worked out. David needed to go all

the way with his bisexuality. Dolly was telling her about a man called Tony who'd be in the Black Room later, who could help David break through. Pardon the pun, she said. She was talking about the importance of getting David relaxed enough to take a length. It was all very technical but these details were just what she needed to stop her thinking. She didn't want to think about it, give it a name, but in the back of her mind was this thought that if she was fucked enough, again and again, she might just miscarry and the decision would be made for her. There would be no need to reschedule at the clinic.

Alice said her bye-byes to Dolly and clicked her mobile shut.

'What did she say?' asked David.

'She was talking about the Black Room,' said Alice.

*   *   *

They weren't going to make it in time, the sun was heading over the hills so he slowed down and forced himself to relax. The sky was turning pink. Like driving through a picture postcard. For some reason he was singing to himself.

'You take the high road and I'll take the low road.'

Something about death.

They turned the bend, headed a mile up a dirt track and there, behind the trees, were the chalets in a circle. A hundred yards from the loch. Idyllic. Some kind of 70s design. Everything made out of rough-hewn wood. Some old hippies must have made it branch by branch. The genius of the guy who thought of this. Rent the whole lot. Perfectly enclosed. Utter privacy, a little refuge from the world. Hippies and nature. Yuppies and sex. Yeah, it made sense.

He parked the car. All the other cars were bigger, more expensive. Alice turned to him.

'What is it?' she said. His plan was shot.

'What? Nothing.'

'You OK. You look . . .'

'I'm . . . I was just . . . just thinking about that song. You know.'

The look on her face, her mind was elsewhere, she knew the song, of course she did, but it wasn't there on her face. The sun had already gone down. There would be no silent moment in the car park. He put his hand on hers, and tried to sing.

'Where me and my true love will never meet again. On the bonny bonny banks.'

'Loch Lomond, sure,' was all she said.

This terrible silence then and this expression on her face which he couldn't read. Thankfully it was interrupted by some man in a kind of Victorian manservant costume walking towards them with a clipboard, asking for their names. And then Dolly was there behind him, running up to them, her vast breasts barely restrained by an antique corset.

'Oh babies, it's you. I'm so glad, so glad you're here.'

Dolly shrieked with excitement. Told them that she was sorry about all the formalities. Thing was they'd had a bunch of couples and some single men turn up uninvited. It must have got out on the net or something. She kept kissing Alice through the car window and she was so, so glad they were here. And they must meet her husband later. Leo. And Sarah, she's astounding, all the men love her. Between you and me she said, no one knows she's really a man. Gorgeous, looks like Christina Aguilera. David sat in silence, his window down. Four or so hours then this would be done and then he would ask Alice. Your chalet is number twelve, Dolly said. The party starts at nine.

*   *   *

They were all standing in a circle in the nude. Leo was the bald man in his fifties, with the large gut that almost concealed his dick. He started by throwing the ball to Dolly. It was like a corporate conference in the nude. Catch the ball, say your name and say what you're looking for.

'We're Steve and Cherry.' Him – late thirties, worked-out body, hung, balding. Her – late twenties, small, plump, huge breasts. He looked middle management. She looked retail. 'We're into full swaps and multiples.'

Alice grabbed his hand. Really, he hoped she would find this as appalling as he did. Like being in HR again. Everyone was butt naked so there was nowhere to stick a name badge. A sticker would have looked even more ridiculous. And the fact that they were taking it all so seriously. He tried not to laugh. But hoped Alice would see the funny side of it.

'Tom and Ruth.' Late thirties. Holding hands. Him – skinny, arty, tattoos and genital piercings. Her – tall, dark, elegant, nipple piercings fastened to a chain round her neck. He looked IT. She looked a nurse. 'We're looking forward to the Black Room,' the woman said.

He swallowed a snigger and looked at Alice. Her face so serious, her grip tight. In a way it was perfect, the more she invested in this the greater would be her disappointment. Just get through it. Throw the ball, catch it. Say your name, get it started, get it over with.

*   *   *

There had been some strangely surreal naked chit-chat, then hand in hand they had watched a pole-dancing demonstration by a slightly overweight housewife called Nancy, and a striptease by some goth girl who looked a lot like the girl in the BMW. They had been invited to skinny-dip at midnight and to join a couple who were into BDSM in their chalet. They had stood by the edge of the massage table watching Dolly being double penetrated and sucking a cock all at the same time. Between mouthfuls, Dolly had explained that this was called 'airlocking'.

Now David sat on the edge of the bed in the chalet. He'd been watching Alice for the last ten minutes as he waited for the Viagra to kick in. She'd fallen silent as soon as he'd taken the tablet. She was standing by the patio doors, looking at the bonfire and the shadows passing before it. She was wearing nothing but hold-ups. As Dolly's guide recommended, women who wanted to use condoms and had a preference for their own brand were advised to carry them in their stockings. He could see the bulge round the rim of both thighs where she had stuffed a pack of ten. Featherlite. He lay back and looked at her body in silhouette, her red hair. He wanted to tell her that at this moment she was unspeakably beautiful. To go up behind her and slowly, gently stroke her skin. But he was anxious about moving. In the last minute the Viagra had started working. His temples were throbbing, his pulse was accelerating and, as it said on the pack, the erectile tissues were filling with the increased blood flow. He didn't want to touch her like this. Would have preferred to have been soft and to feel her softness.

Of course the last time had been a success and he'd wept with gratitude. But Alice had blown it all out of proportion. It had been an almost spiritual experience she'd said. It was almost as if she didn't want to admit that this complex problem they'd struggled with psychologically had been resolved by a 20mg blue pill manufactured by a multi-national pharmaceutical conglomerate.

He would have preferred if he could get hard for her without the drug. He knew she would have too. When you were fucking on Viagra, the emotional bond was gone. You were fastened to a tool, you were a machine. A piston-pumping machine going on for ever. It was like the Prozac he took the year after Hannah. It made you hard too, but in a different way. You became distanced from the world. Anxieties, worries, stressful situations, they just washed over you. Your reaction times were slower. If someone was hit by a bus in front of you, you'd walk past and go, 'OK, someone's been hit by a bus.' They had saved his life but also taken the life out of it. Viagra was not so different. They'd given him back his erection, but taken the feeling out if it. Last week they'd had sex on Viagra and he'd caught himself staring at Alice and thinking, 'Look, there's someone being fucked.'

His dick now resembled the diagram on the instructions. Minutes had passed in total silence and Alice was still staring out of the window. She had one hand raised to her face. Was she biting her nails? They were going through one of their strange states. Stage fright. In ten minutes or so they'd be giving themselves to other people, a large number of other people. He hoped she was having doubts. Good. If he could just find a way to end it now. To ask her his question.

Will you, crazy as it sounds, would you, even though I know you don't believe in it, could you just consider the possibility, could we find a way to, without feeling we were selling out. Could you, will you. Alice, will you?

He got up off the bed and stood beside her. The words in his head. She hardly moved. He touched her shoulder, running over the words.

'You sure you want to do this, baby?' was all he said.

She raised her shoulder to his touch, smoothing her chin against his hand.

'Over there by the fire,' she whispered. Her hand reached for his dick and held him firm. 'She's been fucked by nine guys in the last ten minutes.'

'Really, where?'

'By the fire. Look.'

He looked to where she was pointing, but couldn't see anything clearly. Passing shadows, flashes of skin. He turned to look at her. Her profile lit by the fire. The red flames in her hair. The glow in her face.

'Baby, can we just, just get out of here and go somewhere and talk first before we even think about—'

'The Black Room,' she said. 'I wanna go to the Black Room.'

*   *   *

Cabin two. She'd checked the site map for its exact location. Dolly had told them all about it before and insisted that they join her in there. The Black Room. They'd read online diaries about people's experiences in there. It was described as the place where the old discovered their youth, where the obese felt beautiful, the impotent were virile, the anorgasmic achieved ecstatic bliss, and in which two different swingers in different countries both claimed they had found God. They'd laughed about it at the time. The fountain of youth, the font of wisdom, the Holy Grail. David had said c'mon really – it's just basically a blacked-out room with twenty randy random people fucking each other anonymously.

She was naked but for her hold-ups. David had draped a towel round himself. She led him by the hand past the bonfire. She hardly even noticed the woman being pounded by her tenth man, while other men readied themselves again with the help of hands and mouths. She hardly noticed the waves and invitations to join in, as if they were neighbours at a barbecue.

Cabin two. The lights were off just as she'd expected. There were no questions left about the importance of doing this. As she'd been staring out of the window she'd realised what she was looking for in the Black Room; what had led her here with such impatience was the need to answer her question. For a second, back there, looking out at the twisting human forms, she'd actually thought of what the future could be if she kept the baby. Dropping out, becoming a West End mother. Or like Lysander and Jezebel, raising a child communally. All the options. Terrifying.

In the Black Room she would find the answer. Lose herself and everything she'd been or ever wanted to be. Become anonymous under the touch of anonymous bodies. Of course it was hippie shit. Shit Dolly believed in and that her mother had tried to do in the 70s. Tried but lacked the guts to see through. But tonight she would take all that crap, two generations of failure, and put an end to it. She'd disappear in the darkness and be reborn.

As she marched up the steps to the enclosure the tension in her arm told her that she was pulling David along. Poor David. She had told herself earlier, standing by the window, that if this didn't work then it would be all over. Her and David, but so many other things. She'd go back to the States and start again. Go back to being sixteen. She gripped his hand tighter and pulled him up the steps to the dark draped windows.

*   *   *

Alice parted the curtains and led him in. He caught a brief glimpse illuminated by the firelight. Eight, ten bodies maybe, writhing naked on the bed, floor, against the walls. Hardly any room to move. A head between legs. Darkness again, Alice must have pulled the curtains back. Total darkness. He felt scared and silly at feeling scared, clinging to Alice's hand. The sound of bodies gasping, groaning, the smell of sweat and sex. He took a step in and stood on something, someone.

'Sorry.'

The sound of his voice seemed muffled. Soaked up. Alice's hand slipped from his and for a second he felt lost. But then fingers reached up his calf and the towel fell from his waist and he felt his legs going beneath him. He wanted to call out for her but something told him that talk and names and partners were of no relevance here. A mouth kissed his inner thigh, another hand stroked his ass, a hand held his dick and eased him slowly forward. He tried to resist but was already falling, caught by what seemed many hands. A body, wet with sweat, brushed his cheek. He tried to adjust his eyes to the darkness, but the place was dense dark. Something touched his lips. He opened his mouth and tasted a woman's breast. Who? Dolly? The buxom woman? He couldn't see, but by the feel of the body he guessed she was the goth girl they'd seen earlier on. Eighteen max. The one with the tattoo on the base of her spine. Dark eyeshadow. Purple lipstick and black nail polish on fingers and toes. Maybe, maybe not. It no longer mattered. He sucked on the nipple and as he did a mouth circled the head of his penis. He felt himself falling backwards, although he knew he couldn't be. Fingers ran through his hair. The nipple hard in his mouth and his dick hard in a mouth. Sucking, sucking. Every mouth, lung, tongue in the room, sucking, fucking. He tried to fight it. Resist. No, no. This sense of falling.

Everything as if in slow motion. Every movement counterbalanced by someone else's. You touch and are touched. You reach out with one finger and feel one finger on you. You grip and are gripped. Bite and are bitten. A tongue circling his anus, as his tongue circled the nipple. A cock rubbing in circles over his face as mouths circled his cock. The whole room breathing together, heaving. Second after second, the tongue probing inside him. The mouths taking him in deep and he felt himself slipping under and had to force himself to think about Alice. What the whole point of this was. He'd wanted it to be a disappointment. But if. If. Oh my God. If she was experiencing this. He had wanted so badly for this to be the last time, for it to be a failure for them. To walk away and be Alice and David again. But the more he tried to summon up some semblance of who he was, the more he felt himself slipping away.

Where was she? Unless she was that hand in his hair, that mouth round his cock. Again he resisted the temptation to call her name. Fingers kneaded the muscles in his neck and his head rolled forward to find the wetness of a woman's crotch. Lips brushed his lips. And as he pushed a finger inside someone he felt a finger slowly push into his ass and his muscles tighten round it. Spit, a woman's wetness smeared into his ass. How many people were holding him? Three, four? Alice. She'd wanted this for him, and he was really trying to fight it, but now resistance was over, his muscles were relaxing and he wanted Alice to be part of this. He could sense himself drifting under, struggling not to let himself go. Losing himself. The pressure against his ass, two fingers, a cock. He raised his ass and felt himself opening for it, as he pushed his fingers deeper into a woman. Whoever. Names. He was no longer David, and Alice was no longer Alice. They were just here, bodies breathing, opening. His eyes seeing faint outlines in the dark. But as the pressure pushed deeper inside him he no longer wanted to see. With each slow thrust, each breath, in and out, deeper and deeper, he was turning inside out. Becoming body, breath, nameless. Touch is fingers, taste is mouth. Ass is taste. Taste is touch. Fingers are mouth. Mouth is ass. Touch, taste. Smell. David. Alice. Lost.

*   *   *

The edge of a bed? An elbow, a knee? What, what the hell was that? Alice felt hands all over her. Taking her hand, leading it to a dick. Something, on her face. What? A thigh? A foot? She was pulled backwards, falling. She resisted, tried to stand, but she'd lost her sense of direction, was she going to fall onto the floor, the bed, onto someone else. Strong hands grabbed her ass. Her crotch. Lifted her. She rolled back. Her back hitting something soft with a smack. Flesh. A gasp from beneath her as she landed. A dick in her face. Her foot caught on something. Between someone's legs. Relax, relax she told herself. You wanted this. This is the answer. Something rubbing against her face, a finger, a cock.

She swung her arm round to touch it. But she felt something wet and warm on her toe. Her leg recoiled impulsively. What had that been? Toe sucker. Jesus. Her knee smacked off something – a chin? Someone gasped. She wanted to say sorry. Tried to balance and fell to her right. Her elbow struck something soft. She had wanted to let go, to lose herself, to be open to the experience but it all felt horribly banal. Like being drunk at a gig, squashed in a queue. People being crushed. Fuck, it was absurd. The logistics of it. Was it not possible that there were just too many people in here? Something was pushing against her crotch. There was a dick by her face, trying to find her mouth. OK, OK, go with it. Her mouth found it and sucked on it, and at the same time someone entered her, her hands automatically felt for it, to see if it was wearing a condom, yes, but then fuck. There were fingers pawing her eyeball. Christ, did someone think it was a pussy? A dick jabbed her in her eye. She lashed out to push it away, sticking her finger in something soft. An ass, an eye. Something wet hit her leg, spit, come. Jesus. Someone was humping her leg. What the fuck? Someone whispered something, was it David? The mouth too close to her ear to hear.

As she felt the elbows digging into her sides, the tongues dripping spit over her buttocks, the fingers entering her, the dicks in her face, she lost all sense of where she was, which way she was facing. She wasn't letting go like she thought she would. Losing herself. No. She was resisting. Clinging in fact, clinging, to those little fragments of identity that she'd so wanted to escape. The more she felt her body touched, the more she felt nameless, nobody, the more she told herself, you are Alice, Alice. You went to school at UCLA. Your mother was called Joan. You are pregnant. She clung to an arm, a leg. Let go, Alice, just let go.

It started in the pit of her gut. It rose through her chest, like a drumbeat. Chuck-a-chuck-a. This stupid song starting up in her head.

'Blood hell, Alice. Not here! Not now!'

She tried to hold it in. Took a deep breath trying to push it down. But a violent spasm shot through her, as fast as the dick thrusting in her pussy.

Jesus, no, no. *Paint it Black*.

This stupid song. The more she tried to fight it, the more this energy pushed up from her belly, through her windpipe. She clamped her hand to her mouth. Concentrate on the dick in your pussy. Dick, pussy, dick, pussy. 'Oh my God, I'm going to, I'm going to.'

Giggling, she was giggling.

In the silences between each spasm she sensed the room becoming silent around her. Giggling, fuck. But she couldn't stop. The cock pulled out. The fingers too. The body on top slid off. The more she tried to stop it the worse it got. She put her fist in her mouth, bit on her knuckles, but still it burst out. A snorting guffaw.

'Christ!' a voice said.

Sorry, sorry, she tried to say, but now as she struggled to prop herself up on the other limbs, and the hands left her body, her lungs were given full freedom and it got worse. Not giggling, or even crying. Laughter. Loud deafening laughter. Booming out into the darkness. Hardly able to speak. The words forced out with each lungful.

'Oh God, sorry, I'm sorry.'

She jerked forward, bashing her head against something hard. The wall, keep going. A hand round her arm pulling her down. Bodies were getting up. No sounds of fucking now. A way out, there must be a way out. Her foot hit a hard edge, the bed? She tried to create a mental picture of the room in the dark. It would be the same as her own chalet. A door handle, yes, but it would be the bathroom. No, think about the room, picture it. Stop laughing please, Alice. The laughter was escaping from between her teeth. Tisk tisk tisk. A flash of light. A body visible, a woman, pulling back the heavy curtains to leave.

'For fuck's sake.' A voice to her right.

She couldn't control it. The exclamations and insults

and her own inability to find her way to her feet made it come even harder. Like whooping cough now. Eek, eek.

An elbow struck her cheek. Deliberate? No time to think. Voices muttering, whispering. She managed to get her balance, and tried to make her way through the darkness to the point where the light had been. She tried to focus, distract herself from laughing. But now that she was holding her breath, she felt her face bursting. It was escaping from her, this snorting, chortling, blasting air from the sides of her mouth, making raspberry noises.

Her foot landed on something soft, a breast, an ass. She stumbled and fell forward. Landing on something, someone. Struggling to get out, thrusting, trying to find something to hold onto. Standing on them, trying to find a support, anything. Her head struck a chest, knocking the wind out of someone. She reached out to support herself and grabbed something, her nails digging into flesh. A man let out a gasp.

'Ow! Fucking hell!'

'Sorry, sorry.'

Scrambling over bodies. A hand clawing at her ankle. It was so hilariously awful. People falling over. Slapstick. Hysteria. David. She had to find David. But to call out his name. She'd spoiled it for everyone. They'd blame him. No, leave David here, no way to find him in the dark. Her foot slid in something wet. Gross. Jesus. The laughter, coming now in almost whimpering spasms. She fell forward and reached out. Her fingers finding the curtains. Clinging to them. Tearing them from their rail. Light slashed into the black room. She clawed her way back to her feet, couldn't look back at all the bodies, suddenly illuminated in all their humiliating nudity.

Out. As she put step after step between her and the

black room, the laughter ran out. A hiccup. Her breath caught up with her. Get away from it. Go, as fast as you can. Go. Where though? To the chalet? No, David would come and find her there. Excuses, apologies. A fight. What the fuck was that about, Alice? No. Out of the enclosure. The field. The loch, just away. The chalets were only forty feet from the loch. Good for skinny-dipping in summer, they'd said, but there was a chill breeze. And it was dark. In the opposite direction nothing but marshland and that dirt track they drove down for ten minutes to get here. No point thinking where, just get away. Grab a towel. Wrap it round yourself. Why? No one can see you. Just to feel covered, no longer naked.

Keep going. Don't look at them, the bodies by the fire. The woman being gang banged on the swing. The teenager on her knees sucking cocks. The man with the mask. The woman with the strap-on. Just go.

As her eyes located the end of the wooden walkway, and her fingers found the latch to the gate, her feet felt the soft wet mud of the field and the laughter turned to shivering. She took step after step in the darkness and the light of the bonfire behind faded, as she managed to put enough distance between her and it. Walking where? Nowhere. Into some piece of countryside in the middle of the night wrapped only in a towel.

Why did I laugh?

The faint whisper of the loch ahead. Slight movement in the trees. The grass lit by the party behind. The water seemed black, blacker than black. There were stars, but she couldn't see them in the loch. Not a mirror of the sky at all. More like a hole. Her feet led her towards it as her mind roamed backwards.

OK, clearly, laughing was the one thing you should never do at an orgy. That was a given now. Like you wouldn't at a funeral. But still. It had always been this thing with her. Every time she was forced to face something so grave, so utterly serious, she'd find herself laughing. Like that time aged nine when her mother told her her father had died. The shrink shortly afterwards had assured her mother that this was a natural reaction to extreme grief. Or fear. Like pissing yourself. You laugh. You sing a song.

You take the high road and I'll take the low road.

Tears were a secondary reaction. A conditioned one even. The acceptable thing to do. Laughter was bigger than tears. Laughter was anger, anger at the absurdity of an impossible world. Like that saint who boiled in the cauldron telling the Roman troops to put on more wood. The last gasp of life. The last thing you did before you put the gun in your mouth? Like Cobain, like Plath. Laughing at the sky, singing at the black empty sky. Laughing at God and his hilarious absence. Laughing as if to dare him to reveal himself. Laughing at the stupidity of that. Laughing as you pull the trigger, turn on the gas.

Even in the darkness the loch was becoming clearer. Not the loch but the tiny white splashing waves that hit that thing. That thing that stuck out in the water. A pier. A jetty. Little white waves around it. It was the only thing in the darkness to focus on so she stumbled into the wind, towards it.

All those poor people she'd humiliated. They'd invested so much meaning in it and she'd laughed and made the whole thing seem absurd. A Monty Python sketch. Are there any women at the stoning today? God they must hate her.

Her feet hit the edge of the jetty. Damp. Cold. Slimy wet clawing through her hold-ups. The moon. Hadn't noticed it before. But there it was cutting through the clouds. A half-moon. Its twin in the water. Perfect semi-circle of light in the still dark. A shudder ran through her.

Why had she laughed? Fear. Grief. For what? She was thinking about that image again. The one her mother had shown her when she'd had her first period. Her mother trying to explain to her that this was what adult life was like, that the body was a beautiful thing. A line of hippies against a wall, naked, some commune some-where, her mother in the midst of it. Her long hair barely covering her breasts. Ten naked bodies against a wall smiling at the camera. Then that other one. That photo she'd seen years later. Charles Manson. The naked girls in the desert. Swastikas on their foreheads. Tattooed. Peace and love.

She slowly rolled the wet holds-ups from her legs and let them fall. Dipped her bare toes in the water. Cold, fucking cold.

Knee-jerk. Yes. Maybe it had been that other kind of laughter. That knee-jerk reaction of hers. Like when her painting tutor declared his love for her. Like when her philosophy tutor made love to her so briskly and in-tensely. What was it? Just simple embarrassment. Always this situation when others were passionately involved and she felt detached. Fear of letting go. Fear of this block between her and others. How could a man work himself into a frenzy before her, muttering, pleading, kneeling, kneading her flesh when she felt nothing? Felt like laughing.

The icy bangle crawled up her ankle as she forced her foot in deeper, searching for the bottom.

Disappointment. Yes. The Black Room had not seemed profound or overwhelming, as she had hoped. There was no revelation about childhood, or her mother, or her pregnancy. No sense of finding yourself or even losing yourself. Just bodies breathing, nameless, point-less. No matter how many cocks and fingers pushed into her, she didn't feel connected in any way. All these pathetic attempts at building an identity over the years. She'd told herself that tonight she'd give up on it all, strip it away and find that thing she'd read about so many times, the true self crouching there in the darkness like a small child. Just to see if it was really there. To return to this almost primal state. Crying while she came.

Her teeth were chattering like they were trying to tell her something. Really, the whole thing was laughable. All these sad people in the dark. No, not them. Truth was, she'd been laughing at herself and it was not happy, witty laughter. To want to let go, but lacking the courage. Desperate. Laughing at how shallow you are. You will never let go. Pathetic and superficial. She'd clung to her laughter as a coward would cling to apologies. As the humourless cling to their one good joke. As she and David had for so long clung to their ironic attitude. All she really was was that laugh. That cowardly ironic laugh.

The goose pimples prickling up her leg. The water was how deep? Hard to tell. She pushed her foot in further, halfway up her calf. Deeper deeper. You are so shallow. But as her supporting foot slid on the wet wood, she struggled to regain her balance and fear was with her again.

*   *   *

That laughter. Whoever it was who'd run out had trashed it all. He'd thought for a second he'd recognised the voice, but it couldn't have been. Not Alice. It had been too hysterical. A high-pitched shriek. Some amateur, some newbie maybe. One of the men climbed up and tried to fix the curtains again but it was too late. People sat up. Got to their feet and stumbled towards the opening. He looked down and realised that the woman who'd been sucking him off was not the goth girl at all, but some older woman. Overweight. She smiled at him awkwardly and covered her breasts. Conversations were starting. Awkward. Like a dinner party after someone makes a racist joke.

'Is that the time already? Goodness.'

'God, I feel rather peckish.'

He looked round trying to locate Alice. There was a pile of people on the floor in the shadow of the bed. Maybe six, getting up. It was possible that she was under there somewhere.

People were now trying to introduce themselves. To his left some man was talking about the terrible state of the local B roads.

No, there was no sign of her anywhere. So it must have been her. Jesus, what the hell had come over her? She was unpredictable. Sometimes she'd change just like that. Like someone had flicked a switch inside her.

The man was reassuring everyone that if he could just get some tacks or a hammer or maybe some Scotch tape then he'd have the curtain back up in seconds and they could all resume. But everyone was filing out. David lowered his eyes, climbed through the gap in the curtains, apologising to the man. Outside he scanned the chalets for Alice. Started to worry about her. Really, there was nowhere she could go. Perhaps she was sitting alone back in their chalet.

He went past the bonfire, where a man was being fist-fucked by a woman as he sucked a tall masked man. Past the jacuzzi, and the tattooed man who was going down on a slender woman who was fingering an older woman.

Sandra. Met her earlier, husband Mike. Worked in IT.
Bearsden. Nice folk. He walked past the massage table
where many hands kneaded the flesh of a body that was
hidden from view. He walked up to them.

'Alice?' The faces turned to him.

The body on the bench was Dolly.

'Hey Dave, wanna have a turn?'

'I'm looking for Alice.'

Before Dolly could answer he'd turned and moved on.
He almost ran up to the chalet. It was dark inside and
the windows were like a mirror. He suddenly became
aware of his nudity. His dick was still hard but not
aroused. Damn this Viagra. He decided to cover himself
up before going in to find Alice. She'd be in a real state.
The sight of him with his unstoppable chemical erection
would only upset her more. Going along with this whole
thing had been a mistake. She'd be crying in the back
somewhere. Maybe in the shower. He slid the glass door
open.

'Alice? You there, baby?'

He walked through the bedroom, checked the bathroom. No. Christ, maybe she'd got dressed, taken the
car. Just gone. He checked the wardrobe. Her overnight
bag was still there. He headed back through to the patio
doors but then there was someone there. The big woman
who'd been sucking him off.

'Hi there, can I come in?'

'Well . . .'

'Was just wondering if you wanted to finish off what
we started.'

And she was in. Running her hands over his chest, his
dick. She had some sort of bag with her. 'I brought some
toys,' she said as she sat on the edge of the bed.

He hovered by the doorway. Find Alice first. Tell the

woman you'll be back. No, get rid of her.

'You have a beautiful dick.' Already she was pulling a dildo out of her bag and putting on a show of sucking on her huge breasts.

'Look,' David said. 'Look, I—'

'I swear I have a clit in the back of my throat,' she said. 'I could come just by sucking you.'

Charming, lovely, but not the right time. Get her out of here. If Alice was upset and he managed to bring her back here it would not be good for them to find the big woman jerking off on their bed.

'Look, I'm sorry, but I have a kind of situation here and I have to go.'

She sat upright on the bed. Her breasts were immense. Touching her knees.

'Don't you like me?'

He did, of course he did. That tiny delicate face, that long neck, those almost impossibly large breasts.

'You're a beautiful girl, really. Really beautiful,' he said.

But she seemed in some way angered. She stepped towards him, and went down on her knees. In seconds her head was bobbing on his dick. Wrong, all wrong. She was grabbing his buttocks, forcing it deep into the back of her throat, gagging and moaning. She took his dick from her mouth, and rolled it over her cheek. 'You like me? Tell me you like me.' Then resumed.

He had to hold her face. Remove her forcibly from his dick.

'Look, I think I'm going to go now. Maybe you should too.'

Her eyes said 'You can't refuse me. Don't you know where the fuck you are?' Her eyes said 'Loser.' They said 'Fuck you, needle dick.'

He apologised, wrapped the towel around himself

again. As soon as he could he was out of there. No time
to wait for her to pack up her toys and go. She'd be gone
by the time he got back with Alice. Where the hell was
she?

The circle of chalets, the bonfire, walkway. He scanned
the whole place looking for her. People were pairing off
and returning to their cabins. Nothing. His eyes drifted
to the gate. It was the only place she could have gone.
He walked to the perimeter and mounted the steps to
the wooden promenade. Not wanting to draw attention
to himself he picked up an empty beer bottle on the way.
Mike, the IT guy, waved over at him as he hit the
walkway. Mike was in the line for the spreadeagled
silicone-enhanced girl on the swing. A big-assed older
woman was being fluffer, on her knees, getting the men
ready. David gave a big thumbs-up and raised the bottle
in his hand as if to say 'Off to get another one, want
one?' Mike shook his head and nodded at his dick as if
to say 'Had enough tonight, mate.' David pretended to
laugh. As soon as Mike turned away, David was on his
way, fast. Gone. He went past the bonfire lights, into the
shadows of the last few chalets, as Alice must have done.
At the gate, he turned to see if anyone was watching.
No, too busy. He held his breath, put his hand on the
gate to see if it creaked. It didn't, silly, no one would
notice, he exhaled, pushed and was out.

He stepped off the wood onto the muddy ground.
Slipping. Fuck it was cold. No sight of her. His eyes were
struggling to adjust to the darkness. A breeze on his face.
On his chest. Cold wet feet. Eyes focusing. Something
over there. Far. His forced his eyes to focus and found
he was staring at a plastic bag on a fence, blowing in the
wind. The further he moved, the more he wished he'd
picked up one of the flannel dressing gowns from the

sauna. Then he saw it, a faint flicker. Light colour. Over towards the loch. A towel. Yes. Maybe it was her. Over there by the water.

He found himself running. Not running, if he could have run he would have, but he couldn't see where he was going and the ground beneath his feet was wet.

Yes, it was Alice. There was some kind of pier by the water's edge and she was standing at the end of it, wrapped in her towel.

'Hey!' he shouted out and slipped and fell. 'Alice, you OK, you OK?'

But she didn't turn. In those slow seconds it took for him to get back up and get closer it flashed before him. That she was about to throw herself in. Fear propelled him forward. He slid and fell again, catching himself with his left hand, twisting his wrist. Clambering back up, covered in mud, running, stumbling to get to her. His feet hit the wood of the pier, he gripped her hard by the shoulders. They shivered under his touch. She turned. Smiled.

'You OK? You had me scared in there. You OK? Everything OK? 'Cos, I mean I had, actually, you know you were right. Totally fucking . . . But I mean it's done now, totally and . . . I think from now on . . .'

Her back. Her breathing. A breath. Take a breath.

'I mean, as they say, how was it for you?

'Fine, yeah,' she said.

He was trying to warm her with his touch but her shivering only seemed to increase as he stroked her back.

'I was worried about you, you know, just running off and . . .'

She wrapped her arms round herself, said nothing, just kept staring out at the loch. Shuddering. He stood there staring out at it too. Lifted his hand from her. A sign to the left warned about the depth of the water and not standing on the pier when it was wet. Shit. This was all too melodramatic. One of her poetic tantrums, no doubt.

'So, what's this, some kind of *French Lieutenant's Woman* moment or something?' A stupid joke he regretted even as he said it.

'I guess so,' she said without turning. Why was she being so cold with him? OK, it was cold. That was all.

'It's just . . . was worried.'

'Meryl Streep,' she said. 'On a pier, right?'

He lifted his hand from her back.

'Baby,' he said, 'you OK?'

'Two Oscars – no one really got it.'

'Look, can we just go back in? To our room and talk.'

She crouched by the edge. 'How deep is it, you think?' she asked, still not turning.

'Six, ten, I dunno. Let's go back to the chalet, get warm and talk.'

She turned round. Her smile generous, but distant. Her face shaking. 'See the moon in the water? If I just had a stone or something.' She tippy-toed past him and stepped onto the small beach, bending down to look at the stones.

'I have this thing, Alice, this thing I have to, that we have to talk about and I don't think this is the right place. Can we just—'

'You wanna try and hit the moon?' she said.

'Go back to the chalet or the car. I'm still pretty sober.'

'It's kind of annoying me, the water. You ever seen water so flat?' She picked up a stone and examined it.

'I'd be OK for driving. We should just go home.'

She picked up another stone, examined it and put down the first.

'Baby, please. We need to talk.'

She played with the stone in her hand, feeling its weight. He looked back towards the chalets. Then back at her. She stood up and was practising throwing. What was she doing? Moving to stay warm. Fuck it was cold.

'I mean this whole thing, it kinda disgusts me too, if that's what you're thinking. To be honest I didn't want to, and if you think any of it has meant anything . . .'

She stepped onto the jetty. 'Bet I can hit the moon first,' she said.

'What? What the fuck?'

'Big splash right in the middle.' The words jerking out of her. 'My Uncle Tony – hit a bottle at a hundred yards – lined them up on the fence – had a .357 – was too small to use it – dislocated my shoulder – you know, when it kicks back – he said – used to shoot bottles all the time – let me shoot it once.'

'Alice?'

'A gun. A .357.'

'What? Look, if they made you happy. The men. If that's what this is about I'm fine with that. I'm not jealous or anything. It was you, wasn't it? Who was laughing?'

She turned and stared at him. Shivering. 'Yeah, I was laughing.'

'Alice, please. For Christ's sake, it's fucking freezing. What's wrong, baby?'

She tossed the stone in her hand. Caught it. Pulled her arm back swiftly then threw it forward. The stone skimmed the water, wide of the mark. Ripples across the moon's reflection.

'Close,' she said. 'Not close enough. Need something heavier.'

She stooped to pick up another stone. David leaned down beside her and grabbed her arm as she lifted it.

She looked back at him. Cold. 'OK, we're going home.'

'Look, you wanted this and I didn't . . . I did this for you,' he said.

Her eyes. He lowered his gaze.

'Why? Why don't you try? It's fun. Guys are usually better at this.'

He released his hold. Stood back, gave her her space, slowly braved meeting her gaze. 'Alice.'

'You go on back. I'll see you in a bit.'

Why the fuck couldn't he just say it? What was wrong with him? With her. This big thing to ask her and she was messing around with fucking stones.

'Sorry,' she said. 'I dunno, you're right, I just need my little Meryl Streep moment by myself, OK?'

'OK, OK. See you back in there. I think we should, you know, have a hot shower together, just snuggle up and talk. Talk. We need to talk.'

'OK. See you in a bit, Daddy.'

'See you in a bit.'

And that was all he said as he turned and left her there. He would go back to the chalet and he would wait. From now on, every minute, every day, he would wait and surrender to the waiting. He would wait for Alice to tell him what they were to do with their lives.

*   *   *

She was sorry for having to do this. It was in some way not to do with him. The abortion was booked for eleven a.m. Tuesday. She threw another stone and it landed short. The moon wavered slightly.

He'd tried so hard to make her happy; it wasn't his fault the way she felt. How did she feel anyway? Sad, thoughtful, these words were too clichéd. She just wanted to be alone for a bit. The cold suited her mood. Why did that need justifying?

She watched his silhouette against the lights of the orgy, then he vanished inside. How she needed his clinging love, how she hated it. She could barely see the beach but she decided to walk along it, by the water's edge. Her towel caught on her foot and fell off. She had no strength or desire left to pick it up again. Why this thing she always did, this need to walk away? The cold on her skin was at least something. She stepped in deeper, up to her calves, feeling the freeze grow though her, kicking the water in front of her. Watching the droplets glow in the light.

She stared back at the chalets. They'd started some disco music going. No doubt in an attempt to inject some enthusiasm back into the crowd after her dramatic departure. It was tacky. The whole thing.

Alice kept on wading. Something about the music, the water, seemed horribly familiar. Her mother's third wedding. That was it. The party by Lake Superior, and then as now she'd found herself at night by the edge of the water feeling that the pop music was obscene. Was violating the peace of the lake. Twenty years ago. She'd come so far, only to be confronted yet again by how little she'd moved. Only to be once again confronted with her mother. Her mother and her unwanted child.

She waded deeper into the water, felt the cold bite circling above her knees. No anxiety now about the laughter. That was understood. The moments before. The noises of the other couples. It had seemed in some strange way that everyone in the room was fucking to the same rhythm. As the pounding of the cock inside her came into sync with the moans of others and the beating of her heart, she had felt mortal, for a few seconds, very mortal. She'd thought about her age. About how many more heartbeats she had left. How already she'd reached

an end and was scared of what was next. What would fill
her time till that pounding stopped? More of the same.
The rhythm of a man inside you, as constant as a heartbeat. Filling you. Filling up your time. A child, a heartbeat
inside you that told you to keep on.

The water was up to her thighs now. Cold, so cold.
The chill through her bones, it was so much more
extreme than anything she'd felt tonight.

She waded in deeper. The cold biting round her hips,
crotch. It would not be so hard to go further, feel the
coldness slowly climb over her breasts, her neck, her head,
to hold her breath and push off into the midst of it. To
be out of her depth. But as she looked out something
caught her eye. Pink slowly drifting away. Her towel. And
the feeling of the darkness, slowly sucking her in deeper,
of the rocks sliding beneath her feet, somehow led her to
thinking about it. What it would be like. Her nipples
shrivelling in the cold. Lungs gasping. Like she was no
longer in control. Her body in panic and her lungs. Like
those last hours when her mother lay dying. The lungs,
the heart. All that was left of her. A machine functioning
then stopping. The gasping sound of breath, disgusting.
Hers, her mother's. Bodies. Nothing more.

The depths pulling her. Toes sliding on stones. She
had never learned to swim, could never stand the idea
of putting her head under. For the briefest second, she
felt like letting go. My problem, she told herself, is that
I have spent my life throwing myself into things, then at
the last minute getting scared and pulling out. To just
let go and be pulled in. To really experience life for a
second at the end. Yes, I am one of those unfortunates
who breathes but has never lived. She held her breath
and forced her head underwater. Opened her eyes but
there was only blackness. Her breath running out, her

lungs close to bursting. The bubbles running up the side of her face. She reached for a foothold but found nothing. She gasped and water filled her lungs. Surge of electricity. Hands flailing.

Dry land. It was only after stumbling and falling onto the rocks, shivering, clutching, cutting her knees and shins, that she managed to put it together. How she'd got out. Somehow, found a foothold, pushed up, paddled, got a grip, pulled herself back, fell onto the beach. She sat there, shaking, naked, watching the towel sink finally into the blackness. Yes, she lacked the courage to end it. Her body wanted to live even though her mind could find no reason for doing so. No, that wasn't true. There was this thing inside her that wanted to live. This thing that didn't need a reason.

She sat on the stones, her breath loud in her ears filling the empty space. A tree just to her right. The leaves dangling into vision, framing the loch, as many romantic paintings once did. Pulsing in the red glow from the orgy. Faint red against the black loch. The composition perfect. If she had been a real artist, she would have run back to the chalet, found a pen and made a sketch to be worked up into a canvas. Labouring then, to try to capture the deep dark permanence of the loch, the transience of the leaves, the water – a mirror for the moon. But this was her again. Her through and through. To always be imagining pictures. To sit naked on a beach and see the beauty of things and be unable to do anything with it.

She looked back over her shoulder to the cabins. Choices. Leave now. Alone. Or throw herself back into the midst of it. No it was still the same old trick. Trying to lose yourself then backing away. Finally, now, she had to face what it was she'd been running from. Her mother had struggled all those years trying to find herself. And in turn Alice had spent hers trying to lose her mother. Her mother still, somehow, alive inside her.

It made her laugh. She wanted to go back to the chalets. A little refreshed after the cold wind and water. To go back and stand there, looking at them all. Whispering, shouting commands. 'Fuck her hard.' 'Put it in his ass.' 'Hit him.' 'Make him bleed.' 'Eat her shit.' She'd be the last one to leave. She would no longer even try to participate. She'd take that aesthetic knowledge she had. She'd get them all, those nine other couples, get them to make a human pyramid, body on body, like the Americans did to the Iraqis. She'd take that imagination she had and that distance she couldn't escape from and see it for what it was. Power. She'd do anything, the limits of the imagination, the depths of depravity.

Spasms of tears. Hugging her knees by the water's edge, the stones freezing into her skin. Her eyes adjusting to the dark. The black of the loch no longer so black. The sky seemed purple. Silhouettes of the hills around. There were in fact houses, terribly normal houses around the perimeter. Little boats by the edge. Little boats. Someone's idea of contentment. Sailing, getting away from it all. Nothing natural and profound about it. Little lights on the water. Hotels. Holiday homes. Boating. People boated here. The loch, like everywhere else, was a suburb.

And the cold too. It no longer meant anything. All she wanted to do was find David. To say please, it's not funny any more. I just want you to hold me. Please. Not cling or scratch or hurt him, no more stories, but just to hold him, so gently and share the hot tears. To say 'I don't know what to do.' To say 'Hold me please.' To say it over and over till it became meaningless, and then beyond that for those words to become just a sound.

As she walked, trembling, towards the chalets, she'd already made her mind up. She'd find David, he'd be busy, by himself, packing their bags no doubt, apologising yet again for failing in so many ways. She'd kiss his cheek, whisper in his ear and ask him to come to bed. He'd join her after ten minutes or so. She'd warm herself up. Calm and reassure him as she lifted the quilt to let him in. Tell him everything was going to be fine and that although it scared her, she'd reached a decision.

'David, please, just listen.'

Then she'd say it.

'I want to tell you a story.'

'OK,' he'd say.

'It's about these two people. A man and a woman.'

'Aha.'

'This man and this woman.'

'OK. Who are they? Where do they live?'

'They live in the West End but they don't belong there, they're in this story but they don't want to be, but still, they're together and they have to do this thing together.'

'Sorry, what?'

'They're going to do this thing together, and it scares them, really it does, but they're going to do it.'

'Going to do what?'

'David.'

'What? Tell me.'

'David.'

'Alice.'

'We're going to have a baby.'